Kidnapped by a Stranger . . .

Adrienne's breath came in short quick bursts as she struggled to get a grip on her burgeoning terror. Above her, the man's dark eyes seemed to burn like live coals in his shadowy face. Devil's eyes, she thought hysterically.

His voice, low and dangerously soft, brushed the night like rough silk. "One way or another, *princesse*, I am taking you off this vessel. You have a choice. You may put on some clothes or you may go as you are now, in which case my men are going to get a tantalizing eyeful." As if to emphasize his point, he glided his free hand over her. . . . "Do I have your cooperation?" he asked, his voice oddly hoarse.

At that moment she would have agreed to anything. . . .

A Vow to Keep

Elizabeth Bonner

DIAMOND BOOKS, NEW YORK

This book is a Diamond original edition, and has never been previously published.

A VOW TO KEEP

A Diamond Book/published by arrangement with the author

PRINTING HISTORY
Diamond edition/November 1993

ISBN: 1-55773-957-9

Diamond Books are published by The Berkley Publishing Group, 200 Madison Avenue, New York, NY 10016. DIAMOND and the "D" design are trademarks belonging to Charter Communications, Inc.

PRINTED IN THE UNITED STATES OF AMERICA

10 9 8 7 6 5 4 3 2 1

To my daughter
Adrienne Lee Andersen

Prologue

"AND THE GIRL?" Graeham de Clairmont asked. "What do you intend to do with her?"

Hugh de Clairmont leaned back in the ornately carved chair and lifted a goblet to his lips. As the wine warmed his blood, he thought of what he had been able to find out about Adrienne de Langeais. Her mother had been a tall, dark-haired beauty who turned the head of every man who laid eyes on her, including the king of England. Adrienne was said to have inherited her mother's striking looks along with her father's volatile temperament. Beauty and fire. An intriguing combination, Hugh thought. He was looking forward to taming the girl before disposing of her.

Hugh returned the goblet to the table. His expression was unreadable. "I will use her to lure Richard into Sainte-Croix. Then, when she has served her purpose, I will have her shut away in a convent where she will no longer pose a threat to us."

Graeham looked doubtful. "And if Richard gets to her before we do? What then?"

"We need not concern ourselves with Richard just yet. Until he is crowned, he will be kept busy dealing with contenders for the throne."

The Duke of Lorraine, in whose home this meeting was taking place, had been listening in silence. He now turned away from the window. "Hugh is right," he said. "Even as we speak, Richard is on his way to England for the coronation. John is the one we must watch. Henry promised Sainte-Croix to him. John will be furious when he learns that the inheritance he anticipated was given to his illegitimate half sister as her marriage portion."

The nerve beneath Hugh's left eye twitched. "Henry was a conniving, manipulative scoundrel. Sainte-Croix is my birthright. Mine and Graeham's. I will not rest until the countship has been restored to our family and Henry's heirs have paid for their father's crimes."

"Henry was no ally of mine," the Duke of Lorraine said. "Whatever you choose to do, my men are at your disposal."

Hugh's dark eyes glittered dangerously. He intended to crush every one of Henry Plantagenet's heirs, beginning with Adrienne de Langeais. *Beauty and fire*, he thought again. Yes, he was definitely looking forward to taming the girl.

Chapter One

England

THE FALCON CIRCLED higher and higher until she was nearly a thousand feet above the brook, hovered for several seconds on outstretched wings, then banked and swooped down on the unsuspecting drake as he cleared the reeds. With her talons clenchèd, she turned sharply and came up beneath the drake, striking him with a fierce blow that filled the air with an explosion of feathers. The stunned drake fell to the ground, and the falcon flew after him. Swiftly and cleanly she broke his neck with her strong beak.

Guided by the sound of the bell attached to the falcon's leg, Adrienne made her way along the muddy bank to where the falcon couched on her prey. Talking gently to the falcon as she knelt on the bank, Adrienne grasped the drake's wings and pulled them back to expose the breast. She pierced the flesh at the upper end of the abdomen with her first two fingers, driving them upwards into the drake's breast, and removed the heart. Then she stuffed the drake into the burlap bag with the rest of the day's kill. Standing, she extended her arm and called out, "Adal!" The falcon flew up to perch on the heavy leather gauntlet on Adrienne's hand.

"Adal, you have outdone yourself today," she said as she fed the falcon the heart. "Cook will be pleased. Since

Lysander came home to visit, he and his companions have feasted day and night and made no effort to replenish the larder."

Adrienne frowned as she thought of the younger son of her guardian. Lysander's return to the manor three weeks past had brought her nothing but misery.

It was on her birthday and the eve of Saint Anne's feast day when Lysander had ridden into the inner ward with twenty knights and their squires and the grooms who had accompanied them. He had leapt from his horse and bounded up the stone stairs to the great hall where preparations were under way for the night's festivities.

Oblivious to the onlookers, Lysander had embraced his father, nearly lifting him off his feet in his excitement, and cried out, "Henry is dead! Richard is king of England now. The old lion has been conquered!"

Partially hidden by a stone pillar, she had listened in numb disbelief while Lysander, too caught up in his own swaggering to notice the pain in his father's eyes, regaled Baldhere with the tales being circulated of how Henry's sons had abandoned him in his final hours to join forces with Philip of France. Even Henry's own household servants had made off with his possessions, going so far as to strip the king's corpse as it lay in the chapel at Chinon, Lysander boasted.

In response, the old baron had lifted a reproachful gaze to the knight standing behind Lysander, a seasoned soldier who was responsible for the youth's training. "Gawin," Baldhere said sternly. "While you are instructing my son in the craft of siege and assault, you might also introduce him to the art of diplomacy." With that, Baldhere turned on his heel and strode from the hall.

Stung by the cool reception he had received in his father's house, Lysander swung around to utter a protest to Gawin and noticed Adrienne standing in the shadows. A look of contempt passed across Lysander's features, and Adrienne knew she would be made to suffer for having witnessed his humiliation.

That night, as the rest of the household celebrated Lysander's return, Baldhere had sat through the festivities silent and granite-faced, inwardly mourning the king to whom he had sworn fealty.

Her own grief was of a different nature. For eighteen years, Henry had sent an allowance, first to her mother and then to Baldhere, for her care. Yet not once in those eighteen years had he come to see her or inquired of her welfare or even asked whom she resembled. With his passing, her longing that someday he would acknowledge her also died, leaving a terrible aching void in her heart.

As for Lysander, it did not take long for Adrienne to recognize what disguise his retaliation would wear. Within days the gossip had flared up again. Only now she was not merely a royal embarrassment; she was the bastard daughter of a shamed and defeated king.

Adrienne glanced up at the darkening sky. "We had best go back, Adal. My lord will be angry when he discovers we have ridden out without a groom. If it begins to storm, he will worry." After slipping the leather hood over the falcon's head, she picked up the burlap bag and returned to her tethered mare.

By the time they entered the gates of the Foutreau, the first huge drops of rain had begun to fall.

Clutching Adal's jesses in her fist, Adrienne pulled the hood of the squire's tunic she wore up over her head. She rode astride with Adal held in front of her to keep the wind off the falcon's back. The shopkeepers and craftsmen were rushing to shield their goods from the weather and took little notice of her as she passed. Relieved to be spared for once their whispered remarks and sidelong glances, Adrienne turned her mount up the hill toward the Norman keep that stood sentinel over the village.

After she had relinquished the mare to one of the stableboys, Adrienne took Adal to the mews where Baldhere kept the falcons.

The falconer's apprentice brought her a feathered chicken leg from the kitchen. "A good day's hunt, m'lady?" he asked. Adrienne relaxed. Not everyone had succumbed to Lysander's influence, she thought.

She removed Adal's hood. "Adal did a splendid job today, Peter. She is to be rewarded."

The boy chuckled. "Keep rewarding her, m'lady, and she'll grow fat and lazy like old Rabi."

After Adal had feasted on the chicken leg, Adrienne fastened the falcon's jesses to her swivel and leash and tied her to her perch. She knew Peter would have tended Adal for her, but she had been taught that a good falconer always rewarded his own bird after a hunt. Baldhere had been generous in letting her train with the falcons. With the exception of his prized white Norwegian gyrfalcons, which only the master falconer was allowed to touch, the baron had granted her permission to take out any of the birds in his possession. She did not want to abuse that privilege by shirking her duties.

She picked up the burlap bag and was leaving the mews when Lysander blocked her way and shoved her back into the shadows. Although he was a few months younger than she, he was a full head taller and his squire's training had added muscle to his youthful frame. Seizing her wrist, he wrenched her arm behind her. "Why are they here?" he demanded. "Why does Father meet in secret with them and refuse me admittance to their council?"

Adrienne shook her head. "I don't know what you are talking abou—" She gasped when Lysander increased the pressure on her arm.

"*Henry's knights.* Father has been closeted in his chambers with them all afternoon. He has been asking for *you.*"

A wild, improbable hope surged through Adrienne's thoughts. Was it possible that before his death her sire had experienced a pang of conscience and had finally acknowledged that she was as much his flesh and blood as his legitimate offspring?

Then another more sobering prospect came to mind. All her life she had been a ward of the Crown, her well-being dependent on the annual allowance Henry sent to Baldhere for her care. What was to become of her now that Henry was dead? Would Baldhere permit her to stay at Foutreau? It had never occurred to her that her guardian might cast her out. Now the possibility was suddenly all too real.

Adrienne nervously moistened her lips. "If you wish to know what my lord wants of me, perhaps you should let me go to him."

A sneer curled Lysander's mouth. "Please do go to him. And while you are doing that, I shall be endearing myself to Cook." Before Adrienne realized his intentions, Lysander drove his fist into her stomach.

Adrienne cried out and doubled over in agony. Her grip on the burlap bag loosened, and she felt it being snatched from her hand as she sank to her knees.

Lysander stood with his feet apart, disdain in his pale blue eyes as he looked down on her huddled form. "Take care that you remember your place, *Lady Adrienne*. Unless you want your precious feathered friend preening on the perch there to suffer a tragic accident, you would do well to tread softly when you are in my presence."

After Lysander left the mews, Peter hurried to Adrienne. "Are you all right, m'lady? Did he hurt you?"

Adrienne peered up at the falconer's apprentice through a haze of pain and nausea. "Only my pride," she managed to get out. "Please, help me stand."

Peter gripped her hand and pulled her to her feet. Adrienne pressed her arm against her stomach, wincing as she straightened. "Is it true, Peter, what Lysander said about Henry's knights being here?"

"Aye, m'lady. More'n a dozen of them rode into Foutreau just past midday. There were others with them, but they did not bear the king's arms."

Anxious to know what was happening, Adrienne hurried across the ward toward the keep. The rain was falling heavily now, and by the time she ducked through the kitchen portal, her dark hair was plastered to her head and her tunic clung wetly to her body.

Lysander was nowhere to be seen. Adrienne slipped into the passageway, intent on reaching her chamber and changing into dry clothes before she was spotted, but that hope was dashed when she nearly collided with her foster mother's waiting woman at the foot of the stairs.

Agnes gasped and threw her hands up over her plump face. "Good heavens, m'lady, you gave me a fright! Look at you! Out hawking, no doubt, and the baron ordering us high and low in search of you!" Grasping Adrienne's bloodstained hand, she turned it over and clucked her disapproval. "You'd best go to your chamber and get out of those clothes before anyone sees you. You can't be appearing before the baron dressed like a common lad and drenched to the skin."

Adrienne caught the old woman's sleeve. "Why does my lord seek me, Agnes?" she asked desperately. "Has it to do with Henry's men being here?"

"You are asking the wrong person, m'lady. The baron is taking no one into his confidence, and Lady Joanna has been beside herself, not knowing what he is about."

The revelation that Baldhere had not even apprised his own wife of what was happening did nothing to ease Adrienne's fears. Releasing Agnes's sleeve, she bounded up the narrow stone steps that spiraled steeply up the corner tower.

Two maids were helping Lady Joanna into a chair beside the bed when Adrienne burst into the chamber. Surprise flickered in Lady Joanna's eyes, but her expression otherwise remained serene. After the lap robes had been tucked around her withered legs, she instructed Bertha to inform Baldhere that Adrienne had been found and would appear in the great hall within two hours' time, and Marlys to begin setting up the wooden bathing tub in Adrienne's chamber. Then she extended her gnarled hands toward Adrienne.

A smile softened the lines of her face. "I should have known you would be out with the falcons," she said as Adrienne went to her. "Is it too much to hope that we shall sup tonight on something besides mutton?"

Adrienne kissed an upturned cheek that smelled faintly of lilacs, then knelt beside the chair. "Would a brace of mallards, a pheasant, and a white-tailed hare please my lady?"

"They will please me immensely, my dear. Tell me, did you encounter any trouble?"

Only Lysander, Adrienne thought, but she refused to burden the proud woman with tales of her son's ill doings. She shook her head. "Adal and I would probably still be down at the brook had it not started to rain." She paused, then continued breathlessly, "Lady Joanna, why are Henry's knights here? Agnes said Lord Baldhere had the servants searching for me. Has something happened?"

"If it has, it can only mean good things for you. Baldhere would have sent the men packing had it been otherwise."

"Then you are not going to turn me out?"

"Turn you out! My dear, whatever gave you that idea?"

Adrienne's brows dipped in confusion. "I thought . . . I mean, now that my father is dead, the stipend he always sent . . ."

Lady Joanna took Adrienne's chin in her fragile-boned hand. In spite of her illness, she still had a formidable grip. "Adrienne, listen to me. All the time I was burying four sons and raising two others into brawny young men I scarcely recognized, I begged God to give me just one gentle daughter to whom I might teach all the things I held dear. When you came to us, I knew God had heard my prayers. You were a child not of my womb but of my heart, and from the first time I saw you, I knew I could not have been blessed with a more precious gift. Baldhere and I love you dearly. Even if Henry had never provided for you, we would have wanted to keep you with us. Turning you out has never entered our thoughts."

It was the longest speech Adrienne had ever heard from Lady Joanna, and the most unexpected. Lady Joanna was not particularly demonstrative with any of her children. Adrienne covered the older woman's hand with hers and turned her head to press her cheek to the cool dry palm.

Marlys returned to announce that the bath was being prepared.

Lady Joanna pulled her hand from Adrienne's. "After you have bathed, return to my chamber and I will oversee your toilette. I have a surprise for you—no, no, I am not going to divulge it. Now, off with you. I am tired and I need to rest."

Two hours later, Adrienne stood again in Lady Joanna's chamber, only by now her anxiety had increased a hundredfold. If doffing her braies and chausses and squire's tunic and washing the day's grime from her body made sense, what followed had driven her to a state of near-panic.

Never in Adrienne's life had she spent more than a few minutes getting dressed. Until today it had been sufficient to don a simple chemise and overgown and let her dark hair dry naturally into unruly waves and curls that tumbled down her back without any form of restraint. Today, however, the fundamental act of getting dressed had been raised to a ceremonial ritual.

First had come the chemise, one of Lady Joanna's surprises. Sewn of white sendal silk, it was so soft and sheer that it clung to Adrienne's tall, slender form like a morning mist. Around the close-fitting neck and wrists and in a wide swath around the hem, garlands of roses and ivy had been embroidered in white silk thread. Stitched so finely that it was not even visible until it caught the light at certain angles, the embroidery imparted a richness to the simple fabric.

Next came the bliaud, an overgown of deep wine red silk trimmed with gold, with a fitted bodice and a skirt that fell in graceful folds around her ankles. The neckline was cut into a low square, and the sleeves were very wide and very long, permitting the embroidered neck and wrists of the chemise to be seen. A double gold girdle studded with diamonds, amethysts, and pearls circled her waist and rode low on her hips, its ends nearly trailing on the floor. White silk hose were gartered just below her knees, and her soft kid slippers had been dyed and embroidered with gold to match the bliaud. At Lady Joanna's instruction, the maids brushed Adrienne's thick dark hair back from her face and braided it with strands of pearls, then wound the plaits about her head to form a coronet.

When all was done, the maids stepped back to survey their handiwork, a mixture of delight and envy on their faces. Agnes, who had been in and out of the chamber a dozen times during the transformation, now stood in the doorway, her eyes bright with unshed tears. "You are an angel come down to earth," she murmured, awe in her voice.

"The new clothes were to be your birthday surprise," Lady Joanna said. "But these old fingers could not work fast enough to finish them in time. I had thought to give them to you at Christmastide instead, but since we have important guests, I did not think you would mind having them now."

As Adrienne touched a fingertip to the soft silk, she thought she had never seen anything so beautiful or so meticulously fashioned. With Lady Joanna's pain-ridden hands, the garments must have taken weeks, if not months, to sew; and the ropes of pearls and the jeweled girdle had come from Lady Joanna's own dower chest. If Adrienne had ever questioned the depth of her foster mother's love for her, those doubts had been banished. A swell of emotion pressed against her throat. "They are beautiful," she whispered. "I don't know how to thank you."

"You may thank me by making me proud. Go down there and show them that I have a daughter of whom no one need be ashamed."

When Adrienne entered the great hall through the arched doorway, Baldhere was sitting at the high table, deep in conversation with Father Bernard and four other men whom she did not recognize. Three of the men wore over their chain mail scarlet surcoats emblazoned with three gold lions. In the lower hall, a dozen more similarly clad knights had assembled in small groups with a number of knights from Foutreau. The servants had begun lighting the torches and setting up the trestle tables in preparation for the evening meal. At first no one noticed her, and she used those precious extra seconds to square her shoulders and school her face into a mask that belied the terror churning in the pit of her stomach.

Seeing her, Baldhere stood and extended a hand toward her.

Adrienne crossed the dais toward her guardian with her head held high. What if she tripped and fell? she thought frantically. What if she lost her voice and made a fool of herself? What if—horror of horrors—her stomach growled?

A hush settled over the hall as one by one the knights fell silent. At the high table, a tall wiry knight with a gray beard and a deep scar across his right cheekbone rose to his feet, and his companions followed suit.

Taking her guardian's hand, Adrienne knelt and touched her forehead to the battle-scarred fingers. "My lord," she murmured.

Baldhere gave her hands a reassuring squeeze. "Rise, daughter," he said gruffly.

It was the first time Baldhere had ever called her "daughter." Confused, Adrienne rose. Their gazes met, and behind her guardian's stern countenance, Adrienne saw that his eyes reflected a mixture of pride and concern. Dread sank like a weight in the pit of her stomach. She could not shake the feeling that this meeting did not bode well for her, despite Lady Joanna's assurances to the contrary.

Baldhere placed a hand on her shoulder. "My lords, I present to you my ward, Adrienne de Langeais."

In the silence that followed, it took every ounce of self-control that Adrienne could summon not to turn and run. If she knew why Henry's knights had come here, she might know what to say. As it was, everyone was staring at her with an expectation that made her feel uncomfortable.

From the lower hall a snicker broke the silence. Adrienne saw Lysander whisper something to the group of knights gathered around him. The men glanced in her direction, and a titter rippled throughout the hall.

Adrienne felt her face grow warm. She knotted her hands, wishing she could wrap them around Lysander's neck. Had she not been wearing the new clothes Lady Joanna had so painstakingly sewn for her, she would have leapt off the dais and knocked Lysander to the floor. She knew it would not have taken him long to overpower her and her efforts would have earned her a thrashing, but it would have been worth it to witness the smug look on Lysander's face turn to one of surprise.

Nothing in Adrienne's upbringing had prepared her for what happened next.

The knight with the gray beard and the scar came forward and dropped to one knee in front of her. Bending his head, he extended his hands toward her, palms together, and said solemnly, "My lady, as for years I fought at the side of my lord Henry, king of England, and rendered my services unto him and his heirs, I now offer myself to you and swear before God and all those present to do everything within my power to serve and protect you."

There was a sharp intake of breath from all corners of the hall as everyone realized at the same instant that the knight was swearing an oath of fealty to her.

Adrienne knew that an oath of fealty was a serious matter; it was looked upon as a binding contract, not lightly entered into and even less easily broken. She had seen knights pay homage to Baldhere and had listened to her guardian recount the regal ceremony in which he had sworn an oath of fealty to her father, but this was different. Vassals swore fealty to their overlord, not to the unfortunate legacy of that overlord's indiscretion.

Bewildered, she cast a questioning glance at Baldhere. His grim expression revealed nothing.

She turned back to the knight. The expectant look on his face told her he was waiting, but for what? For her to acknowledge his oath? Dear God, why wouldn't someone tell her what she was supposed to do?

She swallowed hard. "My lord, what is your name?"

"I am called Leland, my lady."

Adrienne's heart pounded. If Sir Leland was rendering his oath in good faith, she had an obligation to accept it.

As she had seen Baldhere do whenever a knight paid homage to him, Adrienne took the knight's hands between hers. Both her hands and her voice shook. "I know not, my lord, what I have done to deserve this honor, but I pray I shall prove worthy of your trust."

Baldhere gave her shoulder a squeeze of approval.

Sir Leland lifted his gaze to hers, and Adrienne thought she saw a flicker of approval in his eyes before they once more became expressionless.

Leland lifted Adrienne's hands to his mouth and brushed his lips across her knuckles. "My lady," he murmured. He rose, and another of Henry's knights took his place.

One by one the king's knights swore an oath of fealty to her. Names paraded by her, gone before she could commit them to memory. Godfrey. Eustace. Giraud . . . and so on. Sometime during the bizarre ceremony, Lysander slipped from the hall. By the time the last of Henry's knights had knelt before her, Adrienne was just beginning to realize the implications of what transpired.

Her heart pounding, Adrienne took the place Baldhere indicated at the long table. After she was seated, Leland sat down next to her. As if responding to a signal, the rest of the knights departed, leaving her alone on the dais with her guardian, Leland, Father Bernard, and the fifth man who had been seated at the high table when she entered the hall.

If she had failed to notice the man before, now she could not tear her gaze from him. Dressed in the drab, somber tones of a cleric, he was a small man with unblinking, heavy-lidded eyes set in a sallow face marred by deep pitted scars. In contrast, his hands, folded serenely on top of the table, were unusually pale and smooth, with long tapered fingers that were almost feminine in their delicacy. Although Adrienne managed to keep her revulsion from showing in her expression, she was unable to purge her mind of the irreverent thought that the man had the hands of a saint and the eyes of a snake.

Clasping his hands behind him, Baldhere began pacing. The tenderness Adrienne had seen earlier in her guardian's expression was gone, and the brusqueness in his voice as he addressed her increased her alarm. "I'll get straight to the purpose of this meeting," Baldhere said. "Before he died, Henry made arrangements to secure your future. 'Tis an unusual pact, but it has been sanctioned by the Church, and the count palatine of the Rhine has endorsed the proposal as well, so there will be no contest from that quarter."

Adrienne's heart missed a beat. Had she heard correctly? Was Baldhere saying that her father had not been unmindful of her existence after all? That, after eighteen years, he was publicly acknowledging that she was truly his daughter?

If so, why did she suddenly feel sick to her stomach?

For the first time she noticed the legal documents on the table.

"You are to be married to Duke Wilhelm of Lachen," Baldhere continued. "The banns will be read on the morrow. If, after seven days, no one comes forward to give reasonable cause to delay the proceedings, the contracts will be signed and the betrothal ceremony performed. Immediately following the ceremony, you will depart Foutreau under the protection of Sir Leland and his men and proceed to Trier where the wedding will take place."

The color drained from Adrienne's face. Shocked into silence, she listened in horror, each "you will" falling on her ears like a physical blow. "You will depart . . . You will be married . . . You will agree . . ."

Disbelief rose up inside her in thick, nauseating waves. Although she had known the day would come when a marriage would be arranged for her, she had thought it would be to someone from the shire. At best, she had prayed that her husband would be an honorable man who would want her for herself and not be distressed by her lack of a dowry. At worst, she had hoped he would not be repulsive.

Then she thought of the gaunt, cheerless man seated at the table with them. Surely *he* could not be Duke Wilhelm? Struggling for composure, she turned her head and forced herself to look at him. He inclined his head toward her, and Adrienne felt the room tilt precariously.

"I am Theobald of Mainz, Duke Wilhelm's chancellor," the man said, as if reading her thoughts. "Since the duke cannot be here for the betrothal ceremony, he sent me to stand in his stead."

Before Adrienne could react to that announcement, Sir Leland began sifting through the documents before him. "As your guardian has already stated," he said, drawing Adrienne's attention away from the chancellor, "you will bring to the marriage as part of your dowry the countship of Sainte-Croix. In return Wilhelm has promised a handsome dower, including the cities of Wiesen and Oftringen." He glanced up. "Shall I read the contracts to you, my lady?"

Too shaken to respond otherwise, Adrienne nodded.

As Leland read aloud one obscure clause after another, Adrienne felt her despair mounting. Although the composer of the contracts had gone to great lengths to ensure her safety—page upon page detailed the penalties that would be exacted should any harm come to her—it was evident that she was not the prize in these negotiations; Sainte-Croix was. Duke Wilhelm, she was willing to wager, would have married a leper in order to gain control of the countship.

It was said that a more unholy place did not exist on the entire Continent. Sainte-Croix was a land of heretics and outlaws. Pilgrims whose travels took them through Sainte-Croix returned to tell of lay priests who performed heathen rituals and of people who worshiped Satan and invoked the souls of the dead. With the Church's blessing, Henry had seized control of the countship and driven the Comte de Sainte-Croix into exile.

"I don't understand," Adrienne said when Leland finished reading the document. "If my father wanted Wilhelm of Lachen to have control of Sainte-Croix, why didn't he just give it to him?"

" 'Tis not that simple," Leland said. "Sainte-Croix provides both England and France with ports of departure from the Continent to the Holy Land. Henry did not want the countship annexed to the Holy Roman Empire, merely placed under its protection so that it would not fall to King Philip. He wanted to ensure that it would remain securely in England's hands."

The truth struck Adrienne like a bucket of icy water. The only reason her father had acknowledged her was to use her for his own purposes. She meant nothing to him, and she had been a fool to think otherwise.

Her throat constricted. All her life she had wanted nothing more than to be acknowledged and accepted by the man who had fathered her. To finally be granted that wish only to have the reality of it turn out to be so debasing was more than she could bear. She stood up. "Please excuse me. I need time to think—"

Baldhere rounded on her. "Sit down!"

Adrienne recoiled as if he'd slapped her. She gripped the edge of the table. "My lord, please don't ask this of me. I'll do anything you want. I shall leave Foutreau if you wish.

But I can't go through with this sham marriage. I would sooner wed the lowest villein in your fief than to—"

"You have no choice."

"I can't do it!"

Baldhere's palm crashed down on the table. His face was a frightening shade of red. "You will go to Trier, if I have to drag you there myself. And you will wed Duke Wilhelm. There will be no more discussion of the matter. You will do as you are told." That said, he turned on his heel and stalked from the hall.

At Baldhere's explosion, conversation in the hall had ceased. Humiliation burned in Adrienne's cheeks as she watched her guardian's departure. Her knees had begun to quake. Aware that everyone was staring at her, she turned a pleading gaze on Leland. "If I repudiate this marriage, what will happen?"

"That choice is not yours to make," Theobald said.

Adrienne whirled on him. "I did not ask for your counsel!" she cried out, her dislike of the man blossoming into outright hatred.

Anger flashed in the chancellor's eyes, but before he could speak, Father Bernard intervened. "My child, please give some thought to your words before you speak, and do not lash out at those who seek to guide you."

Adrienne turned to the priest in desperation. "Father, there must be something you can do to stop this betrothal. Not even the Church sanctions a marriage that does not have the consent of those to be wed."

Father Bernard held out his hands, palms upward, in resignation. "Theoretically you are correct. Given the circumstances, however, I doubt that even the pope would intervene on your behalf. I'm sorry."

Leland gathered up the parchments and stood. "If you refuse this marriage, your life will become a nightmare. You will be prey to any fortune hunter who seeks to gain control of Sainte-Croix."

"But I don't even want Sainte-Croix."

"I fear, my lady, that the terms of your inheritance are inviolable. What you want or don't want is of no consequence."

Feeling backed into a corner, Adrienne struck without thinking. "Why? Because my errant father suffered a twinge of conscience on his deathbed and decided that his bastard daughter should have a dowry?"

"Because," Leland said in a carefully controlled voice, "the *king* decided it should be so."

"Not twelve months ago he announced to the world that Sainte-Croix would go to Prince John so that he might shed that hideous nickname, 'Lackland,' before he took a wife," Adrienne protested. "No one is going to believe, my lord, that Henry would suddenly disinherit his favorite son in favor of a bastard daughter for whom he cared naught."

Leland inclined his head in agreement. "Least of all Prince John," he said. "Unfortunately that is the price one pays for double-crossing one's father."

Even as she obstinately lifted her chin, Adrienne had begun to realize the futility of fighting the mandate. Whether or not she liked it, Henry had made her heiress to the most godforsaken and the most coveted of all his domains. Her future had been decided.

Feeling as if her entire world had shattered, Adrienne pivoted and marched away from the table, her head held so high she could barely see where she was going.

As soon as she was out of the hall, she broke into a run and bolted up the tower stairs. She would have gone into Lady Joanna's chamber, but when she reached the landing, raised voices filtered through the closed door. She froze, her heart pounding as she eavesdropped on the heated exchange.

Baldhere's voice rose to a shout. "For God's sake, woman! Do you think I want to send her away?"

"Of course not, but must we force this on her? 'Tis all so sudden. If we could but give her time to adjust—"

"There is no time. Until she is married, she will be in

danger. Joanna, we have known for years that something like this could happen. 'Tis out of our hands now."

Adrienne fled up the remaining stairs to her own bedchamber. She slammed the door behind her.

She wrapped her arms around her stomach and squeezed her eyes shut against the threatening tears. A sob lodged in her throat, and she choked that back too.

How could they do this to her? How could they tear her away from her home and thrust her into a world where her bastardy would always be paramount in the minds of those around her? Here she could escape the gossip. But in a ducal court where everyone would know she had been wed for the sake of her dowry, every glance in her direction would contain a smirk, every remark an insinuation. She felt betrayed, not only by the father she had never known but also by those she had grown to love and who she had thought loved her.

Behind her, the door opened, then shut again.

Adrienne whirled around to find Lysander leaning against the closed door. Through the high window the setting sun finally broke through the storm clouds and reflected off the downy beginnings of Lysander's pale gold beard. She impaled him with a molten glare. "What do you want?"

"What do you think I want?"

"You have no business here. I want you to leave."

"I beg to differ with you." Lysander pushed himself away from the door. "I have every right to be here. Foutreau is my home. You are the intruder here."

As he came toward her, Adrienne backed away from him. Her mind groped for something to say in her defense. "In a few days I shall be gone. That should make you happy."

Lysander closed the distance between them. A cold smile twisted his mouth. "Ah, yes, seeing you exalted to the rank of duchess while I struggle for mere knighthood will make me ecstatic," he said. "I cannot help but wonder if our dear duke realizes what a treasure he is acquiring. After all, your mother was a whore; why should you be any different?"

Adrienne's nostrils flared. Without thinking, she cracked her open palm against Lysander's cheek.

He shoved her against the wall.

Adrienne threw her hands up between them to push him away. He caught her wrists and forced her hands aside. She started to scream, and Lysander clamped a hand over her mouth.

His face loomed over hers. "How do you think your precious duke will react when he discovers his virgin bride has come to his bed carrying another man's child?"

Adrienne felt his free hand groping beneath her skirts, and the realization of what he intended struck her with terrifying clarity. She wedged her arm between them in an effort to break his hold on her. The hand covering her mouth and nose lifted. She jerked her head to one side and opened her mouth to scream, but he grasped her chin and wrenched her head back to the front. He smothered her cries with his mouth.

Ale had soured his breath, and Adrienne wanted to retch as his mouth covered hers. She clenched her teeth in a desperate refusal to yield to his kiss, but his fingers tightened on her chin, causing her to gasp in pain. He forced her lips apart and invaded her mouth with his tongue.

Without warning the assault stopped.

Leland grasped the neck and belt of Lysander's tunic, pulled him away from her, and hurled him toward the doorway. Lysander landed on his side, just inside the door.

Adrienne braced one hand against the wall as the room reeled around her. She was breathing hard, and her eyes were wide in her flushed face as she watched Leland grab the neck of Lysander's tunic and haul him to his feet. "Come near my lady again, squire," the knight bit out, "and you are liable to find a dagger stuck between your ribs." He shoved Lysander out the door, and the youth stumbled down the stairs.

Leland turned back to her. "Are you hurt?"

She shook her head. "How did you know to come?"

"I saw the boy leave the hall earlier. Judging from the venom in his expression, I thought he might be up to no good."

Adrienne shuddered in relief. "I don't know how to thank you. I am in your debt."

" 'Tis my duty to protect you. I swore an oath of fealty to you. Did you think I would forget my pledge so soon?"

The truth of why fifteen men had sworn their allegiance to her was now painfully clear. It also drove home the terrible finality of her situation. " 'Tis all so overwhelming, my lord," she said shakily. "I fear I have much to learn."

Leland regarded her pensively for a minute. Finally he turned toward the door. "I will post guards outside your chamber door. There is no guessing what further mischief that arrogant young pup might attempt, and I have no wish to return my host's hospitality by murdering his son."

Chapter Two

HER HAND PROTECTED by the gauntlet, Adrienne carried Adal through the low doorway of the mews and fastened the falcon's leash to a stone block in the ward. In a sheltered corner was a shallow stone basin. She washed the basin and filled it with fresh water.

Adal tried to fly toward the sound of the splashing water. Adrienne smiled as she went to her. "You know what that is for, don't you?" she said. Freeing Adal's leash from the block, she took the falcon up on her fist and carried her to the basin, then knelt and tied the leash to a stake driven into the ground. Before she could lower Adal into the water, she saw Sir Leland coming toward them.

Her smile faded.

For the past week, ever since the arrival of Henry's knights, she had been kept under strict surveillance. Marlys now shared her bedchamber, sleeping on a pallet just inside the door, while armed guards occupied the landing without. She was no longer permitted to leave Foutreau, even with a groom, and the few times she had managed to escape the keep, her movements had been confined to the inner ward. She had become a prisoner in her own home.

Six days ago the banns of her impending marriage had been announced in the chapel prior to the morning mass. While tradition held that the banns be read on three successive holy days, she was to be permitted no more than the

23

seven-day wait that was required by law. Unless someone came forth to protest the union, tomorrow morning she would stand before witnesses in the great hall and publicly promise to wed Duke Wilhelm of Lachen. Although the actual wedding would not take place until she reached Trier, the betrothal was as binding as the marriage itself and could be broken only at the risk of penalty to the parties involved.

When Adal spotted Sir Leland, she began bating her wings and straining against the leash. Annoyed, Adrienne turned, blocking the knight from the falcon's view. "Am I to be permitted no solitude at all?" she asked. "Or do you and your men intend to follow me wherever I go?"

"I fear, my lady, that the threat of danger makes solitude a luxury you can no longer afford. There are many who would see your head on a spike rather than permit you to fulfill your father's edict. You would be well advised to keep a close guard about you at all times."

Although Adrienne doubted that she was important enough to warrant that kind of caution, she knew it was useless to argue. She was quickly learning that her thoughts and opinions and wishes were of no consequence. "At least move back," she said, fighting for control of the restless falcon. "You make Adal nervous. She doesn't know you, and she won't bathe while you are standing there."

"That is a fair request, my lady." Leland bent his head toward a stone bench outside the door to the mews. "I shall sit over there."

"Thank you," Adrienne said stiffly. She turned her attention back to Adal.

As the knight looked on, Adrienne lowered the falcon into the basin. With her fingertips she splashed water onto the falcon's breast and under her wings. As soon as Adal settled down and took charge of her own bath, Adrienne stood and moved a discreet distance away to allow the falcon some privacy as she splashed and preened in the basin.

Adrienne cast a covert glance at the knight sitting on the bench near the mews, and her annoyance gave way to curiosity. Over the past few days she had heard numerous bits of gossip about Leland of Nemours, not the least of which was that he had once been in love with her mother. She wondered about that. He was not forward with her in the way that the other men often were, yet sometimes when he looked at her she had the odd feeling that he was seeing someone else. From her limited memory and from what she had been told, she knew that she resembled her mother. She was tall like her mother, and she had her mother's dark hair. She had her father's gray eyes, however. Angevin gray, Baldhere called them, often recounting Henry's ability to reduce a grown man to tears with a mere look from them.

The falcon began to show signs of restlessness. Adrienne removed her from the water and returned her to the block. Adal shivered, spraying Adrienne with water, then spread her wings and tail, obviously enjoying the warm sunshine. Laughing, Adrienne removed the gauntlet and dried her face on the sleeve of her overgown.

Deciding that if her desire for solitude was to be denied, she could at least indulge her curiosity, Adrienne turned and walked across the yard toward Sir Leland.

The knight stood as she approached.

Adrienne motioned toward the bench. "Please, my lord, sit down. There is no need for ceremony. I have lived without it my entire life. My mark on a few documents changes naught. I am still the same person I have always been."

"As you wish, my lady." Leland waited until Adrienne was seated before joining her on the bench.

Adrienne took a deep breath. "I'll not waste your time with idle chatter, my lord. There is something specific I want to ask you."

Leland shook his head. "My lady, if this is regarding the betrothal tomorrow, I fear I cannot—"

" 'Tis about my mother."

Leland turned his head to stare at her. His expression revealed nothing.

"I've heard some of the men say you knew her. Is that true?"

"Yes."

"Did you know her well?"

A shadow passed behind Leland's eyes. He looked away. "Yes."

Adrienne felt a pang of remorse. "I'm sorry. I didn't realize that talking about her would bring back painful memories for you."

Leland smiled pensively. "For a time 'twas my duty to guard her as I am now doing for you. We became friends. Nothing more. If I seem nostalgic, my lady, 'tis for what might have been rather than for what was lost."

"You were in love with her, weren't you?" Adrienne asked softly.

"Everyone who knew her was in love with her. But Isolde loved Henry. There was no room in her heart for anyone else."

"The only things I remember about her were that she was very ill and she spent a great deal of time with the nuns at the abbey." Adrienne was quiet a moment before continuing in a low voice edged with pain. "I never knew my father at all. Sometimes I wish I could see both of them through eyes other than those of a six-year-old who was confused and hurt about being left alone so much of the time."

As they watched Adal groom and anoint her feathers, the knight told Adrienne everything he could remember about Isolde de Langeais, the beautiful young girl who had captured the heart of the king of England. When he finished, a frown puckered Adrienne's brow. "I understand why my father could not abandon Queen Eleanor in order to marry my mother. But if he loved her so much, why did he never return to see her? Why did he never come to see *me*?"

"I cannot answer that. I do know that when you were born, Henry was still battling the furor over Thomas Becket's murder and trying to get the pope to lift the interdict that had been placed on his domains.

"In the meantime, Henry's wife and sons stirred up the barons in a revolt against him. He had his hands full trying to contain the rebellion before it spread across all of France."

Even in her ignorance Adrienne could see that the reasons Sir Leland had given her for her father's neglect were mere excuses. Had Henry wanted to see her or her mother again, he would have made the effort. There was a note of vexation in her sigh. "I wish he had stayed out of my life. After all these years of pretending I did not even exist, why did he have to suddenly take it upon himself to plot my entire future?"

"I have been led to believe, my lady, that before his death, Henry made provisions for all his children."

But those other provisions didn't include this godforsaken marriage, Adrienne thought, again feeling overwhelmed by the fate to which she had been condemned. "I must take Adal inside now." Her voice trembled in spite of her efforts to control it. "She will get overheated if she is kept out in the sun too long."

Adrienne started to stand, but Leland placed a hand on her arm. "My lady, Henry was not a bad man, but a good man who had many faults. Try to remember him for the prosperity he brought to his domains and not for his shortcomings."

Sudden tears of frustration choked Adrienne's throat. "You don't understand," she blurted out. "I don't care what my father did for anyone else. All I ever wanted was to know what he looked like."

Inside the great hall of the castle at Foutreau the mood was grim. Henry's knights stood to one side of the hall, while along the opposite wall Duke Wilhelm's men could be identified by their saffron and black surcoats. All watched and listened in silence as the duke's proxy and Adrienne de Langeais exchanged vows. No villagers were present at the ceremony because there was to be no celebration afterward. No scones and biscuits were to be piled in a heap over which the betrothed couple would ensure their future prosperity by exchanging kisses. No one would follow the ancient custom of showering the couple with kernels of wheat to guarantee fertility. No one felt like celebrating, least of all the bride, who was dressed in a plain lavender bliaud and a gray woolen mantle intended for traveling, and who looked as if she wanted to commit mayhem.

On the dais, Adrienne tried her best not to recoil in disgust when Theobald of Mainz took her right hand. Throughout the ceremony she had vacillated between numbness and impotent rage. Although she had finally yielded to the betrothal out of a sense of duty to Baldhere and Lady Joanna, inwardly she still refused to accept it. Even as Theobald took the heavy gold ring Father Bernard had blessed and slipped it onto her third finger, a part of her clung to the belief that the wedding would not take place.

Adal sensed when Adrienne entered the mews, and began pacing restlessly on her perch. Adrienne picked up a feather and stroked the falcon's breast with it. "This is farewell, my dear friend," she said in a choked voice. She blinked back the tears that gathered in her eyes.

Adal quieted and settled down on her perch.

Adrienne took a deep breath. "Peter will take good care of you. He won't let Lysander near you, and he has promised to take you outside every day so you won't feel cooped up."

A shadow fell across the open doorway. "They are waiting for you," Baldhere said.

Adrienne's throat tightened. "Good-bye, Adal," she whispered brokenly. "I am going to miss you."

She followed Baldhere into the ward where Henry's and Wilhelm's men had assembled on horseback along with a dozen of Baldhere's knights who would accompany them as far as London. Marlys was also going along on the journey as Adrienne's personal maid. The girl's giggle tittered through the courtyard as she tried to accustom herself to the sidesaddle.

Baldhere placed a hand on Adrienne's shoulder. "I would not have agreed to this if I thought it was not for the best. You will have a far more comfortable future than I could ever provide for you."

Adrienne said nothing. She knew she was not making this any easier, but her pride refused to allow her to accept graciously that which neither of them had the power to change.

"Once you are settled in your new home, if your husband is agreeable to the offer, I want to present him with a gift of some of my best falcons. I also want to send Adal to you. You care for that bird more than anyone else does. She belongs with you."

Adrienne turned her head to stare at her guardian in astonishment at his unexpected and generous gesture, and to her surprise she saw that Baldhere's eyes were bright with unshed tears. Her resolve crumbled, and the tears she had been trying so hard to contain streamed down her face. She swallowed hard against the knot that swelled in her throat. "I'm scared," she choked.

Baldhere's arm went around her shoulders, and he drew her against him. "I know you are. But I also know that I would be doing you a disservice to keep you here. Inasmuch as Joanna and I like to think of you as our own, we have always known you were only to be entrusted to us for a short while before leaving us again. We feel blessed to have had you with us for as long as we did. You have a brave and generous heart, my girl. Whatever the future holds for you, I know you will meet it gallantly."

Adrienne wiped her eyes with her fingertips. "I don't feel very gallant," she said. "I fear, my lord, you expect more of me than I am able to give."

Baldhere chuckled. "I disagree. Now, off with you before Marlys annoys the men with her silliness. Why Joanna chose that one to attend you is beyond me, but she will be company for you on the journey nonetheless."

All too soon the last farewells had been said. As they passed through the gates of the outer wall and left the village behind them, Adrienne twisted around in the saddle for a final look at the Norman keep that had been her home for the past twelve years. A feeling of desolation gripped her, and she frantically tried to commit every stone in its massive walls to memory. In spite of the entreaties that she had received to return for a visit, she could not shake the premonition that she would never see Foutreau again.

From the battlements Lysander watched the party ride away. The breeze lifted a lock of his hair, making it shimmer like burnished gold in the sunlight. But his pale blue eyes, focused on the diminishing riders, chilled everything they touched, and an unpleasant smile curled his mouth as a plan began to take shape in his mind.

At the end of the second day, the travelers stopped for the night at an inn on the outskirts of Westminster. As they prepared to depart the next morning, Adrienne noticed that Leland and his men were no longer wearing the distinctive scarlet tabards that identified them as vassals of the king. When she asked Leland about the change in their attire, his answer was guarded. "In a city the size of London, my lady, one cannot always know who one's enemies are. 'Tis best to draw as little attention as possible."

Adrienne did not have to ask who her enemies were. Queen Eleanor was not likely to show compassion for anyone on whom Henry had bestowed a favor, especially when the recipient of that favor was one of her husband's illegitimate offspring.

As a precaution against encountering any of Queen Eleanor's men-at-arms they skirted Westminster where preparations were under way for Richard's coronation and entered the walled part of London through the old Roman Aldersgate. The crowded streets pulsed with excitement. Shopkeepers and eel wives hawked their wares, their voices competing with the squeals of pigs running loose in the streets. On one corner, a few feet away from a friar begging alms, a crier announced that the baths were open and the water hot. All along the way they heard talk of Richard's impending arrival.

As they neared the waterfront, the cobbled lanes narrowed in places to a mere five feet. The half-timbered houses and shops became smaller and closer together, with jutting upper stories that projected out into the street, blocking out the sunlight. Since entering the city, Leland's men had formed a closed circle around Adrienne, shielding her from potential harm. Now Leland moved his horse so close to her that their knees touched. Leaning toward her, he said in a low voice, "From what I can gather, Richard docked in Southampton a few days ago. If we are lucky, by the time he arrives in London, we will be well on our way to Trier."

The dark, airless passageways made Adrienne's heart hammer with trepidation. "I don't like any of this."

"None of us do, my lady."

Adrienne glanced over her shoulder and spotted Theobald in the distance. They had exchanged scarcely two words since the betrothal ceremony, and she had taken to wondering if her affianced husband was as dour as his emissary. She turned back to Leland. "Then why are you escorting me to Trier? I want neither my dowry nor this marriage, so you cannot say you are going to all this trouble for me."

"I made a promise to my king. Would you have me go back on my word?"

The note of chastisement in Leland's voice did not go unnoticed, and Adrienne felt a crimson stain creep up her neck. She shifted uneasily in the sidesaddle and fixed her gaze straight ahead. "Of course not."

Leland regarded Adrienne's stiff-necked pose with a troubled frown. "If I may offer a word of advice, my lady, the sooner you stop fighting the inevitable, the easier this will be on all of us."

"Oooh, m'lady, I think I'm going to die!"

Adrienne stopped pacing and turned an impatient gaze on the other girl. "Marlys, you can't still be sick. The river is as smooth as silk. You can hardly feel the ship move."

From her narrow bunk Marlys peered over the edge of the blanket she was clutching beneath her chin. Tears welled up in her brown eyes. Her pale face had a decidedly greenish cast. "I don't mean to be a bother, m'lady. I'll try harder to be good, I promise."

Adrienne knew Marlys could not help being sick, but she did not know how much longer she could endure being confined in the small cabin she shared with the maid. Marlys was supposed to be attending *her*, yet from the moment the ship left the dock in London, *she* had been the one kept busy emptying the slop basin and bathing Marlys's face with cool damp cloths. And they had not yet left England. If the gentle movement of the merchant-man on the Thames made the girl ill, what was going to happen when they entered the choppy waters of the North Sea?

"Come up on deck for a while," Adrienne suggested. "The fresh air will do us both good."

If it was possible for Marlys's face to turn any paler, it did. She swallowed hard. "Please, m'lady, I can't."

Adrienne thought she would go insane if she had to stay in this wretched cabin another minute. But when she looked at Marlys huddled miserably on the bunk, guilt pricked her conscience. "Rest, then. You will feel better once you get accustomed to the motion of the ship."

Marlys groaned and leaned over the slop basin. Adrienne squeezed her eyes shut and struggled to maintain control of her own stomach. This was going to be a long voyage.

Six days later they dropped anchor in Dordrecht. Leland found Adrienne standing at the rails with the wind whipping through her hair as she watched the ship's cargo being unloaded onto the docks. "I am worried about Marlys," she told him. "I thought she would feel better once she grew accustomed to the motion of the ship, but she only gets worse. Perhaps we should consider traveling the rest of the way by land."

Leland rested his forearms on the railing. His brows drew together. "You will be in more danger on land than on the water. The threat from roving bands of outlaw knights is far greater than the threat of river pirates, especially while we are passing through the border provinces."

Adrienne sighed wearily. "Right now our greatest threat is that Marlys will jump ship."

Two days later, when they were preparing to transfer vessels, Marlys tearfully refused to board the sailing barge that was to carry them up the Rhine River to Coblenz where Duke Wilhelm was to meet them. "I can't do it, m'lady," she choked between sobs. "I've been spewing my guts out ever since we left London. I just can't get on another boat."

Adrienne turned to Leland. "What are we going to do? 'Twill be cruel to force her to continue the journey this way."

Leland's face was flushed from moving chests and horses, and sweat dripped from his hair. The scar across his cheek was more pronounced than usual. He looked at Marlys, but before he could speak, Theobald intervened. "Get on the barge or be left behind. We have endured enough of your antics."

The girl's wailing grew louder.

Adrienne rounded on the chancellor. "Surely you don't think she is feigning her seasickness?"

"What I think, my lady, has no bearing on the matter. Your maidservant will follow orders or suffer the consequences."

Adrienne bristled. It was not right to punish Marlys for something she could not control, and the chancellor's lack of compassion touched a nerve. None of them wanted to be here, she and Marlys least of all. When Theobald turned to walk away, something inside her snapped. "I am not going either," she said.

Theobald turned back to face her, his expression one of disbelief. "I beg your pardon?"

Adrienne lifted her chin and speared Theobald with a look that openly challenged his authority. "Unless arrangements are made to ensure Marlys's comfort, we shall both remain behind."

Theobald glowered at her, and for a moment Adrienne wondered if he intended to force them to board the barge. "Is that a command, my lady?" he asked stiffly.

As she stood there matching his antagonistic stare with one of her own, it occurred to Adrienne that he was deferring to her. It made her feel uneasy. She did not know what to do. Acting in place of Duke Wilhelm, Theobald was responsible for her. Yet she, in turn, was responsible for Marlys. Without answering his question, she turned to Leland. "I wish to speak with you in private."

Leland glanced from Adrienne to Theobald and back again. He motioned down the dock. "This way, my lady."

Adrienne turned and followed Leland. As she walked away, she could feel Theobald's glare burning into her back.

In the end it was agreed that Marlys and twelve of Henry's men would continue the journey overland while

Leland and the two remaining knights, Adrienne, Theobald of Mainz, and Duke Wilhelm's men-at-arms would travel the rest of the way to Coblenz by river barge.

Hugh de Clairmont stood outside his tent with his feet apart and his arms folded over his chest, his dark eyes betraying nothing of the icy satisfaction that settled within him as he watched the prisoners being herded into the encampment. Since word reached him that Henry's daughter and her entourage were on the Continent, his every waking thought had been concentrated on this moment.

His men had followed the party since their departure from Dordrecht a week ago. That so few of Henry's knights were escorting their heiress to her betrothed did not surprise him. By the time he died, Henry had few friends remaining; most of his followers had already abandoned him to swear their allegiance to his son Richard. Of course it was possible that the small size of the party was intended as a diversion; anyone seeking to thwart their plans would be on the lookout for a sizable army. A handful of soldiers bearing no identifying arms would have little trouble slipping across the borders unnoticed.

What did puzzle him was that no lady's maid accompanied Henry's daughter. It appeared that the girl's people valued her reputation as little as they did her safety.

Hugh barked an order to the guard standing nearest him. "Bring the girl to me. And be quick about it." Pivoting, he went inside his tent.

Minutes later the tent flap was raised, and a small, thin brown-haired girl was thrust into the tent. When the guard released her arm, the girl lost her balance and fell to her knees. She sobbed into her hands.

Hugh motioned to the guard. The guard left.

Displeasure creased Hugh's brow as he regarded the trembling, sobbing girl before him. "Get up," he snapped in French. When she did not immediately comply, he reached down and seized her arm. "Get up and stop your sniveling, or I will give you something to cry about."

A panicked cry tore from the girl's throat as he hauled her to her feet. For a moment Hugh just stared at her, thinking this must be a hoax. Not only was the girl far from tall, she was undeniably plain. In fact, she bore no resemblance at all to the fair Isolde despite the stories he had heard. "Look at me," he ordered.

The girl kept her terrified gaze fixed on the middle of his chest. Hugh realized that she was staring at the coiled serpent emblazoned on his surcoat. His patience eroding, he grasped her chin and forced her head up. "When I give you a command, my lady, I expect you to obey. Do you understand me?"

Fresh tears welled up in the girl's eyes, and her bottom lip quivered, but she did not answer.

Hugh released her chin. "Who are you?" he demanded.

Still no answer.

Hugh's eyes turned cold. Was she deaf? Raking his fingers through his hair in frustration, he began to pace like a restless cat within the confines of the tent. The girl who had been brought to him was not the hot-tempered heiress he had been expecting. Had his information regarding Adrienne de Langeais been faulty? Or was there some other explanation? On a whim, he rounded on her and asked again, this time in English, "Who are you?"

The relief that flashed across the girl's face was so pronounced that Hugh nearly laughed aloud. She wiped her wet eyes and sniffled. "Marlys, m'lord."

Hugh's black brows drew together and down. "Then you are not Adrienne de Langeais?"

Astonishment flickered in the girl's eyes, and she vehemently shook her head. "Oh, no, m'lord. Lady Adrienne is my mistress."

Hugh's anger soared at the realization of what must have happened. Of all the idiotic mistakes his men could have made, this one had come close to destroying everything he had worked for. Striding to the tent opening, he lifted the flap. "Find my brother," he told the guard. "Tell him I want to speak with him immediately."

Hugh turned back to Marlys. "I am going to ask you a few questions, my dear. I would not advise you to lie. Is that understood?"

Fear widened the girl's eyes, and she nervously bobbed her head.

A few minutes later Graeham de Clairmont entered the tent. Although neither as tall nor as broad-shouldered as his elder brother, he was formidable in his own right. At the sight of him, Marlys took a step backward.

Graeham threw her a derisive glance. "I hope you were able to get more out of her than I could. The stubborn wench refused to answer any of my questions."

"Probably because she could not understand them," Hugh bit out. "She does not speak French." At his brother's startled expression, Hugh continued in a harsh, punishing tone, "You captured the wrong woman, Graeham. This is not Adrienne de Langeais. This is her maidservant."

Gradually the river narrowed, and the marshes and peat bogs of the lowlands gave way to rolling hills that had been carved into terraced vineyards and dotted with castles. Adrienne stood at the railing, watching the approach of a village lying at the foot of a cliff that jutted high above the river.

After Marlys's departure, the voyage had become much more pleasant, almost relaxing. Each bend in the river unfolded to reveal a landscape that was even more breathtaking than the stretch before. Adrienne could not help thinking that her betrothal, however distasteful, had provided her with an opportunity to see places of beauty that would otherwise have remained beyond her experience.

Ahead of them an iron chain was being stretched across the river to block their passage. The river blocks were occurring with greater frequency the more the river narrowed.

Leland joined her on deck. His expression was grim. "We are about to be stopped again. These river barons with their tolls are thieves and should be dealt with as such."

Adrienne threw him a sharp glance. He seemed more tense than usual. "Are we in any danger?"

Leland shook his head. "They are more of a nuisance than a menace. Although, to be frank, their presence makes me uneasy. It might have behooved us to have made this journey overland after all."

Adrienne slept fitfully. More than once she was awakened by ship's sounds that seemed louder than usual: the groaning of the timbers, the lapping of water against the hull, the footsteps on the deck over her cabin. Annoyed with her inability to rest, she plumped up her pillow and lay back down.

No sooner had she drifted off to sleep than she again jerked awake. She lay without moving, her muscles tensed and her heart pounding. She did not know what had awakened her. All was quiet. Too quiet. It reminded her of the stillness in the forest when the presence of a predator would cause even the birds to stop chirping.

You are being silly, she chastised herself. There was nothing to fear. Sir Pearroc was standing guard outside her cabin door. She took a deep breath, and the sound rattled the stillness. She rolled onto her back. It was uncomfortably warm and stifling in the cabin. As her eyelids drifted shut, she decided that tomorrow night she would ask Sir Leland for permission to make up a pallet on the deck.

Her eyes flew open.

In the blackness a shadowed face loomed inches above hers. A scream swelled inside her, but was silenced by the huge hand that clamped over her mouth and nose. She struck out, raking her nails down the side of that threatening face. Her wrist was caught in a bruising grip, and her arm wrenched aside. She twisted and kicked, but her legs were tangled in the sheets.

Above her a man's harsh whisper pierced the darkness. *"Be still!"*

She stopped struggling. Sobs of terror erupted inside her, and she fought to contain them. Finally the man's hold on her loosened. She sank her teeth into his palm.

He muttered an oath and jerked his hand away.

Before Adrienne could open her mouth to scream, the man lifted her, sheets and all, and pushed her face down onto the bunk. She scrambled to her knees, but before she could get away, he knotted his hand in her hair and shoved her face into the pillow.

Panic rose up inside her in thick, nauseating waves. The pillow smothered her screams and cut off her air. Unable to breathe, she clawed frantically at the hand that held her head, but the man tightened his grip, causing tears to sting the back of her nose. He seemed about to tear her hair from her scalp. She heard the sound of ripping cloth. The man wrenched back her head. She took a huge, ragged breath, filling her starved lungs, but before she could recover, the man inserted a strip torn from the sheet between her teeth and tied it behind her head.

That done, he flipped her onto her back, catching her flailing hands and pinning them over her head. He thrust his knee between her thighs, rendering her kicks ineffective. The feel of his chausses against her bare skin shocked her body into nerve-jangling awareness.

Adrienne's breath came in short quick bursts as she struggled to get a grip on her burgeoning terror. Above her, the man's dark eyes seemed to burn like live coals in his shadowy face. Devil's eyes, she thought hysterically.

His voice, low and dangerously soft, brushed the night like rough silk. "One way or another, *princesse*, I am taking you off this vessel. You have a choice. You may put on some clothes or you may go as you are now, in which case my men are going to get a tantalizing eyeful." As if to emphasize his point, he glided his free hand over her breast, teasing the responsive peak with his thumb.

Adrienne sucked in her breath, and her body went rigid, but the gag in her mouth reduced her shriek of outrage to a pathetic whimper.

He moved his hand downward to caress her hip, then lower still to the sensitive flesh of her inner thigh, and silent screams shrilled through every nerve in her body. "Do I have your cooperation?" he asked, his voice oddly hoarse.

At that moment she would have agreed to anything to make him stop caressing her. Filled with shame and helpless rage, she nodded.

He released her and stood up. "Get dressed."

With quaking limbs, Adrienne did as he ordered. As she slid the chemise over her head, the man opened the door and peered out into the passageway. Adrienne's alarm grew. Sir Pearroc lay in a crumpled heap just outside her door; she did not know whether he was dead or merely unconscious. Where was everyone else? she wondered. Surely someone must have heard the man come onto the barge? Or perhaps he had boarded in Dordrecht and had been waiting for the right moment? Her gaze darted about the tiny cabin as she searched for something to use as a weapon.

Adrienne could see nothing in the cabin sufficiently heavy to strike him with. She fetched her shoes and sat back down on the edge of the bunk. If she could get between him and the door, she thought, she might have a chance. Perhaps she could throw him off balance by hurling her weight against him—

As if she had spoken aloud, he turned and said in a terrifyingly silky voice, "Don't even *think* it."

Alarmed that he had been able to read her mind with such accuracy, Adrienne shrank inside herself, and any thought she had of escaping withered beneath his piercing regard.

When she finished dressing, the man came toward her, took her by the shoulders, and turned her away from him. He tore another strip from the sheet and used it to bind her hands behind her. As he pulled the knot tight, he bent his head and murmured in her ear, "There will be time enough later for cat-and-mouse games should that be your pleasure, *princesse*. For now my concern is getting us off this barge alive."

Chapter Three

UP ON DECK all was still. Even the barge seemed to have stopped moving in the water. Adrienne saw that the sails had been furled. Ahead of them she could see the mast of a smaller boat and hear the barge master's voice raised in disagreement with a toll collector.

Gripping her arm, her captor forced her to the stern of the barge where a second man waited in a rowboat. Before she realized what was happening, her captor picked her up and tossed her over his shoulder, then climbed over the railing and sought a foothold on the rope ladder hanging down the side of the barge. Adrienne stiffened in panic as she found herself staring at the churning, unfriendly water below.

"Take care, *princesse*," came the low, seductive voice she was growing to hate. "Land in the river with your hands bound, and you will sink and drown."

When they reached the bottom of the ladder, he dumped her face down into the rowboat, then lowered his weight in after her, causing the boat to rock precariously. For several terrifying seconds Adrienne was certain the small craft would capsize. She tried to sit up, but her captor threw a blanket over her head and planted a foot between her shoulder blades, forcing her back down. He whispered a stern command to the other man, and she felt the boat begin to move through the water.

Adrienne lay with her cheek pressed against the rough wood, listening to the movement of the oars through the water and trying to calm the frantic pounding of her heart. She had no idea where she was being taken or why. Was this one of the dangers Baldhere and Sir Leland had tried to warn her about? She still found it difficult to believe that she was a threat to anyone, much less of any value. Yet what other explanation was there? If these men were simple bandits, they would have put their efforts into plundering the barge rather than into abducting her.

For one fleeting, unthinking moment, she had the insane urge to laugh. While several times during the past weeks she had entertained herself by imagining how she might avoid marrying Duke Wilhelm, getting herself captured had never entered her thoughts. Then another, more sobering thought occurred to her: marrying a man she had never met could very well be more desirable than whatever fate her captor intended for her. At least her betrothed was legally bound to protect her. Her captor was not. She thought of his devil's eyes glowing at her in the darkness of her cabin, and fear shuddered through her body. It would be a miracle, she thought, if he permitted her to live through the night.

The scraping along the hull of the boat when they ran aground told her when they had reached the shore. The blanket was flung aside, and Adrienne was hauled to her feet. She barely had time to notice the half-dozen mounted knights waiting for them in the woods bordering the riverbank when a punishing hand closed around her upper arm. Her captor dragged her out of the boat and toward a waiting horse.

In desperation she tried to wrench herself away from him, but her bound hands rendered her efforts useless, and the gag effectively silenced the onslaught of questions that begged to be answered. With incredible ease he picked her up and deposited her face down across the back of the destrier, then swung up into the saddle behind her.

He and his men wasted no time putting the river behind them. For what seemed like hours they rode hard and fast, without stopping to rest or to even speak to one another. It was as if each man knew what he had to do, and no one had to be reminded of what was expected of him. If Adrienne had previously doubted that her captors were simple bandits, now she knew they were not. Even the distracting argument between the barge master and the toll collector now seemed too convenient to have been coincidental. Her abduction, Adrienne was beginning to realize with terrifying certainty, had been well planned.

From her undignified position across the back of her captor's horse, Adrienne endured the ride with more willfulness than bravery, refusing to whimper even when an unexpected jolt brought tears to her eyes. As they rode, Adrienne thought of Sir Leland and imagined how he would react to the news of her disappearance. She thought of Marlys and prayed that she and the others had made it safely to Trier. She thought of Foutreau, and her throat constricted as she wondered if she would ever see Baldhere or Lady Joanna again.

You must stop this, she chided herself. *You must remain rational and stay alert to your surroundings. If you permit fear to be your master, you will not be able to think clearly or plan your escape.*

The thought of outwitting her captor had a restorative effect on her, calming her taut nerves and providing her with a sense of purpose. While she knew she was powerless to do anything at the moment, she also knew that he could not keep her bound and gagged indefinitely. Sooner or later he was going to have to remove her restraints, and when he did, she intended to be ready for him.

The sun was just breaking over the horizon when they finally stopped.

As she was lowered to the ground, Adrienne's knees buckled beneath her, but her captor gripped her arm, stopping her from falling. There was little feeling left in her feet, and she stumbled as he steered her away from the others. He shoved her down beside a log. "We are going to rest here for a few hours before continuing our journey. You had best sleep if you can."

It was the first time Adrienne had been able to get a good look at her captor. He was tall and powerfully built, being broader in the shoulders without his armor than other men were while wearing theirs. His tanned skin was stretched taut across his prominent cheekbones, and there was no weakness in his well-defined jaw. A lock of black hair fell across his high forehead to touch black brows that were drawn together in a menacing frown. Three long red parallel scratches marked his left cheek, a token from their earlier struggle.

But it was what she saw in his dark, unfathomable eyes that chilled the blood in her veins.

Revenge.

There was something disturbing, almost erotic, in the bold gaze he fixed on her. He studied her face, not as if it was unfamiliar to him but as if confirming that which he already knew. His gaze dropped to the rapid pulse at the base of her throat, then lower still, and Adrienne's face grew hot as she remembered the insolent manner in which he had touched her on the barge. She had an uneasy feeling that death might be preferable to what he intended for her.

Trying to ignore the knot of fear twisting in her stomach, she glared up at him from beneath her lashes.

Her bravado seemed to amuse him; the corners of his mouth curved upward as he hunkered down before her. He reached toward her, but instead of removing the gag as she had hoped he might do, he merely straightened it, then rested his forearms on top of his muscled thighs. His gaze bored into her. "There appears to be some truth to the rumors," he mused aloud. "You do have your father's eyes. Had Henry glowered at me like that, I might have *handed* Sainte-Croix over to him."

Bewilderment, then surprise, then recognition flickered across Adrienne's face in rapid succession as she realized what he was saying.

The man's smile did not extend to his eyes. "Permit me to introduce myself, *princesse*. I am Hugh de Clairmont, Comte de Sainte-Croix."

The last he had added with chilling deliberation, leaving no doubt in Adrienne's mind that whatever he intended to do with her, letting her live was not likely to be one of her options. He did not need her hand in marriage to exercise his claim to Sainte-Croix. He *was* Sainte-Croix.

Every sacrilege, every outrage ever rumored to have been committed by the godless inhabitants of the countship sprang into Adrienne's mind. While she did not believe that all the people of Sainte-Croix were guilty of invoking the souls of the dead or of worshiping the severed heads of heathen idols, she harbored no such largess toward the man before her now. Hugh de Clairmont, she truly believed, was capable of anything.

Without warning, Hugh stood up. "Get some rest," he said curtly. He signaled to two knights who came to stand guard near her; then he turned and stalked away.

Adrienne closed her eyes and shuddered. The enemy whom her father had defeated but not destroyed was now hers to address. Scared and tired and utterly alone for the first time in her life, she began to pray. While her conscience would only permit her to ask God for guidance and strength, her heart pleaded for divine intervention. She had the unshakable feeling that it was her only hope.

At midday they resumed traveling. The air was hot and thick with moisture. Perspiration trickled from behind Adrienne's ear and into her face, but with her hands tied she could not wipe it away. Lack of sleep and the discomfort of being trussed like the evening's supper had done nothing to soothe her disposition. She suspected that Hugh de Clairmont's purpose in keeping her bound was not to prevent her escape but to humiliate her. What her captor could not know, Adrienne reasoned, was that she had spent too many years deflecting Lysander's taunts to be easily broken.

She was not aware of having fallen asleep until she felt herself being lifted off the back of the horse. She dragged herself up from the depths of unconsciousness just as Hugh de Clairmont slung her over his shoulder. Her exhausted mind groped with the realization that the handful of knights accompanying them had multiplied into an army.

A man's voice cut through the fog in her head. "Do you want her put in the *palissade* with the other prisoners, m'lord?"

Adrienne's heart missed a beat. *Other prisoners?*

As if he had felt her reaction to the man's question, Hugh reached up and gave her backside a proprietary pat, and every muscle in Adrienne's body went rigid. "No, Julien. This one is staying with me. I don't want to risk losing her."

With his arm securely wrapped around her legs, he carried her through the camp.

Pushed beyond reason by her captor's coarse treatment of her, Adrienne felt her fear of him harden into a deadly, smoldering anger. It was the kind of anger that turned caution into daring and invited recklessness. It was a kind of insanity.

Another man fell into step alongside them. "Judging from your wounds, brother, she must have put up quite a struggle. Are you certain she is the right one?"

"Positive."

"She looks as if she is out cold. What did you do? Scare her into a faint?"

Adrienne could have sworn she heard her captor chuckle. "I don't think this one is capable of fainting, Graeham. There is too much of her father in her. More likely she is concocting a plot to kill me."

Lagging behind his brother, Graeham de Clairmont seized a handful of Adrienne's hair and lifted her head.

Had she not been gagged, Adrienne would have spit in his face. Instead she narrowed her eyes and met the man's gaze with a scorching glare. To her annoyance, he grinned at her.

Graeham released her. "You would do well to watch your back, Hugh. I think she means to torture you first."

When they reached the large tent in the middle of the camp, Hugh ducked through the opening, carried her to the far side of the tent, then dumped her on her back atop a pile of furs that had been made into a bed.

For a moment she just lay there, sprawled inelegantly on the furs, unable to push herself upright or demand assistance. She glowered up at Hugh through the shimmering veil of hair that cascaded over her face.

Hugh stood over her, his feet apart and his arms folded across his massive chest. Amusement softened the hatred that glittered in his dark eyes. "You are definitely Henry's daughter," he said. "And no doubt you are just as conniving and just as treacherous as that arrogant scoundrel ever was."

Adrienne kept her gaze fixed solidly on his. Although her heart was racing mercilessly, she vowed she would die before she let him see her fear.

" 'Twould be a simple matter," he continued, "to kill you here and now and save myself the trouble you will no doubt cause me."

Hugh bent and pulled a knife from his boot.

He went down on one knee beside her, and terror streaked through her as the blade flashed before her face. She braced herself for the pain that would come when he plunged the knife into her flesh.

As he reached for her, Adrienne drew up her legs and kicked as hard as she could, slamming both feet against his belly with a force that tore a grunt of pained surprise from his throat and knocked him off balance.

She hurled herself away from him. Too late, she realized that she had rolled in the wrong direction, for she suddenly found herself wedged in the crevice between the bed of furs and the tent wall. She managed to get to her knees, but Hugh caught her around the waist and threw her onto her back. He gripped her shoulders and forced her deeper into the furs. Above her, his face was dark with barely contained rage.

"You stupid little fool! You're lucky I didn't slit your throat!"

Relief swept through Adrienne at the realization that she was still alive, then diminished before the awareness that he had merely been playing games with her mind. Angry and ashamed at the ease with which he had managed to exploit her, she narrowed her eyes, matching his furious glare with a determination she hoped effectively masked the fear still lurking within her.

Scowling, he pulled her upright. "Sit still this time, *princesse*, or you are liable to find yourself wearing this knife instead of admiring it."

Hugh slipped the blade beneath the gag, and the fabric gave way.

Free of the gag at last, Adrienne shook the hair out of her face and took a long, ragged breath. "What do you want of me?" she demanded.

A cutting glance was Hugh's only response.

"If it is Sainte-Croix that you are after, you may have it. I don't want it. I never did."

"I hardly need you, *princesse*, to take what is already mine."

"Then why did you risk life and limb to abduct me off the barge?"

"When I want you to know, I will tell you. For now I have no intention of discussing my plans with you."

"Aren't you at least going to tell me where you are taking me?"

Hugh grasped her chin and forced her to look at him. Much of the anger was gone from his eyes, but the hard, purposeful glint that replaced it and the rough warmth of his hand on her skin made her feel exposed and vulnerable. "No, I am not. And unless you want me to gag you again, you will stop pestering me with your annoying questions."

Anger flashed in Adrienne's eyes, but she wisely kept silent.

Hugh released her and stood up. "I am going to leave you here for a while," he said. "Guards are posted outside this tent, so you may abandon any thoughts you have of trying to escape. Not only will you fail but I cannot guarantee your safety in the presence of three hundred men who have not had a woman in several months. Do I make myself clear?"

He had spoken slowly, as though he thought she might be dim-witted, and his condescension angered her. But right now a far more pressing need demanded her attention, one that refused to wait for her convenience, or for his. Forcing her voice to remain steady, Adrienne lifted her chin, met his stern gaze evenly, and said, "I need to use the garderobe."

Hugh stared at her in disbelief. His jaw clenched, and the veins at his temples looked as if they might burst. Adrienne was already regretting having spoken when he gripped her arm and hauled her to her feet. "Try anything foolish, *princesse*, and I swear I will give you cause to regret it."

Something indefinable in the note of irritation in his voice told Adrienne that she had just won this joust. The small victory made her feel more bold than prudent, and she could not resist one final twist of the lance. "Do not fear that I will try to escape, my lord. It would be foolish to flee on an empty stomach. I have decided to wait until after I have eaten and raided your larder."

Again surprise flickered in Hugh's eyes, but was quickly suppressed. "Then I shall have to see to it that you get a chance to do neither," he said.

Still gripping her arm, he hauled her through the tent opening. All activity in camp suddenly stopped, and every man in sight turned to watch while he steered her past them, past the cooking fires, past the last row of tents at the edge of the clearing. Anger reverberated in his long-legged strides, and Adrienne had to double her pace to keep from being dragged.

By the time they reached the woods, she was out of breath, and her indignation at being treated so callously had neared its zenith. Had her hands been free, she would have had no qualms about fixing them around Hugh de Clairmont's throat. "Has anyone ever told you that you treat your prisoners abominably, my lord?" she said, gasping for air.

"Considering who you are, *princesse*, I am treating you far better than you deserve. You are fortunate that I want you alive."

Fortunate? Adrienne's mind screamed. He had forced her out of her bed in the middle of the night, tied her up, dragged her halfway across the Continent, and mishandled her in front of his men, and she was supposed to feel indebted to him because he was permitting her to live?

He wanted her alive. The realization of what he had said pierced her tired mind and coiled through her thoughts, evaporating her anger at the same time that it fueled her hopes. He wanted her alive! Perhaps there was more to it than that, she reasoned. Perhaps rather than merely wanting her alive, he *needed* her alive. A glance at his rigid countenance told her that she could very well be right. No one who was doing something he *wanted* to do would be likely to look that angry.

If she had guessed correctly, then her safety was ensured. Hugh de Clairmont could humiliate and threaten and torment her all he wanted. As long as he needed her alive, she had an advantage over him that he could not break.

"You are the fortunate one, my lord," she said when they finally stopped. "Were our lots reversed, I would not hesitate to kill *you*."

Hugh grunted. "Spoken like a true Plantagenet," he bit out. Gripping her arm, he spun her around and cut the strip of cloth that bound her wrists. "Perhaps I should warn you to take care with your threats, *princesse*. My temper has been known to hinder my ability to see reason."

Sharp prickly pains stabbed Adrienne's fingers as the circulation suddenly returned to her hands. She was still rubbing the numbness from them when Hugh placed a palm between her shoulder blades and gave her a slight shove. "There is a stream a few feet ahead of you through those trees," he said. "If you are not back here in ten minutes, I will come after you, and I can promise you, you won't enjoy the consequences."

Casting him a scathing glance, Adrienne started off through the trees.

The well-worn trail that led to the water was hemmed in on both sides by undergrowth so tangled and thorny it formed an impenetrable barrier. It was no wonder he trusted her to go to the stream alone, Adrienne thought. The vines and dense brush along the trail discouraged any attempt at escape.

When she reached the stream, Adrienne sank to her knees and wrapped her arms protectively around her stomach as her resolve drained away. She did not know how much longer she could keep up this pretense of bravery. She was tired and hungry and more frightened than she had ever been in her life, and it was through sheer dint of will that she managed to suppress the tears that suddenly threatened.

During the past several weeks, her entire world had been turned upside down and the serenity that had marked her days cruelly shattered. Had she known that gaining her father's acknowledgment would have such far-reaching consequences, she would not have spent so many years longing for it. She would have counted her blessings and shown more gratitude toward those who had taken her in and given her a home. Even her betrothal to Duke Wilhelm, in light of the uncertain future she now faced, was no longer the death sentence it had once seemed to be.

But there was no turning back, she reminded herself. Nor could she permit herself to succumb to self-pity. She already knew that her captor did not intend to kill her. That knowledge alone should give her the strength to endure. She did not know what he did intend to do with her, but right now that was of little importance. What was important was that she not allow herself to be intimidated or defeated by him. Hugh de Clairmont might have the upper hand now, but not for long.

All too soon her time was spent, and she heard Hugh calling her. After drying her face and hands on the hem of her chemise, she straightened her clothes and headed back toward the spot where she had left him.

Adrienne lay on the bed of furs and tried to rest, but even as tired as she was, sleep eluded her. She tried to plan how she might escape, but her concentration failed her. Her thoughts kept returning to Hugh. The things he said, the way he looked at her. The feel of his hand on her skin.

She squeezed her eyes shut and shuddered. Worse than the memories were the unsettling sensations they evoked in her, sensations that were not entirely unpleasant. There was no denying that Hugh de Clairmont was a handsome man. He was also powerful, and dangerous. He was the type of man that other men strove to emulate and that women spun dreams of. Had he ridden into Foutreau as Baldhere's guest, she would likely have been tempted to do some silly girlish thing to attract his attention. Now that she had his attention, however, she was quickly learning reality bore little resemblance to the dream.

She did not know how long he had been gone, but it seemed like hours. He had not retied her hands when they returned to the camp, but had merely warned her not to attempt anything foolish. She had not been certain whether to thank God for her good fortune or feel slighted that Hugh saw no need to take stiffer precautions than to post extra guards outside his tent.

Time after time he had made it clear that he considered her beneath him in both intelligence and cunning. Well, she might be lacking in courage, she mused, but she was far from stupid. Hugh de Clairmont's persistent underestimation of her was her strength. She must never forget that.

After a while she gave up trying to rest and got up from the makeshift bed. Her first priority, she reminded herself, was to escape. There were better ways to spend this time alone than to lie in bed and worry about what was going to become of her.

The tent, while not exceptionally large, had room to stand without stooping. On the side opposite the sleeping pallet were a small table and a chair that could be easily folded for transporting. A large chest and several smaller ones had been placed to the rear of the tent. Surely there was something in one of them she could use as a weapon, she thought.

Taking care not to make a sound, she tiptoed to the chests.

She opened the largest one. It appeared to contain only clothes. Kneeling beside it, Adrienne set aside several pairs of chausses and picked up a handsome tunic of burgundy silk embroidered with gold. Although worn in places, the tunic was well made from cloth of the finest quality. Before his exile, Adrienne mused, Hugh de Clairmont must have lived quite comfortably.

She had neared the bottom of the trunk when she came upon a garment much different from the others. Unlike the knee-length tunics intended for daily wear, this one was cut to extend to the ankles. It was of a cloth she had never seen before, of the deepest black and soft as silk but woven with a short, dense pile that made it feel like sable. Intertwining bands of crimson and gold ran from shoulder to hem, and from the center of the torso a crimson coiled serpent sheathed in an aura of gold, its fangs bared, stared back at her through ruby eyes.

Gooseflesh erupted on her skin, and in spite of the late summer heat she suddenly felt cold. Now she understood why her father and the Church had been able to set aside their differences long enough to secure the downfall of Sainte-Croix: Hugh de Clairmont was more than just her enemy; he was evil.

Her hands shaking, Adrienne folded the tunic. She had just returned it to the trunk when a booted foot fiercely kicked the outside of the tent wall near her, causing her to gasp and topple over backward. She dropped the lid of the trunk. Hugh's voice pierced the canvas. "Get out of my chests, *princesse*. There is nothing in them of value to you."

Her courage fled.

Scrambling to her feet, she pivoted to find one of the guards standing inside the tent, his sword drawn and murder in his eyes. Under his accusing glare, Adrienne went to the pile of furs and sat down to wait for her heart to stop pounding. Not only was Hugh de Clairmont evil, she thought shakily, but he appeared to be clairvoyant as well.

When Hugh entered the tent several hours later he found Adrienne curled atop the furs, sound asleep.

In the flickering light of the candle he held, her face was soft with repose. Lying on her side with one hand tucked beneath her cheek and her long dark hair spread out across the furs, she looked too angelic to be descended from those conniving devils of Anjou who had been trying for two hundred years to unseat the House of Sainte-Croix. Her long thick lashes curled up at the ends, casting shadows on her cheeks. Her lips, slightly parted in sleep, were moist and generous and a deep rose-red, and Hugh felt an unbidden heat unfurl in his loins as he wondered how they would feel against his.

But she *was* the devil's spawn, he reminded himself, reining in the sensual images that flickered through his mind. When the time was right, he would claim her, not in response to his body's demands, but with the singular purpose of crushing that Plantagenet pride and bringing her to her knees. He must not allow himself to forget for even a moment that she was the daughter of his sworn enemy— and the instrument of his revenge.

It was not yet dawn when Hugh aroused Adrienne from a deep sleep. "Come, *princesse*. We must be on our way before morning light."

Adrienne sat up and combed her fingers through her tangled hair. Outside the tent the wind shuddered through the valley, and the air was heavy with moisture from an impending storm. "Where are we going?" she asked sleepily.

Ignoring her question, Hugh pressed a thick slice of coarse bread and a wedge of cheese into her hands. "Eat. We don't have much time." He went outside, leaving her alone in the tent.

Once she was fully awake, Adrienne noticed that the trunks and the furnishings had already been removed from the tent. The only thing that remained to be loaded onto the packhorses, aside from the tent itself, was the pile of furs on which she sat. A warm flush crept into her cheeks as she wondered where Hugh de Clairmont had spent the night.

Lightning briefly illuminated the sky, and through the tent opening Adrienne saw the treetops swaying. If she intended to escape, she had to do it now. She did not know when she would get another chance. She did not even know where Hugh was taking her. At least from here she might be able to find her way back to the river. If you are near a river, Baldhere had once told her, you cannot be lost, for all rivers flow to the sea. She hoped Baldhere was right.

After she had eaten, the men began dismantling the tent. Hugh escorted her back to the stream. The forest, in its unrelenting shroud of black, had turned sinister, and its sounds, from the snapping of a twig beneath her foot to the rustling of the leaves, seemed magnified beyond proportion.

Adrienne's pulse raced. She knew what she had to do. Last night, before she had finally fallen asleep, she had plotted her escape. Yet now that the moment she had awaited was at hand, doubts crowded her mind. What if she was making a mistake? She could be attacked by a wolf in the woods or gored by a wild boar. She wished she had Adal with her to alert her to danger.

"Would you prefer to wait until daylight?"

"No!" she blurted out, vehemently shaking her head. Then, realizing how near she had come to arousing Hugh's suspicions and bungling her chance to flee, she amended, "I'll be fine. I remember the way."

"Don't dawdle," Hugh snapped. "We have no time to waste."

"I won't," Adrienne said, aware of the irony of her promise. As soon as she was out of Hugh's sight, she catapulted into action. She removed her shoes and hose and tied them in her mantle, then hitched her skirts up around her waist. With a glance over her shoulder to be certain she was still alone, she stepped into the water.

The stream, swelled by the rains that had already fallen in the mountains, churned around her feet. Her toes sank into the thick mud, and with each step the water rose higher and higher until it was just below her knees. Lifting her head to stare into the blackness beyond, she tried to tell herself that the night was not her enemy but a great protective cocoon that would grant her asylum.

Taking a deep breath, she stepped into the night and let the darkness claim her.

Hugh rubbed a hand over his eyes, his impatience mounting as the minutes grew long. He had not rested well, and now he was tired and out of sorts. *You are growing soft*, he scolded himself. *You have spent so many months enjoying the Duke of Lorraine's hospitality that a soldier's pallet on the ground leaves you aching like a rheumatic old woman.*

In spite of his self-chastisement, he knew it was not his primitive accommodations that had kept him awake. It was Adrienne.

He wanted her.

Last night, after blowing out the candle, he had undressed in the darkness and stretched out beside her on the furs, not touching her, yet close enough to feel the warmth that emanated from her sleeping form. In spite of his efforts to put her from his mind, he had been unable to stop thinking about her, about the softness of her skin, her beckoning lips, the fire in her smoldering gray eyes. For the first time in his twenty-nine years, he had absolutely no control over his thoughts. Like a sorceress, she had taken possession of his mind.

It would have been better for everyone, he told himself, for him to have simply exercised his dominion over her and gotten the lust out of his system. Instead, he had spent the better part of the night staring at the tent ceiling, silently battling his body's demands.

An especially strong gust of wind shook the trees, forcing his thoughts back to the present. He folded his arms over his chest and shifted impatiently. While he fully respected a woman's need for privacy, it was imperative that they be on their way. His brother's mistake in capturing the wrong girl had cost them valuable time. By now Adrienne's absence from the barge would have been noticed. If the knights traveling with her chose to go on to Trier and alert Lachen, the duke's army would soon be in pursuit. "You need to move faster than that if we are to be away from here before dawn," he called out.

Adrienne did not answer.

Every nerve in Hugh's body suddenly tensed. He squinted into the darkness. "Adrienne!"

Nothing.

Lightning flickered through the trees, followed by the rumble of thunder. Muttering an oath, he shoved a branch aside and hurried to the stream.

Adrienne was gone.

Impossible! He had chosen this spot precisely because it did not offer a ready means of escape!

Except one, he thought, cursing himself for underestimating his captive. He ran back to camp and barked orders to his squire to saddle his horse.

As Gabel ran to do his bidding, Sir Conraed approached Hugh. "Do you want a mount saddled for the lady, my lord, or will she be riding with you?"

"First we must find her. Because of my stupidity, she has managed to escape. She can't have gone far. The only way out of these woods is through the middle of the stream."

A chuckle behind him brought him around sharply to find Graeham grinning at him. His temper snapped. "Is this a private joke, or would you care to share it with me?"

Graeham shrugged. "What can I say? I merely captured the wrong woman. You, on the other hand, had the right one on the end of a tether and you let her slip away. 'Twould seem that yours is the greater blunder."

Hugh's eyes narrowed until they were dark slits in his tense face. Had it not been for Graeham, Hugh would not have lost Sainte-Croix in the first place, and none of this would have been necessary. "If you want to help me find her," he said slowly, carefully enunciating each word, "saddle a horse and follow the stream to the south. Otherwise, *stay out of my way*."

The insolence faded from Graeham's eyes until they were as dangerous and unreadable as his elder brother's. He clicked his heels together and bowed. "As you wish."

Fifteen minutes later, Graeham de Clairmont and five knights rode their horses into the water and headed toward the mountains. Hugh, Conraed, and two other men guided their horses north.

*   *   *

The night had faded into a threatening gray dawn. Out of breath from running, Adrienne stopped and pressed her elbow against the painful stitch in her side. She felt as if she had been running forever, although she knew it could not have been more than an hour. She could not believe her good fortune in having managed to escape. Nor could she believe that Hugh would not soon come after her. Perhaps he would think she had drowned, she thought, then brushed that idea aside. Without a body as proof, he would never accept that excuse for her disappearance. She must not make the mistake of growing too confident.

Gradually the forest grew less dense, and the banks of the stream were now as likely to sport dew-laden grass as thorny underbrush. Several times Adrienne was tempted to leave the water and continue overland, but instinct cautioned her against it. Without the sun to give her a sense of direction, she had only the stream to guide her.

After another quarter of a mile the stream broadened and became shallower with lush grass-covered banks sloping gently upward on either side. As she had done at the last glade she came to, Adrienne waded out of the water.

Resisting the temptation to stop and rest, she trampled a path through the tall grass and several yards into the woods, then retraced her steps to the stream. If Hugh was following her, she hoped to throw him off her trail.

Lightning and thunder ripped the sky simultaneously, and Adrienne froze, her heart pounding. That one had been so close the fine hairs on her skin had stood on end. A raindrop hit her head, and then another. She walked faster. She did not like being in the forest during a storm.

The scent of smoke threaded through the air. Was it from a hearth? she wondered. Or had lightning struck a tree?

The farther downstream she traveled, the stronger the scent became. Most likely she was coming upon a farmhouse or a forester's cottage, she thought. Perhaps whoever lived there would help her find her way back to the Rhine, or at least provide her with shelter until the storm passed.

The rain began coming down harder. Within minutes her hair and clothes were drenched. She was so exhausted that she felt as if she would collapse, and the muscles in her legs burned from plowing her way through the water. Unable to go on, she climbed the bank and sank to the ground beneath a tree.

Drawing her knees up to her chest, she wrapped her arms around them and dropped her forehead onto her knees. Her eyelids drooped shut, and she forced them back open. She did not dare fall asleep.

In spite of her good intentions, fatigue and the steady drumming of the rain soon lulled her into a drugging, hypnotic sleep.

Suddenly a burly fist knotted in her wet hair and jerked her head back.

Her eyes flew open and she stared in shock at the wild-eyed man leaning over her. His beard and hair were unkempt, and his chain mail was in need of repair.

A grin slowly spread across the man's face as he reached for her. His hand snapped around Adrienne's wrist, and fear exploded in her chest.

Chapter Four

ADRIENNE'S SCREAM SHATTERED the stillness.

Hugh gouged his spurs into his mount's sides, sending the war-horse surging forward. Time and distance suddenly became distorted; although Adrienne could not be more than a few hundred yards ahead of him, it seemed to take him forever to reach his destination. He cursed the minutes he had wasted following the false trails Adrienne had left him.

The forest opened into a broad clearing. Hugh sharply reined in his horse, stopping just within the woods. Through the trees, he could see a campfire that was in danger of being doused by the rain. Just beyond that were eight men. Three of the men wore chain mail; the others were protected only by thick leather tunics or quilted gambesons that were usually worn under armor. All were scraggly and unkempt. One man held Adrienne, his burly arm wrapped around her middle. He was trying to subdue her thrashing legs. The others jeered and guffawed and made lewd remarks.

It required every ounce of restraint that Hugh possessed not to rush into the clearing. While he did not know any of the men, he recognized their type. They were renegade knights, the vilest of all human beings. Shunned by their fellow warriors because of their utter lack of conscience, they terrorized the countryside, raping and destroying at will.

"Shall we go in?" Roland whispered. His hand was on the hilt of his sword.

One of the men ripped Adrienne's mantle off and flung it aside. He reached for her gown, and she kicked him, landing her foot squarely in the man's groin. The man grunted and doubled over.

The man holding her spoke sharply to the others, and they closed in on Adrienne. They forced her to the ground, two men holding her arms while two others grabbed her feet and pried her legs apart. The man who had been holding her stepped between her outstretched legs and began removing his hauberk. Adrienne screamed, fury and terror in the piercing shrieks.

A violent rage, unlike anything Hugh had ever felt, surged through him. He was not aware of having drawn his sword. He spurred his horse. A low savage growl that began deep in the bottom of his lungs swelled until it engulfed him, erupting into a bloodcurdling battle yell. Frenzy burning in his eyes, he burst into the clearing. Conraed, Roland, and Etienne followed close behind him.

When the outlaw knights saw them coming, they released Adrienne and scattered, colliding with each other in their attempt to flee the charging horses.

The three knights with Hugh closed in on the outer flanks, swords drawn, while Hugh headed straight for the knight straddling Adrienne. The man's hauberk was half off, and horror was frozen on his face. Shocked into motion, he turned to run.

Hugh swung his sword. The sword struck the outlaw with a force that lifted him off the ground and broke his neck in a single tremendous blow.

Adrienne's initial reaction, the instant the men released her, was to curl into a defensive ball. But the thundering of the war-horses' hooves only inches from her head sent panic screaming through her veins, and she scrambled to her feet.

Chaos erupted all around her. Conraed dismounted and engaged in a sword battle with one of the outlaws while

Etienne pursued another who had managed to reach his horse. Three men lay motionless on the ground, including the man who had been about to rape her, his head at an odd angle and his mouth frozen open in a lifeless scream of terror. Hugh's war-horse charged past her again, kicking clods of dirt and grass into her face. His sword flashed before her eyes as he deflected the blow aimed at him by one of the outlaws. The man swung his sword again, and Hugh countered, driving the man's arm high up over his head. With a quick thrust, Hugh drove his sword into the man's belly. The outlaw staggered and collapsed at Adrienne's feet.

Adrienne turned to run and nearly fell over a branch sticking out from the smoking campfire. A few yards in front of her, Sir Roland's stallion lost his footing on the muddy ground and went down, pinning his rider beneath him. One of the outlaws snatched up the sword that had been knocked from Roland's hand and thrust it into the knight's face. Roland jerked his head aside, barely escaping being blinded. The destrier rolled to his feet, and the outlaw stepped backward to keep from being knocked down.

Without thinking, Adrienne grabbed the stick that she had nearly tripped over and yanked it out of the fire. It was two feet long and as thick as a man's wrist. A crust of white ash covered the end that had been in the fire. Adrienne ran up to the outlaw and slammed the stick down in a powerful blow to his head.

The man threw his hands up over his face to protect it from the flying cinders and stumbled to his knees. He braced one hand on the ground and started to push himself upright. Adrienne struck him again and again. Gripping the sword, he staggered to his feet and turned toward her. His upper lip was drawn back in a snarl. He raised the sword above his head.

Adrienne hurled the stick at him.

The stick struck him in the face. To Adrienne's confusion, he made no attempt to block it but simply stood there with his mouth agape. Then his eyes rolled back and he fell forward. The hilt of a dagger protruded from his back.

Roland, who had risen up on one elbow, closed his eyes and collapsed onto the sodden ground, his war-horse standing protectively over him. Blood ran from one corner of his mouth. Adrienne started toward him, but his destrier snorted threateningly and pawed at the ground.

Hugh shoved her aside. He murmured something to the destrier, calming the animal. Hugh knelt beside Roland. He spoke to the knight in a low voice.

Adrienne wrapped her arms around her stomach and looked around her at the bodies lying on the bloodstained ground. Conraed was gathering up the outlaws' weapons. An eerie quiet engulfed the clearing; the fighting had ended as abruptly as it had begun. Numbness seeped through Adrienne's veins, then slowly began to retreat, leaving every nerve in her body charged with a sharp, unpleasant tingling. She could not stop trembling.

She turned her attention back to Hugh and Roland. Hugh eased Roland onto his back, and the color evacuated the knight's face. Adrienne started forward. "Will he be all right?"

Hugh surged to his feet and rounded on her, his face so dark with rage that Adrienne backed away from him. "Get over there and sit down and stay out of my way!" There was so much fury in his voice that it shook. He leveled a warning finger at her. "If you do one more thing to displease me, I will *kill* you! Do you understand me?"

Certain he would not hesitate to do just that, she nodded jerkily.

Adrienne located her mantle where it had been thrown. Untying it, she removed her shoes and hose and put them on. The clasp on her mantle was broken. Instead of putting the mantle on, she folded it up and held it against her pounding heart. Like the rest of her clothes, it was soaked and covered with grass stains and mud.

Again her gaze was involuntarily drawn to the carnage around her. She had never been squeamish, but now bile rose in her throat as she thought of what had nearly happened. If Hugh had not arrived in time, she would still be on the ground, being used by each man in turn. Her stomach convulsed, and she felt as if she would vomit.

By the time Hugh had helped Roland onto his horse and was leading his own horse toward her, she had managed to steady her quaking nerves, but one look at Hugh's face told her that he had not calmed down one bit. As he bore down on her, she mentally braced herself for whatever retribution might be forthcoming, but when his huge hand suddenly shot out, her courage shattered and she threw her hands up over her face to protect herself from a certain death blow.

Instead of striking her, he seized her wrist and yanked her toward him with enough force to slam her against his massive chest. He shook her so hard her head snapped back. "Do you have any idea how lucky you are? Do you know what those men would have done to you? They would have raped you, not once but over and over again until you were a bloody, beaten pulp. And when they tired of you, they would have left you to die!"

He emphasized that last statement with a jerk so brutal it wrenched a cry from her throat. She opened her mouth to protest, but the undiluted rage she saw in his eyes terrified her into silence.

He spun her around. She put up no resistance when he lifted her onto his horse, not even crying out when her backside smacked painfully against the hard front edge of his saddle.

Hugh swung up into the saddle behind her and wrapped his arm around her waist. The blood was pounding in his head. He could barely remember what had happened. Never in his life had he felt so invincible and so out of control at the same time. Had the outlaws numbered a hundred, he was certain he could have killed every one of them with his bare hands.

They started back to camp. They rode in tense silence, Etienne leading the outlaws' horses and Conraed making sure Roland stayed in the saddle. Roland's face was ashen, and his left arm hung useless at his side.

Adrienne did not have to look at Hugh to feel the fury that still quaked in his powerful form. She felt she should say something, but what? An apology was not exactly in order. After all, she was his prisoner. It was natural—no, it was *expected*—that she would try to escape. Still, he had saved her life. At the very least she owed him a thank-you.

She took a shaky breath. "I am grateful that you came along when you did. I shall always be in your debt for saving me from those men."

Hugh said nothing. He did not even acknowledge that she had spoken.

To Adrienne's horror, a lump swelled in her throat at his obvious rejection of her gratitude. His bellowing she could accept, but this stony silence hurt. Her frustration mounting, she twisted around to look at him. "I am sorry," she blurted out. "I did not mean to cause you so much—"

His arm tightened around her rib cage so abruptly that she sucked in her breath at the unexpected pain. "Sit still!" he ground out.

Biting down on her bottom lip to keep it from quivering, she turned back to the front and stared straight ahead through a haze of tears. She had been a fool to think Hugh de Clairmont might be capable of human understanding. Silent sobs welled up inside her, and she fought them back. She refused to give him the satisfaction of seeing her cry.

Feeling her struggling for control, Hugh relaxed his grip on her. He was not sure what had happened to him. Every time he thought of those men touching her, something inside him threatened to snap. He looked down, his gaze drawn to the wet fabric of her gown where it clung to her breasts, and his stomach clenched.

Careful, a voice in the back of his mind cautioned. *You are letting her get under your skin. What you did back in*

*that clearing you would have done for anyone. The fact that
she is your captive is of no consequence. The fact that she
is beautiful is of no consequence. The fact that your body
reacts like that of an undisciplined youth every time you
look at her is of no consequence. She is your enemy. She
is your means for destroying all the Plantagenets. Forget
that, for even a moment, and you run the risk of subverting
your own plans.*

Graeham and his men had already returned by the time
they reached camp. The look on Hugh's face warned everyone to stay out of his way. Even Graeham kept his distance.

After Roland was treated for his injuries, they broke
camp and resumed traveling, but the weather remained
foul and they made poor progress. Adrienne sat stiffly on
Hugh's horse, trying to keep as much distance as possible
between her and the man seated behind her. But no matter
how hard she tried to avoid bodily contact, she kept sliding
back against Hugh's hard thighs.

She could not stop shaking. She kept thinking of what
had happened back in the clearing. If Hugh had not come
along, what then? She did not want to be indebted to him,
but she was. No matter how she longed to be free of him,
with each passing hour he became more and more inter-
twined in her life. Why could she not take control of her
own fate? Was there some greater force acting against her?
Was her future written in the stars, inevitable, unalterable?
Was Hugh destined to be a part of that future?

You're being silly, she chided herself. *Hugh merely foiled
your escape attempt; that's all. There will be other chances
for escape. This simply wasn't the right time. Next time
you will be better prepared, and all will go as planned.*

Finally, no longer able to ignore the constant friction of
her backside against his groin, Hugh bent his head and
growled in her ear, "Unless you want me to stop right here
and take you into the woods to finish what you have started,
princesse, I suggest you cease your damnable squirming!"

Adrienne stiffened as the full meaning of his words struck her, and hot, humiliating color crept up her neck to smolder in her cheeks. For the rest of the day she sat unnaturally still. She did not even reach up to wipe away the rain that saturated her hair and clothing and streamed into her eyes.

Shortly before nightfall the scouts returned with news of a protected glade well away from the main road. They traveled another hour through dense woods. The glade came into view and Hugh gave the order to stop.

He dismounted and passed his horse's reins to his squire, then reached up to help Adrienne down. Placing his hands beneath her arms, he lifted her off the horse and lowered her to the ground. Her legs were sore from the unaccustomed hours of riding. Wet and exhausted, Adrienne wanted only to find something soft to sit on, but before she could make her wishes known, Hugh's hand snapped around her upper arm and he was hauling her through the clearing.

He directed the squires where he wanted his tent pitched. He ordered the knights to post extra guards. He checked on the supply wagons, making certain nothing had been lost or damaged in the rain. If the day's events had left Adrienne longing for nothing more than a pillow on which to lay her head, they seemed to have fazed Hugh not at all. The man was tireless. He wound his way through the entire camp, making certain that his orders were carried out to the letter. Every step of the way he dragged Adrienne in his wake, until she was seething inwardly and heaping unspoken curses on his head.

He dragged her to the far edge of the camp where his other prisoners stood in the drizzling rain, bound to each other by chains attached to the irons locked around their ankles. Hugh sought out the head guard and demanded a pair of fetters. For a sickening moment, Adrienne thought he was going to chain her with the rest of the prisoners.

Suddenly a woman cried out, "Lady Adrienne!"

Hugh's grip tightened on Adrienne's arm as she twisted around to peer into the group of dirty, exhausted faces. *Marlys?*

The girl was not with the rest of the prisoners but was being kept under separate guard. She ran toward Adrienne.

"Marlys!" Adrienne cried out, overjoyed to see a familiar face. "Are you all right? What are you doing here?"

Marlys gripped her hand. "I'm so glad to see you, m'lady, I am. I thought I'd never see you again. No one here speaks English but Lord Hugh and some of—"

Marlys broke off as one of the guards seized her arm. As the guard pulled her away, Marlys began to cry.

Gripping the irons and chain the guard had given him, Hugh spun Adrienne around and marched her through the clearing, not stopping until he reached the large tent that had been erected in the center of the camp.

How had Marlys come to be here? Were her knights here too? Had the entire group been captured after leaving Dordrecht?

Adrienne wrenched her arm from Hugh's grasp. "My lord, please! Why are you detaining Marlys? What is she to you?"

Aware that they were attracting attention, Hugh struggled to get his temper under control. After spending the better part of the day with Adrienne's bottom wriggling against his loins, he was in a foul mood.

"Your maidservant and your knights are very valuable to me, *princesse*," he drawled sarcastically. "Unless you cooperate, they will be the ones to suffer the consequences. You wouldn't want their fate on your conscience, now, would you?"

"You wouldn't dare!"

The nerve beneath Hugh's left eye twitched. "Are you so certain?"

Adrienne knew what Hugh was trying to do, and she hated him for it. His lack of scruples gave him an unfair advantage. Her voice shook. "I can hardly give you my cooperation, my lord, if I don't know what it is you want of me."

I want you! Hugh's mind screamed. He clenched his teeth so hard the veins at his temples bulged. His gaze, drawn by a power stronger than he, slowly traveled the length of her, pausing to drink in the fullness of her breasts, the curve of her hips, the apex of her thighs where her wet gown clung provocatively to her skin, before rising once more to meet hers.

The color drained from Adrienne's face. She was not so naive that she did not recognize the desire smoldering in his dark eyes. She knew now why he had saved her from the outlaws. It was not because, as a nobleman and a knight, he was bound by a code of honor to protect her from such criminals; it was because he wanted her for himself.

He shoved her into the tent, and she exploded. "If you touch me, I swear I will make you pay, even if I have to wait until you are asleep!"

Hugh seized her shoulders and jerked her against him. Anger heightened the passion in his eyes. "I will touch you whenever and however I please. Do you understand me?"

Although her eyes grew wide and dark, Adrienne returned Hugh's gaze with a fierceness that tested his self-control. Her only answer to his question was a sharp intake of breath when his fingers dug into her shoulders.

Damn, how he wanted her! He wanted her so badly he could feel the heat of his longing surge through his veins. Even the sight of the pulse leaping at the base of her throat was doing odd things to him. Not trusting himself, he flung her away from him. "Get out of those clothes."

Terror streaked through her. "No!"

Anger glinted in Hugh's eyes. "I have already reached my limit on what I will tolerate from you. Either you remove your clothes or I will do it for you."

"But they're all I have!"

Hugh took a step toward her.

"I'll do it!" Casting him a venomous look, Adrienne began removing her shoes and hose with shaking hands. She could not believe she had escaped a horrible fate this morning only to find herself facing it now. Perhaps if she pleaded with him, he would be gentle, she thought. Then she silently chastised herself for thinking such a thing. No matter how much he hurt her, she would not beg for mercy. *She would not!*

As she undressed, Hugh went to his largest clothes chest and removed a clean white linen tunic. When he turned, Adrienne had her back toward him and was working her wet chemise up over her head. His gaze went to the bruises on her buttocks and the backs of her thighs, and his anger evaporated. All day she had been jostled about on his horse, and she had not uttered one word of complaint, whereas he had behaved like a tyrant.

Clutching her chemise and gown protectively in front of her, Adrienne turned around. An angry flush darkened her face as she realized he had been looking at her.

"Put this on."

Sullenly she obeyed, relinquishing her wet clothes to him only after he had handed her the tunic.

Hugh took her soiled clothes to the tent opening and passed them out to his squire. When he turned back to Adrienne, she had managed to get her arms into the sleeves of the tunic and was pulling it down. The bottom of the tunic skimmed over her hips and down her long legs to settle just below her knees. She lifted her hair from beneath the collar and let it fall down her back in a wet, tangled mass. She turned and fixed him with an accusing glare. Again he had been caught staring.

Hugh crossed to his clothes chest, picked it up, and carried it to the pile of furs. He put the chest down at one end of the pallet. "Sit down."

Adrienne sat down on the pile of furs and tucked her legs beneath her. Hugh knelt beside her with the irons, and only then did Adrienne realize what he intended. "Oh, no, you don't!" she cried. She tried to scoot away from him, but he caught a slender ankle in his large tanned fist and gave it a tug that landed her flat on her back. He snapped an iron around her ankle and locked it.

"My apologies, *princesse*," he said as he fastened the other end of the chain to one of the leather carrying straps on the chest. "I cannot take the chance you will escape again."

Adrienne struggled to sit up. She shoved her tangled hair away from her face. "You are contemptible!" she spat. "You have an army at your disposal, yet you resort to irons and threats to keep one helpless female from escaping! My father was right to depose you. You are the vilest snake ever to crawl on the face of the earth!"

Hugh rested his forearm across his thigh and contemplated her stormy face. Damn, she was beautiful even now, looking as if she wanted to kill him. He thought he could have sat and gazed upon her forever. "You are many things, *princesse*," he said in a reflective voice. "Helpless is not one of them."

For a moment they just sat there, their eyes locked in a silent battle of wills. Hugh finally tore his gaze away and stood up. "Get some rest. We shall be leaving before daybreak."

It was well after dark when Hugh returned to the tent, without the heavy mail hauberk, which he had left with his squire to be repaired; several of the metal links had been damaged in the skirmish with the outlaw knights. He found Adrienne sitting with her back against his clothes chest, her knees drawn up and her arms wrapped around her legs. The candlelight that illuminated her stubborn expression reflected like twin torches in her gray eyes. He inclined his head toward the porringer his squire had brought her. "You didn't eat."

"Unchain me," Adrienne demanded.

"No."

"*Why not?* Why won't you tell me what you want with me? Don't I have a right to know what is to become of me? If you were in my shoes, wouldn't you want to know?"

"I am not in your shoes. Furthermore, your incessant prattle is becoming annoying. If you want to speculate on your fate, do it in silence. I am tired of listening to you."

"You are not the only one who has grown weary of his traveling companion," Adrienne shot back. "You might be sick of my questions, but I am thoroughly disgusted with your arrogance, your disregard for propriety, your—" Adrienne broke off, the words sticking in her throat as she watched Hugh remove his boots, set them aside, then begin drawing his tunic off over his head.

Adrienne's annoyance turned into alarm. "What are you doing?"

"I am going to bed."

"*Here?*"

She looked so horrified at the thought that Hugh nearly laughed. "This is my tent. And that"—he bent his head toward the pile of furs she was sitting on—"is my bed."

Her mouth dropped open. "But last night—"

"I slept with you," Hugh finished for her. He paused. "Are you aware that you snore, *princesse*?"

Adrienne colored all the way to the roots of her hair. "I am not going to sleep with you," she blurted out, appalled at the thought of him lying beside her. "I would rather die than sleep with you!"

"Then die quietly," Hugh snapped. "I am not a pleasant man to deal with when my sleep is disturbed."

Hugh reached for the ties at his waist, and Adrienne jerked her gaze away to stare at the tent wall. Her heart pounded. She heard him remove his chausses. Struggling for control, she said sharply, "Will you at least blow out the candles?"

He blew out the candles. Adrienne thought she heard him chuckle.

She waited, every muscle in her body tensed, hardly daring to breathe, as he lowered his tall frame to the furs. *If he touches me*, she thought frantically, *I am going to scream!*

When a full minute passed and he still made no attempt to touch her, she ventured a peek at him.

He was lying on his side on top the furs. His back was toward her. She stared at him, unable to tear her gaze away. Even the darkness failed to hide the sculpted perfection of his heavily muscled back and shoulders. It was no wonder he had been able to wield his sword with such ease this morning, she thought. To him it would have been like swinging a toy.

Her gaze slid down his back to his buttocks, then down the length of his strong legs, and an unbidden warmth was ignited deep down inside her. He was beautiful. Even her hatred of him could not change that.

Like a child drawn to something forbidden, she longed to reach out and touch him.

Clenching her fists to keep herself from inadvertently doing something disgraceful, she asked, "If you won't tell me why you want me, will you at least tell me where we are going?"

"Go to sleep, *princesse*. We have a long ride ahead of us tomorrow."

Exasperated with him for refusing to answer her questions, Adrienne lay down. Her movements caused the chain fastened to her ankle to rattle. "I hate you, Hugh de Clairmont," she whispered at his back. "I hate you because you are just like my father. He never cared about me. All he cared about was getting revenge against those who had betrayed him." A quaver crept into her voice. "He died a lonely man. Just as you will someday."

For a long time Adrienne lay awake, fighting back tears and staring at Hugh's black hair where it curled against his neck.

*   *   *

When Adrienne's breathing finally changed, signaling that she had fallen asleep, Hugh rolled onto his back and released his breath in a long, tense sigh. He stared up at the tent ceiling. For the second night in a row, sleep eluded him.

Chapter Five

THE NEXT MORNING, Hugh removed the chain from around Adrienne's ankle and gave her a squire's tunic and chausses to wear. "They will be more comfortable for traveling," he said.

Adrienne took the clothes. She clutched them in front of her and stood staring down at them, but made no move to put them on. She seemed unusually subdued this morning. Hugh opened his mouth to ask her if she was not feeling well, but before he could say anything, her dark lashes lifted and she impaled him with a brittle glare. "May I please have some privacy?"

Hugh snapped his mouth shut. So much for being concerned, he thought irritably. Beneath that air of wounded innocence she was so good at portraying, the girl had a hide like armor. Pivoting, he stalked from the tent.

After he was gone, Adrienne closed her eyes and rubbed her throbbing temple with her fingertips. She had slept fitfully, jerking awake every time the face of one of the outlaws appeared in her dreams.

After she had changed into the clothes, the guard led her to the bushes at the edge of the camp. Mud oozed up over the tops of her shoes, testing her patience as she tried to scrape them clean. Even though the sun had not yet broken through the trees, the air was already hot and sticky, and the boy's tunic stuck to her skin.

She was trying to comb the tangles from her hair with her fingers when Hugh rode up to her on the great war-horse. He grasped her wrist and hauled her up onto the animal's broad back. She winced as her sore bottom hit the saddle.

Remembering the bruises he had seen yesterday, Hugh shifted his weight to allow her more room. "You will be more comfortable if you ride astride," he said.

"I would rather walk with the other prisoners."

"I'm sure you would."

Adrienne twisted around to look at him. "In fact, we would both be more comfortable if I walked with—"

"No."

"Why not?"

"Because I am not letting you out of my sight. Now swing your right leg over to the other side."

Even though she knew she would be more comfortable if she did as he suggested, the headache and the heavy, suffocating air made her more contrary than usual. "I am comfortable the way I am," she said stubbornly.

Without warning Hugh slid his hand beneath her buttocks, and Adrienne sucked in her breath. "*Princesse*, you have an unsightly bruise right about here," Hugh said in a low, husky voice, cupping her bottom with his large hand. "If you don't change positions, it will only get worse."

Muttering an oath under her breath, Adrienne drew her right leg across the horse's back so that she was straddling him. "You are despicable!" she hissed between clenched teeth.

Hugh withdrew his hand. *And you are beautiful*, he thought. He silently cursed himself. Touching her like that had been a mistake, because now he wanted to touch all of her. Suppressing the urge to slide his hand beneath her tunic, he wrapped his arm around her waist and pulled her against him. For now it would have to be enough.

The ground was wet, making progress slow. The supply wagons kept getting bogged down in the mud. By the time the sun had cleared the treetops, moisture was rising from the ground like steam from a public bath.

Remembering Hugh's impatience the previous day, Adrienne made a noble effort to sit as still as possible, not because of any wish to please him but because she had no desire to listen to his scolding. She felt miserable enough. Sweat soaked her shirt and pooled beneath her breasts to trickle down her skin. She would be glad when they stopped to rest.

Graeham rode his horse up to the front of the column and fell into step alongside them. " 'Tis clouding over again. Do you think we'll get more rain?"

Hugh studied the darkening sky. "I hope not. We have been delayed enough as it is."

As the men talked, Adrienne kept her attention focused on an imaginary point in the distance. She could feel Graeham de Clairmont's scrutinizing gaze on her, and it made her uneasy. Did he plan to take a turn with her when his domineering brother had tired of her?

"Does she speak?" Graeham asked.

"When she wants to," Hugh replied dryly.

Realizing that they were talking about her, Adrienne turned her head to find herself staring into Graeham de Clairmont's dark, piercing eyes.

The first thought that entered Adrienne's mind was that Graeham was an exact likeness of Hugh. Only younger. And not quite so tall, or so muscular. And his face wasn't as harsh or his features so sharply chiseled. And his hair was dark brown instead of black. By the time Adrienne took notice of every detail that differed between the two men, she had reached the conclusion that they did not resemble each other at all.

A slow, steady smile transformed Graeham de Clairmont's face from one of a skilled, battle-hardened knight into that of a devastatingly handsome young courtier. Suddenly Adrienne felt very self-conscious about her soiled, scraggly appearance.

"Now I know why my brother has been spending so much time in his tent," Graeham said. "Forgive me for being so forthright, my lady, but you are the most beautiful creature I have ever beheld."

Every muscle in Hugh's body tensed.

For a moment Adrienne stared at Graeham. She was stunned. The last time she had heard anyone resort to such outlandish flattery was at Foutreau when one of Lord Baldhere's knights was attempting to seduce a maidservant. In fact, the overture was so preposterous that Adrienne felt an unwitting smile tug at the corners of her mouth.

"Ah, so the lady does know how to smile," Graeham teased. His dark eyes twinkled as though he were sharing some private joke with her. "Although I must say, were I the one forced to endure my brother's company all day, I would find little reason even to want to smile."

Adrienne couldn't help it. The harder she tried not to smile, the more futile her efforts became. Her shoulders began to shake with suppressed mirth. Spurring her on even more was the feel of Hugh's strong arm growing more and more rigid with each passing second until it was like an iron band crushing her waist. She could have sworn that he was jealous of his handsome younger brother.

Graeham cast Hugh a disparaging glance. "Don't you think you are being a trifle selfish, Hugh, keeping this vision of loveliness all to yourself?"

Adrienne pressed her lips together to keep from bursting into helpless laughter. The effort heightened the color in her face.

The nerve beneath Hugh's left eye twitched. "Graeham, you are testing my patience."

Graeham ignored him. "If my brother fails to treat you with utmost courtesy, Lady Adrienne, please do not hesitate to send word. Before you can blink, I will be at your side."

"Graeham, if you don't remove yourself from my presence immediately, Lady Adrienne is going to see you get knocked off your horse."

Graeham winked at Adrienne. "My brother is full of threats, my lady, but you need not fear. He really doesn't mean—"

"I haven't forgotten Rougemont, Graeham," Hugh interrupted in a low, ominous voice. "I hope you haven't either."

The color faded from Graeham's face, then returned with a vengeance. His dark eyes narrowed as he regarded Hugh for a long, brittle moment. Then without another word he turned his horse around and rode back down the column.

Adrienne caught her bottom lip between her teeth, and the laughter died in her eyes. Hugh de Clairmont treated his own family with as much high-handed disregard as he did his prisoners.

Hugh's hand moved up from her waist. His thumb brushed against the outer curve of her breast, and she stiffened. "I can sense your disapproval," Hugh murmured against the top of her head. "What were you thinking just now?"

Adrienne thrust her chin out defiantly. The feel of his hand on her breast was having the most unnerving effect. "I was thinking," she said curtly, "that I have never in my entire life known anyone who was so . . . so . . . arrogant."

"Well, I can see we are in complete agreement regarding my brother's character."

"I was referring to you."

Hugh frowned. "Don't tell me I was mistaken in crediting you with more intelligence than to fall for my brother's philandering?"

Adrienne could not tell if she had just been complimented or insulted. "Your brother was being civil to me, whereas you have scarcely acknowledged my presence all morning except to put your cursed hands where they don't belong. *Stop doing that!*"

Hugh had moved his hand up over her breast, and through the linen he was drawing circles around the sensitive peak with his fingertip. Adrienne grabbed his hand, which maddeningly refused to stop its exploration. Hugh bent his head and said in a low voice that only she could hear, "I told you yesterday, *princesse*, that I would touch you whenever I pleased. And right now it pleases me to touch you."

"Everyone will see you!" His closeness, the strength of his muscled thighs pressing against hers, the erotic pattern he was tracing on her breast with his fingertips, the warmth of his breath in her ear, all those things were making the blood rush into her head. Even more confusing was that she found herself actually enjoying them.

"We are at the front of the column," Hugh said. "Unless you raise a hue and cry, no one will suspect a thing."

Exasperation echoed in Adrienne's voice. "It's just that right now I feel . . ."

Hugh rubbed his rough jaw against her cheek. "You feel what, *princesse*?" he prompted gently.

"I feel hot and sweaty and *dirty!*" Adrienne clamped her teeth down on her tongue. With all the valid objections she could have voiced—that his actions were lewd, that they were immoral, that they were highly inappropriate—why had she chosen the one that appealed to the feminine rather than to the rational aspect of her nature?

She had no way of knowing whether he accepted her explanation, because at that moment the scouts returned and Hugh discreetly moved his hand back down to her waist.

By the time they stopped at midday, the heat had taken its toll. Tempers were strained. Hugh was in no mood to listen to Adrienne's protests as he replaced the irons around her ankle and chained her to a tree. As if that was not sufficient, he assigned two guards to keep an eye on her.

She was sitting in the shade with legs bent and her chin resting on her knees when Graeham sauntered over to where she sat. "Well, I see you survived another morning with my brother."

Adrienne's expression immediately became mutinous. "Your brother is the most disagreeable person I have ever known."

"He's been tormenting you, has he?"

Remembering how Hugh had touched her earlier, in full view of God and everyone, Adrienne blushed. She extended her foot to display the fetter locked around her ankle. "Actually, my lord, your brother is a most charming host."

Graeham chuckled. "What did you expect? You wounded his pride yesterday when you escaped from right under his nose."

Adrienne regarded him warily. "Considering how he spoke to you earlier, I am surprised you would defend him."

Graeham lowered his tall frame to the ground and leaned against a tree, stretching his long legs out in front of him. "The trouble with my brother," Graeham said, "is that he has no sense of humor. He takes everything far more seriously than the situation warrants. When we were children, our father used to say that Hugh was liable to die of old age before he even reached manhood."

Adrienne fidgeted and looked away. Graeham's intense gaze made her uneasy. To her bewilderment, Adrienne felt that she was being disloyal to Hugh by talking about him.

Graeham changed the subject. "I heard of your skill with a stick of firewood. I wish I could have been there to see the look on that outlaw's face when you clobbered him over the head."

Adrienne turned her head to stare at him. "Who told you about that?"

"Roland. He has been singing your praises all morning. He says you saved his life."

The compliment made her uncomfortable. Had the knight died, Hugh would never have forgiven her. "Actually, Sir Roland saved mine when he threw his dagger and killed the outlaw." She nervously moistened her lips. "I trust he is mending well?"

"He'll live." Graeham's voice trailed off. Adrienne followed his gaze and saw Hugh coming toward them. Graeham stood up. "If you will pardon me, my lady, I need to check on the horses."

Adrienne watched Graeham join the other knights, cutting a wide path around his brother as he passed. Hugh's presence had a chilling effect on everyone, Adrienne thought. She got to her feet and brushed the dirt off her chausses.

Hugh dismissed the guards, then unlocked her irons. "What were you and my brother talking about?"

"That is none of your business."

"I beg to differ with you, *princesse*. Everything that involves my men is my business."

Adrienne rolled her eyes, then gasped as Hugh caught her chin in his firm grip. He forced her to look at him. His dark gaze bored into her. "Everything," he repeated firmly.

Adrienne jerked her chin out of his grasp. The man's conceit was appalling. "If you must know, we were discussing what a disagreeable excuse for a human being you are."

One dark brow quirked upward, and Hugh's mouth threatened to curve into a smile. He took a step toward her, and Adrienne took an answering step away from him, not realizing that she had done so until she backed into the tree. Hugh reached over her head and placed his palm against the rough bark of the trunk, trapping her between himself and the tree.

Amusement shone in his dark eyes. "Pray tell, *princesse*, what should this errant knight do to make his disposition more pleasing to the lady?"

Without thinking, Adrienne blurted out, "Die."

Surprise flickered across Hugh's face, then dissolved into reluctant admiration. He did not doubt that over the years countless men had wished him dead, but not a single one had ever had the courage to tell him so to his face. He'd had to hear it from one defenseless girl in squire's chausses, her hair in tangles and freckles popping out across the bridge of her sunburned nose as she glared up at him from beneath lashes so long they should have been declared illegal.

Without warning, he threw back his head and laughed. The unaccustomed sound began deep inside him, trembling and swelling until it burst from his chest in a great explosion that drew odd looks from half the men in camp. He laughed so hard his face began to hurt. Tears welled up in his eyes, and his lungs seemed unable to draw enough air. He could not remember the last time he had laughed like that.

When he finally caught his breath, Hugh lifted a dark curl off Adrienne's shoulder and twirled it around his finger. His dark eyes caressed her face. "Since I have no intention of accommodating you in that way, my lady, what would be your next suggestion?"

Adrienne had the distinct feeling that he was mocking her, and it did not please her one bit. "Let me go."

"I think not."

"But why? You have already said you don't need me to retake Sainte-Croix! Why do you insist on keeping me prisoner?"

Hugh was having a hard time keeping his gaze off her rosy mouth. He wanted to kiss her so badly he could taste it. "Because," he said seductively, "having sampled the icing, I have decided that I want the entire tart."

"You mean, you want—" Adrienne broke off, unable to continue. The abrupt widening of her eyes told Hugh that she knew exactly what he meant.

He inclined his head. "Yes."

"Then that makes you no better than those outlaws who tried to defile me yesterday morning!"

"I am afraid there is no comparison, *princesse*. I intend to be civilized about it."

"Meaning you won't force me?"

Hugh's dark gaze sent a liquid warmth coursing through Adrienne's limbs. He lifted the curl to his lips and kissed it. "Meaning I won't have to."

Anger welled up inside her. She stabbed him with the fiercest glare she could manage. "Don't hold your breath. If you ever do decide to rob me of my virtue, my lord, 'twill have to be by force, because I will never willingly surrender it to you."

Hugh said nothing, but a knowing smile teased his mouth, leaving Adrienne with the distressing feeling she had already surrendered far too much.

It was late in the afternoon when they spotted the approaching riders. Hugh raised his hand, signaling to his men to stop. Graeham, Sir Conraed, and Sir Galen rode to the front of the column. Graeham held slightly apart. His expression was sullen. "Who do you think they are?" Conraed asked.

Hugh's eyes narrowed as he watched the four knights approach. "I don't know. They bear no arms."

"Perhaps they want to join up with us?" Sir Galen suggested.

"I don't like it," Graeham said suddenly. "Unless they have good reason for wanting to join up with us, I suggest we send them on their way."

Hugh looked at his brother. For an endless moment tension crackled between them like heat lightning. Finally Hugh looked away. "I agree with Graeham. We don't want to take any chances."

Adrienne shifted her weight to ease the strain on her aching muscles. The slight movement seemed to remind Hugh of her presence, for his arm abruptly tightened around her waist. He brought his head down to hers and murmured, "I am warning you, *princesse*. Don't try anything foolish. You have already caused enough trouble to last me a lifetime. I'll not be so tolerant the next time you seek to defy me."

Adrienne bristled, more at the reminder of his uncanny ability to discern her thoughts than out of any sense of having been affronted. "I might remind you, my lord," she retorted, not caring who heard her, "there are three hundred of you and only four of them. Even I have enough sense not to choose my champion from among the weak."

Graeham snickered. "She has a point."

Hugh glared at his brother, but refrained from responding. Graeham had a way of bringing out the worst in him, and he refused to stoop to petty squabbling.

The four knights slowed their mounts to a walk, finally stopping about twenty yards away. One of them called out, "Are you Hugh de Clairmont?"

Hugh recognized none of the men. "Who wants to know?"

"John de Lancy, under orders from the Duke of Lorraine."

Conraed's hand tightened on his lance. "This could be a trap," he said in a low voice.

"If it is," Hugh whispered back, "they won't ride out of here alive. I want to hear what they have to say." He turned his attention back to the knights. "I am Hugh de Clairmont."

The spokesman for the group hesitated. "How do we know you are who you say you are?" he called out. "We have been instructed to speak with Hugh de Clairmont and no other."

Hugh felt his annoyance building. "Knowing what Lorraine will do to you should you fail to deliver the message, I'd say you would be wise to take the risk."

The four knights conferred among themselves. Finally the leader rode toward them. Adrienne fidgeted under the man's disdainful stare. "May we speak privately?" he asked Hugh.

Hugh and the knight dismounted. Hugh handed his reins to Conraed with a warning not to let Adrienne get away. He fixed her with a meaningful look. "If she does, I'll have both your hides."

When they had walked out of earshot of the others, John de Lancy told Hugh, "I thought we might have missed you. We expected you and your men to pass through this area weeks ago."

"We were delayed," Hugh said. "You said you have a message for me?"

"I do. King Philip has invaded Lorraine. He is holding the duke prisoner at Avenches. Lorraine sent us to warn you not to meet him at Avenches as originally planned. Instead you are to go on to Burg Moudon and await him there. You will be granted safe haven at Moudon."

Burg Moudon was an extra three days' ride. Hugh had hoped to give his men and horses a chance to rest before then. "Philip has no jurisdiction over Lorraine," he said. "Why is he invading now?"

The knight glanced toward Adrienne. "The king knows you have Henry's daughter and that Lorraine assisted you in her abduction. By your actions you have imperiled Philip's truce with Richard and placed France on the brink of war with England. Philip is threatening to have you hauled before the court on charges of treason."

How had Philip learned of his plans so soon? Hugh wondered. Had Lorraine leaked the information, or was it someone else? Either way, he could not risk getting embroiled in a battle with Philip's army. He had no choice but to go on to Burg Moudon as advised and await Lorraine there.

"I don't trust them," Graeham said.

Hugh looked toward one of the campfires where the four knights who had joined them were eating and drinking with some of his own men. The knights had insisted upon accompanying him to Moudon, leading Hugh to wonder if his uninvited guests had been sent to spy on him. He was considering sending men to Avenches to find out for himself if the Duke of Lorraine was really being detained by King Philip. "Nor do I," he said. "That is why I want them watched. If they do anything at all out of the ordinary, I want to know about it." He turned to leave.

"Hugh, wait. I want to know why you mentioned Rougemont earlier. I thought that was in the forgotten past."

"I forget nothing, Graeham."

"Damn it, Hugh! I said I was sorry. I'm sorry you lost Sainte-Croix. I'm sorry about Marie. I'm sorry I caused trouble between you and Vernier. What more do you want from me?"

"I want you to stay away from Adrienne. She is here for a purpose, and that purpose does not include warming your bed."

"I was not aware that merely talking to her was a crime."

"I know you too well, Graeham. You don't know how to *merely* talk to any woman. I am not going to risk everything we have planned because you can't keep your chausses on. Now if you will excuse me, I have other matters to attend to." Hugh started back toward his tent.

For a moment Graeham just stood there, the muscles in his jaw knotting as he watched his brother's departing back. Finally his mounting frustration got the upper hand, and he called out, "Whose bed *is* she warming, Hugh? Yours?"

Hugh paused, every muscle in his body tensed. He refused to be goaded into a fight, especially with Graeham. Forcing himself to be calm, he continued walking. He did not look back.

Until today he thought he had forgiven Graeham for his betrayal. Yet now the memory of that night was as fresh in his mind as if it had happened only five minutes instead of five years ago.

He had gone to Château Rougemont to meet with the Count of Vernier to complete the arrangements for his marriage to Vernier's eldest daughter, Marie. The alliance between the houses of Sainte-Croix and Vernier had been negotiated when Marie was in the cradle. Vernier was getting impatient.

He had no feelings toward Marie one way or another. With her fair hair and blue eyes she was pleasant enough to look upon. She was well educated in the arts and sciences as well as in running a household. And she was soft-spoken and complaisant, not at all the sort of woman who would be given to stirring up rebellious barons in her husband's absence. In fact, she was such a perfect model for a nobleman's wife that Hugh was hard-pressed to find any flaw whatsoever in her. A wedding date was set for the end of May, two weeks after Marie's sixteenth birthday.

That night Vernier hosted a lavish banquet during which he publicly announced the betrothal. Wine flowed, and among those present there was great rejoicing that the two countships were to be officially joined at last. In recent months both King Philip and the Church had been eyeing the southern provinces of France with an interest that was more military than benign. Strong alliances were a necessity.

During the banquet Marie was unusually withdrawn. Hugh asked her if something was wrong. She placed her small hand in his and gave him a gentle smile. " 'Tis merely the headache, my lord. I fear the day's excitement has left me feeling a little tired."

As Hugh observed her youthful face throughout the dinner, he thought she appeared more worried than worn. Her blue eyes darted furtively about the great hall as if seeking someone among the revelers, and more than once he noticed her lips pressed together in a thin line of pique. Midway through the meal, she excused herself from the table. He waited until she left the hall, then discreetly followed her.

She slipped out the side door into the ward, where a man waited in the shadows, and burst into tears. "I don't know what to do," she told the man between sobs. "If only Hugh and I could be married now, I could make him think the babe is his. But by May everyone will know I am with child. Father will be furious!"

Marie was with child? Before Hugh could absorb that revelation, the man spoke. Although Hugh could not clearly make out his reply, the familiarity of the voice sliced through him like a blade to the bone.

Marie sniffled. "Graeham, you have to take me to the old woman in the village. She will help me get rid of this child. Hugh must never know that we have been together!"

Hugh closed his eyes and groaned inwardly. That he might have married Marie not knowing of her deception did not make him half so ill as the thought of his own brother lying with her. Graeham's betrayal infuriated him far more than Marie's.

Before the evening was out, the betrothal that had just been announced was declared null and void.

In spite of her tearful pleas that she be allowed to marry Graeham, Marie was sent to Collombey Abbey along with her nine-year-old sister, Alais, who would replace Marie in the marriage negotiations. In the secluded nunnery, Marie's disgrace would be kept from public attention, and Alais would have no opportunity to follow her sister's example. When Alais was of marriageable age, the wedding would take place. The alliance between Vernier and Sainte-Croix had not been severed; merely bruised.

And Graeham, whose only remorse was for having been caught, had disappeared. No one had heard from him for two years.

Reaching his tent, Hugh jerked open the flap and burst through the opening with a fury that caused Adrienne to scramble to her feet. Her eyes were wide in her freshly scrubbed face.

Hugh stopped short. He had been so lost in thought that he had forgotten Adrienne was in his tent. He went to the table and poured himself a tankard of strong wine. "You may stop looking at me as if you expect me to beat you," he snapped.

Slowly releasing her breath, Adrienne sat back down on the furs and tucked her legs beneath her. The chain fastened to her ankle rattled. "You startled me when you came charging into the tent like a wounded bull," she said.

The note of accusation in her voice was so pronounced that Hugh tensed. Didn't the girl know when to retreat? he thought. Or was she deliberately baiting him? Ignoring her, he lowered himself to the folding camp chair and stretched out his long legs. The wine seeped through his veins, coaxing the tension out of his limbs. He closed his eyes. Until he sat down, Hugh had not realized how tired he was.

From where she sat amid the furs, Adrienne watched him with undisguised curiosity. She did not know if he was asleep or merely resting. She noticed that he had shaved. Without his week-old growth of beard, he looked younger. His black hair, wet from a recent dousing, fell carelessly across his broad forehead and curled around his ears.

As she studied his face in the fading light, Adrienne wondered why she had previously thought his features harsh. They were not harsh, merely well defined. "Elegant" was a word that came to mind. Not the courtly, almost feminine elegance that some nobles affected, but a rugged elegance that made her feel peculiarly light-headed just watching him. Of the two brothers, Graeham was more handsome, but Hugh was more masterful. It occurred to her that most people would do Hugh's bidding not because they wanted to or because he forced them, but because they could not help themselves.

Suddenly his eyes opened.

Adrienne's cheeks, already touched by the sun, turned an even deeper shade of pink. "I thought you were asleep."

" 'Tis difficult to sleep, *princesse*, when one is being stared at."

" 'Tis even more difficult to sleep, my lord, when one is chained like an unruly hound."

Hugh stared at her. He could not believe she would deliberately provoke him; even a fool had his limits. But Adrienne was no fool. She was reckless, perhaps. Headstrong. But hardly a fool. Furthermore, the look in her eyes, he realized with a start, was so direct, so guileless, that suddenly he wasn't certain how to react. He was so accustomed to people hiding their true thoughts from him that he no longer knew how to deal with simple honesty. He raised his tankard toward her in a salute. "More difficult for you, perhaps. I find I have less trouble sleeping when I don't have to worry about you trying to escape."

He brought the tankard to his lips and took a long drink of the wine. His eyes never left her face. Finally he lowered the tankard and rested it against his thigh. "I am puzzled about something," he said. "Most girls marry by the time they are sixteen. Disregarding your betrothal to Lachen, I am surprised someone hasn't snatched you up by now."

The question caught Adrienne by surprise. Usually it was her bastardy, not her spinsterhood, that was examined. "What makes you think I'm not sixteen?" she asked defensively.

"You're not. You turned eighteen in July. Now answer my question. Why haven't you married before now?"

Troubled that a stranger would remember the birthday her own father had never acknowledged, she disguised her hurt with a shrug of indifference. "Who would want me?"

Hugh studied her through narrowed eyes. He could not believe that Adrienne was unaware of her beauty. It was more than just her face that was drawing him ever closer to her, he thought. Yet the more he tried to put a finger on what it was that attracted him, the more the answer eluded him. Just sitting here with her, looking at her, he could feel her subtly yet relentlessly laying siege to his defenses. He wondered if *she* knew what she was doing to him. "You're very beautiful," he said. "What man would not want you?"

Burning color flooded Adrienne's face as she realized that he thought she had been looking for a compliment. "What I meant," she corrected herself, growing flustered, "is that I possess no suitable dowry."

"Don't you consider Sainte-Croix a suitable dowry?"

Adrienne's brow crinkled in annoyance. "Until my father died," she reminded him, "I didn't even have that. But since you asked, no, I do not. Sainte-Croix is a curse. Ever since I found out it was to be my marriage portion, my life has been turned upside down. I never wanted it or this marriage that has been arranged for me. I have never even met Duke Wilhelm, yet I am supposed to meekly surrender to him and accept him as my husband." Aware of how close she had come to revealing her innermost fears, she amended her statement with forced offhandedness, "Although I doubt he will want to marry me now."

"Perhaps 'tis just as well. Lachen is more suited to the priesthood than to marriage. I am sure he welcomes your dowry for its seaports, which provide easy access to the Mediterranean. He has already been on three pilgrimages that I know of to the Holy Land. I doubt they will be his last."

Although she had already surmised that Duke Wilhelm wanted her dowry more than he wanted her, hearing her suspicions verified unexpectedly hurt. She disguised her wounded pride by thrusting out her chin and asking caustically, "Now that we have ascertained Duke Wilhelm's motives for wanting to marry me, are you going to enlighten me as to your motives for abducting me?"

"No, I am not," Hugh said firmly.

At that moment Hugh's squire came into the tent, carrying a large tray. He placed the tray on the table and removed the covers from the trenchers. He began cutting the roasted hare into portions. Hugh signaled to him. Gabel glanced in Adrienne's direction, then put down the knife. He lit the candles, then left the tent.

Standing, Hugh picked up the tray and carried it to the furs. Adrienne eyed him warily. "Wouldn't you be more comfortable at the table?"

"Probably. But there is only one chair, and I would prefer to dine with you rather than looking down upon you." Putting down the tray, Hugh went to the table to retrieve his tankard and the flagon of wine.

The instant Hugh's back was turned, Adrienne slipped one of the two eating knives off the tray and hid it behind her, then shifted her weight so that she was sitting on it. She drew up her knees and wrapped her arms around them and feigned a look of bored indifference as Hugh returned to the furs and sat down. Her heart pounding, she watched him pick up the knife and begin dividing the meat. "Your plans are flawed," she said, wondering if he would notice the missing knife. "As soon as Duke Wilhelm discovers that I have been abducted, he will send his armies after you. And if he doesn't, Richard and Queen Eleanor will."

Hugh glanced up. "What do you know about the king's armies?"

"Only that they will come after you and crush you."

"To protect you?"

At that, Adrienne snorted inelegantly. "Hardly. To have me put away where the queen can forget I exist, more likely. She tried to have my mother sent away to Scotland."

"Instead, Henry kept Isolde within a day's ride of Chinon where he could visit her whenever he wished, and where Eleanor knew he was to be found every time he rode out."

Pricked by the notion that the queen might have been hurt by Henry's liaison with her mother, Adrienne changed the subject. "You seem to know a great deal about me, my lord. Yet I know nothing about you. It puts me at a disadvantage."

Hugh finished serving her. "There is only one knife, so I cut your game for you," he said. He could have used the dagger he kept hidden in his boot, but he did not trust Adrienne with a knife. She was so unpredictable, there was no telling what she might do with it. He picked up his tankard and brought it to his mouth. "What do you want to know?"

Her brows knitted as she pondered the rumors she had heard about the Comte de Sainte-Croix, none of them very flattering. Finally curiosity won out over better judgment. "Is it true that you enjoy roasting and devouring small children?"

Hugh choked on his wine. He wiped the corner of his mouth and speared her with a disapproving glare. "I can see you have been listening to too many troubadours."

"I didn't hear that from a troubadour. Father Bernard told me."

Disdain flashed in Hugh's eyes. "A priest? Why am I not surprised?" He delved into his dinner, his movements rigid with pent-up anger.

Adrienne said calmly, "You have not answered my question."

"And what question was that?" Hugh asked, annoyed.

"Do you enjoy roasting and—"

"No, I do not. Although I have been known to cut down an occasional impudent maiden."

Remembering the stories she had heard about the people of Sainte-Croix worshiping severed heads, she asked warily, "Just what part of her did you cut off, my lord?"

Anger glinted in Hugh's dark eyes. "Don't you have any normal questions to ask me, such as how many brothers and sisters do I have?"

Almost disappointed that her mysterious captor might turn out to be ordinary after all, Adrienne asked dutifully, "How many brothers and sisters do you have?"

"Graeham is my only brother. He is three years younger than I. Our sister, Raissa, is in a convent in Arles. She is your age."

"Is your sister a nun?"

"No. And she won't be if I have anything to say about it. Raissa only thinks she has a calling."

So Hugh de Clairmont thinks himself capable of controlling even his sister's future, Adrienne thought. She secretly hoped Raissa had the determination to do what she wanted with her life and not permit herself to be bullied by her arrogant elder brother. "Why did my father seize Sainte-Croix from you?"

Hugh had been about to take a drink of wine. His hand was arrested in midair. He lowered the tankard to the tray. "Is it your intent to annoy me, *princesse*, or does it come naturally?"

"You said I could ask you questions."

"I changed my mind. Eat your supper."

After refilling his tankard, Hugh leaned back against the clothes chest and studied Adrienne while she ate. Physically he found her pleasing. Not only was she tall and strong and beautiful, but she possessed a rare courage that he admired. It would be an easy matter, he thought, to make her his wife and put an end to this feud between his family and the Crown. Such a marriage would ensure his return to control of Sainte-Croix and would shield Adrienne from having to marry a cold, unsparing man like Lachen.

There was just the small problem of his betrothal to Alais de Vernier.

When they finished eating, Hugh picked up the tray and carried it to the tent opening. He stopped and turned back to Adrienne. Indecision furrowed his brow. He did not like leaving her in irons. It went against everything he believed in to treat any woman so callously. That was why he did not chain Marlys. Yet Adrienne was not Marlys. At the first opportunity Adrienne would flee. He was not willing to take that risk. Shaking his head, he left the tent.

Adrienne released her breath in a slow sigh of relief. She had begun to think he would never leave. Careful not to rattle the chain fastened around her ankle, she rose to her knees and picked up the knife she had been sitting on, the one she had stolen from the supper tray when Hugh turned away to get the wine.

Chapter Six

ADRIENNE CLUTCHED THE eating dagger against her racing heart. She could not believe her good fortune. She had been so shocked to see the dagger lying on the tray that she had nearly missed the opportunity to grab it when Hugh's back was turned. She could not believe that he had not noticed it was missing.

She took a deep breath to steady herself. She had to make plans, and that was best done calmly, not in a state of quaking euphoria.

She thought of waiting for a time when she was not fettered, but quickly dismissed that idea. There was no place to hide the knife where Hugh would not find it. Her best chance for escaping was now, before Hugh returned.

She did not waste time trying to break open the locks on the irons. Instead, she turned her attention to the clothes chest at the foot of the pile of furs. The chain was secured to the leather carrying strap. If she could cut through the strap and free the chain, there would be plenty of time later to worry about getting the iron off her ankle.

She glanced through the tent opening. The guard was standing with his back toward the tent. She scooted up next to the chest and began sawing methodically at the leather strap.

The task was more difficult than she had anticipated. Although the chest appeared to have seen years of use, it had not been abused. The leather carrying handles were as strong and secure as the day they had been attached to the chest. By the time her efforts began to show visible results, dusk had deepened into complete darkness.

After what seemed an eternity, the leather strap gave way.

Adrienne caught the chain as it started to fall and eased it to the ground. She did not know how she was going to get away from the camp without making enough noise to awaken even the soundest sleeper, but she could not worry about that now. First she had to get out of the tent.

She could not leave through the tent opening; it was too well guarded. She was going to have to find another way.

Turning, she pulled back the furs to expose one of the stakes that held the tent wall pegged to the ground. It was driven into the earth at an angle that made it impossible to pull out without being seen from outside. Cutting the tent wall was also out of the question; an untimely rip of the canvas would expose her plans. Only one possibility remained.

Gripping the knife, she began digging at the ground near the stake. She was careful not to press against the canvas and cause any kind of movement that would draw attention. If she could expose enough of the stake, she reasoned, she should be able to pull it out with a minimum of effort.

"It does seem too coincidental," Sir Conraed said after listening to Hugh's concerns regarding their guests. He shook his head. "I do not know Lorraine as well as you do, my lord. But I do know Philip. He would not risk provoking the ire of the Holy Roman Emperor by invading the border provinces. Philip would be more inclined to try to woo Lorraine with expensive gifts and honeyed promises than to launch an attack against him."

"We need to keep traveling if we wish to avoid alerting our visitors to our suspicions. Still, I would feel better knowing exactly what Lorraine is up to. How long would it take you to get to Avenches and return?"

"Barring any unforeseen circumstances, my lord, I could be back within a day or two of your arrival at Burg Moudon, sooner if you travel slowly."

Hugh inclined his head. "I'll make every effort to delay our progress without giving our visitors cause for alarm. Choose your men. In the morning, when we break camp, I'll keep John de Lancy occupied while you slip away."

Adrienne had nearly managed to free the stake when she heard Hugh bark an order to one of the guards. She shoved the knife beneath the furs and smoothed the furs over the place where she had dug. Through the tent opening, she saw Hugh's booted feet as he stopped to talk to the guard. She lay down, her face toward the tent wall, and pretended to be asleep.

Hugh entered the tent.

Adrienne lay very still as he stood looking down on her. Her heart was thumping so loud she was certain he could hear it. Finally, fearing she could not keep up the pretense of sleep much longer, she rolled over. Her eyes flew open, and she found herself staring up at him. In the flickering candlelight, she could see his troubled expression. "I didn't hear you come back," she said. She hoped he did not notice the cut carrying strap on his chest. She pushed herself upright. "Is something wrong?"

Hugh pulled his tunic off over his head. "How many people know of your betrothal to Lachen?"

The question caught Adrienne off guard. "I-I don't know," she stammered. She started to shove her hair back from her face, but when she saw her dirt-encrusted hands, she quickly hid them from view. "My guardian, of course. And the duke. The knights who provided my escort. I have been told that my half brother Geoffrey and William the Marshal were both with my father when he died. I assume they too knew of it. Why?"

Hugh blew out the candle. " 'Tis not important. Go to sleep. We have a long ride ahead of us tomorrow."

Puzzled by Hugh's odd tone, Adrienne lay back down. She was careful not to look his way as he finished undressing. Her heart was only now starting to slow its furious pounding. She had come so close to getting caught. Now she was going to have to wait until Hugh was asleep. She considered changing her mind, but only for an instant. She had no wish to be present in the morning when Hugh noticed the damage she had done to his clothes chest. "May I ask where we are headed?"

"No, you may not."

Adrienne pursed her lips in annoyance. She was beginning to think the man truly enjoyed provoking her; he did it so well.

Hugh stretched out beside her on the furs. Even though their bodies did not touch, Adrienne could feel the tension that emanated from his taut muscles like ribbons of heat shimmering above a meadow on a hot summer day. With a sinking feeling, she realized that it would be a long time before he relaxed enough to fall asleep.

Gradually the noises in the camp lessened until all was still except for an occasional exchange between those who remained awake, or the sound of a log being fed to a campfire. Once she heard the knights changing guard outside the tent.

After what might have been hours or only a few minutes, Adrienne rose up on one elbow. There was no moon to relieve the darkness, and it was difficult to make out Hugh's facial features. "Are you awake?" she whispered.

In the woods just beyond the clearing an owl hooted. The eerie sound raised icy prickles on Adrienne's skin, and she shuddered, wondering if it was an omen.

Moving as quietly as possible, she sat up and turned toward the tent wall. She felt along the ground until her fingers came into contact with the iron stake. She gripped it and pulled. It gave only slightly. After several unsuccessful tries, she knew she was going to have to dig a little deeper to free it completely. She located the dagger where she had hidden it beneath the furs, and resumed chipping away at the ground, occasionally casting a cautious glance in Hugh's direction.

Finally the stake was loose enough so that she was able to pull it from its anchorage.

Although no longer taut, the side wall of the tent was far from slack. Adrienne lifted the edge as far as it would go. The gap afforded precious little room, but if she flattened herself out on the ground, she might be able to slide under it.

Suddenly Hugh moved.

Adrienne's breath caught in her throat. She stared at him. He rolled onto his side, facing her. Her eyes widened in horror as his arm came to rest on the furs where she should have been lying.

Adrienne sat without moving, hardly daring to breathe as the blood pounded in her ears. She must be insane! she told herself. Only a lunatic would try to escape with him lying right beside her. But she was desperate. Captivity was making her do things she would never have attempted otherwise. She had to get away from here. The longer she delayed, the more hopeless her plight became. Even marriage to Duke Wilhelm was no longer as frightening as the uncertain future she faced as Hugh's captive. He might not intend to kill her just yet, but once she had outlived her usefulness, what then? She did not intend to linger for the dubious reward of learning her fate.

When it became evident that Hugh was still asleep, Adrienne breathed a little easier. Afraid the slightest jar would rattle the chain, she moved with excruciating slowness, easing her feet, then her legs, under the edge of the tent wall. Once her legs were completely outside the tent, she lowered herself onto her stomach and edged her way, an inch at a time, toward freedom. The last thing she saw before pulling her head beneath the opening was Hugh, sleeping soundly.

She was just getting to her knees when the guard seized the back of her shirt and a handful of hair at the same time. He yanked her to her feet. "Just where do you think you are going?"

Adrienne swung her hand.

The guard jerked his head to one side, but not quickly enough, and the dagger grazed his temple. Swearing loudly, he gripped her wrist and wrenched her arm up over her head. He pried the knife from her hand.

She brought her heel down hard on the guard's instep. He cried out and lost his hold on her.

Jerking her hand free, Adrienne turned to run. Before she could take two steps, she came up hard against a mail-clad chest. The second guard's arms closed around her. She clawed at his face with both hands, digging her fingers into his eyes and pushing as hard as she could. With a bestial growl, he shoved her away from him. Her foot caught on the chain and she went sprawling.

The guard lunged for her.

Adrienne lashed out with her feet and caught his kneecap with a kick so well placed that he yelped in surprise and went down. The first guard hauled her to her feet, holding her arms in a viselike grip as she kicked and squirmed and tried to tear herself free.

The guard she had kicked slowly pulled himself upright. His expression was dark with rage. Flames from the campfire reflected in his eyes, making them glow like red embers as he limped toward her, his upper lip drawn back in a snarl. He raised his fist, and Adrienne's heart seemed to stop beating. She braced herself for the blow.

Hugh's voice sliced through the darkness. "What in the hell is going on here?" he demanded, tying the drawstring of his chausses as he emerged from his tent.

Suddenly it seemed the entire camp was awake. Knights and men-at-arms were everywhere, swarming around them like bees.

The guard who had been about to strike Adrienne lowered his fist. "She tried to get away," he told Hugh. "She crawled under the tent."

Hugh looked at Adrienne. She was struggling in the guard's imprisoning hold. Even chained she had nearly managed to escape, Hugh thought incredulously. The chain, he saw, was still securely fastened around her ankle.

Gabel, who had been sleeping on a pallet outside the entrance to the tent, appeared at Hugh's side. "She cut the leather handle on your clothes chest, m'lord."

Hugh raised his gaze to Adrienne's face. She lifted her chin and eyed him defiantly, her eyes glittering with that fierce Plantagenet pride that never failed to get under his skin like a thorn. His anger soared. This time she had gone too far.

One of the guards picked up the dagger that had fallen to the ground during the struggle. He passed it to Hugh. "She tried to cut Renard's ear off," he said.

Hugh noticed the blood running down the side of the guard's face from the gash at his temple. "Let her go," he said. His voice was carefully controlled.

"But, my lord, she—"

"I said, let her go. And get that cut looked at."

Reluctantly the guard released her.

Hugh glanced at the men who were gathered around them. Half of them had run straight from their bedrolls and were not clothed. "Don't you have anything better to do?" Hugh snapped. The men shifted uncomfortably, then began drifting back to their tents.

Hugh turned his attention back to Adrienne. She was rubbing some of the feeling back into her arms. "Are you all right?" he asked. His voice was so resonant with concern, so sincere, that Adrienne's defiance wilted beneath a wave of guilt and bewildered relief. She had expected him to be furious with her. She smiled sheepishly. "Yes, thank you."

He extended his hand toward her. "Come here."

An aching lump wedged itself in her throat as she started toward him. She did not deserve to be treated with kindness. Suddenly it was important to her that he understand she was genuinely apologetic. She reached out to take his hand. "I'm sorry for the— *Ouch!*"

He clamped his hand around her wrist and yanked her toward him, causing her head to snap back. "You stupid little fool! After what happened the last time you tried to escape, I thought you would have learned your lesson. What were you trying to prove with this attempt? That you can continue to defy me and not suffer the consequences?"

Coming as it did after a show of carefully crafted calm, his outburst of rage shattered her composure. "I wasn't trying to prove anything!" she cried out. "I was trying to escape—something any prisoner with even a shred of dignity left has an obligation to do. Were our places reversed, my lord, I would hardly expect *you* to meekly surrender to your captor's whims!"

Hugh's expression turned ugly. His hand tightened on her wrist. He lowered his face to hers and spoke in a low, menacing voice that sent a shiver of terror racing through her veins. "Let me remind you, *princesse*, that you have never once suffered unduly at my hands. And had I granted the slightest concession to my whims, you would at this moment be in that tent, in my bed, doing your damnedest to pleasure me. Do you understand?"

In spite of the fact that her knees were quaking so badly she could barely stand, there was defiance in the look Adrienne gave him. "What I understand, my lord, is that I am forced to spend my days enduring your touch and my nights sharing your bed, never knowing when you are going to fondle me in front of your men or when your threats of defilement might become a reality."

Hugh's eyes narrowed. "Since you find my company so distasteful," he spat, "you should be pleased to know you won't be forced to endure it any longer. From now on, you will be treated like any other prisoner. Instead of game and wine, you will sup on bread and water. Instead of on a pallet, you will sleep on the ground. When we move out in the morning, you will not ride, but will walk with the rest of the prisoners. If you think you have fared badly before now, *Your Highness*, you are due for a rude awakening."

Before Adrienne could make sense of what he was saying, Hugh spun her around and shoved her ahead of him. She stumbled. He caught her arm, breaking her fall, and jerked her along in his wake. When she frantically took a running step to keep from being dragged, the chain dangling from her ankle swung around and caught Hugh across the heel with an impact that wrenched a violent curse from his throat. He rounded on her, his expression so replete with rage that Adrienne threw her hands up over her face, thinking he meant to strike her.

Instead, he picked her up and tossed her over his shoulder like a sack of flour. So much raw fury reverberated in his stride that Adrienne had to grit her teeth to keep them from knocking together as he carried her, not into his tent but across the camp to the *palissade* where the other prisoners were confined.

"Where are you ta-aking me?" Adrienne managed to get out between clenched teeth.

Hugh ignored her. "Open the gate!" he bellowed at the startled guards.

The two guards nearly collided with each other as they hurried to do his bidding.

The iron hinges on the temporary structure creaked, and the nauseating stench of excrement and unwashed bodies wafted through the gate as it was swung open. Inside the *palissade*'s vertical stake walls, about thirty prisoners huddled in a miserable group. There was barely enough room for them to sit, much less lie down. Those who had been awakened by the commotion eyed warily the tall, unpredictable man who had ordered their imprisonment. Before anyone realized what he intended, he dumped Adrienne into their midst.

There was a loud rattling of chains as some of the men scrambled to get out of the way. Hugh barked an order to one of the guards. The guard seized the chain fastened to Adrienne's ankle and attached it to a second chain before locking it around her other ankle. Now not only were her feet fastened together but she was chained to the other prisoners as well.

Pushing herself into a sitting position, she shoved her hair out of her eyes and impaled Hugh with a virulent glower. "I hate you," she spat.

Hugh's lips curled into a leering smile. "Since you found your last accommodations so lacking, *princesse*, perhaps these will be more to your liking." He bent at the waist in an insulting mockery of a bow. "Enjoy."

The gate slammed shut.

Terrified at the thought of being left in this den of filth and unwashed bodies, Adrienne surged to her feet. Her chains brought her up short and upset those nearest her.

"Sit down!" one man snapped. Someone else grabbed the hem of her tunic and yanked, bringing her crashing to the ground.

A hand closed around her breast. "Would you look at what his lordship brought us," a man sneered. "He must have gotten tired of her."

Adrienne slapped the man's hand away, but he caught her wrist and hauled her onto his lap. "Now, that's no way to treat a fellow prisoner," he chided. He slid his hand up her thigh.

A silent scream exploded in Adrienne's throat. Placing her hands against the man's chest, she shoved as hard as she could. "Get your hands off me!"

Suddenly another man took her by the shoulders and pulled her away, then quickly put himself between Adrienne and her assailant. "I'm warning you," he told the man in a quiet but threatening tone. "If you want to see daylight, you'll not lay a hand on her again. Is that clear?"

The man could not answer. Another prisoner behind him had looped a chain around his neck and was pulling hard. The prisoner gasped and sputtered and clawed at his throat. Finally he nodded.

The man who had pulled Adrienne away from him now turned toward her. She had scooted as far away from the others as she could get and was sitting with her back pressed against the *palissade* wall, her knees drawn up tight. Her entire body was quaking. The man reached toward her, and she cringed away from him. "Don't touch me!"

He dropped his hand. "Are you hurt, my lady?"

There was something oddly familiar about his voice, but Adrienne did not recognize him with his scraggly, unkempt beard. She started to shake her head, as much in confusion as in answer to his question.

"I am Eustace, my lady," the man prompted gently. "I swore an oath of fealty to you."

One of Henry's knights! Adrienne nearly crumpled in relief. "Wh-where are the others?" she stammered.

One by one the other knights spoke up, identifying themselves. Sir Godfrey. Sir Talbot. Sir Guillaume . . . Ten of the twelve knights who had left the ship with Marlys.

"I know not what gutter the rest of this scum springs from," Sir Eustace said derisively, "but if anyone touches you again, he'll not live to tell of it. You have our word, my lady."

Adrienne searched the sea of shadowed faces staring back at her. "Where is Marlys?"

"She is safe. She is kept apart from us so no one here will harm her."

"She's fornicatin' with the guards!" one man called out. He was silenced by a fist that seemed to come at him out of nowhere.

"She is safe," Eustace repeated firmly.

Hugging her knees against her chest, Adrienne rested her forehead on them and swallowed hard against the tears that choked her throat. She refused to let any of them see her cry. She was the daughter of a king, she reminded herself. No matter how hard her father had tried to disavow her, she was a Plantagenet, descended of that noble house of Anjou that had withstood centuries of adversity, and this was but a test of her strength. This was her chance, she thought crazily, to prove that she was as worthy of her lineage as any of her father's legitimate children.

It was the most farfetched fantasy she had ever concocted, but she clung to it nonetheless, and as the night stretched out agonizingly, it brought her a small measure of comfort.

Morning dawned gray and threatening. As the men broke camp, Sir Conraed and five other knights slipped unseen into the forest. If Hugh had wondered what diversion he would have to create so his uninvited guests would not notice his knights' departure, he need not have worried. Graeham provided enough of a diversion to draw the attention of everyone in camp.

"*You left her there all night?*" Graeham's face was white with shock. "My God! Are you crazy? You know what those men will do to her! You might as well have thrown her to the wolves!"

"They won't touch her," Hugh said tersely, his brittle tone masking the sick churning in the pit of his stomach. No sooner had the *palissade* gate closed last night than he had regretted his rash decision, but to retreat now would invite rebellion. He finished adjusting his war-horse's girth strap and straightened. His eyes were cold and emotionless in a face as unyielding as granite. "If they do, they will answer to me."

Hugh started to turn away, but Graeham grabbed the sleeve of his tunic and swung him back around. "*You bastard!* If you had even an ounce of decency in you,

you would never have subjected Adrienne to such vile treatment!"

Hugh jerked his arm out of Graeham's grasp. His dark eyes smoldered. "Were you not my brother, I would kill you for that. Adrienne will remain with the other prisoners until she learns not to defy me. That is my decision, and you had best accept it." Placing his foot in the stirrup, Hugh swung up into the saddle. "This discussion is finished. Do not mention Adrienne to me again."

He issued the order to move out.

Disbelief frozen on his face, Graeham watched his brother turn his horse and ride to the front of the column. The other riders started forward, leaving him standing in their dust. Sick with disgust, he pivoted and went back to his own horse.

Roland, his arm in a sling, was waiting for him. "Did he change his mind?"

Graeham shook his head. "The man is insane. Adrienne escaped from under his nose yet again, and he is determined to make her suffer for his wounded pride. I don't think he cares how much he hurts her."

Roland, who had witnessed Hugh's transformation into a raging madman when they fought the outlaw knights, said nothing. Something in Hugh had been changed forever that day. Roland was not certain exactly what it was, but he did not agree with Graeham's assessment that Hugh did not care about Adrienne. If anything, Roland thought, Hugh cared too much.

The jangling of chains as the prisoners shuffled forward could be heard over the rumble of the supply wagons. Graeham's stomach clenched. It was all he could do to keep his head turned to the front. He could not believe Hugh was making Adrienne walk, chained to the other prisoners. Even the girl, Marlys, was permitted to ride in one of the wagons.

Graeham was not the only one disturbed by Hugh's actions. The other knights were unusually quiet, their gloom reflecting the oppressive sky that bore down on them. To them, Adrienne's attempted escape had been a diversion. A source of entertainment at best. At worst, an annoyance. No one thought she deserved the punishment Hugh had meted out. With the exception of John de Lancy, everyone avoided Hugh.

"I heard you had trouble with your hostage last night," John de Lancy said as he rode alongside Hugh.

Hugh's expression was unreadable. "It's been dealt with."

John de Lancy glanced over his shoulder at the sullen soldiers following them. "It appears, my lord, that your solution to the problem isn't meeting with much enthusiasm."

Hugh said nothing.

After a few minutes of silence, John de Lancy spoke again. " 'Tis a formidable task you have taken upon yourself, challenging the powers of two monarchs in order to claim a province they both want. Should they decide to join forces against you, they will cut you to pieces."

Years of dealing with devious men had taught Hugh to be cautious, and something told him John de Lancy was fishing for information regarding his plans to retake Sainte-Croix. "You could be right," he said noncommittally. "But I am willing to take the chance that you are wrong. Now if you will excuse me, I need to confer with some of my men." Before the knight could question him further, Hugh guided his horse out of the formation and fell back, leaving John de Lancy alone to lead the column.

When they stopped at midday to rest, it took all the self-control that Hugh possessed not to have Adrienne brought to him. He knew what would happen if he saw her: he would change his mind about keeping her with the other prisoners. And that, he was acutely aware, would jeopardize not only his authority over his men but his own objectivity toward Adrienne as well. He had veered dangerously close to losing that objectivity. Every time she looked at him with those haunting gray eyes, he found himself seeing her as a beautiful, desirable woman instead of as the daughter of his enemy. He should have put her with the other prisoners from the beginning. She was a distraction he did not need.

Yet that night when Hugh retired to his tent, he found himself thinking about her to the point of obsession. If having her sleeping beside him at night had been a distraction, *not* having her at his side was even more of one. His resolve nearly collapsed when the head guard in charge of the prisoners sought him out.

The guard shifted nervously. "M'lord, begging your pardon, but I don't think 'tis a good idea for Lady Adrienne to be penned with the other prisoners at night."

Hugh schooled his expression into one of bored indifference. "Has anyone harmed her?"

"Well, no, m'lord. King Henry's men are looking out for her. But some of the others, they've been getting ideas."

With an outward calm that he was far from feeling, Hugh said, "You may relay a warning to all the prisoners. Should anyone so much as lay a finger on her, I'll have his right hand cut off. Should it happen again, 'twill be the left."

The guard stared at him, open-mouthed. "Isn't that a bit severe, m'lord?" he ventured hesitantly.

Hugh's dark gaze bored into him. "Jules, when you were in Palestine with my brother, did you ever witness the punishment most commonly dealt out to those caught stealing another man's property?"

"Well, yes, m'lord, but Lady Adrienne—"

"—is my property," Hugh finished for him. "And you, Jules, are responsible for safeguarding that property. Should I find you have been derelict in your duties, you know what will happen, don't you?"

The guard paled. "Yes, m'lord," he mumbled.

"Will there be anything else, Jules?"

"No, m'lord."

"You are dismissed."

After Jules left, Hugh filled his tankard and drained it in a single long draft. He barely tasted the wine, and his hand shook as he set down the tankard. *Damn, but you are a cold, heartless brute*, his conscience shrieked at him. He felt as if he would be sick. There were a hundred other ways he could have bent Adrienne to his will. Had he not already warned her that he would vent his ire on Marlys or on her knights should she defy him again? That would have been a simple solution. He was relatively certain that Adrienne would swear to anything to prevent her maidservant or her knights from being punished in her stead. Why had he not thought of that instead of acting so impulsively?

Yet he had made his choice. Now he must see it through.

Sitting on the ground, Adrienne leaned back against the *palissade* wall and closed her eyes. Every bone, every muscle, in her body throbbed with pain. Never before in her life had she walked as many miles as she had today. The bottoms of her feet burned, and the muscles in her legs quivered from the unaccustomed exertion. She hurt so badly that she no longer cared that her clothes were soiled or that her face was streaked with dirt and sweat or that her hair was matted. All she wanted to do was go to sleep and never wake up.

A hand settled on her shoulder. She forced her eyes open.

Sir Eustace was leaning over her. "Your supper, my lady."

Adrienne looked at the chunk of dark coarse bread he held out to her, and her stomach rebelled. She shook her head. "I'm not hungry."

Concern clouded the knight's eyes. "My lady, you need to eat if you are to keep up your strength."

Hugh's face flickered through her mind, igniting a spark of anger deep down inside her. Sir Eustace was right. She had to keep up her strength, if only to spite *him*. She had to show him that she could not be conquered. And one day, she vowed, she would have her revenge.

She took the bread.

Chapter Seven

FOR THREE DAYS the moving army followed the same routine: rising before dawn, traveling until noon, stopping for an hour's rest, then continuing until sunset. During all that time, Hugh avoided going near the prisoners. Adrienne's confinement had become as much of a punishment for him as for her. Complaints reached him by the hour—she was not being given enough food; she was tired and needed to rest; she had no privacy.

Amazingly, the complaints came not from her but from Hugh's men. They approached him, sometimes in groups, sometimes singly, but always with the same concern for Adrienne's welfare. He had thought to avoid dissent among his men by treating Adrienne no differently than he would one of them who had defied him. Yet instead of unity, he was very near to having a rebellion on his hands.

"My lord, if we take turns watching her, in addition to the regular guards, will you free her?" Sir Roland asked when they had stopped for the night. It had been raining on and off for most of the day, and the discomfort of wet clothing combined with the steamy heat had brought tempers to a peak.

His expression rigid, Hugh looked in turn at each of the six knights assembled outside his tent. That Graeham was among them did nothing to further their cause. "God's teeth!" he thundered. "What hold does she have on you that you have all gone as soft as overripe plums?"

Roland raked his good hand through his hair in frustration. "My lord, whatever her crime, 'tis unfair to treat Lady Adrienne like a hardened soldier accustomed to the rigors of a march."

"I might remind you, Roland, that she has already made two escape attempts, not to mention being responsible for nearly getting you killed. She is hardly the weak, helpless female you men seem to think she is. And if I cannot control her, what makes you think you will be able to keep her in line?"

Graeham, who had managed to keep silent until now, suddenly exploded. "Damn it, Hugh! Your problem is that she has outwitted you twice and you are too vain to admit it. All you can think of is how to control her! Has it never occurred to you that brute force might not be the answer to everything?"

There was an unpleasant element of truth in Graeham's accusation that struck a nerve. "I did not go to the trouble of capturing her just to risk losing her again simply because my *men* insist upon behaving like sentimental old women," he bit out. "Adrienne will remain with the other prisoners until we reach Burg Moudon. Only when she is safe behind the fortress walls can I be sure she will not flee."

They reached the castle at midday. The prisoners were herded into a windowless storeroom on the ground floor of the keep. A short time later a guard came and removed Adrienne's irons. He escorted her up a winding staircase to a tower chamber where Marlys, pacing anxiously, awaited her.

"Oh, m'lady, what have they done to you?" Marlys blurted out. Her frightened brown eyes filled with tears. "Your beautiful hair. It's so . . . so—"

"It itches," Adrienne finished for her, resisting the temptation to scratch. It had been so long since her hair had seen soap or a comb that there was no guessing what might be nesting amid the mass of tangles.

"Marlys, I can't bear being like this," she said wearily. "I need a bath."

Marlys glanced nervously toward the door. "Now?"

"Yes, please." Adrienne plucked at her soiled tunic. "And something clean to wear."

Marlys bit down on her bottom lip. After several seconds of wrestling with indecision, she went to the door and opened it. She spoke slowly to the guards posted outside the door. The two men glanced at each other, and one man replied haltingly in a mixture of French and English. Marlys bobbed her head excitedly. "Yes, yes, a bath," she said.

The guard peered into the room. Adrienne lifted her chin and met his curious stare with as much dignity as she could summon. "A bath," she repeated in French. "And clean clothes. These are crawling with vermin."

The guard nodded his understanding and closed the door.

Marlys flashed Adrienne a grateful smile. "We'll get you out of those dirty rags, m'lady, and I'll wash your hair and comb the snarls out, and then you'll feel better."

Marlys continued rambling aimlessly, but Adrienne barely heard her. She was so exhausted, all she could think of was lying down on the great bed that stood against the far wall. Yet she knew she dared not touch the linens until she had bathed.

A tapestry, painstakingly executed in wool and silk with tiny stitches, hung over the bed. The embroidery depicted a woman sitting beneath a tree, caressing the face of the man who reclined near her, his head in her lap. The woman's golden hair cascaded over her shoulders and spilled around them, blanketing them both in a golden aura. That the two were very much in love was evident. At one time Adrienne would have thought the scene touching and would have longed for such a love of her own. Experience had taught her otherwise. As in her own situation, people married not for love but for political or economic reasons. Even the secret liaisons that abounded in most courts reflected jealous rivalry more often than genuine affection.

Besides, Adrienne thought cynically, no woman would ever be foolish enough to allow herself to love any man that much.

A copper bathing tub was carried into the chamber and set before the hearth. Since it was still unseasonably warm, no fire burned on the hearth. The servants carried bucket after bucket of hot water up from the kitchens and poured it into the tub. Finally the last servant left the chamber. Marlys closed the door.

Marlys helped Adrienne undress and step into the bath. An uncontrollable shudder that was part pleasure, part shock, rippled through her as she lowered her aching muscles into the steaming water. Too exhausted to protest Marlys's fussing, she closed her eyes and relinquished herself to the girl's care. Oddly, the maidservant's incessant chatter was like a balm to her weary nerves. By the time every inch of her had been scrubbed clean, her head had cleared and she was able to think logically once again.

She had no idea why she had been freed of her chains upon arrival at Burg Moudon or why she had been given a private bedchamber and her own maidservant. Over the last few days, news had reached her of the bickering between Hugh and his knights regarding his treatment of her. Perhaps he was merely bowing to the wishes of his men, she thought. She doubted that he felt any remorse. She did not think Hugh de Clairmont was even capable of remorse.

Whatever his reason for separating her from the others, she mused, she was not going to permit him the luxury of growing complacent. If he had thought to teach her a lesson by placing her in chains, he had seriously underestimated her. The only thing he had accomplished was to make her more determined than ever to elude him.

After the bath, Adrienne wrapped herself in a linen towel and sat on the huge bed while Marlys worked the tangles out of her wet hair with a comb. The comb snagged on a particularly stubborn snarl, and she winced. "How many guards are posted outside the door?" she asked.

"There are two on the landing, m'lady, and two more at the bottom of the stairs."

Adrienne's brows drew together in concentration. "We have to find a way out of here."

Marlys looked aghast. "Escape?"

"Yes."

"But, m'lady, after what happened the last time you tried to get away, aren't you afraid of what Lord Hugh will do to you?"

The light in Adrienne's eyes turned as hard and deadly as steel. "No."

Confusion shadowed Marlys's face. "I-I don't know if I can escape," she stammered. "He scares me. He's so b-big. And when he gets angry, he's like a demon!"

Adrienne turned around to face Marlys. "Marlys, listen to me. He won't hurt us. Whatever his reasons for taking us prisoner, he wants us alive. If he did not, he would have killed us already. You have to remember that."

Marlys nodded, but Adrienne could tell by her wary expression that she was not convinced. "If you are afraid of him, you need not take the risk. I will go alone."

Horror flashed across the other girl's face. "Please don't leave me here, m'lady! I want to go home too. I don't want to stay here by myself!"

"Then you will come with me?"

Marlys chewed her bottom lip. Finally she nodded.

"Good. We won't attempt anything foolish. I promise. We shall wait until the time is right and our freedom is ensured. But I shall need your help, Marlys. I cannot do it without you."

"M-me?"

"Yes, you. I doubt that Hugh will grant me the freedom of movement that he will permit you. You will have to be my eyes and ears. Whenever you go to the kitchens or pass through the hall, you must always be on the alert for anything that might be of use to us. Take notice of where the guards are posted. See if there is an unmanned door to the outside. Listen in on conversations. Watch for any sign of discontent that we might be able to use to create a diversion. Do you understand?"

Marlys nodded, less reluctantly this time. Just looking and listening was not as frightening as actually doing anything.

Marlys finished combing the tangles from Adrienne's hair, then went in search of clean clothes for her mistress.

"Remember what I told you," Adrienne reminded her before she left the bedchamber. "You are my eyes and ears."

Hugh did not like what he saw. Not only was the fortress poorly defended but it was built too near the tree line. It would be easy for a marauding army to sneak up on them unseen. As a precaution he had given the order for the bulk of his men to set up camp in a protected clearing some distance away in the woods. If Burg Moudon was attacked, he did not want his men trapped inside the castle walls.

Hugh left the parapet and descended the stone stairs to the great hall, where long trestle tables were being set up for the evening meal. Their host, the Baron of Riehen, was giving a lavish banquet tonight honoring the birth of his son. Hugh and his men had been invited to attend.

Hugh looked around the hall. None of the knights garrisoned at Burg Moudon were known to him, and that made him uneasy. He had been allied with the House of Lorraine for fifteen years, having initially served as a squire in the duke's army at the age of fourteen. It was unusual for him to enter any of the duke's holdings and not encounter a familiar face.

John de Lancy approached him. He was carrying a tankard. "This is good," he said, indicating the wine. "Not like that moldy ferment Lorraine usually stocks. Will you join me?"

Hugh shook his head. "Perhaps later," he said. A movement at the corner of his eye caught his attention, and he turned his head in time to see Marlys slip furtively behind the passage screen. A black, heavy look curtained his face. He had given specific orders that neither girl was to leave the tower. Excusing himself, he strode across the hall. Whatever plot Adrienne was hatching this time, she was not going to get away with it.

His displeasure soared when he saw that the guards he had ordered posted at the bottom of the tower stairs were not at their stations. Had they been his guards and not Lorraine's, he would have seen that they were severely punished. He did not tolerate such indolence from his men. He took the stairs two at a time.

Only one of the two guards on the landing was still at his post. The man jumped to attention when Hugh appeared.

"Where is the other guard?" Hugh demanded.

"He went to relieve himself, m'lord."

Hugh's jaw knotted. If Adrienne managed to escape again, he was going to claim a few hides. Giving the guard a blistering look, he threw open the door to the bedchamber.

He stopped short, stunned by the unexpected assault on his senses. The air in the chamber was warm and damp and scented with lavender and rosemary. A tub, still filled with water, sat before the hearth. A wet towel lay beside it on the floor. Adrienne stood beside the bed, clutching around her a towel that revealed more than it covered. Her dark hair spilled all around her in a disorderly confusion of damp curls, and her eyes were huge with indignation and uncertainty.

A jolt of awareness slammed into Hugh with the power of a bolt of lightning, shattering his self-deceptions. With excruciating clarity he suddenly understood why he had put Adrienne with the other prisoners. He had thought that by putting her out of his sight, he could also put her out of his mind. He was wrong. Instead of dampening his desire for her, the days apart had only served to make him want her even more.

Hugh pushed the door shut.

Adrienne's fingers tightened on the towel, and her chin shot up mutinously. "What do you want?" she demanded. The tremor in her voice belied the fury in her eyes.

Plantagenet eyes, Hugh thought. Angevin gray, and alive with a fire that kindled his hunger, making him even more determined to have her. He started toward her. "I want you."

Adrienne stood, trapped in the smoldering sexuality of his gaze like a rabbit caught in a snare. She could not have fled even if her life had depended upon it. Instead, she threw back her head and met his steady advance with a glare of scathing contempt. Her heart pounded mercilessly, yet she did not retreat. As much as he terrified her, she could not deny that she derived a perverse satisfaction from defying him.

Hugh stopped before her, his gaze locked with hers in an intense clash of wills that seemed to suck the air from the chamber. In Hugh's eyes, Adrienne saw the disturbing reflection of her own dark passions, and she trembled. Unlike the predator and his prey, there was no definitive distinction between the seducer and the seduced. They were one and the same.

Hugh closed his big hand around both of hers and he gently but firmly pried her fingers open. The towel slid to the floor.

His eyes darkened as they devoured the sensual feast before him. Adrienne's breasts lifted and fell with each breath she took, their dusky rose tips peeking tantalizingly from behind the dark curls that spilled over her shoulders. A waist so slender he could span it with his hands blossomed erotically into full, womanly hips and long, shapely legs. Her skin was still warm and moist from her bath.

Still holding both her hands in one of his, Hugh drew her against him. He lifted his gaze to her eyes and saw both victory and surrender in their smoky depths. A low groan tore from his throat. Plunging his fingers into her fragrant curls, he tilted her head back and lowered his head.

Adrienne gasped as his mouth claimed hers. Startled into senselessness by the savage intensity of his kiss, she unthinkingly leaned into his arms. His lips were hard and possessive, ruthlessly demanding all that she had to give, and more. Instead of fighting him, Adrienne found herself clutching the front of his tunic and rising up on tiptoe to meet the impassioned thrust of his tongue.

His callused hands glided down her back and stroked her satiny skin. He cupped her buttocks and pulled her higher and closer against him. His arms tightened around her like bands of iron, crushing her breasts against the broad, hard wall of his chest. His lips and tongue teased and tormented hers, alternately punishing, then caressing, seducing her with painfully sweet sensations unlike anything she had ever known. The rest of the world had ceased to exist. She felt as if she were being swept away on a giant wave and pulled into a sea of uncontrollable passions from which she had neither the strength nor the desire to escape.

Marlys's voice pierced the illusion. "Oh, my God!"

Adrienne tore her mouth away, horrified at the realization of what she was doing.

Hugh slowly released her, and Adrienne shuddered, shaken by what had just happened. Her eyes were wide and dark in her flushed face, and her breathing labored. Painfully aware of Marlys standing in the doorway gawking at them in open-mouthed shock, she self-consciously crossed her arms in front of her as the molten passions that had so recently engulfed her solidified into a pillar of shame. She did not know what had come over her. Never in her life had she behaved in such a shameful manner.

Hugh bent and picked up the towel that had fallen to the floor. He pressed it into her hands. "One of the guards will escort you downstairs as soon as you are dressed," he said in a low, strained voice. Pivoting, he strode from the chamber.

Clutching the clothes she had brought with her, Marlys rushed forward. "Oh, m'lady! He didn't hurt you, did he?"

Adrienne felt sick to her stomach. Her knees were shaking so badly they threatened to fail her, and her face had drained of all color. She slumped onto the edge of the bed. "What have I done?" she whispered.

Marlys sat down beside her. "It was not your fault, m'lady. 'Twas he who forced himself in here and took advantage of you."

Adrienne slowly shook her head. "He didn't force me, Marlys. I did nothing to stop him."

"As if you could!"

Tears of humiliation filled Adrienne's eyes. "I didn't even try," she croaked.

Marlys looked confused. "Did he hurt you, m'lady?"

Adrienne did not know what it was she felt. It was not pain but an unrelieved ache deep down inside her. A longing. For what, she did not know. She shook her head.

Marlys fidgeted. "These were the only clothes I could find for you to wear," she said. "They're not cut of the best cloth, but they are clean. Let me help you dress, m'lady. Then mayhap we can find something to eat. The servants are setting up the tables now. I think supper is not far off."

Adrienne remembered Hugh telling her that one of the guards would take her downstairs when she had dressed. No doubt he intended that she dine with him. Shame pinkened her cheeks. She had no wish to see him again, much less to spend the evening in his company. Furthermore, she was exhausted. The forced march of the past several days had sapped her strength. The only thing she desired more than a chance to escape was a good night's sleep in a decent bed. She considered sending Marlys down with a message that she was feeling ill, then thought better of it. She would be a fool to forfeit what might be her only opportunity to leave this bedchamber.

The clothing Marlys had brought her was too large and too short. The linen chemise barely reached her ankles, and the dark blue gown hung from her shoulders like a sack. It needed a girdle to lend some shape to its graceless form, but Adrienne refused Marlys's request to go in search of one. "Lord Hugh has already seen far more of me than is decent," she said bitterly. "For tonight I would prefer that he forget I have a body."

Hugh was seated at the high table on the dais, talking with the Baron of Riehen, when the guard led Adrienne into the great hall. It was the first time since arriving at Burg Moudon that she had seen their host. She took an immediate dislike to the spare, cold-eyed man.

Riehen stood when he saw her. His hawklike gaze raked over her with an insolence that left no doubt in Adrienne's mind what he was thinking. Concealing her uneasiness behind an air of regal arrogance, Adrienne lifted her chin and returned the man's assessing gaze with cold disdain as she approached the table. She dropped into a formal curtsy before him. "My lord."

Riehen chuckled and glanced over his shoulder at Hugh. "You failed to tell me she was beautiful," he said. There was a note of accusation in his tone. "You merely said that she was as formidable an opponent as her father."

Adrienne straightened. Her gaze traveled past the baron to Hugh. His veiled expression hinted at the passion that had raged between them, and Adrienne felt a disconcerting heat creep up her neck.

"An oversight on my part, surely," Hugh said cryptically.

The servants had already begun bringing dishes from the kitchens. The savory aroma of meats and pastries hit Adrienne like a physical blow, causing her to sway slightly. For several days she had had nothing but bread and water, and now the richness of the cooking smells made her feel peculiar. Her mouth watered. She felt ravenous and sick to her stomach all at the same time.

Hugh took her elbow and guided her to one of the benches at the table. After she was seated, he sat down beside her. Some of the fog that had shrouded her cleared, and she realized that he was speaking to her. She turned her head toward him to find him studying her. The earlier lasciviousness that she had seen in his eyes was gone. He placed a jeweled goblet on the table in front of her. "Perhaps you should take a drink," he suggested gently.

She shook her head. "I-I'm fine."

"For a moment, *princesse*, you were so pale I feared you might faint."

Adrienne wished he would not be so solicitous. His kindness weakened her resolve to seek revenge against him for his treatment of her. "Unless my memory fails me, my lord," she said, " 'twas you who said I was not capable of fainting."

"Perhaps I misjudged you."

His willingness to admit that he might have been wrong coupled with the genuine concern she read in his expression served only to increase her confusion. Her skin still burned where his hands had roamed, and her lips were tender from his passionate kisses. Just being near him agitated the responses he had awakened in her with his touch. She had withstood threats and deprivation only to surrender to his caresses. "You did not misjudge me," she said shakily. "I have never fainted in my life."

But when a first course of venison with pepper sauce was served, the gamy smell of the roasted meat sent a spasm of nausea twisting through her stomach. She gripped the edge of the table to steady herself. Noticing the sudden evacuation of color from her face, Hugh broke a piece from the warm crusty loaf that had been placed between them and handed it to her, along with his goblet. Because they shared both trencher and cup, she had no choice but to accept his attentions.

The bread and wine had the desired effect, however, and by the time the venison was replaced with a course of roasted wild boar, she was feeling much improved. After the boar came roasted and stuffed peacocks and swans, followed by all manner of waterfowl and small game, meat pasties, fish, and eel pies, all to be washed down with copious amounts of strong wine. Adrienne sampled some of the courses and abstained from others. She managed to sip enough wine from Hugh's goblet to partially numb herself to his presence, even though he seemed to make a point of brushing his hand or his thigh against hers at every opportunity.

The hall was crowded with revelers, all growing louder and rowdier as the evening progressed. It was difficult to hear the harpers and minstrels above the din. Adrienne thought it odd that Riehen's wife was not present. Hugh had told her the feast was to honor the baron's newborn son.

Adrienne turned her head in the direction of a loud feminine squeal and saw their host pull a pretty serving maid onto his lap. He shoved his hand beneath the girl's skirts. Embarrassed by the baron's crudity, Adrienne looked away and tried to concentrate on the meal and the entertainment. She saw Graeham seated some distance away from the high table with John de Lancy and a group of knights. One of the knights stood up and emptied a jug of wine over another knight's head, and the men burst into raucous laughter.

Glancing at Hugh to see his reaction to the incident, Adrienne saw him rub his thumbnail along the bridge of his nose as though scratching it. He was not looking at his brother, but was staring across the hall. She followed his gaze and saw a knight leave through the side doors. Certain that a signal had been sent, she vowed to be more alert. If something was afoot, she did not intend to be caught by surprise.

Brightly dressed jugglers and acrobats replaced the musicians. As she watched them perform, Adrienne tried not to notice the attention that a buxom serving girl was lavishing upon Hugh. All evening the girl had hovered conspicuously near, returning time and again to refill Hugh's goblet or place a new delicacy before him. But when the comely servant drew attention to herself with her offending giggle,

Adrienne glared at her with smoldering resentment.

Her reaction did not go unnoticed.

Hugh chuckled. He put his arm around Adrienne's shoulders and brushed his lips against her temple. "Is that a spark of jealousy I see in your eyes, *princesse*?"

Mortified that he had seen her unguarded reaction, Adrienne pulled out of his grasp. "No, it is not," she shot back. Still, despite her denial, she felt the uncomfortable prick of truth in Hugh's observation.

Before he could comment further, a great shout went up, followed by the thunder of applause. Riehen was cutting into a large meat pie. As he broke the crust, a dozen song sparrows flew up out of the pastry shell. At the same moment someone unleashed into the hall a number of falcons. To the accompaniment of drunken cheering, the falcons aggressively pursued the hapless sparrows. One falcon seized her prey directly over the high table, showering the diners with feathers and splattering the white linen tablecloth with blood.

Adrienne's appetite fled. Although she had heard knights tell of the bizarre custom of releasing birds from a pie, it was the first time she had ever witnessed it with her own eyes. It made her stomach roil. To kill for food conformed to the laws of nature; to kill for sport was a cruelty only mankind was capable of inflicting. Without bothering to excuse herself, she rose from the bench.

Hugh grabbed her arm. "Sit down," he commanded. The humor had fled his expression, and his tone was dead serious. Too angry to heed the warning she saw in his eyes, she jerked her arm free and bolted from the hall.

All eyes at the high table suddenly focused on Hugh. His expression turned murderous. He downed his wine in a single swallow, then slammed the goblet down on the table and stood up. "The wench forgets who holds the reins," he ground out. "A sound thrashing will improve her memory."

Riehen regarded him with amusement as he stepped over the bench and started after Adrienne. "Beat her well," he called out to Hugh's departing back.

"I intend to," Hugh said angrily over his shoulder.

When he reached the corner tower, Hugh did not follow Adrienne, but stopped and dropped his facade of anger. He glanced up the stairs as the furious slamming of a chamber door echoed throughout the tower. The ruse had worked. In her innocence, Adrienne had unknowingly presented him with a finer diversion than any he might have planned. He glanced back toward the hall to make sure he had not been followed, then slipped out the side door.

Adrienne collapsed against the door and closed her eyes. Her color was high and her breathing ragged.

Marlys approached her cautiously. "M'lady, what happened?"

Adrienne's eyes flew open. "Nothing happened," she said, struggling to catch her breath. "I just don't understand these people. I don't understand them and I don't like them. Lord Baldhere would never allow such behavior at Foutreau. Even our highest feasts were never as extravagant as this common banquet. I cannot help but think that if these people had ever suffered the loss of a crop to an unseasonable rain or had to wonder where their next meal might come from, they would not be so given to excess."

Marlys took Adrienne's arm. "Come, m'lady, and sit down."

"I'll be fine."

"But, m'lady, you're shaking!"

The vision of Hugh flirting with the pretty servant flashed before Adrienne's eyes, fueling her anger. "I am shaking because I am angry. Marlys, you should have seen them! 'Tis not enough that the men drink themselves into a stupor; they must also drench each other with expensive wine!"

Marlys listened, wide-eyed, while Adrienne told her of the meal, of a procession of courses so endless it was difficult to remember what one had just eaten. She told

of the drunken revelry, of the brawling that had broken
out in the lower hall, of the baron pawing a defenseless
serving girl right at the table, of the pie filled with live
sparrows.

Adrienne saw the look of awe on her maidservant's face,
and she had to bite her tongue to keep from lashing out
at her. She could understand why Marlys might think it
all wonderfully rich and lavish, but to her, schooled in
frugality, the banquet was obscene. "Please, let's not talk
of it anymore. All I want to do is go to sleep. Prison though
it is, at least this chamber has a bed."

Marlys brushed Adrienne's hair and turned back the
covers. She started to make up a pallet for herself on the
floor at the foot of the bed.

Adrienne stopped her. "You need not sleep on the floor.
This bed is big enough for an army."

"But, m'lady, if Lord Hugh comes back—"

"If he comes back, he will have to find some other bed in
which to plant his drunken carcass," Adrienne said testily.
She resented the implication that Hugh would be sharing
her bed, although after what had happened between them
earlier, she would not have been surprised if he'd tried to
force himself upon her. With as much as he had drunk at
dinner, he was not likely to pay heed to her objections.
"You and I will share the bed," she said. "But you must
help me move it first."

Marlys gawked at her. "Begging your pardon, m'lady?
We can't move that bed. It must weigh as much as an
oxcart!"

"We have no choice. There is no bolt on the chamber
door, and I wish to spend the night undisturbed."

Although obviously skeptical of the wisdom of their
action—Marlys had surely seen enough of Hugh's temper that she dreaded having it directed at her—she lent
Adrienne a hand. Between the two of them, they managed
to shove the heavy bed in front of the door, barring access
to any who might seek to enter.

*   *   *

Sir Conraed was waiting for Hugh in the stables. "Lorraine is being held prisoner at Avenches. But not by Philip. Prince John is using Philip's arms to make all think he has the king's support. If what we heard tell is true, Philip knows nothing of the ploy."

The news did not sit well with Hugh. "Then John, not Philip, is the one who knows we have Adrienne. It sheds a different light on the matter."

Conraed agreed. "It did not sit well with John to learn that Henry conferred Sainte-Croix upon the girl instead of upon him as promised. John wants the countship, and he will stop at nothing to get it."

Hugh swore under his breath. "Where is John now?"

"No more than a few hours' ride behind us. We tried to get here as quickly as we could, but John and his men were close on our heels. The Count of Flanders is helping him, and they have amassed a sizable army. John de Lancy and Riehen are under orders to hold you here. When Prince John and his men have surrounded the castle, the baron will turn on you and take you prisoner."

Hugh cursed himself for not having realized the full import of the situation sooner. "I should have guessed Riehen was not allied to Lorraine when I recognized none of his knights. But I never expected him to hold loyalties to John. No doubt tonight's banquet was intended to get us to drop our guard.

"Most of my men are camped in a clearing between here and the river," Hugh continued. "I'll need to get word to them of the impending attack. I want them to prepare to retreat, if necessary. Their position is safe enough, but I don't want them trapped between John's army and the castle."

"If we leave now, my lord, we can be well away from here before morning."

" 'Tis impossible. Fortunately, only a handful of us are quartered within the castle. The problem is getting Adrienne away from here without being seen. If the baron is working for John, I dare not risk arousing his suspicions. I know John too well. He may have ordered Riehen to kill Adrienne should it appear we have become wise to his plans."

After several more minutes spent hastily formulating plans for a counterattack, Conraed slipped away to rejoin his men. Hugh returned to the keep.

The guards posted both at the foot of the tower stairs and on the landing were on duty. Hugh swore silently. At a time when he needed the guards to be lax in their duties, they seemed unusually alert. He wondered if the attack was planned for tonight. Perhaps John had managed to get word to the baron of his arrival.

Feigning drunkenness, Hugh raised his voice in a ribald ditty and staggered up the stairs. None of the guards tried to stop him. They moved out of his way when he tried to open the door to Adrienne's chamber. To his alarm, it would not budge. He tried again.

Something was wrong. He had taken precautions to put Adrienne in a chamber that could not be bolted from the inside. He pounded on the door with his fist. "Open this door!"

No response. He pounded again.

Behind him, one of the guards cleared his throat. "She's in there, m'lord. We saw her go in. Pretty upset she was, too. We heard a loud scraping noise soon after. We think she and her maidservant might have pushed the bed across the door."

Masking his apprehension behind a spurt of rage, Hugh smashed his fist into the heavy wooden door. "Stubborn wench! You push me too far, woman! When I get my hands on you, I'll teach you a lesson you won't soon forget!"

Muttering under his breath about going in search of a willing woman, he turned and stumbled down the stairs.

Back in the hall, Riehen was dividing his attentions between the girl on his lap—a different one—and dessert. Forgoing the syrupy sweet pastries and confections that had been brought to the tables on huge silver trays, Riehen alternated between downing slices of preserved ginger and cooling his blazing palate with gulps of wine. He eyeballed Hugh drunkenly. "Where's the girl?"

Hugh refilled his goblet. "I left her to nurse her bruised backside and contemplate the folly of disobeying me," he said. He lifted his goblet in a toast and fixed the baron with a sly grin. "She'll receive me later, well chastened and compliant, just the way I like them."

Riehen laughed. "I saw the look in her eyes. That one would as soon stab you in your sleep. I'd watch my back if I were you."

In the lower hall, Graeham had drawn his sword and was challenging one of Riehen's knights. The other men had formed a circle around them and were cheering them on.

Hugh set down his goblet and strode purposefully toward them. He pushed his way through the circle just as the other knight drew his sword, and stepped between the knight and his brother. He glared at Graeham. "We are guests here. There will be no bloodshed."

Graeham's dark eyes, brightened by anger and an excess of wine, smoldered. "This is my fight. Stay out of it."

"I said there will be no fighting."

"And I told you to stay out of it!" Graeham's voice rose to a shout. His face, contorted with anger, flushed feverishly. "You are not my keeper, Hugh. You have no right to interfere."

Hugh swept his gaze through the crowd. "Go back to your food and drink," he ordered. "There will be no fight."

There was a rumble of disappointment among the onlookers, most of whom were apparently hoping for some excitement to crown an evening already steeped in excess.

The knight Graeham had challenged started to protest Hugh's intervention, but he was a young man who had only recently earned his spurs. One look at Hugh's ferocious expression was enough to quell his objections.

Graeham was not so easily swayed. He came at Hugh with his sword drawn. "I warned you to stay out of my affairs!"

Hugh threw up his arm, deflecting the blow. Graeham cursed and grabbed his bruised arm. His sword clattered to the floor. Seizing the front of Graeham's tunic, Hugh shoved him through the crowd and up against the stone wall. "Listen to me," he said in a voice just loud enough for his brother to hear. "We are all in danger here."

Although his expression remained fierce, Graeham stopped fighting him.

Hugh continued in a low, controlled voice, "I have learned that the baron is going to order his men to turn on us, possibly tonight. I need you to alert the others within the castle and get through the wall before Riehen suspects we know his scheme."

The muscle in Graeham's jaw knotted, but the alarm that pierced the intoxicated haze in his eyes told Hugh that he had comprehended his warning. "Why should I believe you?" Graeham spat. "Even if what you say is true, why are you telling me? After all that has passed between us, I would think you would want to see the end of me."

That there should be so much rancor between him and his only brother suddenly filled Hugh with an intense sadness. "Because you were right and I was wrong," he said slowly. "Rougemont is in the past. The forgotten past." He hesitated. "And because you are my brother."

Hugh sensed Graeham's struggle with this unexpected change, and he silently vowed to be less rigid in the future. Life was too short to spend trying to bend everyone to his will.

"Adrienne and her maid have barricaded themselves in their chamber," Hugh continued with quiet urgency. "After the others are asleep, I need to get them out."

"We are being watched," Graeham responded under his breath.

"I know."

"You get Lady Adrienne out. I'll alert the others."

"John de Lancy is working for Riehen. Watch out for him."

"I will." Graeham drew a deep breath and shoved his arms up between them, breaking Hugh's hold on him. "From now on," he bellowed, "stay out of my affairs and I'll stay out of yours." Retrieving his sword, he sauntered over to the trestle table, straddled the bench, and sat down. He ignored Hugh.

Gradually the revelry began to die down as the excesses of food and wine took their toll. The music and dancing gave way to a lone jongleur strumming a psaltery and reciting an epic poem of the battles of Charlemagne. Riehen left the hall with the girl who had recently occupied his knee, and several other knights followed his lead. No one bothered to inquire if the drawbridge was raised or if the night guards were at their posts. The defense of the castle, Hugh noted, seemed to have been left entirely to chance.

Finally Hugh was able to slip from the hall unnoticed.

Gabel was waiting for him behind the passage screen. "Sir Conraed said you might need this," the squire said. He handed Hugh a stout rope of considerable length. "Julien found a raft hidden in the bushes on the outer bank of the moat. 'Tis rickety, but 'twill serve our purpose."

"Where is Julien now?"

"He's with the raft, m'lord."

Hugh took the rope. "I want you and Julien to move the raft to the base of the southwest tower and wait for me there."

Adrienne rose up on one elbow and looked around the moonlit chamber. She was not certain what had awakened her. "Marlys?" she whispered.

No answer.

Adrienne called out again. Although there was an indentation in the pillow where the girl had laid her head, the sheets were cold. Marlys was not in the chamber. Adrienne was confused. How could Marlys have gotten out with the bed pushed across the door?

Then Adrienne heard the scraping noise on the outer wall.

She eased out of bed and slipped her chemise on over her head. The wine she had drunk at dinner made her head feel heavy and her movements clumsy. She looked around for a weapon, finally settling on a brass candlestick that stood on the washstand. She removed the candle.

A shadow passed across the moonlight that illuminated the window.

Adrienne scampered out of the way and pressed her back to the stone wall.

A pair of booted feet emerged through the open window, followed by long, powerful legs and a man's massive torso. Fighting the terrified quaking of her limbs, Adrienne raised the candlestick high. Just as the intruder's feet struck the floor with catlike softness, Adrienne brought the candlestick down hard.

A searing pain jolted through her shoulder. The intruder wrenched her arm up over her head and shoved her so hard she knocked the back of her head against the wall. A large leather gloved hand clamped brutally over her mouth.

Hugh's harsh whisper rasped against her ear. "Be quiet, you little fool, or you'll get us both killed!"

Relief surged through her at the sound of his voice.

Hugh eased his hand away from her mouth.

"You frightened me to death," Adrienne whispered hoarsely. Her heart was still pounding. "Is it a habit of yours to enter a chamber by unconventional means?"

"I've not stayed alive these twenty-nine years by limiting myself to doors," Hugh retorted. "You are lucky I was able to get to you before it was too late, *princesse*. Heaven knows what possessed you to barricade yourself in this chamber, but you nearly sealed your death warrant with your childish prank."

"My death warrant!"

"Be silent!" Hugh hissed. "My God, woman, you'll arouse every guard within these walls! Even your magpie of a maidservant managed to be quieter than you."

Adrienne's alarm increased. "Where is Marlys? What have you done with her?"

"I've already taken her down the wall. Get dressed. We must be gone."

As Adrienne put on the ill-fitting gown and slippers, Hugh kept watch out the tower window. Although he could see nothing out of the ordinary, every nerve in his body was attuned to the danger that permeated the night air. Prince John's men were out there somewhere. He could feel their presence.

When Adrienne was dressed, Hugh hoisted himself up onto the window ledge and grabbed the rope he had tied around one of the merlons on the crenellated battlement directly above the window. "Have you ever climbed down a rope?" he asked.

"No."

"Then I'll have to carry you down the same way I carried your maid, on my back—"

"On your back?"

"It's the safest way. There's a raft directly below us in the moat. When we reach the end of the rope, I'll step onto the raft and you can slide down off my back. Do you think you can manage that?"

"Do I have any other choice?"

Hugh looked at her long and hard, trying to see her face in the darkness. Although she sounded calm, he knew she was afraid; he could sense the fear that pulsed in her veins. "None," he said quietly.

Adrienne waited while Hugh pushed himself out the window and wrapped his strong legs around the rope. Then she climbed onto the ledge. Her gown rode up above her knees, exposing her legs, but this was no time for modesty. She strained to see where the rope was suspended from the battlement. "How did you get up there without alerting the guards?"

"I went up another tower and crossed over," he said. Gripping the rope with his hands and legs, he eased his weight over the edge and lowered himself until his head was level with hers. "Get behind me and wrap your legs around my waist and your arms around my neck. Cross your arms in front of my chest and grip your wrists."

Adrienne did as she was told, incredulous to find herself following his orders without protest. She had no reason to trust him, yet she did. She remembered the signal she had seen exchanged in the great hall; Hugh had been expecting trouble.

"Scoot off the ledge," Hugh ordered.

Her heart pounding, Adrienne timidly inched forward until her bottom was barely supported by the stone window ledge.

"If you hesitate, you'll hurt us both," Hugh said impatiently, his voice strained.

In the moonlight, Adrienne could see the cords bulging in his neck. That he was able to support his own weight, much less hers, attested to his strength. Her arms were already burning from the effort of clinging to him.

She scooted the rest of the way off the ledge, and her legs settled around Hugh's hips. Her chest was pinned against his back and her cheek pressed against his neck. His hair was damp with sweat.

"I'm going to have to turn around," Hugh said. "Just hold on tight."

Even with advance warning, Adrienne was not prepared for the terror that surged through her when Hugh swung around and she no longer had the security of the stone wall against her back. For several agonizing seconds they swayed dangerously in midair. Below them the moat loomed dark and uninviting. Adrienne spotted the raft and realized for the first time just how far down it was. She bit down on her bottom lip to keep from crying out. Her arms and legs ached mercilessly.

Hugh eased the hold his legs had on the rope and planted his feet against the stone wall. "We're going down. Are you ready?"

"Y-yes." The single word came out like a choked sob.

"You're doing fine. Don't look down."

Hugh shoved away from the wall. Adrienne gasped and buried her face against his neck. She was certain they were going to plunge to their death.

Using his feet to keep them from crashing against the wall, Hugh lowered them, hand by hand, down the rope. Their progress was painfully slow. The bright moonlight that illuminated the castle walls also exposed them to anyone who might be waiting in the woods or might spot them from the adjoining tower. Hugh hoped he could get Adrienne down before they were seen.

Suddenly an arrow sliced through the air. It struck the man who waited with the raft. The man cried out and tumbled headlong into the water. Hugh swore as he saw the raft bob out from under them and start to drift away.

Up on the battlements, a nerve-jangling battle yell shattered the stillness of the night.

Arrows came at them from nowhere, hundreds of them, striking the stone wall and falling into the moat. Adrienne choked back a scream. She did not want to believe that they had made it this far only to be killed before they even reached the ground.

"*Princesse*, can you swim?"

Adrienne frantically shook her head. "No."

" 'Tis not important. I will help you. Whatever happens, don't panic." Hugh braced his feet against the wall and shoved. They swung out over the middle of the moat.

Hugh released his hold on the rope.

Chapter Eight

THE WATER CLOSED over Adrienne's head, filling her mouth and nose. Hugh landed on top of her, and she lashed out in terror as his weight bore her deeper and deeper into the water. Her lungs began to burn from the effort of holding her breath.

Just when she thought she could stand it no longer, an arm went around her waist and suddenly she was being pulled upward through the cold, murky water. Her head broke the surface and she swallowed a huge gulp of air.

With one arm securely around her middle, Hugh swam to the bank. He hoisted Adrienne to safety, then climbed out of the water after her.

Adrienne collapsed on the ground, her heart pounding so hard it hurt. No matter how hard she breathed, she felt as if she could not get enough air.

Shouts went up from the parapet.

Behind the castle walls, flames darted into the night sky, and the acrid smell of smoke filled the air as fire ignited one thatched roof after another inside the compound.

Hugh clambered to his feet. He grabbed Adrienne's arm and pulled her upright.

Adrienne choked back a scream as an arrow whistled past her ear.

Hugh began running, dragging Adrienne along in his wake. She had lost her slippers when she landed in the water. Rocks and twigs bruised her feet.

Graeham was waiting on horseback in the cover of the trees. He held the reins to Hugh's horse and was carrying Hugh's chain mail and sword. "Prince John cut us off," Graeham said. "We had to move the camp away from the river. Conraed will lead a counterattack from the north."

Hugh put the heavy mail hauberk on over his wet tunic, then buckled on his short sword. "Take Adrienne back to camp," he ordered. "Then I want you and fifty men to circle around John and cut off any possibility of retreat."

Hugh mounted his horse. Gripping the reins, he turned and looked down at Adrienne. "Don't be foolish enough to try to escape, *princesse*. John thinks you are the only one standing in the way of his claim to Sainte-Croix. Should you fall into his hands, you'll not live to see another day."

Adrienne's gratitude toward Hugh for rescuing her from Burg Moudon fled. "I am not stupid, my lord. I know full well what fate would await me at Prince John's hands. No doubt it would be remarkably similar to what I have endured at yours."

Adrienne could not see the sudden anger that flashed in Hugh's eyes, but she heard it in his voice. "John," he bit out, "would have let you drown. Don't you ever forget that." He spurred his horse and rode back toward the castle.

The full import of what Hugh had revealed suddenly struck Adrienne. She rounded on Graeham. "What Hugh said about John, is it true? Is Prince John here?"

"Who do you think ordered the attack on Burg Moudon?" Graeham asked sarcastically. Reaching down, he took Adrienne's hand and hauled her up in front of him. "Come. There is no time to waste. 'Twill be light soon."

They had not gone more than a hundred yards when an arrow struck Graeham's horse in the neck.

The animal screamed and reared up on its hind legs.

Terror surged through Adrienne. She clung to Graeham's tunic in a desperate attempt to keep from falling as Graeham tried to bring the panicked horse back under control. The horse lost its footing and went down.

Adrienne went flying. She hit the ground hard.

"*Run!*" Graeham yelled.

Adrienne pushed herself upright. She gritted her teeth against the violent spinning in her head.

Hoofbeats thundered in her ears.

Somehow she managed to get to her feet. She began to run. Her wet gown clung to her legs and slowed her down.

Tree branches slapped at her face as she ran. She could see nothing in the darkness, and she had no sense of where she was headed.

A rider quickly closed the distance between them. As he drew up alongside her, he leaned far to the right and reached for her. His hand closed around a fistful of her gown.

Shortly after dawn, Hugh's men gained control of the keep, and the fighting moved away from the castle. The dead littered the ward and floated in the moat. Hugh ordered his men to carry the wounded into the safety of the keep hall. Built of stone with a roof of tile, it was the only building in the compound capable of withstanding the attackers' torches. Nothing remained of the outbuildings but burned, blackened shells.

By midday Prince John's men had retreated. As they crossed the river to safety, Hugh's rage mounted. Where was Graeham? Why had he not moved his men into position and stopped John from getting away? Graeham had better have a damn good reason for disobeying his orders, he thought angrily.

Hugh went inside the keep hall where the wounded were being treated. The rushes covering the stone floor of the hall were stained with blood and urine. Hugh passed by the rows of injured men stretched out on the floor and went up the stairs to the tower chamber where the Baron of Riehen was being detained.

One of the guards removed the heavy iron lock from the door.

Riehen turned away from the window when Hugh entered the chamber. There were dark circles beneath his eyes, and he had not shaved. A wry smile touched his mouth. "I see you have forced Prince John to retreat across the river," he said. "My congratulations to you on your victory."

Hugh was in no mood for casual conversation. He had learned from one of Riehen's men whom he had taken prisoner that the baron's wife had not just given birth to a son but was in Cologne visiting relatives. As he had suspected, last night's banquet had been part of a plot to weaken his defenses and trap him inside the castle. "I understand you want to talk," he said tersely.

Riehen motioned toward a table that was laid out with cold meats and a flagon of wine. "Will you join me?"

"No."

Riehen went to the table and poured himself a goblet of wine. "Then you won't mind if I help myself," he said. It was not a question but an assumption.

Hugh glanced at the repast and thought that all prisoners should be treated so well. "What do you want?"

"My freedom."

"Denied."

"I ask no favors. I am willing to reward you quite handsomely for my release."

"With what?" Hugh asked dryly.

"I have information of value to offer you . . . for a price."

"And that price is your freedom?"

"Yes."

"You turned on me and my men while we were guests in your home," Hugh reminded him. "Do not be surprised if what you say carries little weight with me."

Riehen chuckled. "There is no need to take my alliance personally. I was paid well."

"By whom?"

"Richard."

Hugh was careful not to let his surprise show on his face.

"John mobilized his forces as soon as he learned that Lady Adrienne had inherited Sainte-Croix," Riehen continued. "He had hoped to seize the countship before Richard learned it had passed out of control of the Crown. What he did not know was that Richard had already been informed of Lady Adrienne's betrothal.

"Richard does not want Sainte-Croix to fall into his brother's hands any more than he wants it annexed to the Holy Roman Empire. Or returned to you, for that matter. He planted his own agents among Prince John's ranks. John de Lancy was one of them. I was another. Our orders were to take Lady Adrienne prisoner before John could capture her, then turn her over to Richard."

Hugh eyed the other man closely. "And now that you and John de Lancy have failed in your endeavor to capture Lady Adrienne, what scheme does Richard propose next?"

A sly smile spread across Riehen's face. "What makes you think we failed?"

They were interrupted by a knock on the door.

Hugh strode to the door and opened it. Graeham was on the landing. His face was flushed, and his dark hair was plastered to his head with sweat. His shoulders heaved as he struggled to catch his breath. "Lady Adrienne," he managed to get out, "is gone."

A dozen men watched while John de Lancy lowered Adrienne from the back of his horse. He dismounted and handed the reins to his squire. The strip of cloth that had been wrapped around de Lancy's left hand was blood-soaked, and blood had crusted over a scrape on his cheek-bone.

Gripping Adrienne's arm with his good hand, he marched her to the campfire. Her hands were tied together in front of her with a leather thong. Her lips were pressed into an angry line, and rebellion flashed in her gray eyes. De Lancy shoved her down near the fire. "My orders are to deliver you to Richard," he said tersely. "He said nothing about wanting you alive. If you value your life, Lady Adrienne, you'll not attempt any more of your tricks."

De Lancy barked orders to one of his men to bring medicants and clean bandages, then stalked off through the trees.

After he was out of her sight, Adrienne closed her eyes and let the tension flow out of her limbs. Her body ached. John de Lancy had been far from gentle in his treatment of her, especially after he sliced open his left hand trying to wrest his dagger back from her. She suspected that her back carried more than a few bruises as tokens of his temper.

At least she was alive, she reasoned, but the thought brought her little joy. What had become of Graeham? She had no way of knowing if he had been hurt or even killed. And what would Hugh think when he discovered she was missing? She had already tried to escape twice; no doubt he would believe she had tried yet again.

And this time, she thought miserably, he might decide to let her go.

Her throat tightened.

She no longer knew how she felt about Hugh. He had abducted her, threatened her, humiliated her in front of his men, and placed her in irons. For that she hated him. Yet he had also come to her rescue twice, once to save her from the outlaw knights and again from the attack on Burg Moudon. She could no more forget the risks he had taken for her than she could forget the havoc he had wreaked in her life.

Nor could she forget the desire that had burned in his eyes when he said he wanted her, or the pleasurable sensations he had awakened in her with his touch.

Why couldn't her hatred for him be simple and uncomplicated rather than clouded by conflicting emotions that had nothing whatsoever to do with hatred?

"Where are your loyal vassals now, *Lady* Adrienne? Did they, like the rest of Henry's subjects, turn tail and run?"

Adrienne's eyes flew open. If the words had startled her, the familiarity of the voice jolted her like a slap. Pale blond hair and pale blue eyes shifted in and out of focus. She blinked, her mind refusing to acknowledge what her eyes saw. She opened her mouth to speak, but no sound would come out. Her lips silently formed his name: *Lysander*.

Her foster brother hunkered down before her. A cold smile burned in his eyes. "You seem surprised. Surely you did not think you had seen the last of me?"

Adrienne finally found her voice. "What are you doing here?" she whispered, disbelieving.

"I am carrying out Richard's orders and returning to him his rightful property," Lysander said. "Did you think you would get away with stealing Sainte-Croix from the Crown?"

So John de Lancy was working for King Richard rather than for Philip, Adrienne thought, trying to piece together the few scraps of information that she knew. But Lysander? He was merely a squire apprenticed to the Duke of Leicester. He had not even earned his spurs.

Adrienne eyed him suspiciously. "You still have not explained how you come to be here. Why would Richard send you to fetch me back to England when he has thousands of trained knights at his command?"

"Surely you did not expect me to stand aside and do nothing while a domain that rightfully belongs to Richard slipped from his hands because of Henry's plotting? Richard was quite pleased with the information that I was able to provide him."

John de Lancy appeared behind Lysander. "If you think to help the girl escape, you will find that I would sooner slit your throat than continue playing nursemaid to you."

Lysander rolled to his feet. His eyes burned like blue ice. "You forget, my lord, were it not for me, Richard would have lost Sainte-Croix. You would do well to take care how you speak to me."

De Lancy snorted. "You may have curried Richard's favor, squire, but you'll get no special treatment here. Unlike the king, I have no preference for smooth-faced boys in my bed."

Lysander's face turned red, but before he could defend himself, John de Lancy barked, "If I catch you near the prisoner again, you will find yourself returning to England in irons. And don't think Richard will be swayed by your protests of innocence. It would be an easy matter to convince him that the subject he thought so loyal was in reality an enemy of the Crown. Now, get out of here!"

Lysander stalked away, his shoulders hunched in anger and humiliation. In spite of herself, Adrienne almost felt sorry for him. For what was probably the first time in his life, Lysander was faced with someone who was not intimidated by his bullying.

With his right hand John de Lancy grasped Adrienne's bound wrists and pulled her to her feet. "What did the boy say to you?" he demanded.

Adrienne noticed that the strip of cloth the knight had torn off the bottom of her chemise and wrapped around his left hand to stanch the flow of blood had been replaced by a clean linen bandage. She lifted her chin and met his suspicious gaze defiantly. "Unfortunately, Lysander was too busy gloating to tell me anything of importance."

De Lancy knotted his fist in her hair and wrenched her head back. His eyes narrowed. "Do not make the mistake of antagonizing me, my lady. I am not Hugh de Clairmont. I have no intention of allowing myself to become enamored of you."

Adrienne's eyes smarted with pain. Her haughtiness fled.

John de Lancy released her hair. He gave the order for his men to prepare to move out.

Hugh waited.

It would be morning soon. From where he crouched in the underbrush, he could see the campsite where John de

Lancy and his men were spending the night. They were a few yards from the river. Hugh saw Adrienne sleeping on the ground. She lay on her side with her knees drawn up against her chest. Her hands were tied together in front of her. One end of a short rope was tied to her hands; the other end was secured to John de Lancy's belt. The slightest movement by either of them would awaken the other.

The weather had turned cool during the night, but it was not the brisk chill of autumn. The air was heavy, and the ground damp. A white mist rose from the river. It was the type of weather that gave rise to sudden fevers and caused the bones to ache.

Hugh felt that ache now. He exercised his left arm, trying to work some of the soreness out of it. When the time came to seize Adrienne, he needed to be able to move quickly. He could not risk being slowed by joints stiffened as if with gout.

Finding Adrienne had been relatively simple. Although Graeham had not been able to get a good look at Adrienne's captor, Riehen had already divulged enough information to allow Hugh to be reasonably certain of the man's identity. It had not taken long for Hugh and his men to find John de Lancy's trail. His hunch had been correct. Now all he had to do was wait.

Soon the two men who had taken the last watch of the night stoked the campfire and began to awaken the others. Hugh saw de Lancy stir. The knight awakened Adrienne. She pushed herself into a sitting position and shoved her hair away from her face. With her hands bound and her body still drugged with sleep, her movements were clumsy.

John de Lancy untied the rope from his belt and wrapped the end several times around his fist. He stood up and hauled Adrienne to her feet.

Hugh slipped soundlessly from his hiding place and retreated into the woods.

*   *   *

John de Lancy led Adrienne to the riverbank.

Unsteady on her feet, she stumbled along after him. Her head throbbed. She had spent the entire previous day in wet clothes, and now every bone in her body hurt.

John de Lancy secured the rope to a tree. "Do not waste your time trying to escape, my dear," he said as he pulled the knot tight. " 'Twill be a long ride before we stop to rest again. Use your time foolishly and you will soon regret it."

The knight started back to camp. Adrienne waited until he had disappeared from sight, then turned her attention to the leather thong that bound her wrists. Last night, after John de Lancy had fallen asleep, she had nearly managed to work one hand loose. If she could repeat the same movements now, she thought, she might be able to free herself.

Her frustration mounted as her efforts soon proved futile. Last night's attempts had chafed her wrists and caused them to swell, and now the thong was even tighter than before.

Suddenly a man's hand reached around her from behind and clamped over her mouth.

Adrienne jumped and a smothered cry of fright burst in her throat.

A familiar voice rasped in her ear. "Be quiet and no harm will come to you. Do you understand?"

Lysander!

Fear pounded in her veins. After John de Lancy's warning, Lysander had kept his distance. What did he want with her now? She nodded.

Lysander eased his hand off her mouth. He moved in front of her, and Adrienne saw the dagger he held. "What are you doing?" she whispered.

"I am taking you back to England. I was the one who led Richard's men to you. I refuse to sit in the shadows while that arrogant scoundrel reaps the reward for bringing you back."

Adrienne stared at him in disbelief, thinking he must be insane. "Lysander, don't do this," she whispered frantically. " 'Tis not worth the risk. Should you be found out, John de Lancy will kill you!"

Lysander snickered. "Your compassion is most touching. I was not aware you cared so deeply for my welfare." He slipped his dagger between her hands and cut the leather thong and the rope that bound her wrists.

Adrienne winced and sucked in her breath as the restraints gave way and feeling surged through her hands. "You flatter yourself," she retorted, rubbing her tingling hands. "My concern is not for you but for the pain your death would cause Lord Baldhere and Lady Joanna. Were it not for them, I would raise a shout myself to bring John de Lancy running."

Anger flashed in Lysander's pale eyes. He pressed the tip of the dagger into Adrienne's throat and backed her into a tree. "Try it and you die."

Adrienne could feel the point of the blade digging into her skin. 'Twas a mistake to provoke Lysander, she reminded herself. At least if she went with him, she might find a chance to escape. Lysander was so desperate to win Richard's favor that he was bound to make a mistake sooner or later. John de Lancy, on the other hand, was too cunning, too calculating; she would never be able to get away from him on her own. She sucked in her breath as Lysander increased the pressure on the dagger. "I-I won't betray you to John de Lancy," she stammered. "I swear it."

Lysander hesitated a moment. Finally he released her and slipped the dagger into his belt. "I have horses waiting not far from here," he said. "If we hurry, we can be well on our way before anyone even knows we are gone."

A movement behind Lysander caught Adrienne's eye. The figure of a man emerged from the mist. Adrienne gasped.

Lysander whirled around and came up hard against a broad wall of muscle and chain mail.

Chapter Nine

LYSANDER WENT FOR the dagger at his waist.

In that instant Adrienne recognized Hugh. Relief surged through her. "Hugh, look out!"

Hugh caught Lysander's wrist in a bruising grip and wrenched his arm up over his head.

Lysander clung to the dagger as if to his life.

"Let it go, boy," Hugh commanded.

Lysander spat in Hugh's face.

Hugh increased the pressure on Lysander's wrist.

A pained grunt sounded in Lysander's throat. He released his grip on the dagger. It fell to the ground.

Hugh kicked the dagger out of the way.

Lysander swung with his fist.

Hugh threw up his left arm, blocking the blow.

Lysander swung again and again, delivering useless blows that failed to meet their intended target. His frustration mounted as Hugh easily deflected his punches. He lashed out blindly.

Hugh smashed his fist into Lysander's jaw, sending him reeling. Lysander scrambled to his feet. He slipped and fell on the muddy bank. He pushed himself upright. There was a crazed look in his pale eyes.

Adrienne's heart pounded in terror. Lysander was no match for Hugh. Hugh could break him like a reed. "Lysander, stop!" she cried out. "He'll kill you!"

Lysander lunged at Hugh, and Adrienne shoved a fist against her mouth to stifle a scream as Lysander barreled headfirst into Hugh's abdomen.

Hugh barely swayed. Catching the youth by the shoulders, he picked him up and hurled him into the river. Lysander struck the water with a loud splash.

Shouts sounded in the woods a few yards away.

Hugh turned to Adrienne and seized her arm. "Let's get out of here."

Adrienne twisted around to look back at the river. Lysander's head bobbed above the water, and his arms flailed wildly. "Help me!" he screamed. "*Help!*"

Panic surged through Adrienne. Like her, Lysander had never learned to swim. She dug her heels into the ground. "My lord, please! We can't just leave him to drown!"

Hugh stared at Adrienne in furious disbelief. Tightening his grip on her arm, he dragged her roughly after him as he plowed his way through the mist and trees. Adrienne had to run to keep up. Behind them, the voices of their pursuers grew louder.

Finally they reached a clearing where five of Hugh's men waited on their horses. Conraed tossed the reins of Hugh's war-horse to him. Hugh hoisted Adrienne up onto the animal's back, then swung up into the saddle behind her. The men spurred their horses forward.

As they rode, Adrienne huddled within the protective circle of Hugh's arm, but no comfort was to be found there. Hugh's powerful form was rigid with pent-up anger, and his chain mail was hard and cold against her cheek. She could not stop shaking.

She kept seeing Lysander's head bobbing in the water, and hearing his screams for help.

She tried to tell herself that she was not to blame for what had happened; 'twas Lysander's eagerness to please Richard that might have cost him his life. But inwardly she knew the truth did not matter. If Lysander died, Baldhere and Lady Joanna would never forgive her.

Tears gathered in her eyes, and her shoulders began to jerk convulsively from the strain of holding them back. If Lysander died, she would never be able to return to Foutreau; she would not be welcome there. Her home would be lost to her. Everyone she held close to her heart would be lost to her.

Feelings of helplessness and rage filled her. Once again the events in her life seemed to be hurtling out of her control, and there was nothing she could do to stop them.

Please, God, don't let Lysander die.

When they had put a safe distance between them and John de Lancy's men, Hugh gave the order to stop.

Sunlight had brightened the fog but had not yet burned it off, and it surrounded them like a thick white blanket. The mist seemed to smother sound, deadening it. Adrienne found the stillness unnerving.

Hugh dismounted, then helped Adrienne down. Before she was able to get her bearings, Hugh's hand snapped around her arm and he steered her away from the others.

He spun her around to face him.

Adrienne instinctively shrank from the raw fury that blazed in his eyes, but her retreat was halted by the brutal grip he had on her arm. "Who is he?" Hugh demanded.

Adrienne started to shake her head. "I don't know what you are talking ab—"

"Don't lie to me! Your hesitation back there could have gotten us both killed. What is that boy to you that you were willing to risk our lives for him?"

In her mind, Adrienne saw Lysander fighting the water, and the tears she had been trying to hold back sprang readily to her eyes. In her misery and confusion, she wished unthinkingly that Hugh would hold her and tell her that Lysander was not going to die. She gasped as his hand tightened on her arm. "My lord, please, you are hurting—"

"Answer me!"

"He is my guardian's younger son!" she cried out.

Hugh recoiled in surprise. He had seen the boy cut Adrienne's bonds. He had also seen him threaten her with the dagger. It made no sense to him.

He released Adrienne's arm. "The boy was trying to free you?" he asked, incredulous.

Adrienne folded her arms defensively in front of her. "No," she said in a choked voice, unable to meet Hugh's gaze. "He hoped to turn me over to Richard himself, so that he, instead of John de Lancy, would win the king's favor."

Hugh regarded her through narrowed eyes. "Why would your guardian's son betray you?"

"Why would he not? He hated me . . . and I him. When Henry's knights came to Foutreau for me, Lysander saw a way to punish me and earn Richard's praise at the same time." A tear streaked down Adrienne's cheek, and she dashed it away with the back of her hand. Suddenly the terrible secret that she had been harboring for years tumbled forth before she could stop it. "I hated him so much," she blurted out. "When we were children, I used to lie awake at night and wish that something terrible would happen to him. I thought that if I squeezed my eyes shut and concentrated hard enough, I could make him . . . die." Her voice broke.

In that instant Hugh understood why she had hesitated, why she had panicked at the sight of the youth struggling in the water. Had Lysander died, she would have spent the rest of her life blaming herself for having caused his death.

His expression gentled. "*Princesse*, 'tis highly unlikely that the boy drowned. For one thing, he was making so much noise that John de Lancy's men would have quickly found him. For another, the water near that bank was barely chest deep. Had the boy thought to put his feet down, he would have touched the bottom."

Although it was not the soothing embrace that she had longed for, she knew that Hugh's attempt to comfort her was sincere, and for that she was grateful. "Thank you," she whispered.

Reaching out, Hugh placed a finger beneath her chin and tilted her face up toward his. Her eyes were huge and bright with unshed tears. Hugh's stomach clenched. "I have known many young men such as he, *princesse*. Being a reckless lot, they often meet with an untimely demise. Should something happen to your guardian's son, 'twill be brought about by his own imprudence, not because of anything you might have wished."

Adrienne took a shuddering breath, and then another, in a futile attempt to calm her shattered nerves. She tried to smile. "You're right, my lord," she said shakily. " 'Twas foolish of me to worry so about a childish conceit."

Hugh's hand slid down to her shoulder. He gave it a reassuring squeeze. "Come. We must be on our way."

All day they rode at a brutal pace, stopping from time to time just long enough to water and rest the horses. During one such stop early in the day, Adrienne asked about Graeham and was relieved to hear that he was unharmed. She learned from Hugh's men that they had taken control of the keep and were holding the Baron of Riehen prisoner. She also learned that their losses in the fighting had been high—twenty-two killed and more than a hundred wounded.

After that, no one spoke much. The men seemed subdued, even troubled.

Several times during the day, Hugh inquired after Adrienne's welfare; otherwise, he spoke not at all. Had he not been as uncommunicative with his men as with her, Adrienne might have been insulted, but the dark shadows beneath his eyes and the lines of fatigue in his face reminded her that he had not slept for several nights. In spite of his earlier anger, she realized that his silence probably had nothing to do with her.

As they rode, disquieting thoughts churned in Adrienne's mind. Thoughts of what would happen to her when they returned to Burg Moudon. Thoughts of what might become of her knights and of Marlys. Thoughts of a future that looked more and more bleak with each passing day.

She no longer knew what to do.

She could try again to escape, but that path was beginning to look less and less attractive. Even if she did manage to get away, where would she go? Back to Foutreau?

Even if Lysander lived, she knew that Foutreau was no longer the safe haven it had been in the past. Richard wanted Sainte-Croix so badly he would stop at nothing to get it. If she returned to England, she would likely be imprisoned, or worse.

Or perhaps she could try to reach Trier?

She glanced down at her betrothal ring with its distinctive labyrinthine design etched in the heavy gold.

She doubted Duke Wilhelm would want her now. He would assume that she had already been sullied by the men who had abducted her. Of course, Wilhelm might still be willing to go through with the wedding, if only to secure his claim to Sainte-Croix. But what would happen to her after that? Would he shut her away someplace where she would not be a daily reminder of the shame she had brought to his household?

A dull ache in her jaw made her realize she was clenching her teeth. She forced herself to relax.

She had not wanted this betrothal, she reminded herself; it had been forced upon her. Nor had she asked to be abducted or held prisoner or used as a pawn by the very same men who would hold her responsible if *their* plans for *her* life went awry.

She had no answers. She did not know what she was going to do or where she would go. She only knew that she was weary of being forever at the mercy of those who conspired to shape her destiny.

By the time they reached Burg Moudon, darkness had fallen. Hugh's men had set up camp outside the castle walls.

Fires burned brightly, breaking the damp chill of the night. The smell of charred timbers hung in the air. Hugh escorted Adrienne to the large tent in the center of the camp and left her there under heavy guard while he went to the keep in search of his brother.

A short time later, Marlys was brought to the tent.

She ran to Adrienne and threw her arms around her. "Oh, m'lady, I was worried about you! I'm so glad you're safe. I don't know what I'd do if you didn't come back."

Adrienne held the other girl tightly, finally finding the comfort she had craved all day. Marlys had a kind heart. For the first time since leaving Foutreau, she was truly grateful to have the girl with her. "I'm fine," she said wearily. "I'm just tired and hungry. But what of you? Are you all right? You weren't hurt in the fighting, were you?"

Marlys shook her head. "It scared ten years off my life when Lord Hugh carried me down that wall. I kept thinking I was going to fall into the moat and drown. But he got me down without a bit of trouble, and I waited here for him to bring you, but he never came back. We didn't know what had become of you. When we found out you'd been taken, we feared for your life."

Adrienne lowered her voice. "Marlys, I saw Lysander."

"Lysander!"

"Shhh!" Adrienne glanced at the guard standing just outside the tent opening. "Lysander was with the men who abducted me," she whispered. "He led them to us." Adrienne quickly recounted all that had happened, from John de Lancy's abduction of her to Lysander's unwilling plunge in the river.

When she finished, Marlys's eyes sparked with righteous fury. " 'Twould serve him right if he did drown!" she said hotly. "How dare Lysander betray you to King Richard! If Lord Baldhere knew what he was up to, he'd give him the thrashing of his life! Why, when we get back to Foutreau, I'm sorely tempted to tell Lord Baldhere myself just what his son has been doing!"

Adrienne's expression sobered. "Marlys, what if we never go back?"

The other girl opened her mouth to refute that possibility, then stopped. Her eyes widened. "Do you think we might not?" she asked in a wavering voice.

Adrienne shook her head. "I wish I knew. But, Marlys, I've been thinking . . ." Adrienne hesitated and looked around. "Come, sit down."

They sat down on the bed of furs. Adrienne tucked her legs beneath her. She leaned toward Marlys and spoke in a hushed tone. "We cannot depend upon Lord Baldhere to come to our aid; his protection was taken from us when we left Foutreau. We must look out for ourselves and do what is best for us, regardless of whether it is what Lord Baldhere would have wished."

"But where will we go? With King Richard after you, no place in England will be safe for us!"

"Nor in most of France."

Realization of the hopelessness of their situation reflected in Marlys's eyes.

Adrienne thought for a moment. "We might seek asylum in Brittany."

Marlys frowned. "I don't even know where Brittany is."

Adrienne did, and therein lay the problem. Just getting there entailed crossing Richard's domains. "Or we could appeal to King Philip," she said.

Marlys's face lit up. "Or to Duke Wilhelm?"

"No."

"But, m'lady, he's your betrothed, and he—"

"I don't want to marry him, Marlys."

The other girl's mouth dropped open. "Not want to marry . . . but, m'lady, 'twas decreed by the king."

"I don't want to marry him," Adrienne repeated firmly. Stubbornly. "Marlys, I know I must sound demented, but I have thought of little else all day. I am afraid of Wilhelm. I don't know what manner of person he is. I don't know if he is kind or cruel. I don't know what he will do to us—either of us—once we reach Trier. *If* we could reach Trier."

"Then what are we going to do?"

Adrienne hesitated. "We could ally ourselves with Hugh."

Marlys's eyes grew as round as spinning wheels. "But he's our enemy!"

"And Richard should, by rights, be our friend. But he is not. Hugh, in keeping us from Richard, has protected us from him, although I doubt that was his intention."

Adrienne could tell from the look on Marlys's face that she had never thought of it quite like that.

Adrienne continued, "Hugh wants Sainte-Croix. I can't condemn him for that; 'tis his birthright. Were I to become Hugh's vassal, then Sainte-Croix would once again be his, without any blood being shed, and we would be entitled to his protection. This fighting between Hugh and the Crown can't last forever. When he has made his peace with Richard, we will be able to return to England without fear of reprisal."

Adrienne had spoken quickly, too quickly. She was not certain whether she was trying to convince Marlys or herself. But speaking her thoughts aloud made them seem more real, and more attainable.

Marlys fidgeted and twisted her fingers in the folds of her gown. She avoided Adrienne's gaze.

"Marlys, what is it?"

"M'lady, I know 'tis not my place to speak of such matters, but Lord Hugh . . . I mean, the way he looks at you . . . you would forever be at his mercy." The girl's face reddened.

Adrienne knew what she was thinking; the same memory was never far from her own thoughts. She was remembering the night of the banquet when Hugh came into their bed-chamber. When he had held her. Kissed her.

He wanted her; he had said as much.

She was not so naive that she did not recognize how she could use that to her advantage. "Women are at a man's mercy from the day they are born, be that man their father or their husband or their overlord," Adrienne said. "Would it not be to our benefit to *choose* the man who will have control over our lives?"

Marlys stared at her as if she had uttered a heresy. In a way, she had. She supposed that somewhere in the world there lived headstrong daughters and wives who rebelled against the restrictions placed on them by society and by the Church, but she knew of none. And she had never considered herself particularly rebellious. Even when she did not like the path her elders chose for her, she had always followed it, albeit reluctantly. The thought of having a voice in her own future was utterly foreign to her, but now that the notion had planted itself in her mind, she could not dislodge it.

She could see, however, that Marlys was going to take a little longer to warm to the idea. She took the other girl's hand. "Please think about it," she said. "I know 'tis a big decision, and it was never my intent to burden you with it. But whatever I decide, 'twill affect you too. I want to do what will be best for both of us."

Before Marlys could respond, a guard entered the tent carrying a tray laden with covered dishes. He put the tray down. "If you require anything else, m'lady," he told Adrienne, "send your maidservant to me. I shall be just outside."

After the guard had gone, Marlys peeked under the cover of one of the dishes. The aroma of venison roasted with garlic and herbs filled the tent.

Marlys took a deep, appreciative breath and cast Adrienne a sheepish glance. Laughter danced in her brown eyes and a smile tugged at the corners of her mouth. "I think we should choose the one who feeds us best."

In the keep hall, Hugh noticed that much work had been done while he was away. The injured men had been moved to other quarters and the hall returned to its intended use. Servants were setting up the trestle tables in preparation for the evening meal. The debris had been cleared away and the stone floors scrubbed clean. Hugh had never cared for the northern custom of strewing rushes on the floor, and the change pleased him.

Hugh located the seneschal and praised him on the altered appearance of the keep.

The stooped white-haired man relaxed his guard, and some of the wariness left his expression. " 'Twas Lord Graeham's doing. He's been keeping the servants hopping, but he's a fair man, and none mind doing his bidding." He hesitated. "My lord, the chamber you occupied when you first arrived here has been made ready for your return. Water is now being heated for a bath, and a meal can be brought up to you if you wish to dine in private."

Hugh thanked him. They spent the next few minutes discussing the keep's supply of winter rations; then Hugh took his leave and went upstairs to the solar that had once served as Riehen's private sitting room.

When Hugh entered the chamber, he found Graeham, Conraed, Roland, and Etienne engaged in a heated conversation. Roland still wore his arm in a sling—a visible reminder of Adrienne's first escape attempt. The men fell silent when they saw Hugh.

Graeham's face was rigid with barely contained rage.

Hugh glanced around the small group of knights. "What is wrong?"

"They suspect me of betraying us to Richard," Graeham said hotly.

"No one has accused you," Conraed said.

" 'Tis what you are all thinking."

"What are we supposed to think?" Etienne asked. " 'Tis well known that there is no love lost between you and Hugh, and you have much to gain by your brother's downfall."

"So do Toulouse and Lorraine!"

"Enough!" Hugh ordered. "I will not tolerate petty bickering among my men, nor will I permit accusations to be leveled without due cause. If there is a problem, we shall discuss it and we shall find a solution."

Hugh looked at each man in turn. Graeham's expression was surly. Roland and Conraed exchanged glances.

Etienne was the first to speak. "My lord, we were trying to determine how the king learned of our plans so quickly. For Richard to have summoned an army to intercept us this soon, he had to have known of our plans weeks ago."

"Richard's intent was to capture Lady Adrienne," Roland reminded him. "He could have had his men following her long before she fell into our hands."

"Roland is right," Conraed said. "We lost valuable time in Dordrecht."

Graeham bristled. "Say it, Conraed. I'm to blame for that blunder too."

"I said that is enough!" Hugh barked. "Richard learned of Adrienne's betrothal from the son of one of Henry's favorite barons. He had his army in pursuit before she ever left England."

"You're certain of that?" Conraed asked.

Hugh glowered at the knight, annoyed that Conraed would question him.

An awkward silence descended over the group.

Etienne glanced at Graeham. "I spoke rashly, my lord. I'm sorry."

Graeham's stiff-necked posture did not soften. He refused to meet the other man's gaze.

Hugh changed the subject. "I want all of you to prepare to move out in the morning. Only the most seriously wounded will remain behind; everyone else is to be ready to depart at first light. Roland, find my squire and have him bring me a change of clothing. Graeham, remain here. I need to speak with you alone."

"My lord, at this moment your squire is lying abed with an arrow wound in his shoulder," Roland said.

Hugh's brows dipped in annoyance. "I examined Gabel's wound myself before I left to find Adrienne. 'Tis but a scratch, and a paltry one at that. If I know Gabel, he has found some comely wench to anticipate his every need.

Tell the boy to get his lazy bones out of bed and tend to my bath or I shall put him to work in the kitchens."

After the others had gone, Hugh turned to Graeham. "This keep is poorly defended. However, if the forest is cleared between here and the river, and an outer curtain wall erected, it could become a formidable fortress. The dwellings and outbuildings that burned will need to be rebuilt. If you are up to the task, Burg Moudon is yours. You may choose your men. Anyone who wishes to stay with you will be released from his oath to me."

"Are you sure you can trust me not to turn traitor and release Riehen?" Graeham asked sarcastically.

"I trust you more than I trust anyone else."

Graeham cast Hugh a sharp glance. When he realized that Hugh was serious, some of his anger abated. He took a deep breath. "I apologize. You didn't deserve that."

Hugh regarded his brother for a moment. "Graeham, when I said Rougemont was in the forgotten past, I meant it."

"Unfortunately, no one else seems to have forgotten it."

"Give them time. You and I have been at each other's throats since we returned from Jerusalem. When the others see that we are no longer at odds, they too will begin to forget."

It was late when Hugh finally retired to his bedchamber. A welcoming fire burned on the hearth. As the seneschal had promised, supper and a bath awaited him. Hugh poured himself a tankard of wine, then sat down in a chair near the hearth and stretched out his long legs. Taking a long drink, he let the wine seep through his limbs, warming him, as he watched the steam rise from the copper tub that had been set up before the hearth and filled with hot water. He wondered idly if it was the same tub that Adrienne had bathed in just two nights ago, and the longing he had been trying to suppress all day leapt in his veins.

He closed his eyes and groaned inwardly. All day he had been trying unsuccessfully to ignore his body's demands, but Adrienne's closeness and the feel of her body pressed against his had made that virtually impossible. All day he'd kept remembering the softness of her skin, the feel of her lips against his, her impassioned response to his kisses.

Had it only been two nights ago?

It seemed a lifetime had passed since then.

He had never felt such fear as when he discovered she was missing. He knew that the men who had taken her would kill her should she provoke them. He doubted that Adrienne had ever been exposed to men who used others to further their own interests and who did not hesitate to kill anyone who stood in their way. For all her stubbornness and fire, Adrienne was remarkably naive; he suspected that until now she had led an extremely sheltered life.

Then there was Lysander.

Lysander. Lysander. Lysander.

Like a litany, the name had echoed over and over in his head as he rode. Until he learned the youth's identity, the unknown had taunted him. He had wondered obsessively who the young man was. Was he Adrienne's friend? A childhood companion?

A lover?

Until this morning, he had never given thought to Adrienne having had a lover. But once the idea entered his mind, he could not let it go. He kept visualizing her in another man's arms. Seeing them kiss. Seeing them make love.

Just thinking about it had filled him with such fury that he had been tempted to go back, find the youth, and crush the life out of him.

He had been jealous. Insanely so.

He had never felt that way about a woman before, and it troubled him.

He did not know what he was going to do with her. His plan to use her to wreak revenge on the Plantagenet heirs no longer appealed to him. Adrienne had been as much a victim of her father's political ambitions as he; punishing her for Henry's actions would serve no purpose. He doubted he would even derive any enjoyment from it.

He couldn't let her go; he needed her to lure Richard into Sainte-Croix.

But afterward?

The thought of locking her away in a nunnery left a foul taste in his mouth. Adrienne was too headstrong, too full of life. Unless she had a calling, the convent would be like a prison to her.

That was not the only reason he hesitated to have her cloistered.

He wanted her for himself.

Kissing her had ignited his hunger for her beyond anything he had ever felt for a woman. He was not certain what it was that drew him to her. It was more than her beauty; he had never been one to lose his objectivity over a perfect nose or a well-turned leg. Yet every time he let down his guard, a soft, kissable mouth and a pair of Angevin gray eyes invaded his thoughts.

They were Henry's eyes. Every time he looked into them, he was reminded that Adrienne was Henry's daughter. They challenged and provoked and seduced him with a degree of skill that was all the more maddening because he was certain that Adrienne did not even know she was doing it. The difference between Adrienne and her father, Hugh thought, was that Henry had known how to use his personal charm and overwhelming presence to bend others to his will; Adrienne did it unconsciously.

The door to Hugh's bedchamber creaked, and Hugh's eyes flew open. It took his tired mind several seconds to realize that it was not his squire who stood on the threshold; it was the rosy-cheeked serving girl who had waited in attendance on him the night of the banquet, the one whose flirtations had sparked Adrienne's ire.

The girl glanced shyly at him from beneath her lashes, but there was nothing innocent about the knowing smile that touched her mouth as she pushed the door shut behind her.

*   *   *

Adrienne lay on the bed of furs and stared up at the shadows the candles cast on the tent ceiling. She had bathed and changed into clean clothes and eaten a light supper. Marlys had kept her company until exhaustion and the lateness of the hour took her back to her own tent. She had thought Hugh would have returned by now, but he had not. She felt an odd emptiness at his absence.

She had learned from one of Hugh's guards that they were going to move out in the morning. What Hugh intended to do with her and her knights no one knew. If she was to influence his decision, she had to act tonight. By morning it might be too late.

She and Marlys had finally decided to cast their lot with Hugh. The girl was still terrified of him, but when they had narrowed their choices down to Hugh and Duke Wilhelm, even Marlys admitted that staying with Hugh was preferable to trusting their fate to a man they had never met. A known adversary was less frightening than an unknown one.

Then there was John de Lancy's puzzling statement that Hugh had grown enamored of her.

Adrienne was skeptical. Considering how Hugh had treated her these past weeks, she would hate to find out how he treated women he *didn't* like. Still, she had to admit, she had not fared all that badly. At Foutreau she had heard enough stories from the servants to know that women usually suffered far worse at the hands of their aggressors.

And he had rescued her yet again. Why? she wondered. Why did he keep risking his life for her? Was it possible that in some bizarre way he did care for her? Or was she merely trying to justify her own confused feelings toward him?

She was still trying to find the answer to that when the tent flap was pulled aside.

Adrienne bolted upright, fighting her disappointment when she realized that it was not Hugh but his squire who had entered the tent.

Gabel stopped short when he saw her. His hair was tousled, and his clothes hung askew. He looked as if he had just crawled out of bed. Mumbling an apology, he went to Hugh's clothes chest and opened it.

Adrienne shoved her hair away from her face. "Gabel, is it?"

The boy turned and eyed her warily. "Aye."

"Do you know where Lord Hugh is?"

"Aye, m'lady." Gabel sounded unusually put out. "He's at the keep. I'm to fetch him clean clothes."

The realization that Hugh might not have intended to return to the tent at all unexpectedly stung. Adrienne struggled to keep her wounded pride from showing on her face.

Gabel turned back to the trunk and began going through its contents. Adrienne's mind raced. She needed to speak with Hugh, but judging from Gabel's disgruntled tone, she doubted she could trust the squire to relay a message to his lord. More than that, she feared Hugh might refuse to see her.

When Gabel closed the trunk, Adrienne pushed back the furs and scrambled to her feet. "I'll take the clothes to him."

Gabel's mouth dropped open, and he regarded her as if she were possessed. He started to shake his head. "I-I can't let you do that, m'lady," he stammered.

"Please, Gabel. I must see Lord Hugh."

"Then I shall tell him you want—"

"No!" Adrienne softened her outburst with a pleading smile. "Suppose he won't see me?"

"Then you will have to abide by his wishes." Gabel paused, then added, "Just as the rest of us do."

Adrienne thought frantically. "Gabel, the men who attacked Graeham and abducted me—they were sent by Richard."

"By Richard? But I thought—" Gabel broke off and clamped his mouth shut. "My lady, I will tell Lord Hugh that you want to see him, but that's all I will do."

Adrienne knew by the boy's reaction that he thought Prince John's men had seized her. Having heard the guards talking, she realized that most of the men believed that. Apparently only Hugh and the few knights closest to him knew the truth. Wondering just how much she could confuse the issue without arousing the squire's suspicions, she said, "Gabel, Lord Hugh knows 'twas Prince John and his men who led the attack on Burg Moudon. What he doesn't know is that King Richard sent them. I overheard John's men talking. Richard is plotting against Lord Hugh."

She glanced toward the tent opening, and her voice dropped conspiratorially. "Richard plans to kill him." *God, forgive me for lying.*

Adrienne saw the uncertainty in the squire's face, and she felt a twinge of guilt for deceiving him. If Gabel carried out her request, he risked provoking his lord's temper. If he refused, and by chance something did happen to Hugh, he would forever blame himself.

Gabel drew in a deep breath as if it could be his last. "I'll take the clothes to Lord Hugh myself," he said hesitantly. "But if the guards will permit you to leave the tent, you may come with me."

Hugh leaned back in the small tub and watched the serving girl through half-closed eyes as she passed the soapy sponge over his chest in ever-widening circles. Every time she reached across him, her bodice gaped, exposing her breasts to his view. There was no subtlety in the ploy, and Hugh knew she would not protest should he decide to act upon her invitation.

The girl was comely enough. Her skin was fair and unblemished, her figure full and inviting. A few weeks ago he would have eagerly taken her to his bed. Now her efforts to entice him to that end succeeded only in making him think of another.

He kept remembering when Adrienne had told him of her hatred for her guardian's son and her wish that he would die. He could not forget the anguish in her voice or the way her eyes had pleaded with him, as if begging him not to hate her for her admission. He remembered his own longing to take her in his arms and comfort her.

Hugh frowned. He was becoming obsessed, he thought sourly. That the unwelcome intrusion of one woman into his thoughts could prevent him from enjoying the charms another did not sit well with him.

He forced himself to concentrate on the girl who was leaning so close to him that he could smell her musky feminine scent. He was willing to wager a handsome sum that she knew well how to please a man, for she was skillfully arousing his body despite his lack of interest in her. Her hand dipped beneath the water as the circles she was soaping on his chest widened.

Hugh caught her hand, stilling it. "What is your name?" he asked suddenly.

The girl glanced at him, and a dimple appeared at each corner of her mouth. "Petra, my lord."

Hugh's gaze rested on her mouth. Her pink tongue darted over her lips, moistening them, and Hugh's eyes darkened. Still holding her hand imprisoned against his chest, he slid his free hand into her hair and drew her head down to his.

A sharp knock sounded on the chamber door.

Hugh swore aloud. He released Petra, and the girl scrambled to her feet. From the panicked look that passed across her features, Hugh suspected she was more afraid than embarrassed at being caught in his bedchamber. "Enter!" he bellowed.

The door swung open, and Gabel stepped into the chamber, a pile of clothing in his arms. He stopped short, his startled gaze traveling from Hugh to Petra, then back to Hugh again, and his face turned a brilliant red.

Hugh looked past Gabel to the open doorway.

Adrienne stood on the threshold.

Desire and fury surged through him at once.

She was clad once again in a squire's tunic and chausses, and her dark hair curled damply around her freshly scrubbed face. Her gaze alighted on Petra, and in the next few seconds Hugh saw shock, then fury, then disdain flash across her expressive face before she regained control of her emotions.

Hugh gripped the sides of the tub. "I gave specific orders that you were not to leave my tent. Why are you here?"

Lifting her chin, Adrienne turned her gaze on him and regarded him with regal reserve. It was the same haughty stance that Henry had often taken when someone displeased him, and the startling similarity caught Hugh by surprise.

"I wish to speak with you, my lord," Adrienne said coolly.

Any other time, Hugh might have found the situation funny.

Petra was glowering at Adrienne with undisguised resentment, while Adrienne was doing her best to ignore her and appear unruffled. Hugh's squire looked as if he expected to be slain on the spot. And Hugh was trapped in a bathtub with less than eight inches of water to hide his irrefutable condition.

His gaze bored into Adrienne's. "Leave us," he ordered.

Gabel did not need to be told twice. A comical look of relief flooding his face, he deposited Hugh's clothes on the nearest chair and bolted from the chamber.

Petra followed Gabel, dragging her feet and casting Adrienne venomous glances on her way out of the chamber.

Hugh sat where he was, not trusting himself to behave rationally should he leave the confinement of the tub. He was tempted to throttle Adrienne, yet he knew that once he touched her, he would be lost. In the span of a few seconds his desire for her had increased a hundredfold.

"Close the door," he said thickly.

Chapter Ten

ALTHOUGH HUGH HAD spoken quietly, the command sounded to Adrienne like a death sentence. Her knees trembled, but it was not courage that kept her from fleeing; it was jealousy.

Seeing Hugh with the serving girl who had fawned over him the night of the banquet had unleashed in her a jealous fury unlike anything she had ever felt. She would have preferred to be flayed alive rather than to leave Hugh alone for five minutes with that woman. The intensity of her reaction stunned and frightened her.

John de Lancy was wrong, she thought shakily. Hugh was not enamored of her; 'twas she who was in danger of losing her heart.

She pushed the door shut.

She turned to find Hugh watching her. He had not moved from the tub. His wet hair was tousled, making him look disarmingly boyish. Amusement and something else she could not define smoldered in his eyes. "Had I known you were so eager to assist with my bath, *princesse*, I would have sent for you rather than for Gabel."

"It appeared to me, my lord, that assistance was already in ample supply."

"Jealous?"

"No."

One dark brow angled upward.

"I am not jealous!" Until the words were out of her mouth Adrienne didn't realize that she had raised her voice. Not for all the gold and finery in the world would she ever admit to him that she was jealous. Terribly so. The thought of that other woman touching Hugh made her blood boil. She did not even want to think of what would have transpired had the girl stayed with him. She lifted her chin and glowered at him. "Shall I call the girl back so that she can finish what she started?" she asked stiffly.

"That will not be necessary." Hugh splashed water over his chest and shoulders with cupped hands. "Instead, you may tell me what is so important that it cannot wait until morning."

Although Adrienne had already surmised that he had intended to spend the night in the keep, knowing that he had intended to spend it in another woman's arms made her all the more determined to follow through with her plan. Forcing a calm she was far from feeling, she said, "I want to swear an oath of fealty to you."

Hugh froze. "You want to *what*?"

"I know you must think this is a trick, my lord, but I swear 'tis not." Adrienne spoke quickly. Too quickly, allowing the words to tumble out before her courage waned. "There are practical reasons for my request," she continued. "First, there are my knights. They are bound to me by their oath. Were I your vassal, they would be obligated to serve you as they do me. Instead of having twelve prisoners to feed and shelter and confine, and who serve no purpose but to encumber you, you would have a dozen more soldiers to fight for you and do your bidding."

Hugh wasn't certain whether he was more stunned by Adrienne's proposal to swear fealty to him or by her request to free her knights. "You don't ask for much, do you, *princesse*?" he retorted.

Adrienne chose to ignore the sarcasm in his voice. "In truth, my lord, no. All I ask for in return is your protection as my overlord."

Hugh drew back and regarded her through narrowed eyes. "You are amazing," he said slowly. "Even your father never had the gall to ask me to release a bunch of brigands and welcome them to my ranks as allies."

Adrienne had the uncomfortable feeling that he was mocking her. "They are not brigands," she said defensively. "They are skilled knights whose only crime is their loyalty to me."

"And to Henry," Hugh reminded her.

Adrienne's frustration mounted. "Considering the extent of your losses in taking this keep, my lord, I thought you would welcome the addition of trained knights to your army."

"You forget, *princesse*, those very same knights helped your father seize Sainte-Croix from me. As far as I am concerned, they are common thieves." Hugh inclined his head toward the bed. "Hand me a towel."

There was no mistaking the tone of dismissal in his voice. Adrienne realized with a sinking feeling that Hugh had no intention of even considering her offer. What he couldn't know, however, was that *she* had no intention of giving up.

Adrienne crossed the bedchamber and picked up one of the linen drying cloths that lay on the foot of the bed. She turned back to Hugh. "There is also the matter of Sainte-Croix. Were I your vassal, Sainte-Croix would be yours to do with as you saw fit. You would be able to—"

"Sainte-Croix is already mine, as are your knights. I fear you bargain with an empty purse, *princesse*."

"But, my lord, I—"

"You are my prisoner. Everything you own, or think you own, now belongs to me."

Anger flashed in Adrienne's eyes. She clutched the towel against her pounding heart. "Not everything," she said in a low, determined voice.

"Everything," Hugh repeated flatly. He extended his hand. "Now, bring me the towel," he ordered.

Pricked by his imperious tone, Adrienne flung the towel onto the bed. Before Hugh realized what she intended, she gripped the hem of her tunic and pulled it off over her head. She shook her head, allowing her hair to tumble down over her bare shoulders.

Hugh stared at her, too stunned to move. Only once before had he ever been shocked into immobility, and that was ten years ago, the first and only time he had ever been thrown from his horse in the midst of a battle. The experience had so unnerved him that he had sworn he would never permit it to happen again. It hadn't.

Until now.

Hugh gripped the sides of the tub. His face was rigid with barely controlled fury, and when he spoke, his voice was strained. "Put on your clothes and get out of this chamber, or I will not be responsible for my actions."

Adrienne lifted her chin and eyed him defiantly. Although she had never done anything so brazen in her life, she knew intuitively that she had Hugh at a disadvantage. John de Lancy had been right after all: Hugh's one weakness was his attraction to her. The knowledge both thrilled and terrified her. Never letting her gaze waver from Hugh's, she released the tunic and let it slide to the floor. Her hands went to the waist of her chausses. Locating the ties that held them up, she grasped one end and pulled the knot free.

Hugh swore aloud. He pushed himself to his feet, sending water surging onto the floor, and stepped out of the tub.

Adrienne braced herself as he closed the distance between them in angry strides. Her breathing quickened. Any other time her gaze might have been drawn to his body—lean and powerful and glistening—but she could not tear her eyes away from his face. Rage and desire burned darkly in his eyes. He seized her shoulders, and a cry that was part surprise, part triumph, tore from her throat.

For a moment they just stood there, their gazes locked. Hugh's fingers tightened on her arms, digging painfully into her flesh. Then his gaze dropped to her mouth, and he groaned. He pulled her toward him. "Damn you," he bit out.

His head descended.

Adrienne lifted her face to his kiss. When his lips touched hers, a shock surged through her, causing every nerve in her body to come alive with forbidden longings.

His arms went around her, and he crushed her to him, fitting her tightly against his hard contours. Adrienne's lips parted, and Hugh thrust his tongue into her mouth, withdrew it, then thrust again and again in a provocative imitation of the act that was to follow.

Adrienne wrapped her arms around him and clung to him as her entire world reeled. She felt the way she had as a child when she twirled around and around in circles, then collapsed onto the ground to watch the clouds spin dizzily above her.

Hugh buried one hand in her hair and tilted her head back, while his other hand pressed against the small of her back. He kissed her lips, her eyelids, her throat. A moan broke from her lips, and she put her hands on his shoulders to steady herself as her center of balance shifted. His mouth traced a searing path down her throat to her breasts. Still bracing her lower back, he withdrew his hand from her hair and cupped her breast, stroking and caressing it as he lifted it to his mouth.

His lips closed around her nipple, and Adrienne felt the floor drop from beneath her feet. Her fingers tightened on his shoulders as a shudder of pure pleasure rippled through her. Her entire body quaked with excitement and terror. She was afraid, not of what he was doing to her, but of surrendering, of losing control, of passing a point beyond which there would be no hope of return. He drew her nipple deeper into his mouth, and her resolve slipped. *I love you!* she thought insanely, barely choking back the words.

Suddenly Hugh straightened. Before Adrienne's world had a chance to stop spinning, Hugh bent and slid one arm behind her knees, then lifted her in his arms. She clung to him, pulling him down with her as he lowered her to the bed.

He hovered over her, nudging her thighs apart with his knees, then settling between them. He supported his weight with his arms as he lowered himself just until his chest came into contact with her breasts. Then he began moving, brushing the black hair on his chest against her breasts and coaxing her nipples into aching awareness, teasing her skin with thousands of tiny pleasurable tickling sensations that kept building and building until they could no longer be ignored.

Suddenly something burst inside her, filling her with a liquid warmth.

She gasped and arched her back, bringing her breasts hard against his chest. Hugh lowered his weight fully against her and reclaimed her lips, smothering her cry with his mouth. He kissed her deeply, thoroughly, drinking in her exotic sweetness. He circled her tongue with his, teasing and caressing it, then drawing it into his own mouth where she began returning his kisses with an impassioned eagerness that wrought an involuntary shudder of delight from him.

As they kissed, he began moving his hips against hers in slow erotic circles that heightened their awareness of each other. Through her chausses, Adrienne could feel his probing hardness, and she unthinkingly parted her legs farther, allowing him to settle deeper against her. She slid her hands over his back and buttocks, thrilling in the feel of the taut, well-honed muscles as she pulled him even closer against her in answer to her body's increasing demands. His body was still wet and sleek from his bath, and everywhere she touched, her fingers glided effortlessly over his skin.

The feather-light touch of her fingers against his skin was almost more than Hugh could bear. He wanted her so badly that it took all of his self-control to restrain himself. Intuition told him that Adrienne was acting from instinct rather than experience, and he did not want to hurt her by taking her before she was ready.

He rolled onto his back, pulling her with him. She sprawled against his chest, straddling his hips. The sudden movement surprised her, and for a moment she stared at him in confusion, her eyes dark with longing and her lips swollen from his kisses. Hugh buried his hands in her hair and drew her down to him. Her hair cascaded down over both of them, engulfing them in a sweetly scented veil of brown-black curls as she rested her breasts against his chest and lowered her head.

She touched her lips to his, hesitantly at first, then boldly. She brushed her lips back and forth over his. She kissed the corners of his mouth. She caught his bottom lip between her teeth and tugged gently. Finally she touched his lips with the tip of her tongue.

Hugh relaxed and allowed himself to enjoy her explorations, the sweetness of her tongue as she teased his lips, and the caressing warmth of her breath against his mouth. He slid his hands down her back, her silky skin like a balm against his callused fingers. He eased his hands beneath the waist of her chausses and clasped her bare buttocks, kneading the smooth flesh and pulling her tighter against his arousal.

The feel of his hands holding her so intimately awakened in Adrienne something that was foreign to her yet completely natural. Her breathing quickened, and she pushed her buttocks against his hands, increasing the pressure he was exerting on them. She trailed her lips down over Hugh's face, then followed with her cheek, enjoying the prickly roughness of his unshaven jaw against her skin. She kissed the leaping pulse in the side of his neck, then followed the line of the artery downward to the vulnerable hollow at the base of his throat, then lower still.

She slid down over Hugh's thighs as she left a trail of soft, moist kisses on his broad, tanned chest with its mat of black hair. His chest was covered with scars, some knotted, others long and deep. The thought of wounds severe enough to cause such pronounced scarring made her throat tighten and brought sudden tears to her eyes. She kissed each scar as if by doing so she could take away the pain he had endured, until only one scar remained. With a deliberation that bordered upon reverence, she traced with her lips the long, pale arc that sliced downward over his hard, flat belly.

The muscles in Hugh's abdomen shuddered, and he sucked in his breath. He caught Adrienne beneath the arms and turned over, lifting her off him and rolling her onto her back in a single unbroken movement. "Damn, but you are a sorceress," he ground out. Grasping the waist of her chausses, he pulled them down over her hips, then off, and flung them aside. He positioned himself between her thighs.

Adrienne instinctively lifted her hips to meet his thrust as he quickly entered her.

A cry that was part surprise, part pain, burst in her throat. She had known that the first time might hurt, but she had naively thought herself to be immune to the pain. A tear streaked down her cheek. She tried to pull away, but it was too late. Hugh withdrew partway, then drove into her again and again. In the flickering candlelight, she saw his face, taut with the effort of holding back, and for a split second she felt a shiver of fear as she mistook the burning intensity in his eyes for revenge. Gradually the pain subsided, and Adrienne became aware of him inside her, filling her. As she began to understand the real reason for Hugh's savage expression, it lost its power to frighten her, and she relaxed.

As a result, her pleasure surged.

He drove into her, and she gasped as he touched something deep inside her that she had never felt before. It was as if he had unlocked some private part of her that she had not known existed, and once opened, that door refused to be shut.

He drove into her again, and a molten warmth began to seep through her limbs. She closed her eyes and let herself be carried away on a wave of pleasurable sensations that lifted her higher and higher until she felt as if she were suspended over the edge of a steep precipice, ready to fall at the slightest provocation.

He drove into her harder and faster, no longer able to restrain the force of his thrusts, and Adrienne lost all control. Her back arched, and she cried out his name as the wave carried her completely over the edge.

I love you! she screamed mindlessly, and this time she could not be certain whether or not she had spoken the words aloud. She gripped Hugh's shoulders, digging her nails into the bunched muscles as he drove into her one last time, finally joining her in sweet oblivion.

As Adrienne slowly drifted back down to earth, Hugh wrapped his arms around her, carrying her with him as he rolled onto his side. She nestled closer against him and rested her cheek against his pounding heart. She forced her mind to block out the distressing thoughts that conspired to ruin the warm contentment she was feeling. She did not want to think about what had made her come here tonight. Nor did she want to think about what her impulsiveness was going to cost her. She wanted only to savor this moment, to commit to memory the feeling of Hugh's strong arms around her. For the first time in her life she felt secure and protected and wanted.

Hugh slid his hand into her hair and held her head against his chest. Resting his chin against the top of her head, he stared across the chamber at the candles next to his uneaten supper on the table. The wicks had burned low, and the flames flickered and smoked. A frown troubled his brow. He had wanted Adrienne from the first time he saw her that night on the barge, and now when the opportunity presented itself, instead of taking his time and making it pleasurable for her, he had rushed at her like an untried youth.

He had never lost control like that before. He told himself that it was because he had gone several months without a woman. He told himself it was because Petra had done a thorough job of arousing him. He told himself it was because he had spent the better part of the day with his arms locked around Adrienne and his mind locked around the idea of her having a lover. But no matter how he tried to justify his actions, he could not deny that he had failed to make certain Adrienne was ready to receive him, and he had hurt her.

He had called her a sorceress, partly in anger and partly in jest. Now he was beginning to wonder if there might be some truth to the accusation.

Adrienne stirred in his arms and tilted her head back to look at him. Her face was flushed, and there was a sleepy, contented look in her eyes. Hugh lifted a curl off her cheek. "I seem to recall you telling me that you would never come willingly to my bed."

Adrienne detected a teasing note in his voice. "I had an ulterior motive."

"Ah, yes. The release of your knights."

"Which you will grant me."

"And how do you figure that?"

She smiled lazily. "Because you are an honorable man."

Her smile was infectious, and Hugh felt an involuntary tug at the corners of his own mouth. "Henry would roll over in his grave if he heard you say that."

" 'Tis true."

Hugh chuckled. "I fear you suffer from delusions, *princesse*."

Adrienne traced a forefinger along his jaw. She wondered uneasily if he had heard her say she loved him. "You could have forced me to your bed long before now, my lord," she said thoughtfully. "Yet you did not. Why?"

"Because it was not convenient to do so."

"I think 'twas because that thick hide of yours truly harbors a conscience."

Her smile, the dreamy look in her eyes, and the sultry innocence in her voice all served to reawaken Hugh's desire. Adrienne *must* be a sorceress; she had certainly cast a spell over him.

Hugh rolled her onto her back. Bracing himself on one elbow, he cupped her breast with his free hand and began stroking it and teasing the sensitive peak with his fingers. His gaze never left her face. "I have no conscience."

"Meaning you won't release my knights?"

"We will discuss your knights in the morning. Right now I have other plans."

Hugh deepened his caresses, and Adrienne's breath caught in her throat. Her pupils suddenly expanded, making her eyes seem large and smoky. Still she made no move to stop him. "What are you doing?"

"I am going to make love to you again, and this time I am going to make certain we both enjoy it."

A stab of doubt pierced Adrienne's sense of contentment. Since she still felt as if she were floating, she could only assume that Hugh had not enjoyed their lovemaking. "Did you not enjoy it before, my lord?" she asked hesitantly.

"I enjoyed it immensely."

"Then why are you—"

Hugh covered her mouth with his, and the question she had been about to ask was lost in his kiss.

The fire had nearly burned itself out. The remaining embers glowed red in the darkness. The rest of the castle had long since settled in for the night, and all was still.

Content and sated from their lovemaking, Adrienne lay on her side and gazed sleepily into the hearth. Hugh lay behind her with one arm around her middle, tracing abstract patterns on her breast with his fingers. Their legs were entwined. Hugh's breath was warm against her ear. He pressed a kiss into her hair. "Tell me about your guardian's son," he prompted gently. "Why does he dislike you so much?"

Adrienne took a deep, unsteady breath. She did not want to spoil the night by talking about Lysander. Yet if she refused to talk about him, Hugh might draw conclusions that were even more damaging. "Lysander resented me from the first day I arrived at Foutreau. I never understood why. Sometimes I thought he was jealous of me, although he had no reason to be."

She hesitated, then continued in a low, distant voice, "When I was a child, I had a pet kitten. She was gold and orange, with big orange eyes. I loved her so much. She used to follow me everywhere and get into everything. Lady Joanna made me put her outside whenever we were in the weaving room, because she would get into the embroidery silks and tangle them terribly. She was so playful . . ." Her voice wavered. "One day when I finished my duties in the weaving room, I went looking for her. I called and called, but she never came. I found her later. Lysander had killed her and placed her skinned carcass on my bed."

"My God," Hugh whispered. "Did your guardian punish him for it?"

"Lord Baldhere wasn't there when it happened."

"But when he returned, surely someone told him what his son had done."

"Yes . . . I told him. He gave Lysander the thrashing of his life. Then he gave me one for bearing tales. I learned to keep silent where Lysander was concerned."

Hugh's brows knitted together. "You must forgive me if I don't approve of your guardian's methods."

"That day I wasn't very fond of them myself. Eventually I realized that Baldhere was right. Lysander might someday be the lord of the manor. I needed to learn to treat him with the respect that is his birthright." Adrienne chuckled, then added, "I fear I failed miserably in that regard."

"*Princesse*, respect is not an entitlement," Hugh said quietly. "It must be earned."

Adrienne placed her hand over Hugh's and pulled his arm more tightly around her. "I said I failed, my lord. I did not say I felt guilty about it."

Hugh said nothing. He was remembering this morning at the river. Had he known then what he knew now, he would have given the youth more than just a dunking in the water.

"There was another time, when I was twelve." Adrienne spoke so softly, Hugh had to strain to hear her. " 'Twas on All Hallows' Eve. A girl in the village told me that if I waited until dark, then looked into a mirror while holding a lighted candle, I would see over my shoulder the likeness of my future husband. Well, I begged a candle from the steward, and when Lady Joanna was napping, I sneaked into her bedchamber and borrowed her silver hand mirror. I could hardly wait for night to fall. Never in my life had a day dragged on for so long."

In spite of himself, Hugh began to laugh.

" 'Twas not funny, my lord. At the time I took the matter quite seriously."

"I'm not laughing at you, *princesse*. I was thinking of my sister. Raissa fell prey to that very same superstition. *She* saw nothing, which is why she decided she was fated to become a nun." Hugh fought to contain his mirth. "Tell me, what prophetic apparition filled your mirror?"

"Well, Lysander had found out what I planned and was hiding in the garderobe when I slipped up to my bedchamber. After lighting the candle, I spoke aloud three times the charm that the girl had taught me. Then, just as I peered into the mirror, Lysander emerged from the shadows behind me, holding in front of him the severed head of a wild boar that he had stolen from the kitchens."

Adrienne suppressed a shudder. Even now the memory of that night chilled her blood. "You never heard anyone scream so loud. For weeks afterward I disrupted the entire household with my nightmares. Lord Baldhere took to the field with his men so he could get a decent night's sleep."

Hugh's smile had faded. There was an element of cruelty in Lysander's pranks that went beyond youthful enthusiasm.

Now he understood why Adrienne had not been afraid of him, why she had continued to defy him, no matter how severely he punished her. Nothing he could do to her, short of taking her life, would ever be as bad as what she had already endured from her guardian's son. Should their paths cross again, he vowed, Lysander of Foutreau would get more than his clothes dampened.

When Hugh remained silent, Adrienne turned her head to look at him. In the near darkness his expression was solemn. "I did not tell you about Lysander to make you pity me," she said. "Merely to explain why I am not as fond of him as people expect me to be. Lysander is not a kind person. Had I not been there, he would have found someone else to torment."

Hugh lifted his hand to her face and stroked her cheek. Her skin was as soft and fragrant as rose petals. "Pity is a useless emotion, *princesse*, demeaning to the giver as well as to the recipient. I indulge in it as seldom as possible, and not at all where you are concerned."

"Then what were you thinking just now to cause you to look so full of gloom?"

"The truth? I was congratulating myself on having discovered why you are such a formidable enemy."

Adrienne sighed wearily and turned her gaze back toward the hearth. "I'm not your enemy, my lord. I'm your prisoner."

"There is a difference?"

"Aye, there is a difference. As your prisoner, 'tis my duty to try to escape. As your enemy, I would have been obligated to kill you." She hesitated, then added softly, "At that I would not have failed."

Hugh chuckled. "I believe you."

Neither of them spoke after that. Hugh drew Adrienne closer against him and shifted his weight to get more comfortable. His cheek rested against the back of her head. The subtle fragrance of her hair, the warmth of her body next to his, and the memories of their lovemaking worked together like a drug, dulling his resistance and coaxing him into a pleasant lethargy.

He was nearly asleep when Adrienne's groggy voice pierced his consciousness. "My lord, have you ever been in love?"

Hugh's eyes flew open, and every nerve in his body was suddenly alert. "Why do you want to know?"

Adrienne yawned. "I was wondering if it felt . . . anything at all . . . like . . ." Her voice trailed off.

"Like what?" Hugh prompted.

No answer.

Hugh rose up on one elbow. He could barely make out the contours of her face in the darkness. "*Princesse?*"

Adrienne was sound asleep.

The sun slanted across the bedchamber, filling it with a thin golden light. Adrienne snuggled deeper beneath the covers, seeking warmth in the morning chill. Images of the night floated through her memory, tokens of the dream world from which she was reluctantly emerging.

A contented smile touched her lips. Hugh had made love to her several times last night, lingering over her for hours and bringing her from one delicious peak to another. Every time she thought her senses could climb no higher, he had proved her wrong. If she could relive last night, she would not change a thing. And she would have no regrets.

The door to the bedchamber creaked, but Adrienne ignored the sound. She did not want to relinquish the night. She wanted this warm, groggy, sated feeling to last forever.

Suddenly the mattress dipped and a kiss brushed her cheek. "Good morning, sleepyhead."

Her eyes flew open.

Hugh was leaning over her, his hands braced on either side of her head. Adrienne rolled onto her back and smiled sleepily up at him. He had bathed and shaved and was fully dressed. Adrienne's heart turned over in her chest. She wondered why she had not noticed before how handsome he was. *Good morning, my love*, she thought. "Good morning, my lord," she said.

Hugh grinned at her. "You are the laziest wench I have ever known," he teased. "While everyone else is looking forward to the midday meal, you have yet to break your fast. Do you intend to lie abed all day?"

Adrienne felt a blush flood her cheeks as the memories of their lovemaking rushed back to her with even greater clarity. "I've never slept this late in my life," she said sheepishly.

Hugh slid his hand beneath the covers and caressed her breasts. Beneath his fingertips, her nipples immediately hardened. "That's what comes of staying awake all night, *princesse*," he said in a low, seductive voice.

Her defenses unusually weak, Adrienne was just starting to melt to his touch when a sharp knock at the door jolted her back to reality. She clutched the covers to her chin and tried to dodge the distractions of Hugh's teasing hand. "My lord, please!"

Pulling his hand from beneath the covers, Hugh winked at her and stood up. "Enter," he called out.

The door opened and one of the serving girls came into the bedchamber, then stopped and cast a hesitant glance about her. She was carrying a tray of covered dishes. To Adrienne's relief, it was not the same girl she had found in Hugh's chamber last night.

Hugh indicated the table where his own dinner had awaited him yesterday evening. The dishes had been cleared away while Adrienne slept. "You may put the tray there," he said.

The girl obeyed. Keeping her head bowed, she turned and cast Hugh an uncertain glance from beneath her lashes. Unlike the looks the other serving girl had given Hugh, there was nothing seductive in the girl's manner. If anything, she appeared to be terrified of him. "M-m'lord, the lady's b-bath is being pr-prepared now," she stammered.

Hugh inclined his head. "Thank you."

The girl bolted from the chamber.

Hugh turned back to Adrienne. His dark brows were drawn together in a puzzled frown.

Adrienne stifled a laugh. "What did you do to her to make her so afraid of you?"

"I didn't do anything to her. I've been too occupied with meeting *your* demands, *princesse*."

He chuckled at the affronted look Adrienne threw him. Before she could protest his suggestive remark, he said, "I need to check on our supplies. We will depart Burg Moudon as soon as you have dressed and eaten. Gabel will wait for you on the landing outside this chamber door. When you are ready, he will escort you down to the ward." He turned to leave.

Both the lateness of the hour and the realization that she was to be accompanied by Hugh's squire rather than by armed guards struck her at once. "My lord, wait!"

Clutching the covers over her breasts, Adrienne sat up and clambered from the bed. The floor was cold beneath her bare feet. "I thought you had plans to leave at dawn. Is something amiss?"

Hugh grinned at her. His dark eyes sparkled. "I too slept later than is my custom. At dawn our bedchamber was very nearly besieged by a score of armed knights, worried that I might have met with an untimely end during the night. You may thank Gabel that they stopped at the door."

Before Adrienne could say anything else, Hugh left the bedchamber, closing the door behind him.

She sank down onto the edge of the bed. She was mortified at the thought of Hugh's men barging into the bedchamber while she lay naked in Hugh's arms. Had they seen her . . .

She squeezed her eyes shut and groaned. What did it matter? What was done was done.

Although she was not ashamed of what had transpired during the night, she was already dreading the knowing glances and ribald comments that were sure to pass her way.

She took a deep breath. There was nothing to be gained by worrying about that which could not be changed. She had withstood insults before; she could withstand them now.

She looked down at the betrothal ring on her finger. The labyrinth's convoluted path made her head ache as she tried to follow it with her gaze. With a sigh, she pulled the ring off her finger and placed it on the pillow where only moments ago her head had lain. The future that ring had promised was lost to her now. She had made her choice.

Hugh was in the ward talking with his brother when Gabel escorted Adrienne from the keep. She had just learned that Graeham would be staying behind when they left Burg Moudon, and she realized with a pang that she was going to miss him. His playful teasing had provided a welcome respite from Hugh's sometimes gloomy moods. She had found out from Gabel that Hugh and Graeham had called a truce; the ghosts that haunted their past had been laid to rest.

Graeham swept into a chivalrous bow when he saw her. "My fair lady, you grow more beautiful with each passing day. I am tempted to steal you away from my brother and detain you here."

Adrienne was acutely aware of Hugh's caressing gaze upon her. He actually seemed *pleased* to see her. Buoyed by the warmth in his eyes and by Graeham's joking, she could not help but laugh. She cast Graeham a look of mock horror. "Surely not in the lower chambers of the donjon, my lord, where the rats vie with the prisoners for moldy crumbs? I shall perish!"

Graeham leaned close to her. His eyes twinkled with mischief. "Actually, my lady, the prison I had in mind was my—"

"Hrrrmph!" Hugh cleared his throat loudly.

Both Adrienne and Graeham turned to stare at him. His black brows were knitted together ominously, and a nerve twitched beneath his left eye. Graeham laughed. "Just as I suspected," he said. He took Adrienne's hand. "My lady, I wish you a safe journey. It has been five years since I last saw my homeland, and it may be months more before I am so indulged. When you see the olive groves and the sunflower fields, and smell the lavender that grows wild on the mountainsides, I hope you will think of me. Those are the things I have missed the most."

"Graeham, you have said enough," Hugh said in a low, meaningful voice.

Graeham had the good grace to look apologetic as he glanced at Hugh. Turning back to Adrienne, he brought her hand to his mouth and brushed a kiss across her knuckles. "I hope we meet again, my lady."

Adrienne had not missed the exchange between the two brothers. A dozen questions sprang to mind, but there was no time to ask them. Hugh took her arm and led her to a saddled horse that stood beside his. The horse was smaller than Hugh's and was chestnut-colored with a white blaze on its forehead. "I thought you would be more comfortable with your own mount," Hugh said. "I hope you have no objection to riding astride."

Happiness filled Adrienne to the point of bursting. That Hugh trusted her to ride alone told her that he had accepted the proposal she had put before him last night. At least she had not bargained away her virginity in vain, she thought. "I don't mind at all, my lord," she said lightly.

She was glad now that she had decided to wear the squire's tunic and chausses that she had been given last night rather than accepting the timid maidservant's offer of a gown and chemise. The cumbersome gown would have made riding astride inconvenient at best. She had, however, accepted the loan of a mantle. The soft wool kept out the unseasonable chill.

Hugh helped her up into the saddle. She sucked in her breath at the unexpected pain that shot through her legs.

"Are you all right?" Hugh asked.

Adrienne fought the rising tide of color in her face; there was only one explanation for her soreness this morning. Hoping no one else had heard her gasp, she took the reins and managed a woeful smile. "I'm fine."

Hugh took one last look around at the ward and the keep. "You have your work laid out for you," he told Graeham. "It won't be easy."

Graeham chuckled. "Nothing worth having ever is."

Hugh started to mount his horse, but Graeham placed a hand on his arm, stopping him. "Don't let her get away," he said in a low voice, just loud enough for Hugh to hear.

"Don't worry. She won't escape again."

"That isn't what I meant."

Hugh glowered at his brother. "I know what you meant."

Graeham stepped back as Hugh swung up into the saddle. This time when he spoke, his voice was loud enough for everyone to hear. "I suppose you will do what you want, regardless of whether it is good for you. You are as hardheaded and unyielding as ever, Hugh de Clairmont."

Adrienne glanced from Hugh to Graeham and wondered what had happened. Graeham sounded as if he was teasing, but there was a barb to his words. Judging from the look on Hugh's face, she suspected that he had just been pricked by that barb.

Hugh and Adrienne joined the rest of Hugh's men outside the castle gates. Adrienne tried to ignore the looks that followed them as they rode to the front of the column. She did not know why she felt so vulnerable, except that this time she was being judged for a situation that was of her own making.

She glanced at Hugh and caught him watching her, his expression pensive. Again she was struck by his handsomeness and by the power and strength he exuded. Her gaze darted briefly to his mouth, and she felt her face grow warm as she remembered those firm, sensual lips kissing her—all over. She forced her gaze back to the front. "Is what Graeham said true?" she asked. "Are we going to Sainte-Croix?"

"My brother talks too much."

Adrienne cast Hugh a sideways glance. In spite of his tense reply, she found herself suppressing a smile. She did not think anything could dampen her spirits this morning. "I would have figured it out eventually," she pointed out.

"I'm sure you would have," Hugh said dryly. He gave the order to move out.

Adrienne and Hugh headed the column. Riding alongside Hugh, Adrienne felt a strange mixture of pleasure and pride. She knew she should not feel this way, that she should hate Hugh for abducting her and turning her life upside down. Yet she didn't. She felt that she was riding alongside him not as his prisoner but as his partner—his wife.

She knew she was being silly. There had been no real change in her status; she was still his prisoner. Yet he was allowing her a measure of freedom that she had not been granted since leaving the barge. Riding her own horse might not make it any easier for her to escape, but it did give her an added advantage. Oddly, she felt no desire to abuse her newfound freedom.

Again she looked at Hugh. He was staring straight ahead, but there was strengthened determination, a renewed sense of purpose, in the set of his shoulders and the tilt of his jaw. Adrienne realized that he was glad to be going home, and she felt a bittersweet happiness for him. "May I ask you a question, my lord?"

"As long as you keep it civilized. Your questions, *princesse*, tend to be barbaric."

" 'Tis your reputation and that of Sainte-Croix that are barbaric," she corrected. "*I* am merely curious."

Hugh could not argue with that. In trying to justify seizing the countship, Henry had spread many bizarre rumors about Sainte-Croix and had succeeded in blackening Hugh's name. "What do you wish to know?" he asked.

"Until now you have kept me tied up, in irons, or under heavy guard. Why are you now permitting me to ride my own horse?"

Because I want you so badly that sitting with you so close makes me insane with longing, Hugh thought. He cast her a guarded glance. "Would you prefer to ride with me?"

"Most certainly not." Afraid of revealing her feelings, Adrienne gave her head an arrogant toss and fixed her gaze straight ahead. "I don't suppose 'tis because you have decided to trust me?"

Hugh laughed softly. "No."

"I thought not." Adrienne chewed on her bottom lip. "You have not yet given me an answer to my proposal. Is it possible that this change in our traveling arrangements means that you have decided to accept my oath of fealty?"

"No."

"No, you have not decided, or no, you will not accept my pledge?"

"As much as I would like to accept your pledge, *princesse*, I cannot in good conscience do so. Should you end up in Richard's hands, you may have to swear an oath of fealty to him in return for your life, and you will want to be certain Richard *believes* you. If he were to learn that you had already promised fealty to me, your credibility would suffer."

A sudden constriction in Adrienne's chest made it difficult to breathe. Although Hugh's reason for not accepting her oath of fealty made perfectly good sense, a vague uneasiness clouded her earlier happiness. "I see."

Hugh saw her troubled expression and smiled. "You need not worry, *princesse*. I have no intention of letting Richard get his hands on you. As long as you are with me, I promise that no harm will come to you."

His reassurance brought her little comfort. The more she thought about the situation she was in, the worse she felt. She had bargained away her virginity for nothing. *Nothing*.

Although she had known that she was taking a risk when she bargained with Hugh, his change in attitude toward her had given her reason to hope that he would accept her proposal. Instead, he had taken her virtue—no matter that she had given it to him; were he a man of honor, he would have refused it—and offered her nothing in return. She was still his prisoner. She was still headed for an uncertain future in a strange land.

She looked down at the pale mark that her betrothal ring had left on the third finger of her right hand, a visible reminder of the life she had traded away for a single night of passion. At the time it had seemed worth the risk; now she was beginning to realize just how foolhardy she had been. If hers had been the only life at stake, she would not have minded so much. But she had her knights to think of. And Marlys.

After a few minutes Hugh spoke. "You are suddenly very quiet. I fear that I have offended you. I assure you, that was never my intent."

Adrienne gripped the reins. "I was thinking about my knights and Marlys, and wondering what is to become of them. Will you continue to hold them prisoner indefinitely because of me?"

When Hugh did not answer, Adrienne felt an unreasoning sense of disquiet. She twisted around in the saddle and peered down the column, trying to spot a familiar face.

"They're not back there, *princesse*."

Adrienne sharply reined in her horse as uneasiness turned into panic.

Behind them, the column came to a halt.

"*Princesse*, you are holding everyone up."

"Where are my knights?" Adrienne demanded. "What have you done with them?"

Hugh grasped Adrienne's bridle and turned her horse back in the right direction. "Your knights and your maidservant were released this morning while you slept. They are on their way back to England."

Chapter Eleven

HUGH'S FACE BLURRED and shifted before Adrienne's eyes. She felt as if the ground had opened up and she was being sucked down into a dark, cold netherworld. She felt betrayed.

Gripping the reins, she resumed riding. She kept her gaze fixed straight ahead, not even acknowledging Hugh when he brought his horse into step with hers.

Hugh made no attempt to hide his annoyance. "I thought you would be pleased," he said brusquely. " 'Twas what you wanted—to have them released."

Released, yes! But not sent away where I will never see them again!

Adrienne fought to regain her composure. "You're right," she managed to get out, not looking at Hugh. "I-I am grateful to you. 'Tis only that the news came as a surprise. I had hoped . . ."

I had hoped to keep Marlys and the others with me so that I would not be surrounded entirely by enemies.

Adrienne fought back the tears that clogged her throat. "I wish I could have said good-bye to Marlys."

Hugh felt a twinge of guilt. His decision to send Adrienne's knights and Marlys back to England had not been selflessly motivated; the knights were under his orders to carry a message to King Richard. In planning how he was going to lure Richard into Sainte-Croix, he had forgotten

194

that Marlys had been Adrienne's only female companion since leaving her guardian's home. "It never crossed my mind that you would want to bid the girl farewell," he said. "I apologize for being so thoughtless."

Adrienne acknowledged his apology with a stiff nod. " 'Tis done. There is nothing to be gained by dwelling upon the matter."

They spoke little after that. The few times Hugh tried to initiate a conversation, Adrienne responded to his remarks in a lifeless monotone that invited no return comment. She felt like crying. The warmth and security that she had felt last night in his arms was gone. The lazy, groggy contentment that she had awakened to this morning was gone. The memories of their lovemaking no longer brought her a rush of pleasure, but made her ache with humiliation. She felt as if she had crawled too far out on a limb to claim a pear that was just beyond her reach, and the limb had snapped. The worst part was not knowing why she felt so miserable.

She tried to tell herself that she was glad her knights and Marlys were no longer Hugh's prisoners, but inwardly she was resentful that she too had not been freed. She tried to tell herself that Hugh had been magnanimous in honoring her request to release her knights and Marlys, but a less than gracious part of her was piqued that he had managed to do so in a way that made her feel as if she had lost more than she had gained.

"*Princesse*, I asked you a question."

Adrienne turned her head to stare blankly at him. "I'm sorry. I didn't hear you."

A nerve beneath Hugh's left eye began to twitch. His jaw tightened. "Forget it," he bit out. "Talking to you this past hour has been like trying to talk to a corpse. I am tired of humoring you." He turned his angry gaze back to the front.

Adrienne caught her bottom lip between her teeth and looked away. A terrible pressure swelled in her chest, and she was dangerously close to bursting into tears. She knew she was ruining this day for both of them. He had not meant to hurt her, and she was not being fair to him by punishing him for granting a request that she herself had made. She had already destroyed the intimacy that had blossomed between them. If this day was to be salvaged at all, it was up to her to stop wallowing in self-pity and make the first move toward reconciliation. She took a shaky breath. "I know I haven't been very good company today. I-I'm sorry."

Her apology was greeted with a stony wall of silence. Hugh did not look at her; he gave no acknowledgment whatsoever that she had even spoken.

Tears stung the back of Adrienne's nose. She steeled herself against the hurt she felt at Hugh's refusal to talk to her; after all, she had brought his anger upon herself. She tried again. " 'Tis very quiet without Graeham to entertain us with his teasing," she ventured. "I rather miss him. Don't you?"

Still no response from Hugh.

Adrienne fought the urge to turn around to see if anyone was listening to her make a fool of herself. "Let's talk about something else." She tried to force a lightness into her voice, but did not quite succeed. "Tell me about Sainte-Croix. What is it like there?"

Hugh snorted inelegantly. "Finally showing an interest in your dowry, *princesse*?"

Adrienne flinched at the unsheathed sarcasm in his voice. "I just thought that if I knew more about it"—her throat constricted—"then I wouldn't feel so . . . frightened."

At her unexpected admission, Hugh's anger abruptly evaporated. He turned his head to look at her. She was sitting stiffly in the saddle, clutching the reins in a white-knuckled grip, staring fixedly to the front. The color had drained from her face. He realized with a start that she truly was frightened, and he regretted having been so impatient with her. "You have no cause to be afraid," he said. "I gave you my word that I would protect you."

Adrienne took a deep breath and fought to get her emotions back under control. "I cannot change my feelings simply because you tell me I'm not entitled to them," she said defensively.

"I never said you were not entitled to your feelings, *princesse*. I'm merely trying to figure out what it is you are afraid of."

Adrienne did not respond. If anything, she seemed to withdraw even further.

They rode in silence for several minutes. "Are you afraid of me?" Hugh finally asked. When she did not immediately answer, he added quietly, "I've given you every reason to be."

Adrienne glanced at him. He was right; he *had* given her reason to fear him. Marlys was terrified of him, and he had treated Marlys far more kindly than he had her. Yet, in spite of all that had happened, in spite of all that he had done to her, she did not fear him nearly so much as she feared being without him. The irony of that realization caused an involuntary smile to tug at the corners of her mouth.

She averted her gaze, but not before Hugh had seen the break in her composure. "What?" he asked.

She shook her head. " 'Tis nothing."

"I saw you smile, *princesse*. Don't try to deny it."

Adrienne felt her face growing warm. " 'Tis nothing," she repeated.

Hugh shot her a look of exasperation. "You are the most infuriating woman I have ever known," he said peevishly. "First you are sullen, then you are afraid, and now you are smirking, and you refuse to tell me why. I am beginning to feel like a court jester who has been put on this earth for your amusement and who is falling short of your expectations."

In spite of his curt tone, there was an undercurrent of vulnerability in Hugh's statement that touched something deep inside her; and she realized that, although he would probably deny it, he too had an inherent need to feel loved and accepted. "If you must know," she said, "I was thinking that I feel safe when I am with you."

Inwardly, Hugh felt an immense pleasure at her confession. Outwardly, he eyed her with skepticism. "And that made you smirk?"

"It made me *smile*," she corrected him. Then she added in a low, pensive voice, "And it makes me afraid, too, because I don't *want* to need you."

Several minutes passed before Hugh spoke. "Why did you come to my chamber last night?"

Because I couldn't bear to be away from you.

Adrienne shrugged. "Because I was weary of feeling helpless. Because I wanted to take control of my own fate."

When he did not answer, Adrienne glanced at him. His expression was unreadable.

"Is that so hard to understand?" she asked.

Hugh regarded her thoughtfully for a moment. "If you could do it over again, would you stay away?"

A combination of embarrassment and sadness filled her expressive eyes.

"No," she said softly.

On the fourth day they reached the foothills of the Alps. Although it was not yet nightfall, Hugh ordered his men to set up camp.

When she returned from tending to her private needs, Adrienne looked around her in bewilderment at the tents that were going up. "Why are we stopping here?" she asked.

Hugh relinquished his war-horse to his squire's care and started across the camp toward his tent. "My men need to rest, and they need to clean and repair their weapons and armor," he said.

Although Adrienne suspected he was keeping something from her, she refrained from pressing the matter. As she walked alongside him, she rubbed her arms to warm them and looked around her at the rolling hills that were showing the first traces of the bright golds and reds of autumn. The air was distinctly cooler here and not as heavy as it had been in the lower elevations. "Are we close to Sainte-Croix?" she asked.

"Sainte-Croix is on the other side of the mountains. The nearest border is about a six-day march from here."

The men's gazes followed them across the camp. Although their stares made Adrienne self-conscious, she was learning to ignore them. One of the benefits of Hugh's protection was that the men dared do no more than stare. Knowing full well the penalty for touching her, they wisely kept their distance.

Adrienne knew that the men were aware that she shared Hugh's bed at night, and the knowledge caused her no small amount of worry. At times she felt consumed by shame; at other times she reacted with proud defiance, unwilling to concede to any wrongdoing. She would awaken in the morning after a night of lovemaking with the unshakable confidence of a woman who knew she was wanted and cherished, and by midday she would be despondent with the certain knowledge that she was doomed to burn in hell.

But no matter how she felt throughout the day, at night, when Hugh rolled toward her and took her in his arms, the rest of the world ceased to exist. His touch had succeeded where irons had failed—he no longer needed chains to keep her at his side; she had lost her will to flee.

When they reached his tent, Hugh went straight to a large chest that had been placed beside his. It was of a dark polished wood held together by wide brass bands and inlaid with gold and ivory and shell pearl. Adrienne recognized immediately that it was not one of Hugh's, and when he bent and raised the lid, her curiosity got the best of her and she strained her neck to see what the chest held.

Hugh straightened and turned to fix her with a boyish grin. "These bolts of cloth are for you, *princesse*. Since we are going to be here for a few days, I thought you might welcome the chance to expand your wardrobe."

Since her wardrobe consisted of one squire's tunic and a pair of chausses that were becoming the worse for wear, Adrienne was hard-pressed to contain her excitement. She looked at the chest and then at Hugh, her eyes bright with obvious pleasure. "You are very generous, my lord. I-I don't know how to thank you."

Although her smile was reward enough, Hugh was not about to let an opportunity pass without taking full advantage of it. His eyes darkened. "Come here," he said huskily.

A few days ago Adrienne would have balked at his arbitrary order. Now she went to him without hesitation. As his arms went around her, she rose up on tiptoe and reached around his neck to draw his head down.

Hugh crushed her to him, and Adrienne surrendered to his kiss, reveling in the strength of his arms around her and the feel of his lips on hers.

His touch was like an opiate, satisfying her body's cravings as it awakened new ones in her. She could not get enough of him. She wished that this moment could last forever and that she could spend the rest of her life wrapped securely in the protective warmth of his arms, where the rest of the world could not intrude.

When Hugh finally lifted his head, she could not suppress a pang of disappointment. She tilted back her head and smiled up at him. "Thank you," she said.

Still holding her tightly against him, Hugh lifted a wayward curl away from her face. Laughter threaded through the passion that darkened his eyes. "For the kiss?" he teased.

Adrienne wrinkled her brow with feigned annoyance. "For the *cloth*," she said.

Hugh's expression became unreadable. "Thank *you* for the kiss," he said quietly.

He brushed his lips against her forehead before releasing her. "I will be gone for a few hours. There are needles and thread and other sewing implements in the chest. If you find you need anything else, tell Gabel and he will get it for you. Don't leave the camp. After my men have scouted the area and set up perimeters, you will be free to roam farther afield."

'Twas a far cry from the days when Hugh had resorted to extreme measures to control her movements, and Adrienne could not resist a jest. She clasped her hands behind her back and tilted her head to one side. "What, no ropes? No chains? No armed guards to keep me from taking flight?"

When Hugh turned to look at her, she punctuated her query with an imperious lifting of her brows that took Hugh by surprise. That she could joke about something that had caused her pain and humiliation deepened his respect for her. He also found himself fighting the urge to take her in his arms again and kiss her senseless.

"Insolent wench," he growled.

Adrienne's spontaneous laugh followed him to the tent opening. Hugh reached for the tent flap, then hesitated. He regarded her sternly. "I'll have your word, *princesse*, that you'll not try to escape."

Dimples appeared at the corners of Adrienne's mouth. "My lord, you have my word."

After Hugh left the tent, Adrienne's smile faded, and a terrible weight settled in her chest. "And my heart," she added achingly.

During the three weeks that Hugh's men stayed in their temporary camp, the weather held. The days were sunny and warm, the nights crisp with the promise of winter. As Hugh gradually permitted Adrienne more and more freedom, she fell into the habit of carrying her sewing up a nearby hill where she could sit in the soft grass in full view of the camp, sheltered from the wind, and enjoy the warmth of the sun.

On one particularly pleasant afternoon as they neared the end of their stay, Hugh joined her on the hill. She glanced up from her sewing and smiled a greeting. A tingling quickened inside her at his approach. She never ceased to be amazed at her body's reaction to him. Just recalling their lovemaking was often enough to bring her to the brink of release; at times he had but to barely touch her to shatter her control.

She thought he looked particularly handsome today. He was not wearing his chain mail but was clad in a plain brown knee-length tunic and chausses that hugged his long powerful legs like a second skin. Days spent in the sun had turned his skin a deep bronze that perfectly complemented his black hair and dark, piercing eyes, and Adrienne knew firsthand that if he removed his tunic, his tan would extend all the way to his waist.

Without warning, she jabbed herself with the needle.

"Ouch!" She dropped the needle and shook her hand as if to shake off the sting. She frowned at the bead of crimson that formed on the pad of her forefinger. "Weeks of idleness have made me clumsy. I've had to learn to sew all over again."

Hugh lowered himself to the ground beside her and gave her a wounded look. "And here I thought 'twas my presence that rattled your composure."

Adrienne snorted inelegantly. "You flatter yourself, my lord. You are not nearly so fearsome a foe as an unco-operative needle and a tangled thread."

"Is that so?" Hugh took hold of her hand.

Adrienne's breath caught in her throat as Hugh lifted her hand to his mouth. He drew her wounded finger into his mouth and sucked on it, all the while watching her through hooded eyes. The rough-gentle feel of his tongue teasing her finger was nearly Adrienne's undoing. She could not move, even to withdraw her hand. It was as if he held her captive with those dark, hypnotic eyes of his. "Aye, 'tis so," she said shakily.

Finally Hugh released her hand.

With trembling fingers, Adrienne secured her needle in the soft russet wool of the mantle she had been making and set the half-sewn garment aside. Acutely aware of his nearness and of his caressing gaze on her, she turned her attention toward the valley spread out before them. " 'Tis beautiful here," she said.

"I agree. That color suits you."

"I was talking about the *mountains*."

Hugh's gaze roamed over her. "I wasn't."

Feeling self-conscious, Adrienne looked down at the bliaud she had completed two days ago, and fingered the dark blue wool. "The cloth is the finest I have ever seen, my lord. Thank you for giving it to me."

"You wear it well, *princesse*. I regret that I could not have given it to you sooner."

Adrienne felt her face grow warm. Eager to change the subject, she pointed to a bird circling above a rocky ledge on the next hill. "Oh, look!"

Hugh followed her gaze. "A falcon," he said.

"A tiercel," Adrienne corrected him without thinking. Then, realizing what she had done, she quickly added, "The only reason I know the difference is because I've been watching him for the past few days. His mate is close by. They look like peregrines, although I can't be certain at this distance."

Hugh regarded her with interest. "You're right. That one is a peregrine."

Adrienne's expression became pensive. "My guardian has several peregrines. Adal is my favorite. She is not at all temperamental with me, although she becomes nervous around strangers. I used to take her hunting every chance I got."

Adrienne pulled back her sleeve to show Hugh the raised white scars on her left forearm. "See these scars? Before I learned how to hold the jesses, Adal would perch on my arm instead of on the gauntlet. And she would try to climb up my arm if she thought I had a treat for her." Adrienne's voice dropped. "I miss her so much. Lord Baldhere was going to send her to me once I was wed, but now I suppose

I'll never see her again. She was more than just a falcon; she was my best friend. My only friend. Whenever I felt sad or frightened, I would tell her my troubles. Sometimes I could have sworn she knew what I was saying."

Understanding reflected in Hugh's eyes. "Animals sense our moods, *princesse*, even if they cannot interpret our words. In that way they are superior to human beings. *We* can be remarkably obtuse."

"Did you have a favored animal as a child, my lord?"

"A horse," Hugh said without hesitation. "He was coal black and full of fire. I took him out one day without permission. He was not yet trained, but I was certain I could control him. He broke his neck in a fall."

"I'm sorry."

Hugh drew up one knee and rested his arm across it. His eyes clouded as the painful memories surfaced. "I paid a price for my eagerness. Unfortunately, my horse paid an even greater price."

Although he had spoken in a voice that was devoid of emotion, there was no mistaking the pain that shadowed his eyes. Adrienne remembered Graeham telling her that even as a child Hugh had been far too serious, and she wondered if he was solemn by nature or if the guilt he felt for causing his horse's death had crushed whatever boyish exuberance he might have had. " 'Twas an accident, my lord," she said softly. "You cannot hold yourself to blame for something that could not be helped."

"I was eight years old, *princesse*, old enough to know better."

Adrienne thought Hugh was being unduly harsh on himself, but she sensed from his tone that he would not welcome either her opinion or her continued pursuit of the matter.

"There is a falcon mews at Château Clairmont," Hugh said, diverting the conversation away from a memory that still pained him, even after all these years. "Unless it has been destroyed in my absence," he added.

Adrienne felt her stomach knot. The reminder of why they were here cast a pall on her contentment. "How long have you been away?" she asked softly.

Hugh stared out across the valley. "Two years," he said absently, as though his thoughts were far away. "I traveled to Jerusalem with the intention of being gone only a few months; instead, I returned to find that my lands had been seized and that I had a price on my head."

"Jerusalem! My lord, the Truce of God forbids seizure of a man's lands while he is in the Holy Land!"

"Only if he goes there to fight for the cross, *princesse*. I went there to secure Graeham's release from a Saracen jail."

"But that is no cause to confiscate Sainte-Croix and drive you into exile. My father must have been mad!"

The vehemence of Adrienne's protest made Hugh think of a she-bear defending her cubs, and he caught himself wondering what kind of mother she would be to her children.

" 'Twas not the countship Henry wanted, but Sainte-Croix's seaports," Hugh said. "Both England and France desire use of the ports to launch an invasion of Jerusalem, something I would not permit as long as I was in control of Sainte-Croix."

Adrienne frowned. "I don't understand. Why would you not allow my father to use the seaports to do God's work? Do you not want the infidels driven from the Holy Land?"

"It does not matter to me who rules Jerusalem as long as he is fair-minded. In spite of what the Church would have us believe, *princesse*, holy wars are the unholiest wars of all."

Instead of satisfying her curiosity, Hugh's comments rekindled an unease that had been with her from the day she learned Sainte-Croix was to be her dowry. Although Adrienne could find no logical argument against Hugh's refusal to allow Sainte-Croix to be used as a point of departure to the Holy Land, it troubled her that he could defy the Church with such unwavering conviction. She had nearly convinced herself that there was no truth to the ugly rumors that she had heard about Sainte-Croix, but now she was not so certain.

Hugh chuckled softly at her distressed expression. "You look as cheerful as a condemned felon on the way to his hanging," he teased.

"My lord, the better I have come to know you during these past weeks, the more I believe you are truly honorable, and justified in trying to reclaim the land that is your birthright. Yet I cannot help fearing for your soul."

One dark brow quirked upward in surprise. "Assuming I even have a soul, why would it be in jeopardy?"

Adrienne fidgeted. "I know it angers you when I speak of this, but I've heard so many unsettling rumors about Sainte-Croix—and about you—that 'tis impossible for me to know wherein lies the truth."

Understanding dawned in Hugh's eyes. "Such as my supposed fondness for roasting and eating children?"

Adrienne colored hotly. "Yes. I know now that I was mistaken about that, yet pilgrims who traveled through Foutreau spoke of other evils as well. They told of people worshiping the severed heads of heathen idols and invoking the souls of the dead and denying the cross. Everything I have ever heard about Sainte-Croix makes me think it is a dark, godless land full of heretics."

Which would explain why Adrienne was so afraid of going there, Hugh thought. "Tell me, *princesse*, how do you justify the thousands of God-fearing Christians who, at mass, resort to consuming the body and blood of the man they hold most holy?"

Adrienne's expression changed from one of horror to one of bewilderment. "But my lord, 'tis not really the body and blood of Christ. I mean, we are supposed to believe it is, but in reality 'tis merely bread and wine."

"Yet the Church would have you believe otherwise."

"Yes, but—"

"Just as the Church would have you believe that the symbolic rituals practiced by those of other faiths are satanic and should be crushed. The Church wants Sainte-Croix as much as Henry did, as much as Richard and John do now, and it will resort to any excuse to justify seizing the countship, including slandering its inhabitants."

"Then they are not heretics?"

"*Princesse*, one man's heretic is another man's believer," Hugh said gently. "The people of Sainte-Croix consider themselves as Christian as those who follow the Church in Rome. They do not deny the existence of Christ; they merely question his divinity. They believe he was a human being who was persecuted by his government the way they are persecuted by the pope. Many abstain from eating meat. Some believe that marriage is a sin because its purpose is to bring more children into a world that they believe is inherently evil. They allow women to give sermons and even to become priests."

"Women priests!"

"Why not? Is a woman less capable of delivering God's word than a man?"

Adrienne cast Hugh an embarrassed glance from beneath her lashes. "In truth, my lord, I sometimes think women are better suited to the task because we are more sympathetic to the human plight, yet 'tis heresy!"

"Not to the people of Sainte-Croix. To them, the followers of the Roman Church are the heretics."

Adrienne was beginning to feel defensive. While Hugh had not exactly attacked her beliefs, he had shaken her ability to accept them without question. She shook her head. "I'm sorry, my lord, but I find it hard to accept the integrity of a people who owe their fealty to a man who adorns his surcoats and his shields with the likeness of a *serpent*. Of all the beasts of the wild, why could you not have chosen for your badge a noble creature such as a lion or an eagle?"

At the unexpected twist in the conversation, Hugh threw back his head and laughed.

Adrienne bristled. She did not like being laughed at.
" 'Tis not funny, my lord," she said. "Any who see the
serpent of Sainte-Croix are likely to jump to the conclusion
that you yourself are an agent of the devil. How can you
bear to be so maligned in the eyes of your peers and those
who would serve you?"

Mirth sparkled in Hugh's eyes. "Ah, *princesse*, the tale
behind my serpent badge is so mundane that you are likely
to be disappointed."

When Adrienne tilted her head to one side and eyed him
expectantly, Hugh explained. "When one of my ancestors
was trying to decide the best location for siting the château,
he discovered numerous caves in the area. Some of those
caves were infested with snakes. He found that people
would stay away if they thought snakes were present, so
he stored his valuables within the caves and posted banners
warning of poisonous vipers. The ruse worked so well that
he carried it a step further and adopted the serpent for his
arms. The sign of the serpent was enough to strike fear into
the hearts of even the bravest men, and served to keep his
enemies at bay."

Adrienne regarded him warily. "That is all? The serpent
is not intended to represent the earthly guise of Satan?"

"That is all," Hugh said flatly. "There is nothing symbolic or mysterious about my family's use of the serpent
on our arms. 'Twas merely a practical solution to the eter-
nal problem of how to guard one's valuables and one's
life."

Although Adrienne could not help feeling that Hugh was
intentionally keeping something from her, the subject made
her so uneasy that she readily dropped it. "You said you
went to Jerusalem to free Graeham from jail. How did he
come to be there when you are so adamantly opposed to the
Church's efforts to keep the kingdom of Jerusalem under
Christian rule?"

"Graeham does not share my reluctance to meddle in foreign affairs. He fought in Palestine with Girard de Ridefort.

When Saladin captured Jerusalem, Graeham was taken prisoner. I went to the Holy Land to pay his ransom."

Drawing her legs up, Adrienne wrapped her arms around them and rested her chin on her knees. Her expression was pensive. "And while you were gone, my father seized Sainte-Croix."

"Yes."

Adrienne mulled that one over for a few minutes. "Is that why you and Graeham had a falling-out?" she asked at last. "Do you blame him for losing Sainte-Croix?"

Hugh's expression became closed. "No."

At Hugh's obvious unwillingness to continue discussing either his brother or Sainte-Croix, the conversation turned to other topics. But Adrienne's mind still churned with dozens of unasked questions, and she could not help wondering what had happened to drive the two brothers apart.

That night in Hugh's tent, as they lay in each other's arms, Adrienne broached the subject of Sainte-Croix again. "May I ask you a question?" she whispered in the darkness.

Hugh's hand slid down over her abdomen and into the triangle of soft hair between her thighs. Although he had just made love to her a short time ago, his need for her was insatiable. He wanted her again. "Considering where your questions lead, *princesse*, are you sure that's wise?" he murmured into her ear.

"Only one question, my lord. I promise." Adrienne sucked in her breath as Hugh's exploring fingers touched a particularly sensitive spot.

Hugh reluctantly relented. "One question. No more."

"Do you remember those things you told me about your people's beliefs?"

Hugh trailed his lips down her neck. "Mmmm."

Adrienne wasn't certain if he had said yes or no. She was finding it more and more difficult to maintain her concentration. Every time Hugh touched her, it was as if she lost her will to resist him. Assuming he had answered in the affirmative, she continued, "Do you believe those things also, my lord?"

Although Hugh lifted his head to study her face in the darkness, his fingers continued with their seduction. "That was two questions, *princesse*."

A delicious warmth swept over Adrienne, and she shuddered. "My lord, please!"

Hugh shifted his weight over her and parted her thighs with his knee. "I don't believe in anything," he said thickly.

As his words began to sink in, Adrienne felt an overwhelming sadness for him. It must be terribly lonely, she thought, to have not even God to talk to. *Please, God, watch over him. He is a good man who doesn't realize the error of his beliefs.*

Then Hugh eased his engorged shaft into her, and Adrienne forgot what she was praying for.

For the second time in his life, Sir Leland found himself waiting in the antechamber of Duke Wilhelm's private quarters. The first time was when he carried Henry's missive to the duke. The room had not changed. A crucifix made from a dark fine-grained wood hung on one wall. Although the eyes of the carved likeness of the Jesus appeared to be closed when observed head on, when Leland turned, they seemed to open and follow him about the chamber. A chill touched Leland's spine. The oppressive, joyless atmosphere of the ducal palace reminded him of a tomb.

He hoped, for Lady Adrienne's sake, that Duke Wilhelm possessed a more forgiving disposition than his living quarters would imply.

Sir Leland had discovered that Lady Adrienne was missing from the barge when he went to her cabin to take over guard duty from Sir Pearroc and found the knight unconscious from a blow to the back of the head. After several long, tense days of searching the riverbanks, Henry's knights located the spot where a small boat had been dragged ashore. They had then found a trail that eventually brought them to a large clearing where Leland estimated that several hundred men had made camp.

A group that large, mounted on horseback, could only be an army, or part of one.

No one knew who had taken Lady Adrienne, although nearly everyone had an opinion. Some of the men said it was King Richard. Others thought Prince John had the strongest motive for abducting her.

From the campsite the trail became easier to follow, although the reasons for its direction were not always easy to determine. The trail appeared to be leading into Lorraine, then made an abrupt turn toward the south. What had happened? Leland wondered. Had they met up with an adversary or merely been warned of the approach of one? There were no signs of fighting, so Leland was inclined to believe the latter.

When Leland and his men reached Burg Moudon, the answers began to fall rapidly into place.

For a week they quartered at Burg Moudon under the pretense of being pilgrims en route to the Holy Land. They learned that the castle had recently seen heavy fighting; that the Comte de Sainte-Croix had taken control of the keep, and Prince John's forces had fled across the river.

For a week they observed the rebuilding of dwellings that had been damaged in the battle. They saw laborers clearing away the forest between the keep and the river, and surveyors marking off the location of a new outer curtain wall. During the day they offered suggestions for strengthening the keep's defenses; at night they enjoyed its hospitality.

The more Leland got to know his host, the more he liked him. Graeham de Clairmont was an affable, intelligent young man who inspired his followers by his example and with his enthusiasm rather than by giving orders and issuing threats. Yet he was also, Leland noticed, remarkably closemouthed when it came to divulging any information regarding his elder brother.

Because he did not want to arouse Graeham de Clairmont's suspicions, Leland had to take care when questioning the servants. He was able to learn that Hugh de Clairmont had left Burg Moudon with a female companion. However, because the woman had apparently gone with Hugh of her own free will and on her own horse, Leland doubted she was Lady Adrienne. From his own acquaintance with Henry's daughter, Leland could not visualize that strong-willed beauty going anywhere with her captor without putting up a fierce struggle.

After a week, neither he nor Theobald of Mainz nor any of their men were able to turn up any evidence that Lady Adrienne had ever been at Burg Moudon. Acknowledging defeat, they prepared to move out after spending one final night at the keep.

Graeham de Clairmont saw to it that they were adequately provisioned for their journey. He gave them the names of knights who had fought with him in Palestine and asked that he be remembered to them should their paths cross. And that night he had a sumptuous feast prepared in their honor.

Leland had found himself reluctant to leave Burg Moudon. He was no longer a young man, and knighthood was a calling better suited to those with more resilience in their bones. Graeham de Clairmont seemed to be an honorable man and one who would be a fair overlord. Had he not already been bound by an oath of fealty, Leland would not have minded remaining at Burg Moudon.

But his loyalty was to Lady Adrienne. She was more to him than the daughter of the king he had once served; she was also the daughter of the woman he had never stopped loving. Had Isolde de Langeais accepted his marriage proposal, they might have had a daughter together. In a way he had come to think of Adrienne as his daughter. He could not abandon her now.

That night there was much gaiety and revelry at the high table at Burg Moudon. Food was plentiful and well prepared, and the wine flowed with a plentitude that guaranteed them all heavy heads come morning. Graeham called everyone in the great hall to attention. He stood and raised his goblet high. "I wish to propose a toast," he announced.

Servants scrambled to refill goblets and tankards.

Graeham grinned. "First, to my brother. May he come to his senses in time to realize what is good for him."

That one drew a burst of laughter from all corners of the hall. Leland saw no hidden meaning in Graeham's comment, and he laughed along with the others. Many young noblemen were afflicted with an overabundance of stubbornness; he doubted Hugh de Clairmont was any different.

Graeham continued. "And to our guests. May they have a safe journey, and may they succeed where those before them have failed, in driving Saladin and his infidels out of Jerusalem!"

The cheers that accompanied Graeham's toast were shattered by the sound of a wine jug crashing to the floor and a shriek from one of the serving girls.

Leland instinctively leapt to his feet and reached for his sword.

On Graeham's right, Theobald of Mainz had seized the wrist of the girl who had been filling his goblet.

"What are you doing?" Graeham demanded of the chancellor.

Theobald of Mainz wrenched the girl's hand up into the air. The light of the torches reflected in his snakelike eyes, making them glow red in his scarred face. "Where did you get this ring?" he bit out.

The frightened serving girl began to cry. "I-I didn't steal it, m'lord; I swear," she stammered between sobs. "I found it in one of the b-bedchambers."

Leland's gaze dropped to the ornate gold ring on the girl's finger, and his heart seemed to stop beating.

It was Lady Adrienne's betrothal ring.

Leland's thoughts snapped back to the present as the massive wooden doors leading to Duke Wilhelm's private apartment swung open and six guards exited the chamber escorting a fettered and manacled prisoner. As he was being led from the chamber, Graeham de Clairmont turned his head and boldly met Leland's gaze. His dark eyes burned with the promise of revenge.

Theobald of Mainz appeared on the threshold. "Duke Wilhelm will see you now," he said.

Leland gritted his teeth. If a man had ever gotten under his skin more than Theobald, he had not yet met him. During the past two months he had fallen into the habit of amusing himself by plotting the chancellor's demise, and more than once he had come close to killing the sanctimonious little man with his bare hands.

As if he could read the knight's mind, Theobald smiled thinly and said, "Duke Wilhelm has been generous in granting you an audience. Try not to waste his time."

Duke Wilhelm's private study was as stark and devoid of ornamentation as the rest of the palace. There were no tapestries to warm the walls, and no fire burned on the hearth to lessen the bite of the chill that permeated the chamber. Furnishings were few, consisting of a long table and a single upright chest whose doors were carved with a labyrinth design that matched the one on Adrienne's betrothal ring. Stacked on one end of the table were a number of scrolls with cracked and discolored edges that hinted at their antiquity.

Duke Wilhelm sat at the table in the chamber's only chair, a massive high-backed affair with arms carved in the shape of a lion's paws. The last time Leland had met the duke, his judgment had been unclouded by emotional attachment. He had been acting on Henry's command, carrying out Henry's last wishes. He had not yet known Lady Adrienne, nor had he cared how she might feel about her betrothed husband. Now he regarded the duke with the critical eye of a father assessing his own daughter's future happiness. Henry, he thought bleakly, must have been mad.

Duke Wilhelm appeared to be approaching his sixtieth year. His features were gaunt and hawklike, and his skin and the whites of his eyes possessed a jaundiced tinge, as if he suffered from frequent attacks of yellow bile. His hair was long and unkempt and was thinning on the top of his head. He did not stand when Leland entered the chamber, but observed the knight's approach with bright, feverish eyes.

Leland dutifully dropped to one knee before the duke in a gesture of obeisance.

"Rise," Wilhelm commanded.

Leland obeyed.

Wilhelm placed his folded hands on top of the table. "I am not at all pleased that you allowed my affianced wife to be seized by outlaws," he said. "She was entrusted to you to be delivered unto me without incident. That you were so careless in executing your duties leads me to wonder at the rabble on which King Henry was forced to rely in his final days."

Leland stiffened but did not respond. He knew it was useless to try to defend himself. Those such as Wilhelm of Lachen were seldom swayed in their opinions.

"My bride is in the hands of that heretic, Hugh de Clairmont," Wilhelm continued. "If I lose Sainte-Croix because of your stupidity, I shall hold you responsible."

Leland could not help thinking that Lady Adrienne was better off with Hugh de Clairmont than she would ever be with Wilhelm of Lachen. "All is not lost, my lord," Leland said, carefully choosing his words. "I shall go after Lady Adrienne, and I shall bring her back."

"*My men* will go after the girl," Wilhelm corrected. "You and your companions will remove yourselves from my presence without delay. I no longer have need of your services."

Leland felt as if the duke had just delivered him a blow to the gut. " 'Tis not my intent to contradict you, my lord, but I cannot leave. Lady Adrienne is my mistress. My allegiance is to her until she releases me from my vow."

The duke's feverish, fanatical gaze bored into him. "I speak for the girl, knight. You are now a free agent. You have twenty-four hours to leave this principality. Should you cross these borders again, you will be hanged as a criminal."

Leland bowed stiffly at the waist. "Yes, my lord."

"You are dismissed."

Leland turned toward the door to find Theobald eyeing him with self-righteous disdain. The chancellor opened the door for him and stepped back. Fighting the urge to fly at Theobald and wrap his hands around the man's neck, Leland left the chamber.

After Leland had gone, Wilhelm glanced at Theobald. "Have him followed," he ordered.

Chapter Twelve

HUGH'S ARMY ABANDONED its temporary camp in the foothills of the Alps and pressed southward. After several weeks of idleness, it felt good to Hugh to be on the move again. He glanced over at Adrienne who was riding next to him on her own mount. She sat tall in the saddle, with her head held high. The wind whipped her dark hair away from her face and pinkened her cheeks. Her expression was open and inquisitive as she observed everything around her with a childlike absorption.

"Are you warm enough?" Hugh asked.

Adrienne turned her head to look at him. Her gray wool mantle heightened the gray of her eyes. She smiled, and dimples appeared at the corners of her mouth. "I'm fine, thank you. Tell me, my lord, is Sainte-Croix as beautiful as this?"

Only with you in it, Hugh thought. " 'Tis more rugged," he said. "In some places there is not an inch of level ground for building and planting. The towns cling like eagles' nests to the sides of the mountains and are often accessible only by a single steep road."

Adrienne's brows drew together as she tried to envision a landscape totally unlike the gently rolling hills of the shire where she had spent her childhood. "It must be terribly desolate," she mused aloud.

Hugh chuckled. "Not at all, *princesse*. Farmers have

tamed the slopes with terraced vineyards and olive groves, and they produce some of the best wine on the Continent as well as a fine oil flavored with rosemary. I think you will find Sainte-Croix to be quite civilized."

As they rode, Hugh told her about the lavender that grew wild on the hillsides, filling the air with its aromatic scent every summer when it bloomed. He told her of limestone houses with tile roofs, of farmers who hauled their produce into town on donkey-drawn carts, and of flocks of sheep that often blocked the roads, making passage impossible until the astute traveler bribed the attendant shepherd with a jug of wine. He told her how the late summer rains would wash the dust out of the air and leave the sky so clear that from many of the towns one could see all the way to the sea.

"You make it sound like a paradise," Adrienne said.

"Paradise tempered with reality," Hugh conceded. "There are days in midsummer when it is unwise for those of a weaker constitution to venture out into the sun without a head covering. And in the winter, when the master wind roars down from the mountains, even the most stouthearted choose to stay inside near a warming fire."

"It seems like a land of such extremes. Sometimes I don't think I will ever understand it—or its people."

"Are you still afraid of going there?"

Adrienne cast Hugh an impish glance. "I have had a master wind roaring at me these two months past," she said lightly. "If I can tolerate *him*, I can learn to live with anything."

Hugh threw back his head and laughed.

At noon the next day they met up with the counts of Toulouse, Foix, and Vernier and their armies. Hugh rode ahead to greet them, leaving Adrienne behind with Sir Conraed and the rest of his men.

From her vantage point it appeared to Adrienne as if the newcomers numbered in the hundreds, if not the thousands.

"Is everything all right?" she asked Conraed.

"You need not worry," the knight assured her. "They are allies."

Allies or not, their arrival made Adrienne uneasy.

Adrienne saw nothing of Hugh the rest of the day. Conraed and Roland and Etienne took turns trying to keep her entertained as they traveled, amusing her with tales of their travels and of their youth. While Adrienne appreciated their efforts, she could not help straining her neck from time to time in hopes of catching a glimpse of Hugh.

Seeing where her attention strayed, Roland asked, "You are fond of him, aren't you?"

Adrienne turned her head to look at the man who had nearly given his life for her that day she had been attacked by the outlaw knights. Conraed and Etienne had ridden ahead to confer with Hugh. Although she did not know Roland well, Adrienne felt a quiet kinship with him, as if that fateful day in the clearing had cemented a permanent bond between them. "I love him," she said simply.

Roland did not laugh as another might have done, nor did he tell her she was being foolish. If anything, his expression seemed to grow even more serious. "Lord Hugh is not an easy man to love, my lady," he said.

" 'Twas not my will to fall in love, my lord. I would gladly have chosen a less painful fate."

Roland regarded her thoughtfully. "If he loved you in return, would you still choose otherwise?"

"If he loved me in return, my lord, we would not be having this conversation."

Hugh does love you, Roland thought. "You have a point, my lady," he said.

Adrienne's grin failed to mask the raw ache that darkened her eyes. "Are you conceding defeat, my lord?"

"Only for the sake of chivalry. I have four sisters, my lady. Each of them spent years impressing upon me that it is impolite to argue with a lady."

"Impolite, my lord? Or futile?"

Roland could not help laughing. "Dangerous," he corrected.

Night was well upon them when they finally made camp. Conraed escorted Adrienne to a tent in the middle of the camp and left her there with instructions to send for him should she need anything.

Taking the lighted candle Conraed had given her, Adrienne went inside the tent. She stopped and looked around her in bewilderment.

At first she thought Conraed might have made a mistake. The tent was smaller than the one she shared with Hugh, and it did not contain Hugh's trunks or any of the usual furnishings. A pile of folded furs and blankets lay on the ground against a side wall, ready to be turned into a sleeping pallet. Beside the bedding stood two small chests: the ornate one that held the fabrics and sewing implements that Hugh had brought from Burg Moudon, and another, plainer, one that Hugh had given to her to hold her clothing and her growing assortment of personal belongings.

Unwilling to accept what she saw, Adrienne turned and ducked through the tent opening. She was brought up short by two lances that suddenly crossed in front of her. She gasped and drew back in surprise, then stared in disbelief at the knights who blocked her exit. After weeks of relative freedom she had not been prepared for the sight of armed guards posted outside her tent. "I-I was looking for Lord Hugh," she stammered.

"Lord Hugh does not wish to be disturbed," one of the knights said.

"But I was only going to—"

"I am sorry, m'lady. Those were his orders."

A terrible pain swelled in Adrienne's chest, cutting off her air. "I see."

"If you wish, m'lady, I can send for Sir Conraed."

Adrienne shoved her hair away from her face with her free hand and struggled to regain her composure. The memory of how Hugh had abandoned her after the arrival of his allies and the realization that he was intentionally avoiding her now made her feel as if she might be ill. "That won't be necessary," she said in a low, hollow voice. She turned and went back inside the tent.

Her hand shook, causing the candle flame to dip and flicker. She looked around her at the erratic shadows on the tent walls. Desolation swept over her. Not once since that night at Burg Moudon when she had gone to Hugh's bedchamber had they spent a night apart. Now not only had he relegated her to her own tent but he had offered no explanation.

If only he had given her a reason, she thought dismally, she would be able to understand why she was suddenly being cast off. She would understand why he no longer wanted her. She would understand why . . .

She squeezed her eyes shut and fought back the threatening tears. In truth, no explanation would have been sufficient to ease the crushing ache in her heart. She had misled herself into thinking that she would be safe as long as she was with Hugh. She had misled herself into thinking that she could make him fall in love with her as she had fallen in love with him.

She had been wrong, terribly wrong. Hugh would never love her. To him she was no more than a temporary diversion, a common wench who had been willing to warm his bed for a time.

A whore.

Her shoulders lurched forward and began to jerk with sobs. She had given herself to Hugh without the benefit of marriage, and now she was paying the price.

Hugh told his allies of the treachery involving Prince John and the Duke of Lorraine and of the attack on Burg Moudon. The men sat by the campfire. "Lorraine has been invaluable," Hugh said. "Without his help, we would never have been able to capture Lady Adrienne. But now that he is being detained by Prince John, we will have to proceed without him."

"We don't need Lorraine's help," Vernier said. "Our joint armies number well over sixteen hundred, not including Lorraine's men. We can easily retake Sainte-Croix without him."

Although Hugh had counted on having at least twice that number of men, he kept his misgivings to himself. "I have no siege equipment," he reminded Vernier. "I lost everything when Henry seized Sainte-Croix."

"You won't need any equipment," Vernier said. "We brought enough battering rams and trebuchets and siege towers with us to enable us to launch an attack on Paris."

"I'm not concerned with taking Sainte-Croix so much as with holding on to it afterward. Richard will not surrender the countship without a fight. We shall have a long winter ahead of us defending Sainte-Croix against Richard's army."

"As long as your ports remain open," Raymond of Toulouse said, "we will be able to hold out indefinitely. As we speak, my ships are preparing to depart Saint-Gilles with provisions in the event of a siege."

Hugh looked at Raymond with a guarded expression. He had no reason to trust the Toulousian; the counts of Toulouse had an annoying habit of switching their loyalties whenever it suited their interests. He hoped Raymond's desire to keep King Richard from renewing Eleanor's claim to Toulouse was strong enough to allow them to accomplish their purpose.

Without Lorraine's help, Hugh felt uneasy with his remaining allies. Foix's support, which was substantial, could be withdrawn at any moment should the Count of Armagnac decide to take advantage of Foix's absence to launch an attack on his countship. Toulouse was fickle. And Vernier he knew well enough not to trust. Hugh raised his tankard. "Here's to victory."

"So where is our little heiress?" Vernier asked after the men had drunk. "We have seen naught of her."

"She is being kept under guard," Hugh said.

"Is she as fair as rumor says?" Foix asked. "I have heard that she is even more beautiful than her mother."

Raymond laughed. "The question is, how well does she pleasure a man?"

The muscle in Hugh's jaw knotted. "She resembles her mother," he bit out.

The men exchanged glances. "You are incredibly touchy," Raymond commented. "Can it be that you have become enamored of Lady Adrienne?"

Hugh gave Raymond a look that would have quelled the curiosity of a younger man, or one with less wine under his belt. He had no wish to discuss Adrienne with anyone, yet he knew his silence would generate even more unwanted questions. "In the past two months," he said, "Lady Adrienne has caused me countless delays. She has tried twice to escape. She was abducted once. She caused one of my men to be seriously injured and succeeded in bringing the rest of my men to the brink of rebellion." *And she has made me laugh more times than I can remember.* "If I am touchy, 'tis with good reason."

"She sounds to me like Henry's daughter," Raymond said. "Are you certain she had a mortal mother, or did she descend directly from the devil like the rest of the Plantagenet's issue?"

Although Hugh laughed, his smile did not extend to his eyes. "Lady Adrienne is no devil. She is, however, a tremendous drain on my patience."

The men talked for a while longer. Then Toulouse and Foix excused themselves to retire for the night.

Vernier lingered behind. "So tell me," he began as he lifted his tankard to his mouth. "Have you fallen for Henry's daughter?"

Hugh shot him a glance of annoyance. "In case you have forgotten, my lord, I am betrothed to *your* daughter."

Vernier regarded him through narrowed eyes. "I haven't forgotten. I merely wondered if *you* had."

*   *   *

The army broke camp at daybreak. The vast number of knights and men-at-arms and the cumbersome supply wagons and siege equipment made traveling slow.

Adrienne no longer rode at the front of the column with Hugh but farther back with Sir Conraed and a score of Hugh's most trusted knights. The knights kept their mounts close to hers, forming a protective, impenetrable circle around her.

The separation from Hugh, coming so abruptly after the intimacy they had attained, hurt. Adrienne tried to tell herself that she should have expected it, that the idyllic days and nights they had spent together in the temporary camp were bound to end eventually. What she had not expected, however, was the renewed sense of powerlessness that had come with that end, the cruel reminder that she was nothing more than a pawn in a political struggle that she wanted no part of.

Adrienne was so engrossed in her own thoughts that she did not realize Hugh had joined her until he spoke.

"Good morning, *princesse*."

Adrienne stiffened. She did not look at him. She did not want him to know she had cried herself to sleep last night. "Good morning, my lord," she said woodenly.

After spending a sleepless night with thoughts of her occupying his mind, Hugh had been looking forward to seeing her this morning. Instead of being glad to see him, however, she was angry. He could not pretend that he did not know why. Nor could he blame her. "I should have explained to you last night why I stayed away from you," he said.

"I am merely a prisoner, my lord. You don't owe me any explanations."

"I disagree."

Adrienne was stubbornly silent. She stared straight ahead and refused to look at him.

"Of the men who joined us yesterday, only a few are

known to me. As for the rest, I know nothing of their integrity or their manners. That is why I thought it best that you have your own tent and that I keep my distance. I did not want to give them the opportunity to make you an object of ridicule. I hoped to spare you that humiliation."

"You never cared about my feelings before."

Hugh was silent a moment before saying, "*Princesse*, look at me."

Adrienne obeyed, but there was no disguising the resentment in her expression.

Hugh's chest tightened when he saw her swollen eyelids and the violet shadows beneath her eyes. He wanted to kick himself for having hurt her. "*Princesse*, I would be lying if I tried to deny that accusation. You're right; at first I gave no thought whatsoever to your feelings. But the situation has changed. I've changed. I wish I could tell you what will happen when all this is behind us, but I cannot. Right now my first priority is routing Henry's men—who are now Richard's men—from Sainte-Croix. Then and only then will I be able to concentrate on putting my personal affairs in order. I hope to work out an arrangement with you that will be mutually agreeable, but what that arrangement might be, I do not know. I cannot make any promises. I'm sorry."

That he had even considered a future for her which entailed something besides death or imprisonment went a long way toward relieving Adrienne's anxieties. Of late she had stopped thinking about the future at all because that was less frightening than trying to accept its very uncertainty. Still, Hugh's sudden reversion to treating her like a prisoner rankled. "Is it absolutely necessary to post armed guards outside my tent?" she asked. "I thought I had demonstrated to you that I would not try to escape."

"The guards are for your protection. After what happened at Burg Moudon, I don't want to take any unnecessary risks with your safety."

She sighed. "I suppose you're right." Although she was

fairly certain that she would be safe, she knew Hugh had a legitimate concern.

The unmistakable reluctance in her admission brought a smile to Hugh's lips. "If it is any consolation to you, *princesse*, I too spent a miserable night."

I missed you terribly, Adrienne thought. She lifted her head and regarded him with disdain. "Good," she said flatly.

Inwardly glad to see that she had retained her sense of humor, even if it was being exercised at his expense, Hugh scowled at her. "Heartless wench," he grumbled.

On a clear, brisk day near the end of November Hugh and his army entered Sainte-Croix. They surrounded Salers, outnumbering the inhabitants nine to one. By nightfall Hugh's men had taken control of the village; at dawn the keep on nearby Montsoreau surrendered. As the sun broke over the mountains, Hugh's men lowered the flags bearing the gold lions of Anjou, which had flown from the castle towers during his absence, and raised the coiled serpent of Sainte-Croix.

After assigning a number of men to the keep to maintain control, Hugh pressed on deeper into Sainte-Croix.

Pully fell next.

Martigny surrendered after minimal fighting.

The château at Argent held out against three days of almost ceaseless attack before surrendering.

From the moment the siege on Argent began, Adrienne was kept under close guard away from the fighting, yet not so far away that she could not hear the incessant hammering of the battering rams against the fortress walls. Nor could she escape the thick, choking smoke from houses that had been torched, or the shrill screams of the wounded.

Adrienne was sitting on a low stool near one of the cooking fires, cutting linen into strips of a width suitable for use as bandages, when guards herded a throng of women and children through the temporary camp that had been set up to safeguard the supplies while Hugh's army launched an attack on Bise, and to provide a place away from the fighting where the wounded could be carried to safety. The tortured wails of the women who had lost their homes and loved ones filled the camp. Frightened children cried and clung to their mothers' skirts.

One woman broke away from the others and headed straight toward Adrienne. She threw herself on the ground at Adrienne's feet.

Startled, Adrienne surged to her feet, dropping the bandages she had been preparing.

"M'lady, help us!" the woman begged, sobbing. "They burned our houses and threw our belongings out into the streets, and now they are forcing us to go with them and be their whores!"

Roland, who had been ordered to stay with Adrienne, took her arm. "My lady, please, come away from here."

The woman grabbed the hem of Adrienne's gown. Her voice rose to a shriek. "They killed my sister's girl. They forced themselves on her and then they killed her! Now they're going to kill us!"

One of the guards rode his horse over to them. He prodded the woman with the blunt end of his lance. "Get up!" he ordered. The woman curled up into a ball and began sobbing violently. The guard jabbed her again.

"Leave her alone!" Adrienne cried out. She started to reach for the woman, but Roland pulled her back.

The knight's hand tightened on her arm. "Come away, my lady. 'Tis none of our affair." He firmly steered Adrienne away from the wailing woman.

Before they had gone more than a few yards, Adrienne dug in her heels and yanked her arm from Roland's grasp. "Is it true?" she demanded. "Are the men going to use these women as whores?"

Roland's expression became closed. "The women will come to no harm as long as they do as they are told."

"My lord, that woman said her sister's daughter was raped and murdered!"

Another guard joined the first one. Between the two of them, they dragged the screaming woman back to the others.

Adrienne turned away and squeezed her eyes shut. She felt as if she would be sick.

"My lady, are you all right?"

Adrienne pressed her fingertips against her throbbing temples. "I cannot bear to see any more misery and suffering," she cried out. "What is wrong with Hugh? Has he no thought for the innocent victims of his aggression?"

"My lady, a siege always claims unintended victims. 'Tis the way of it."

"And that justifies the men's crimes?"

"If the people surrendered peaceably, there would be no need to attack."

"My lord, these people are not warriors! They are farmers and craftsmen and shopkeepers. What gives Hugh the right to burn their homes and destroy their livelihoods? And what of the women and children? What have they done to deserve such a cruel punishment?"

"My lady, 'tis a matter not of punishing the innocent but of returning Sainte-Croix to its rightful overlord."

"Lord Hugh might claim Sainte-Croix by right of birth," Adrienne shot back, "but his methods of exercising that claim are no different from the methods used by his enemies who would seize the countship by force. My God! Is there to be no end to the misery these people must endure simply because men who would be in control turn to warfare with no regard for those who will be hurt by their actions?"

Roland was quickly becoming frustrated by his inability to make Adrienne see reason. "My lady, war is unpleasant, yes, but at times it is a necessary evil."

"Necessary to whom? Certainly not to the people whose lives are shattered by it!"

Roland did not respond. His gaze darted past Adrienne, and he shifted uncomfortably.

Adrienne turned to see what the knight was looking at, and her breath caught in her throat. She had not seen Hugh ride up.

His expression was hard. "Perhaps you should direct your questions to me, *princesse*, instead of unleashing your venom on Roland."

Stung by the reprimand, Adrienne stiffened. "You are a hypocrite," she said, lashing out. "You refuse to fight against the infidels in Jerusalem because you say it doesn't matter who rules, as long as he is fair-minded. Yet you attack your own people simply to regain control over them. How is this war any different from the holy wars you are so opposed to?"

"It's not," Hugh said curtly. He dismounted, and Adrienne sucked in her breath when she saw the blood seeping from beneath his hauberk. He moved slowly, as if the effort pained him.

Roland motioned to a squire hovering nearby, then rushed to Hugh's side and caught his arm to keep him from falling.

The squire ran up with a folding camp chair.

Roland steadied Hugh as he sat down, then helped him remove his hauberk and his tunic.

Blood pumped from a vicious gash between Hugh's shoulder and neck. It looked as if someone had succeeded in driving his lance into the vulnerable neck opening of Hugh's chain mail. The sight of his wounds caused Adrienne's stomach to knot. Suddenly the possibility of losing him seemed all too imminent. Tears filled her eyes, and she had to steel herself against going to him. "Dear God, is retaking Sainte-Croix worth getting yourself maimed or killed?" she asked in a quavering voice. "Is it worth all this senseless destruction?"

Hugh's expression was rigid from the sheer effort required to conquer his pain. "*Princesse*, I refuse to justify my actions to you or to anyone. If you cannot control your tongue, I suggest you return to your tent and stay there."

Anger and despair flashed in Adrienne's eyes. "I was beginning to think you were a kind, principled man, Hugh de Clairmont. I was wrong. You are a barbarian, just like the rest of them!"

Adrienne whirled around and nearly collided with the Count of Vernier. "Excuse me, my lord," she murmured. She shoved past him and stumbled blindly toward her tent.

Vernier watched her stormy departure with barely veiled interest. After Adrienne had disappeared from sight, he turned to Hugh. One brow arched quizzically. "A lovers' spat?" he asked.

The color drained from Hugh's face as Roland probed his wound with the point of his dagger in an attempt to remove the broken lance tip that was embedded in the muscle. "A prisoner," Hugh corrected him, forcing out the words between clenched teeth, "who is too outspoken for her own good."

"Your prisoner seems to enjoy an inordinate amount of freedom," Vernier said.

Hugh eyed the other man evenly. "Perhaps you should worry a little less about my prisoner and concentrate on controlling your men."

Vernier laughed mirthlessly. "You must be speaking of the girl in the village. A pretty young thing. She could have warmed many a bed come winter. 'Twas a pity she refused to cooperate."

"Your men brutally murdered her," Hugh ground out. "I will not tolerate that kind of behavior from my own knights, much less from yours."

Vernier's eyes narrowed. "You are hardly in a position to dictate what you will or will not tolerate," he reminded Hugh. "Without my army you haven't the manpower either to retake Sainte-Croix or to hold on to it when Richard arrives to claim sovereignty. Like it or not, you need me far more than I need you."

In spite of having lashed out at Adrienne, Hugh harbored some of the same distressing feelings as she about the terror and destruction his army was unleashing on the countryside. Still, Vernier spoke the truth: he needed the military support of men like Vernier and Toulouse. He took a deep breath and tried to ignore Roland's ministrations. "You might think of your daughter," he said, changing tactics. "Alais will someday be the mistress of this countship. If the wounds we inflict on these people are too deep to heal, Alais will bear the brunt of their anger. Do you want your daughter to spend the rest of her life enduring their hatred because you refused to exercise control over your men?"

"Alais will do as she is told. As for my men, as long as they uphold their oath of fealty to me, they may do whatever they want and behave in whatever manner pleases them. The loss of a common wench here and there is a small price to pay to retain the loyalty of men who have served one well over the years."

Vernier started to leave, then turned back. "One more thing," he said. His eyes glittered dangerously. "I was betrayed once by the house of Sainte-Croix when your brother lay with Marie and got her with child. I will not tolerate another betrayal. If you so much as try to break your betrothal to Alais, I will come after you. And I will kill you."

Chapter Thirteen

WORD OF HUGH'S advance through Sainte-Croix
preceded him. By the time his army reached Château
Clairmont, the occupants of the castle had fled, leaving
behind a handful of faithful servants who were doing their
best to stave off looters.

Hugh strode through the vast hall of the castle, his joy
at being home again tempered by his anger at the filth and
decay that were the legacy of two years of occupancy by
Henry's agents. Mice and cockroaches scurried through the
soiled rushes that covered the stone floors. Cobwebs hung
from the rafters. Priceless tapestries were stained and torn,
and a stench like that of soured milk permeated the very
walls of the hall.

"Saints preserve us, 'tis a miracle!"

Hugh turned at the sound of the familiar voice, and a
grin split his face from ear to ear. "Paschal!" The seneschal, whose white hair hung about his shoulders and
who had been at Château Clairmont since Hugh's father
was a child, had visibly aged in the past two years but
was otherwise unchanged. Hugh went to the old man and
wrapped his arms around his withered form. "My God, 'tis
good to see you!"

"And you, my lord. I never thought to see you within
these walls again."

"I've come home, Paschal. And I have no intention of leaving. Henry is dead, and Richard doesn't have an army big enough to drive me away."

"It has not been the same since you left for the Holy Land. Have you had word of Lord Graeham? Were you able to find him?"

Hugh laughed. "Find him? Paschal, my brother has been making a nuisance of himself for the past twelve months. I left him at Burg Moudon, hearty and hale and building a new life for himself, although I doubt he will ever outgrow his adventurer's ways. I expect any day to hear that he has taken off again for Palestine or Egypt or some other exotic corner of the world. Graeham's feet are planted in air; they were never intended to take root in one place and stay."

The old man's expression saddened. "Verna died this past spring, my lord."

The quietly spoken announcement hit Hugh with the force of a physical blow. Verna, Paschal's wife, had raised him and his brother and sister after their mother's death when Raissa was still in the cradle. He had fonder memories of Verna than of his own mother. "I didn't know," he said, stunned.

"Until the end," Paschal continued, "she held on to the hope that you would come home. She prayed daily for your return."

"Did Henry's men hurt her?"

"They did not lay a finger on her, my lord. But their presence broke her spirit. She tried to keep your home clean, but they destroyed her efforts and deliberately sullied the hall and the chambers until the burden of keeping them up became too much for her."

The nerve beneath Hugh's left eye began to jerk. "I brought approximately two hundred women with me. They are not prisoners but were left widowed and homeless in the siege on Sainte-Croix. They will stay here until their homes have been rebuilt and they can return to their villages. Put them to work cleaning. By nightfall Château Clairmont will be as Verna would have wanted it."

Clad only in a plain linen chemise, Adrienne sat without moving on a chair in the spacious second floor bedchamber that Hugh had assigned to her last night, while Lina, a cheerful young girl of no more than thirteen or fourteen, braided colored ribbons into her long, dark hair. Two other girls moved about the bedchamber, talking and giggling as they made the bed and laid out the bliauds that Adrienne was to choose from.

Except that Adrienne did not feel up to making a choice. All she wanted to do was go back to bed.

It had been late yesterday when Hugh showed her to the chamber. Neither of them had spoken much; Hugh seemed in an unusually foul temper for a man who had just won a major victory, and she was still struggling with the images of agony and destruction that had accompanied their progress across Sainte-Croix. Hugh had left her in the care of the same three maidservants who were torturing her now with their incessant chatter. After washing the grime from her body, she had fallen into bed and drifted immediately into a deep, dreamless sleep.

She had arisen early, having been awakened by the sunlight streaming in through the bank of windows that pierced the east wall of the bedchamber. But within an hour a crippling lethargy had overtaken her and she'd returned to bed where she spent the rest of the day.

The chamber had been thoroughly cleaned the day before, and the lingering smell of strong soap made Adrienne queasy. She clamped her lips together and swallowed, but the harder she tried to ignore the smell, the more her stomach rebelled. The girls' giggling annoyed her, but she bit back the sarcastic remark that sprang to the tip of her tongue. Tears stung her eyes, but she forced them back too.

She did not know what was wrong with her. She felt overwhelmingly tired all the time. And ever since that day at Bise when Hugh had reprimanded her, she had been thin-skinned and teary-eyed. She took affront where none was due and lost her temper over every slight, real or imagined. One minute she was vilifying Hugh's name with every damning curse she could think of; the next she was to be found crying her eyes out and praying that he would not be killed in the fighting. She was as inconsolable as she was unapproachable.

She squeezed her eyes shut and shuddered as a wave of nausea swept over her.

Lina suddenly stopped braiding her hair. "Are you cold, m'lady? Shall we light a fire?"

Adrienne shook her head. Perspiration had broken out across her upper lip, and she felt as if she might faint. "No, I'm fine," she said unevenly. "If anything, 'tis too warm in here. Perhaps we can open a window."

The girls exchanged glances as if they thought she was possessed; they had been doing their best not to shiver in the chilling drafts that invaded the chamber from all sides. However, the girl who had been straightening the bed went to one of the tall, narrow casements on the east wall and opened it.

"I think you should wear the blue one, m'lady," one of the girls said. "It suits your coloring better than the others."

"Fine," Adrienne said wearily. She didn't care which bliaud she wore. She was getting dressed only because Hugh had asked—*ordered*—her to join him in the great hall for supper. She supposed he might have left it as a simple request had she not slammed the chamber door in his face. She did not know what had made her react that way except that she had grown to hate him these past few weeks. She hated him and she did not want to be anywhere near him.

She also wished he would put his arms around her and hold her and tell her that everything was going to be all right, that she was not losing her sanity, and that there would be no more bloodshed.

She wanted him to say he loved her.

They were interrupted by a knock on the chamber door.

One of the maidservants went to the door and opened it. Hugh's squire stood on the landing, holding a rose. He shifted nervously and blushed. "Lord Hugh b-bade me to give this to Lady Adrienne," he stammered. "And he wants to know how much longer she will be."

The girl took the rose and turned to Adrienne. "Oh, look, m'lady! 'Tis the last rose of the season! I saw the bud this morning in a sunny corner of the garden. It was just starting to open!"

Filled with a sudden unreasoning rage, Adrienne surged to her feet. "Give me that!" she demanded.

Startled, the girl gave the rose to her.

Adrienne hardly noticed the thorns that pierced her fingers as she tore at the crimson petals, shredding them. Tears flooded her eyes and streamed down her face. "You may tell Lord Hugh that I have no intention of joining him for supper, now or ever." Her voice shook. She handed the ruined rose back to Gabel. "You may tell him that *this* is what I think of his miserable summons *and of him!*"

A horrified silence fell over the chamber.

Gabel stared, appalled, at the destroyed flower in his hand.

The girl who had opened the window hastily crossed herself.

Everyone backed away from Adrienne as if she were the embodiment of evil.

Adrienne doubled over as a painful spasm gripped her stomach. "Get out, all of you," she ordered, sobbing. Stumbling to the bed, she collapsed onto it and buried her face in the covers. Violent sobs racked her entire body.

Lina went to her and hesitantly laid a hand on her shoulder. "M'lady, you will make yourself sick if you don't stop crying."

"Please, just go . . . away . . . and leave me alone."

Two of the girls looked uncertainly at each other, but the one who had crossed herself had no doubts about what to do. "I'm getting out of here," she said. "I don't care if Lord Hugh did tell us to wait on her. She's King Henry's daughter, and *he* was descended from the devil."

The girl left the chamber with Gabel close on her heels.

The remaining two girls exchanged glances. "Maybe we should go get Marthe," Lina whispered desperately. "She will know what to do."

"I'll go," the other girl said, anxious to get away from their unpredictable guest.

After she had gone, Lina stood by the bed, wringing her hands. She didn't know what to do. Lady Adrienne was crying as if her heart was broken, and Lina did not know how to make her stop.

Down in the great hall, Hugh sat at the high table with the counts whose armies had helped him regain control of Sainte-Croix. An extravagant dinner celebrating their victory had been prepared, and the festivities had already begun, but Hugh did not feel like celebrating.

He was worried about Adrienne. Nothing had been right between them since the siege began. She was distant and uncommunicative, and his few encounters with her had ended in disaster.

He told himself that with Vernier present it was just as well that they stay apart. Until he and Alais were safely married and Vernier removed his army, he needed to tread carefully. He did not like being at Vernier's mercy, but for the time being he had little choice; he did not take Vernier's threat of reprisal lightly.

For the tenth time Hugh glanced toward the arched opening that led to the stair tower and wondered why Gabel was taking so long to return. He took a drink of wine from his goblet and smiled to himself as he imagined Adrienne's reaction to the rose he had sent to her. Unlike other women he had known, who measured their happiness against the vastness of a man's holdings or the weight of a jewel chest, Adrienne found pleasure in simple things: the colors of a sunset, the ever-changing patterns of the clouds, a bird taking flight.

Hugh was just reminding himself to show Adrienne the mews when Gabel returned to the hall. His face was drained of all color. He looked as if he had seen a specter.

Sensing that something was wrong, Hugh immediately stood up. Conversation at the high table ceased, and all heads turned toward him.

Gabel went to Hugh. "My lord, I gave her the rose like you said, but she . . . she . . ." Gabel faltered.

"She what?" Hugh demanded, his impatience mounting.

Gabel placed the shredded flower in Hugh's hand.

There was a sharp intake of breath around the table.

Hugh's face turned a bright red. He swore aloud, and his fingers closed around the rose as if he wished they were around Adrienne's neck. Pivoting, he strode angrily from the hall.

When Hugh was out of sight, Raymond of Toulouse turned to his companions and lifted his goblet in a salute. "The girl has guts. Although when Hugh finishes with her, she will think twice before she defies him again."

Everyone but Vernier laughed. He excused himself from the table and went to one of the trestle tables in the lower hall where the knights who formed his personal guard were seated. He motioned to one. The knight got up from the table, and he and Vernier left the hall.

"I want you to choose a hundred men and make haste to Collombey Abbey," Vernier said. "Bring Alais back here."

The knight inclined his head. "Yes, my lord. We will depart at daybreak."

"You will depart *now*. I want the wedding between my daughter and Hugh de Clairmont to take place without further delay."

The knight looked surprised. "But my lord, 'tis Advent, and the Church forbids—"

"Do as you are told." Vernier bit out the order. "Let me worry about the Church."

The door to Adrienne's bedchamber crashed open.

Lina jumped, terror frozen on her face.

At the intrusion, Adrienne sat up and dragged the sleeve of her chemise across her eyes. "What are you d-doing here?" she stammered.

Taken aback by the unexpected sight of Adrienne's tear-ravaged face, Hugh quickly recovered, glanced at the serving girl, and jerked his head toward the door. "Get out."

Lina glanced uncertainly at Adrienne, and Hugh exploded. "When I give you an order, I expect you to obey it!"

The girl uttered a frightened cry and fled from the bedchamber.

Hugh slammed the door shut and strode purposefully toward the bed.

Suddenly afraid, Adrienne scrambled off the far side of the bed, putting it between them. She stood warily, poised to flee should Hugh come near her.

Hugh flung the rose onto the bed. The shredded petals hovered in midair before drifting down onto the embroidered coverlet. "You had better have a good explanation for this, *princesse*. I am getting weary of your sulking and your needling and your outbursts of ill temper. You are becoming a shrew."

Adrienne lifted her chin and met his furious gaze with open rebellion, but the effect was destroyed by an untimely hiccup. "After what you have done to the people of this countship these past weeks, don't you dare accuse *me* of unseemly behavior," she choked. "You are just like that vile serpent you wear as a badge. You talk to me of fairness and goodness, making me think that my father was wrong about you and that you are truly a kind, just man. Yet all the while you are wrapping your coils around my heart, and then, when I am your prisoner in soul as well as in body, you strike, killing my image of you with your poison."

In spite of her harsh words, Hugh saw as much pain as anger in her eyes, and some of his own anger abated. "*Princesse*, we have been over this before. I am sorry you had to witness the bloodshed, but the siege was necessary if I was to retake the countship."

"If Sainte-Croix was all you truly wanted, my lord, you could have had it by far less bloody means. You could have married me."

Adrienne did not know where that idea had come from, and she could tell by Hugh's expression that he was as startled by it as she was.

His eyes narrowed. "Would you have agreed?" he asked cautiously.

Adrienne hiccuped again. "A fortnight ago I might have said yes. But you have destroyed any sympathy I ever felt for you. I h-hate you."

Hugh slowly circled the bed toward her. "There is a fine line between hate and love, *princesse*. Some say they are opposite sides of the same coin."

Adrienne backed away from him. She felt as if she might vomit. "Don't flatter yourself, Hugh de Clairmont. I feel as much love for you as I do for a snake. That's all you are, a deceitful, evil sn-snake."

Hugh's hand closed around her arm, and Adrienne's knees buckled.

With a tortured moan, she clamped one hand over her mouth and wrested her arm out of Hugh's grip. She shoved her way past him and stumbled to the washstand, reaching the bronze laver at the same instant that she lost control over her stomach.

Because she had not eaten all day, her stomach was empty. She coughed and gagged as spasm after spasm gripped her body, but there was nothing to come up. She was vaguely aware of Hugh's hands resting on her shoulders, steadying her as she bent over the laver. Feeling utterly wretched, she began to cry again.

There was a brisk knock at the chamber door, and then the door opened.

Relief swept over Hugh's face when he saw Marthe. Broad-hipped and with a heart as big as all of France, Marthe had been in charge of the kitchens at Château Clairmont for as long as Hugh could remember. She also knew the secrets of the herbs and was the first one anyone went to when there was an illness or injury.

Entering the chamber, Marthe took one look at Adrienne, hunched over the laver, weeping and trying to rid herself of a dry stomach, and promptly ordered Hugh to get her into bed.

Adrienne protested loudly when Hugh turned her and scooped her up in his strong arms, then carried her across the chamber. But when he tried to put her down on the bed, she clutched the front of his tunic and refused to let go. "Please don't leave me," she begged while sobbing harder than ever.

Hugh didn't know whether to laugh or be angry. Only moments ago she had been telling him how much she hated him; now she was clinging to him as if for her life.

"Is she bewitched?" asked a timid voice from the doorway. It was the girl who had gone after Marthe.

Marthe turned and glowered at the girl. "No, she is not," she said sternly. "Get yourself down to the kitchen and fetch my herb pouch and a flagon of hot water. And be quick about it."

Finally Hugh succeeded in prying Adrienne's fingers off his tunic.

Marthe shooed him away from the bed and bent over Adrienne. "Off with you, my lord," Marthe told Hugh. "You'll only get in the way. And for heaven's sake, someone close that window! 'Tis colder than a Norman's soul in here!"

Hugh waited on the landing outside Adrienne's bedchamber for what seemed like hours. Downstairs he could hear the sounds of the celebration taking place; the feast had gone on without him. He had no appetite. His immediate concern was Adrienne, and until he knew what was wrong with her, he intended to stay close by.

Her behavior tonight disturbed him. He had seen signs of it coming: the sudden tears, the inappropriate outbursts of temper. At first he had thought she was reacting to the events of the past several weeks; if Adrienne had hitherto led as sheltered a life as he suspected, she would understandably have been upset by the siege.

But somehow that explanation did not sit well with him.

Adrienne had demonstrated time and again that she was remarkably resilient. Events that would have broken a weaker person had made her more determined than ever to fight back. He only hoped that the cumulative effects of all that had happened since he took her off the barge had not become too much for her to bear. He had seen it happen before: seasoned warriors who had survived one military campaign after another with no outward signs of distress only to break down and weep like babies at the sight of something as inconsequential as a tree limb broken in a storm.

Suddenly the door opened, and Lina and another girl slipped quietly out of the chamber. Lina cast him a wary glance and edged as far away from him as she could get. The two girls descended the stairs.

Hugh was just starting to enter the chamber when Marthe emerged. "Is she all right?" Hugh asked, unable to disguise the worry in his voice. "What's wrong with her?"

"There is nothing wrong with her that time and a little more patience on your part won't cure. She is in perfect health."

"Don't tell me there's nothing wrong, Marthe. I saw with my own eyes—"

"What you saw, my lord, was a woman whose body is changing. She is not ill; she is with child."

Hugh drew back and stared at the old woman in disbelief.

Marthe chuckled. "There is no cause to look so surprised. You should know better than anyone how she got that way."

Hugh took a deep, steadying breath. "May I see her?"

"This is your home, my lord," Marthe reminded him. "You may do whatever pleases you. But please try not to upset her. She needs to stay calm for the baby's sake."

Hugh entered the bedchamber and quietly pushed the door shut behind him.

A fire had been built on the hearth. Adrienne was in bed, with the covers pulled up to her chin. Hugh went to the bed and stood looking down at her. Her dark hair was spread out across the pillows. Her eyes were closed, and her long lashes fanned out across cheeks that were splotched with pink from her bout of tears. Her breathing was even, however, and she finally seemed at peace with herself.

Hugh bent down and brushed his lips against her brow.

Adrienne's eyes opened.

Hugh sat down on the edge of the bed. "How do you feel?"

"Much better. Marthe gave me an herbal tea to calm my stomach and to help me sleep." Adrienne hesitated. "Did she tell you?"

The realization that he was going to be a father was just starting to sink in. In spite of himself, Hugh felt his face grow warm. "She told me."

Even though she had not yet accepted the fact that she was going to have a baby, Adrienne had hoped that Hugh would be pleased. Obviously he wasn't. She turned her head away and fought the fresh wave of tears that threatened.

"I was worried about you," Hugh said. "You gave me a fright."

Adrienne withdrew one hand from beneath the covers and wiped her eyes. "Marthe said some women are given to crying during the first weeks. Others need an inordinate amount of sleep, and yet others cannot keep anything on their stomachs. I fear, my lord, that I have been afflicted with *all* the symptoms."

"I'm just glad you're all right."

An awkward silence settled between them. After a few minutes Adrienne said in a low voice, "After all the tormenting I endured as a child, I always told myself that I would never bring an unwanted child into the world."

Hugh winced at the bitterness in her words. He also felt a sense of panic at the thought that Adrienne might not want the baby and might try to get rid of it. He took her hand. "*I* want the child," he said quietly but firmly.

Adrienne met his gaze evenly. "Enough to marry me?"

A cloud passed behind Hugh's eyes. "*Princesse*, I will provide for you and for the baby, so you need not worry about what will become of you. But I cannot marry you. I'm sorry."

Adrienne felt as if he had struck her. She started to pull her hand away, but Hugh's grip on it tightened. "Let me explain."

Adrienne fought to stay calm. "You need not justify your actions to me, my lord. I am a prisoner. 'Twas foolish of me to think you might want to marry me."

"This has nothing to do with what I want. Like you, I have little say in the matter."

There was such a look of impotent frustration in his eyes that Adrienne could not refuse him. Even though she knew his explanation would probably hurt her, she nodded. "I'm listening."

Still holding her hand, Hugh began to talk about Rougemont. He told her of his betrothal to Marie de Vernier. He told her how, during the banquet celebrating the betrothal and making it public, he had learned that Marie was pregnant with Graeham's child.

He told her of Graeham's disappearance, of Marie's confinement in a convent, and of his own subsequent betrothal to Vernier's younger daughter, Alais.

He told her things he had never confided to anyone else, and as the story unfolded, he felt as if a tremendous weight was being lifted off his shoulders.

He told her of Vernier's threat should he attempt to break his betrothal to Alais.

When he finished, Adrienne said, "It would appear, my lord, that you have complicated your life beyond salvation."

"If only I had not been so determined to get revenge against Henry's heirs, I would not be in this predicament," Hugh said harshly, punishing himself. "I feel like an unmitigated fool."

Adrienne rose up on one elbow and braced her head on her hand. "Had you not been so determined, I would at this moment be wed to a man who wanted me only for my dowry." Her expression became pensive. "Wilhelm of Lachen might be a good man, but every time I think of him, I feel a chill. Perhaps I am speaking from the heart instead of from the mind, but I am glad you are my child's father."

Hugh felt a swell of emotion unlike anything he had ever known. He grazed his thumb back and forth across her knuckles. "You won't want for anything. I promise."

Except a husband, Adrienne thought. It distressed her to know that by bearing a child out of wedlock she would be subjecting that child to the same cruel taunts that she had endured. There was one thing that she could change, however. "I ask for only one thing, my lord: a father for my child. I don't want my child to grow up the way I did, not even knowing what his own father looks like."

Hugh brought her hand to his mouth and kissed it. "I'm not Henry, *princesse*. I have no intention of neglecting either you or our child. You have my word."

They talked for a while longer. Finally the tea Adrienne had drunk made her eyelids heavy, and she yawned. Hugh released her hand and stood up.

Dismay flickered across Adrienne's face. "Please stay," she said sleepily.

"You need your rest, *princesse*. I don't want Marthe
scolding me because I tired you. Besides, I need to make
sure my guests are not destroying the hall."

Adrienne laughed at the thought of Hugh being afraid of
Marthe. "You missed your banquet," she said ruefully.

Hugh blew out the candles and tucked the covers around
her. "Perhaps I am making a mistake by telling you this,
princesse—knowing you, you will find a way to use it
against me—but there is no one at that banquet whose
company I enjoy more than yours." He gently kissed her
lips. "Sleep well."

Adrienne remembered little beyond the door closing after
him; by then the full effect of the tea was upon her. But
sometime during the night she was aware of a weight
settling next to her on the bed. Hugh folded his arms
around her and drew her against him. "I couldn't stay
away," he murmured into her hair.

"Are you sure you're not too tired?" Hugh asked.

Adrienne laughed. "My lord, that is the third time you
have asked me that!"

They were partway up the steep spiral staircase that
led to the battlements. Hugh was taking Adrienne up to
the parapet so that she could get a commanding view of
Sainte-Croix.

" 'Tis a matter of self-preservation, *princesse*. Marthe
will have my hide if I tire you."

"And I will throw a childish fit if you don't let me see
this magnificent view you have been boasting of."

Hugh looked undecided. "I had forgotten how steep these
stairs are. Perhaps I should carry you."

"Now, that is a fool talking. If I start feeling winded, I
will tell you, and we can stop to rest. I promise."

By the time they reached the parapet, Adrienne had
begun to feel ill, not from climbing but from the sensation
of being trapped in the dark, enclosed stairwell. She felt a
great sense of relief when Hugh opened the small arched

door at the top of the tower and they stepped out into the bright sunshine.

Adrienne went to the crenellated outer wall, and her heart missed a beat. "Oh, my lord! 'Tis glorious!"

Château Clairmont, Adrienne had learned, was located on the highest point in Sainte-Croix. From their lofty perch at the top of the southwest tower, they could see for miles and miles without obstruction.

The mountains were not nearly as tall as the Alps, but they were just as beautiful, their rugged slopes dotted with white and pink limestone outcroppings and deep nearly black crevasses which hinted at the intricate network of caves that stretched throughout the countship. It was easy to see, Adrienne thought, how the superstitions and the fear surrounding the mysterious serpent of Sainte-Croix could take root and flourish in such a land.

It was not a barren land, however. Even though winter was nearly upon them, the south sides of the mountains, which were covered with olive trees and wild juniper and rosemary and lavender, were still green. Just as Hugh had told her, villages, their buildings stacked nearly vertical against the steep slopes, clung to the sides of the mountains like eagles' nests. Stone walls hinted at secluded gardens behind tall wooden gates, and narrow winding paths connected villages and farms. And to the south, beyond the farthest ridge, the blue-green waters of the Mediterranean stretched all the way to the horizon.

Yet the landscape was not without blight; tents—thousands of them, set up to house the invading armies—were crowded near the base of the castle's outer curtain wall. Ignoring their disturbing presence, Adrienne turned to Hugh, her eyes bright with excitement. "My lord, 'tis the most beautiful place in the world! The sky is so clear and the sun so bright—not at all like the English mists that I am accustomed to. I have never seen anything like it."

With the sunlight glancing off her dark hair and shimmering about her head like a halo, Hugh thought

Adrienne had never looked so beautiful. Her color had returned, and she had not been sick at all during the past two days. He was glad he had brought her up here. He laughed. " 'Tis hardly the dark, gloomy wasteland you were expecting, is it, *princesse*?"

"I was wrong about Sainte-Croix," Adrienne conceded. "And so was my father. He wanted it for all the wrong reasons. If he'd had any sense at all, he would have forgone the seaports in favor of establishing a residence where he could bask in the sunshine while looking out over the mountains."

Hugh's expression gentled. "Come here."

Feeling better than she had in days, Adrienne went to him without protest. Hugh took her hand and pulled her to him. Burying his hands in her hair, he lowered his head to hers and kissed her, gently at first, then with a passion that made Adrienne's head spin and her knees weaken beneath her. Her hands moving over his back, pressing him closer to her, she savored his kiss as if it might be his last; she knew that the day would soon come when she would not be free to express her love for him, and she was determined to enjoy the time they had left to themselves.

When Hugh finally lifted his head, there was genuine regret in his expression. "Your father was a fool," he said quietly.

Still clasping him tightly to her, Adrienne tilted her head back and smiled as she gazed into his dark eyes. "Why do you say that?"

"For neglecting you all these years. Had Henry paid some attention to you, he would have seen how beautiful and intelligent you are. Through your marriage, he could have negotiated the most powerful alliances in the civilized world."

Adrienne grimaced. "Just what I have always wanted— to be sold to the highest bidder like a prize sow."

"Or a rare jewel?"

Adrienne blushed, but before she could comment, one of Hugh's knights appeared in the doorway. "My lord, you are needed in the hall. There has been trouble between Vernier's men and some of the villagers."

Swearing silently, Hugh released Adrienne. "I'll be there shortly," he told the knight before dismissing him.

After the knight had gone, Hugh turned back to Adrienne. "I'm sorry, *princesse*, but we will have to cut this rendez-vous short. We can come back another day."

Adrienne was not able to hide her disappointment. "Please let me stay up here a while longer. I'll not try anything foolish or dangerous. I just want to enjoy the sunshine and the freedom from being watched every moment of the day."

Hugh hesitated. He did not like the idea of leaving Adrienne unattended. He did not think she would jump or even try to escape down the tower wall. Rather, he worried that Vernier would discover that she was alone. He did not trust the count; there was no telling what Vernier might attempt.

Finally he relented. "You may stay. I will post guards on the nearest landing. When you are ready to come inside, call for them and they will escort you down. I don't want you descending these stairs alone."

Adrienne's expression turned mutinous. "My lord, I am quite capable of—"

"The alternative is to leave with me now," Hugh said sternly.

Adrienne sighed. "As you wish. I will call for the guards when I am ready to come down."

At her obvious reluctance, Hugh reached out and brushed his knuckle across her cheek. "I don't want to take any chances with your safety, *princesse*. It would sadden me greatly should anything happen to you or our child."

That unexpected admission went a long way toward softening the edge on Adrienne's annoyance. "Don't worry, my lord. I won't do anything to endanger either of us."

"I didn't think you would," Hugh said.

It wasn't until after Hugh had gone and Adrienne had time to mull over his words that she realized he had not been speaking of the possibility of her falling; he had been referring to a far more sinister threat.

She turned her head to stare out over the sun-drenched mountains, and a frown creased her brow as the argument between Baldhere and Lady Joanna that she had overheard returned to haunt her: "There is no time. Until she is married, she will be in danger. . . . 'Tis out of our hands now."

A chilling melancholy settled over her. Even with her chances of marriage shattered, she was still at the mercy of forces beyond her control. If anything, she was in even more danger than before. If, as Sir Leland had said, the conditions of her inheritance were truly inviolable, then the child she carried had an even greater claim to Sainte-Croix than either she or Hugh—and posed even more of a threat to their enemies.

Chapter Fourteen

ALTHOUGH THE DAYS grew shorter, they remained mild and sunny; winter seemed content to postpone its arrival. Hugh showed Adrienne the falcon mews, and she fell into the habit of going there as often as possible. The mews had been neglected during Hugh's absence, and the few birds remaining were hostile and uncooperative. One of the squires, however, had managed to trap a young female kite, and when his own patience in training her proved inadequate, he gave the falcon to Adrienne. With little else to occupy her time except sewing new clothes for herself and her baby, Adrienne welcomed the moments when she could escape the confines of the castle.

She named the graceful forked-tailed falcon Sperantia, which meant "hope."

Sperantia took to her immediately, feeding from the fist with a readiness that made Adrienne wonder if she was truly wild or if she had escaped from captivity elsewhere. The falcon rebelled against the hood, however, and it was several days before Adrienne was able to slip the soft leather hood over the falcon's head without Sperantia panicking and trying to pull it off.

With the falcon's head covered, Adrienne walked slowly from the mews out into the ward, all the while talking to the bird and stroking her with a feather. Sperantia bated her wings and tried to climb up Adrienne's arm, but Adrienne managed to keep a firm grip on the jesses. The falcon's talons dug into the leather gauntlet on Adrienne's hand.

"There, there," Adrienne cooed softly, still stroking the falcon with the feather. "Doesn't that warm sun feel good on your back?"

She had just managed to get the bird calmed down when Sir Conraed approached her. Sensing the nearness of a stranger, Sperantia began to bate her wings even more fiercely than before. Adrienne's arm was quickly tiring from the effort of controlling her. "Shhh," she whispered soothingly. "There is nothing to fear. I won't let anyone hurt you."

"I'm sorry," Conraed said when the falcon had finally stopped trying to fly away. "I didn't mean to startle her. I just thought I would join you for a few minutes. My uncle used to enjoy falconry. It has been many years since I've watched the young ones in training."

"You don't need to apologize. Sperantia needs to learn not to panic when other people are around." She laughed. "I'm dreading the first time the dogs start barking while I have her out in the ward. She may succeed in carrying us both over that wall."

Although she had spoken in jest, Conraed eyed her oddly. Adrienne knew that his appearance had not been coincidental and that his reason for joining her was merely a pretext. Although she was permitted to pass from the keep to the ward with relative freedom, she had noticed that whenever she went outside, one of Hugh's men soon joined her.

She had asked Hugh about it, and he readily admitted to assigning his men to guard her, citing his concern for her safety as the reason. Some of the men had taken to fighting among themselves and causing trouble in the village, he told her. And he assured her that while it was nothing for her to worry about, he did not want her to fall victim to their restlessness.

Although she had found it annoying to be followed, she had no choice but to accept Hugh's decision, and she soon learned to judge the seriousness of the situation by which man he sent to guard her. She cast Conraed a sidelong glance as they strolled across the ward. "Would you care to tell me what is going on that I'm not supposed to know about?" she asked sweetly.

Conraed feigned ignorance. "What makes you think something is going on, my lady?"

A dimple appeared at one corner of Adrienne's mouth. "I have come to learn that the extent of Hugh's worry influences his choice of bodyguards for me. Given that you are his most trusted knight, my lord, I am inclined to believe that something of great significance has happened or is about to happen."

Conraed scowled at her, but he soon lost control and began to smile. "I pity the man who underestimates you, my lady. He is in for a surprise."

Adrienne refused to be diverted. "You haven't answered my question, Sir Conraed."

"Nor do I intend to. I am here to watch over you, not to answer your questions."

After several more unsuccessful attempts to needle information out of Conraed, Adrienne reached the conclusion that he was Hugh's most trusted knight precisely *because* he was so closemouthed.

They were just returning to the mews when Adrienne noticed a crowd gathering outside the door to the great hall. There were perhaps fifty or sixty people, mostly men from the village. Those closest to the building were shouting and pounding on the door with their fists. Eight of Hugh's knights were trying to maintain order.

Had the commotion not caused Sperantia to strain at her jesses, Adrienne might have stayed to see what was happening, but the falcon was becoming difficult to control. Reluctantly she accompanied Conraed back to the mews.

That evening, when Adrienne was changing into a clean chemise and bliaud for dinner, she learned from Lina that some of the soldiers who were camped outside the castle walls had gone into the village and ransacked a *boucherie*.

"They tied up the butcher," Lina said as she helped ease the wine-red bliaud over Adrienne's head. "Then they made him look on while they raped his wife. Four of them had their way with her before they were caught."

Adrienne gasped.

"She was with child, about six months gone," Lina continued. She tugged the overgown into place, and the hem settled around Adrienne's ankles in graceful folds. "Marthe says she might lose the baby."

Adrienne unthinkingly placed her hand against her abdomen in an unconscious gesture of empathy for the woman. "My God!"

"And that's not the half of it," Lina continued. "They were the Count of Vernier's men, and he won't punish them for it. He says his men are growing restless, and they need some diversion. The townspeople are furious. They sent men to speak with Lord Hugh and demand that justice be done."

Adrienne sank down onto the bed. She had not been ill for several days; now her stomach was churning miserably. This was not the first time Vernier's men had caused trouble. She knew they had been responsible for brutally murdering a girl during the siege on Bise. And there had been other incidents as well: grain stored for the winter destroyed, orchards burned, chickens and goats stolen from the peasants and tormented for the sport of watching them die an agonizing death, an old man hanged in the village square. "I don't understand why Hugh lets those men stay here. He doesn't need them any more. Why doesn't he send them away?"

Lina fidgeted. "I suppose Lord Hugh has his reasons."

Adrienne looked at the girl. "You know something."

Lina shook her head adamantly. "Oh, no, m'lady, 'tis nothing."

"Lina, tell me!"

Lina glanced at the door as if she expected someone to barge through it at any moment and cut out her tongue. "Well, m'lady, I heard—I mean, everyone knows, so 'tis not as if it is a secret—that Lord Hugh is betrothed to the Count of Vernier's daughter. He doesn't love her," she added in a rush. "The betrothal was arranged years ago. 'Tis supposed to be good for Sainte-Croix, because Vernier's army is so strong and Sainte-Croix is so small."

"Lina, I already know that. I, too, am already betrothed, although I doubt there will be any wedding now."

Relief flooded the girl's face. "I thought you didn't know. Marthe made us promise we wouldn't say anything to you about it because it might upset you."

" 'Tis futile to fret about something we have no power to change," Adrienne said. "But Hugh's betrothal still does not explain why Vernier doesn't take his army and leave. Hugh only needed him to retake Sainte-Croix, and he has already accomplished that."

Lina's expression turned conspiratorial. "I heard some of the other servants talking. They said that Vernier has already sent for his daughter and that the wedding will take place as soon as she arrives."

That news caught Adrienne by surprise. She had assumed that the wedding would not take place for some time yet— at least not until after her baby was born. "She is coming here now?"

Lina nodded.

Adrienne's mind raced. The Church forbade weddings from taking place during Advent and also during the Twelve Days of Christmas. And with winter soon to be upon them, the weather might slow the travelers down, delaying their arrival until too late to perform the ceremony before Lent. . . .

Adrienne groaned inwardly and rubbed her fingertips across her brow in frustration. She was only dreaming of postponing the inevitable. The wedding was going to take place, possibly sooner than anyone had expected. She had no claim on Hugh's life, and she had only his word that he would not neglect their child.

"Are you feeling ill, m'lady? Shall I go get Marthe?"

Adrienne shook her head. "No, Lina. You have already done more than enough for me. I often grow lonely for someone to talk to. You have made my stay at Sainte-Croix far more bearable than it would have been otherwise."

Lina beamed. "I'll wait for you, m'lady, while you eat. Then I'll brush your hair for you before you retire for the night."

Adrienne started to refuse the girl's offer, but the look of expectation on Lina's face silenced her. For many young girls who served in their overlord's household, it was an honor to be assigned a position as a waiting woman, far preferable to hours of drudgery in the kitchens. She missed Marlys's companionship, and Lina seemed eager to please. "I might be a while," she said. "Are you certain no one will object?"

"Oh, no, m'lady. There's plenty of mending for me to do to keep my hands from being idle while I wait—that is, if I may use your candles to see by. Paschal complains that we use too many candles."

Adrienne could not help smiling at the thought of the elderly seneschal guarding the stores of candles. During the weeks she had been at Sainte-Croix, she had noticed that Paschal was fiercely protective of both Hugh and Hugh's home. "Of course you may use my candles. And, Lina, thank you for being so good to me."

"I would do anything for you, m'lady. You're good and kind and beautiful, and Lord Hugh is right to love you so—" Fearing that she had said too much, Lina broke off. Her face turned a brilliant crimson.

Although she reasoned that it was unlikely that Hugh felt the same way about her, Adrienne felt her heart leap at the mere suggestion that he loved her. Her throat constricted. "I love him too, Lina," she said achingly. "Far more than he will ever know."

* * *

Adrienne did not enter the great hall immediately, but stood by the passage screen and watched Hugh and Vernier. They were seated at the high table, and they appeared to be engaged in a quarrel. Hugh's face was dark with rage, and the cords stood out on his neck. One hand gripped his goblet, and the other was knotted into a fist. From where she stood, Adrienne could not see the Count of Vernier's face, but whatever he was saying had the effect of increasing Hugh's anger. Hugh slammed his goblet down on the table and started to rise when he spotted Adrienne.

No longer able to hide in the shadows, Adrienne walked toward the high table. Hugh rose the remainder of the way and extended his hand toward her. There was no sign of the anger she had seen only a moment ago, and his expression was unreadable. Had she not witnessed the argument with her own eyes, she would never have known that anything untoward had just taken place.

Her own feelings were in turmoil. She wanted to run to Hugh and hold him, to selfishly guard the precious moments they had remaining. And yet another part of her wanted to lash out at him—at anyone—in frustration at the unfairness of their situation. Just as she had the first night she had given herself to Hugh, she felt a desperate need to take control of her own fate. She wanted that which her mother had been denied—a husband and a father for her child. She was no longer willing to settle for a political match arranged by her elders; she wanted a husband who would also be a friend and a confidant and a lover. She wanted someone who would love and honor her as much as she did him.

She wanted Hugh.

As she neared the table, her gaze drifted away from Hugh and rested on Vernier, and alarm touched a finger to her spine. The count's face was flushed, and there was a bright, glassy look in his eyes. She did not need to smell the wine on his breath to know that he was well on his way to becoming drunk. Uneasy, she glanced away.

She could not even look at Vernier without thinking of the incident in the village, but she was acutely aware of Vernier's predatory gaze on her. She walked past him without acknowledging his presence and placed her hand in Hugh's. "Good evening, my lord."

Hugh brought her hand to his lips. "Good evening, *princesse*," he said, lingering over her hand longer than was prudent. "I trust you spent an enjoyable afternoon."

"Yes, thank you. Sperantia finally seems to be taking to the hood. In a few weeks, if the weather holds, I want to start training her to the lure."

Hugh seated her at his right, on the bench next to his chair, putting himself between her and Vernier. Although the implied message was clear, it did not stop Vernier from leaning forward to engage Adrienne in conversation. "Your father was quite fond of hunting with falcons, Lady Adrienne. Did your interest in the sport come from him?"

"Leave her alone," Hugh snapped.

Adrienne immediately grew defensive, both at Vernier's tactless inquiry and at Hugh's interference. Forcing her face into a mask that gave no hint of the revulsion she felt for Vernier, she turned her head and met his gaze without flinching. "If such traits are truly passed from father to child, my lord, then 'tis more likely that I inherited his passion for expanding my holdings at the expense of my allies—and my children."

In spite of her outward calm, the venom in her voice and the double meaning of her words caused Vernier to draw back in surprise.

Raymond of Toulouse began to laugh—hearty, loud guffaws that drew the attention of everyone in the hall. He lifted his goblet toward Vernier. "That makes one wonder," he said meaningfully. "Does the girl speak of Henry, or is she referring to you?"

Toulouse's remark sparked laughter along the length of the table. Vernier's face darkened ominously. Hugh's hand descended on Adrienne's shoulder in a warning gesture. He leaned toward her and said in a low voice that only she could hear, "Silence your tongue, *princesse*, or you will find yourself courting powerful enemies you neither need nor want."

Once incited, Adrienne's rebellion refused to be quelled. "I know what his men did in the village today," she shot back. "And I know that he is protecting them."

"That is not your concern."

"But, my lord, what they did to that poor—"

"That will be enough. I refuse to discuss it with you."

Adrienne's stomach felt as if it were trying to work its way up into her throat. She swallowed hard and averted her gaze, wondering frantically how she was going to endure the evening without being sick. She already regretted having come down to the great hall.

Mistaking her sudden silence for compliance—and feeling justifiably suspicious of that compliance—Hugh released her shoulder.

The servants brought in the first of the dishes, roasted pork and the ever-present fish for those who did not eat meat, and everyone's attention turned to the food.

The rich, fatty smell of the roasted pork disagreed with Adrienne's stomach, but to keep from drawing attention to herself by refusing to have any, she accepted a very small slice of the meat. She considered asking Hugh if he would permit one of the servants to bring her some of Marthe's herb tea, but pride got in her way, and she kept silent. Instead, she took a drink from the goblet she shared with Hugh. The wine was strong, and it settled in her empty stomach like a live coal.

The tension that tainted the high table also seemed to have spread to the lower hall. Because there was room for only a fraction of the warriors and men-at-arms camped outside the castle walls, only the counts' favored knights were permitted to take their meals inside the hall. Even that small number filled the hall to capacity, and usually the trestle tables were crowded and noisy. Tonight, however, the usual revelry was absent. Many of the knights who were in the habit of joining them for the evening meal had chosen to remain in the camp with their fellow soldiers. The few knights who did arrive huddled in small groups, whispering among themselves.

Suddenly Adrienne realized that someone had spoken to her, and she turned her head. The Count of Foix had just returned from the lower hall where he had been speaking with some of his men. "May I sit next to you, my lady?" he asked.

Adrienne nodded.

The count stepped over the bench and sat down.

Adrienne glanced at Hugh. He had turned toward Vernier, and the two seemed to be quarreling again, although they kept their voices low enough to make eavesdropping difficult.

With a sigh, Adrienne turned back to her food. She nibbled on a sliver of the meat and a piece of dry bread.

"I wouldn't take it personally," the Count of Foix said. "Those two have been at each other's throats all day."

Adrienne glanced at the Count of Foix, but she hesitated to speak, not knowing where he stood.

Sensing her uncertainty, Foix chuckled. "Vernier brings out the worst in everyone—myself included."

Adrienne took another sip of the wine, then pushed the goblet away. The wine had an odd taste. "And yet you are friends," she said.

"Allies," the count said, correcting her. "Vernier doesn't have any friends."

Adrienne looked at Vernier. He drained his goblet, then barked at one of the servants to refill it. He started to speak to Hugh, but stopped when he saw her watching him. Adrienne colored hotly and turned away, but not quickly enough to escape the hatred that flamed in Vernier's eyes.

After what seemed an eternity, the trays were carried away, and the second course arrived. By this time a dull ache was pressing against Adrienne's forehead and increasing her feelings of nausea.

The outright animosity that Vernier had displayed troubled her. She knew Hugh did not trust him, and she was beginning to worry, not for herself so much as for the safety of her baby. If Vernier even suspected that she was carrying Hugh's child, there was no telling what he might do.

"You look pale," Hugh said in a low voice. "Are you feeling all right?"

"I'm fine." Adrienne did not look at Hugh. She was beginning to have trouble turning her head without feeling as if she would be sick.

Mistaking her restrained response for pique, Hugh slipped his hand beneath the table and laid it on Adrienne's thigh. "I apologize for neglecting you. And for my burst of temper. It was wrong of me to take my frustration out on you."

I love you so much, and I'm so afraid, Adrienne thought. Unable to voice the feelings that welled up inside her, she placed her hand on Hugh's, and he shifted his hand so that he could hold hers. She took a deep breath. " 'Tis the Count of Vernier, my lord," she whispered. "I know you are betrothed to his daughter, but I cannot smile and pretend that I don't see what he is doing to the people of this countship."

"I know," Hugh said wearily.

When the betrothals—first to Marie and then to Alais— were arranged, they had seemed like a good idea. In spite of its coveted seaports, Sainte-Croix was small and vulnerable whereas Vernier, while landlocked, was powerfully armed. The fact that the two countships shared a border made an alliance between them all the more desirable. Now Hugh was beginning to wonder just how high a price he and his people would have to pay for such an alliance.

"I hate him," Adrienne said under her breath. "I wish he would take his army and go away."

Hugh squeezed her hand. "So do I, *princesse*."

Adrienne pressed the fingertips of her free hand against her temple as a wave of heat washed over her, followed by a chill that caused her skin to erupt into gooseflesh. "My lord, I'm feeling a little faint. I think it would be best if I returned to my bedchamber."

Worry creased Hugh's brow. He moved his hand to her elbow and steadied her as she rose to her feet, then stood up himself. "I'll take you."

"That isn't necessary, my lord. I'll be fine. I just want to lie down for a while."

"I insist."

"You might as well enjoy what time you have left with him," Vernier said sarcastically. "Once Richard arrives, your lover will no longer have any use for you."

Adrienne gripped the edge of the table as the floor shifted beneath her, and stared at Vernier in icy shock. The news of Richard's imminent arrival stunned her more than the reference to Hugh.

Hugh gripped Adrienne's arm. His face was dark with rage. "Go to your bedchamber," he ordered. "I will handle this."

Adrienne turned a bewildered gaze on Hugh. "Is it true, my lord? Is Richard coming here?"

"Go to your bedchamber," Hugh repeated, more firmly this time. He started to steer Adrienne away from the table.

Ignoring Hugh's attempts to get Adrienne to leave the hall, Vernier said harshly, "Why else do you think you are here, you love-struck little fool, but to lure Richard into Sainte-Croix?"

Adrienne's face went bloodless.

Hugh rounded on Vernier. "That will be enough!"

Vernier's cold laugh rattled in the tense silence that had descended over the hall. His hard gaze never leaving Adrienne's face, he took another drink of wine. He dragged the back of his hand across his mouth. "You look surprised, Lady Adrienne. I would have thought that you, of all people, would know of Hugh's plans to use you to wreak his revenge on the Plantagenet's heirs, then banish you to a convent where you would no longer pose a threat to his claim to Sainte-Croix."

A low, murderous growl sounded deep in Hugh's throat. He released Adrienne's arm and lunged at Vernier.

Adrienne screamed.

Vernier jumped to his feet. Hugh crashed into him, and they both went sprawling across the table, knocking over goblets and sending trenchers and platters crashing to the floor.

Within seconds the entire hall erupted into chaos. Swords were drawn, and the awful sound of metal striking metal filled the air. Servants screamed and ran from the hall. Knights who had been sharing trenchers suddenly found themselves facing each other in a fight to the death.

On the dais, Adrienne backed into the wall and pressed her fist against her mouth to smother the screams that welled up inside her as Hugh and Vernier rolled over and over on the table. Hugh's hands were locked around Vernier's neck. Vernier shoved one hand against Hugh's face, his fingers gouging into Hugh's eyes. The counts of Foix and Toulouse grabbed Hugh from behind and dragged him off Vernier.

Filled with rage, Hugh threw his arms up over his head, breaking the hold the two men had on him. Foix, the smaller of the two, flew backward and crashed into the wall.

Vernier snatched a dagger up off the table and rolled to his feet.

Hugh grabbed his chair and hurled it at Vernier. The chair was massive and heavy, and its weight knocked Vernier down. The dagger clattered to the floor. Toulouse stepped between Hugh and Vernier. "You must stop this fighting! With Richard on his way here, we cannot risk weakening our ranks with petty bickering!"

Hugh's shoulders heaved as he struggled to catch his breath.

Vernier slowly pushed himself upright. His face was florid, and he was unsteady on his feet.

Casting Vernier a scorching look, Hugh leapt off the dais and into the thick of the fighting. The action was as suicidal as it was brave, and Adrienne's heart missed a beat as she watched Hugh seize a knight by the back of his tunic and fling him away from his opponent. He then shoved one of the heavy benches between two men, tripping them as they lunged at each other with their swords drawn. He bellowed orders to stop fighting, his deep voice reverberating off the stone walls.

The skirmish ceased as quickly as it had begun. The knights looked bewildered, as if they were not certain why they had been battling each other. Fortunately no one had been killed, but several of the men had been injured, some of them seriously.

The great hall was in shambles. Tables and benches were overturned, and the stone floor was slippery with spilled wine. The dogs ran through the hall barking, their tails wagging, sniffing and stopping to gulp the meat that lay on the floor.

Hugh ordered everyone out of the hall.

The men left. Two of them had to be carried out. Soon the hall was empty except for Hugh and Adrienne, Vernier, Toulouse, and Foix. Where only moments ago there had been chaos, now there was a thick, choking silence, broken only by the sounds of the dogs devouring the food.

Adrienne stood stiffly on the dais, engulfed in a haze of pain and torment so intense that nothing around her felt quite real. It was as if she were caught in the middle of a dream—a recurring dream from which she would awaken just before the end, leaving her wondering at the outcome.

Only now, with the danger over, did she allow herself to think about what had happened. Although the trouble had erupted suddenly, in retrospect, she realized that she should have seen it coming. Vernier had been drinking heavily. Hugh and Vernier had been at odds all day. And she had made the mistake of antagonizing Vernier instead of ignoring what she was certain had been a deliberate taunt regarding her father.

That the consequences had not been worse was a miracle.

Then Vernier had told her about Hugh's plan to use her and put her in a convent where she would not be a threat to him.

Where her baby would not be a threat to him.

Her chest tightened, and the tears that came to her so easily these days flooded her eyes.

Hugh had promised to provide for her and for her baby. *He had promised!* Yet he had not specified how he intended to do that. He had not said he intended to put her in a nunnery, nor had he said he would not.

A spasm, stronger than the previous ones, gripped her stomach.

Whirling about, Adrienne bolted from the hall and stumbled blindly up the tower stairs. She threw open the door to her bedchamber.

Lina, who had been sitting in a chair by the hearth, her head bent over her mending, jumped to her feet. Her eyes were wide with shock. "M'lady! You look like you've seen a ghost! What happened?"

Adrienne stood hunched over just inside the door with her hands pressed over her mouth, fighting against the bile that filled her throat.

Finally the spasm ended. Adrienne straightened slightly and took a shaky breath. She felt weak and unsteady. "Lina, please go down to the kitchen and get some of Marthe's herbal tea."

Lina looked worried. "Will you be all right here by yourself?"

She nodded. "I'll be fine . . . as soon as my stomach settles."

Lina dropped her sewing onto the chair and hurried from the bedchamber.

As soon as she was gone, Adrienne's control broke. She ran to the laver and heaved up what little she had been able to get down.

One by one, the servants returned to the hall and began cleaning up the mess.

Hugh stood in the middle of the lower hall and plowed his fingers through his hair. He was dangerously close to snapping. He was just beginning to realize that the anger and frustration which had been building inside him during the past few weeks were merely outward manifestations of something far more debilitating: fear.

His hatred for Henry had eaten at his soul for so long that he had lost his objectivity—and his humanity. He ate, slept, and breathed plans for revenge without giving thought to those who would be hurt by those plans. He had even anticipated the eventuality of his own death, structuring his plans so well that the events themselves, once set into motion, would bring his scheme to fruition with or without him.

What he had not counted on was losing the will to seek revenge.

He knew precisely when he had begun to change. It was the morning Adrienne escaped only to be attacked by the outlaw knights. Hearing her screams and seeing her in danger of being violated had shattered the armor he had worn around his heart for as long as he could remember.

He had never been quite the same after that day.

His desire for revenge against Henry and Henry's heirs, once so clear and self-sustaining, was now muddied with doubt.

Hugh looked at Vernier and wondered if there was any way to sever the alliance between them without provoking the count's rage, but before he had even formed the question in his own mind, he knew the answer: Vernier would not be satisfied with killing him; he would also punish the people of Sainte-Croix. And what would become of

Adrienne? Hugh shuddered to think of the cruelties Vernier would inflict on Adrienne were she left at his mercy.

Vernier, his own rage far from appeased, took a swipe at a goblet that lay on the table, sending it flying, then stormed from the hall.

Toulouse and Foix quietly followed him.

Perhaps, Hugh thought dismally, it was best to leave matters alone until tempers had had a chance to cool.

There was one matter, however, that could not wait.

When Hugh reached Adrienne's bedchamber, she was standing at the window, staring out into the darkness. She turned when he entered the chamber. Hugh stopped just inside the doorway, and his stomach clenched when he saw the accusation that glittered in her eyes.

Adrienne lifted her chin and eyed him coldly. "Is it true?" she asked in a choked voice. "Did you use me to lure Richard into Sainte-Croix?"

There was no point in denying the truth. "Yes."

Adrienne winced.

Hugh started toward her. "*Princesse*, listen to me—"

"Why?" Adrienne demanded. "What is your purpose in bringing Richard here? What are you going to do—kill him?"

"If necessary, yes."

"Why? What did Richard ever do to you?"

"He helped your father seize Sainte-Croix."

Understanding dawned in Adrienne's eyes. Her mouth fell open. "You intend to wreak revenge on all my father's children, don't you?" she asked when she finally found her voice.

"*Princesse*—"

"Once you have gotten rid of Richard, who is next? John? Or me?" Her voice rose. "What do you intend to do to me? Are you going to kill me too? Or are you going to have me immured in a nunnery where I will be out of your way and you will be free of your obligations to me and to our child?"

"No."

"I don't believe you."

Hugh went to her and took her hands, and he was startled by how cold they were. They felt not at all like flesh and muscle and bone, but like ice. Adrienne started to pull away, but he tightened his hold on her hands. He began to massage them in an attempt to rub some warmth back into them. "That was my original intent, yes. But no longer. I promised you that I would take care of you, and I meant it."

For how long? Adrienne thought. Until she became an inconvenience or an embarrassment? And what of Alais de Vernier? How could she expect Alais to meekly stand aside and allow her husband to entertain his mistress beneath her roof, when *she* could hardly bear the thought of Hugh even marrying the girl?

"*Princesse*, if it were within my power to do so, I would like nothing better than to abandon Sainte-Croix to those who seek to control it and go somewhere far, far away where you and I and our child could live in peace. But I cannot do that; too many people are depending on me. Thousands of lives are in danger, and I cannot abandon my people. Not now, when they face certain attack by Richard's army. That is why, no matter how much I would like to, I cannot send Vernier away. I need his men. Without Vernier's army, the people of Sainte-Croix will be slaughtered."

Adrienne shook her head. "It doesn't have to be that way, my lord. My father is dead, and Sainte-Croix is once more in your hands. What is to be gained by continuing this feud that existed between you? 'Tis not too late to make your peace with Richard. With Richard as your ally, you would have no need of Vernier."

"If it were only that simple—"

"It *is* that simple," Adrienne said hotly, gripping Hugh's hands in desperation. "Yes, you might have to swallow your pride. Yes, you might have to make some concessions. You might even have to agree to grant Richard the use of your seaports for *his* purposes rather than your own. But is that such a terrible price to pay if it will keep Sainte-Croix from being attacked?"

Hugh's face darkened. He threw off Adrienne's hands. "To hell with Sainte-Croix's seaports!" he bellowed. "If I thought it would end the violence, I would give the infernal seaports to the pope himself!"

"My lord, there is no need to blaspheme—" Adrienne broke off and shrank away from the fury in Hugh's eyes. "I-I'm sorry," she stammered. " 'Tis not my place to tell you what to do."

Hugh struggled to get his temper under control. "I don't blame you, *princesse*. And I'm not angry with you. I'm angry at myself for embroiling all of us in a situation that I no longer have the power to get us out of." He hesitated, then added in a low voice, "And I'm scared to death that no matter which path I choose, it will be the wrong one."

For the first time, Adrienne truly appreciated the bind Hugh was in. If he remained allied with Vernier, he risked subjecting Sainte-Croix to attack by Richard's army. If he sided with Richard, Vernier would likely turn on him and vent his own ire on the countship. While a part of her secretly hoped he would choose Richard over Vernier, simply because it would mean the end of his betrothal to Vernier's daughter, she knew that in the end both the decision and the responsibility for that decision must be Hugh's. She went to him and placed her hands flat on his chest, drawing strength from the steady heartbeat she felt beneath his tunic. She lifted her gaze to his, and her own heart ached when she saw the bruises on his face from the fight with Vernier. "My lord, it takes a brave man to admit his fear. But whether you decide to cast your lot with Richard or with Vernier, I know that when the time comes you will do what is right."

Hugh took her face between his hands and kissed her forehead. Despair darkened his eyes. Adrienne was going to learn the truth sooner or later, and he preferred to have her hear it from him rather than from someone like Vernier. "*Princesse*, if it were only a matter of choosing between Richard and Vernier, I could readily accept the consequences of that choice. But tell me, how do I choose between my brother and you and our unborn child?"

Chapter Fifteen

ADRIENNE LOOKED AT Hugh in bewilderment. The subject of the conversation had switched from King Richard and the Count of Vernier to her and Graeham. It made no sense—unless something else had happened, something she knew nothing about. "I'm not sure I understand."

"We received word this morning that Wilhelm of Lachen's men attacked Burg Moudon. They took Graeham prisoner. Lachen has promised to release Graeham if I deliver you to him and relinquish control of Sainte-Croix."

Adrienne felt the floor shift beneath her. She had not forgotten about Duke Wilhelm, but she had convinced herself that he no longer wanted her, making it easier for her to pretend he was no longer a threat to her.

Hugh caught her by the shoulders as she started to sway. "*Princesse*, I have no intention of turning you over to Lachen. Please believe that."

"My lord, how can you say that? Graeham is your brother!"

"And you are my . . ." Hugh faltered. *You are my beloved*, he thought, suddenly painfully aware of how much he had come to care for Adrienne in the short time he had known her. It unsettled him to realize just how empty his life would be without her. He wasn't even certain he would have the will to live should anything happen to her. "You are the mother of my child," he finished.

"Hugh, listen to me. Duke Wilhelm cannot hurt me except at great penalty to himself; my betrothal contracts are explicit on that point. But he can kill Graeham, and if his demands aren't met, he may do just that."

"Your betrothal agreement might protect you, *princesse*, but it won't guarantee our baby's safety. I hardly expect Lachen to welcome another man's child with open arms."

The truth of what Hugh was saying tore at Adrienne's heart, but she knew she had no choice. "My lord, if Duke Wilhelm won't accept my child," she said shakily, "then I will request that the baby be given to you to raise."

Hugh stared at her in stunned outrage. "My God, woman! Are you so eager to return to Lachen that you are willing to abandon your own child?"

"No!" A sob broke in Adrienne's throat. "Just the thought of having to give up my child breaks my heart. But if I do not take that chance and Duke Wilhelm kills Graeham, I will not be able to live with myself, knowing that I could have done something to stop him. Nor can I bear the thought of spending the rest of my life enduring your hatred."

Hugh's expression gentled. "I could never hate you. Not for that."

A tear streaked down Adrienne's cheek. " 'Tis easy enough to say, my lord, but until it happens, you don't know how you would react."

Hugh frowned. That Adrienne was right did not make the situation easier to accept. Before he could speak, there was a faint knock on the door, and he turned to find Lina standing in the doorway, holding a tray. The girl looked uncertainly from him to Adrienne. "I brought the tea Lady Adrienne wanted," she said in a frightened voice.

Adrienne sniffled and wiped her eyes, and Hugh went to the door to take the tray. "Thank you," he said.

Some of the stiffness left Lina's body. "Will there be anything else?" she asked.

Adrienne shook her head. "No, thank you."

"Yes, there is something else." Hugh corrected. He looked at Lina. "I want a cot moved into this bedchamber. Starting tonight, you will sleep in here."

Lina bobbed her head. "Yes, m'lord."

Adrienne started across the chamber. "My lord, that isn't necessary."

Hugh set the tray down on the table. "It is necessary," he said, "for my peace of mind. I will rest better knowing that you are not alone."

Hugh's meaning was clear; he would not be returning to her bed. Not tonight. Perhaps never.

Adrienne looked away, but not before Hugh had seen the dismay in her eyes. Going to her, he tilted her face toward his. He spoke in a low, urgent voice. "Under the circumstances, I think it would be best if we kept our distance from each other. At least for now."

Tears stung the back of Adrienne's nose. "I understand," she whispered achingly.

I love you, Hugh thought. He searched her face, unconsciously committing to memory every feature, his gaze finally coming to rest on her gray eyes, bright with unshed tears. They were Henry's eyes, and for once he was glad that Henry's blood flowed in her veins; during the coming weeks, Adrienne was going to need every bit of the Plantagenet's strength and courage. His thumb grazed across her cheekbone. "Stay safe, *princesse*."

Adrienne saw little of Hugh during the weeks that followed. He was usually to be found with his men preparing the castle for defense against a siege. Temporary wooden galleries were built and installed along the tops of the inner and outer curtain walls and around the tops of the towers. Projecting beyond the walls, the galleries would provide secure footing for the archers and would enable the defenders to protect the base of the wall. Thousands of arrows were made, and boulders were gathered, to be used as missiles in the catapults or dropped over the castle walls on the attackers below.

As promised, the ships sent by Raymond of Toulouse began to arrive. Food and grain were taken off the ships and loaded onto wagons and pack animals, then carried overland and stored in every available space in the castle and the village as well as in the caves that riddled the surrounding mountains.

Adrienne's movements were confined to the keep and the inner ward. Since the unfortunate evening when fighting had broken out in the great hall, she had taken her meals in her bedchamber, with Lina to keep her company. Occasionally she ventured down to the kitchens where Paschal and Marthe and Lina went out of their way to make her feel welcome, but the sidelong glances and the whispered remarks of the other servants made her uneasy, and she seldom stayed long.

If she saw little of Hugh, she saw more than she wanted of Vernier. Everywhere she turned, the count seemed to be nearby, watching her with a hard, predatory gaze that chilled her blood. When she descended the stairs, she would find him standing at the bottom as if waiting for her. He would not speak. He would merely nod. When she trained in the ward with Sperantia, she would sometimes look up and see Vernier standing on the battlement, watching her. Always watching.

Although the days remained sunny, the nights turned bitter cold. At night Adrienne would lie awake in her bed, listening to the wind howling outside her chamber windows and to Lina muttering in her sleep from her cot against the far wall. Sometimes laughter drifted up from the great hall, and she would wonder what Hugh was doing.

Christmas came and went without the boisterous two-week-long celebration that Adrienne was accustomed to. Rather, it was a rather solemn affair marked by a prayerful mass and a curious little mystery play performed on Christmas Eve by some of the villagers who portrayed shepherds praying to Our Lady to curse their cruel over-lords. The seeming incongruity of the play and the absence of the familiar rituals made Adrienne homesick; she missed the feasting and the exchanging of gifts and the holly boughs with their bright red berries, and even the forbidden sprig of mistletoe that always managed to find its way into the keep over Father Bernard's objections.

Rumors reached them, sporadically at first, then almost daily: Richard was on the Continent; Richard's army was being quartered at Chinon while preparing for the march south; heavy rains in the north had flooded the Loire Valley, delaying Richard's passage; Richard was in Poitiers; Wilhelm of Lachen had amassed a sizable force and was headed toward Lyons.

Tension hung in the air.

No more was said of Hugh trading Adrienne for Graeham, although the thought was never far from Adrienne's mind. She alternated between wondering at Hugh's sanity in refusing to even consider the possibility—after all, Graeham's life was at stake—and thanking God for saving her from a marriage she had never wanted. One day she would pray that she could find something, anything, to do that would help get Hugh out of the mess he was in; the next day would find her angrily reminding herself that Hugh de Clairmont and his brother were getting no more than they deserved.

The only thing that remained constant was the worry that shadowed her days and haunted her nights with troubled dreams: if Château Clairmont came under attack, she and her baby could die, regardless of what Hugh decided to do.

A fire blazed on the hearth in Adrienne's bedchamber, chasing away the chill that inevitably crept into the air when the sun went down. Because of the impending siege, firewood was hoarded, and Adrienne saved her meager ration for use on the nights when she bathed.

A copper tub had been set up before the hearth and filled with hot water. Steam rose from the tub, filling the chamber with its scented warmth. Sitting in the tub with her knees drawn up, Adrienne leaned back as far as the restricted space would allow and closed her eyes. Lina had gone down to the kitchen to fetch more hot water, and she relished the respite from the girl's fawning.

Lina meant well, and Adrienne truly enjoyed the girl's company, but she was growing tired of being waited on hand and foot as if she were incapable of helping herself. She knew some women relished the attentions of their waiting maids, who sometimes became beloved confidantes and were often a woman's only source of female companionship. And other women, like Lady Joanna, whose illness kept her confined to her bedchamber, had a legitimate need for their services.

She, on the other hand, was accustomed to solitude and usually preferred it.

There was one person, though, whose company she sorely missed: Hugh.

She had seen him earlier in the day when she took Sperantia out into the ward for a lesson with the lure. He was up on the wall walk with Sir Conraed. Judging from their pointing gestures and the occasional sweep of Hugh's hand, she had surmised that they were discussing the lay of the land and potential strategies for defending Château Clairmont from attack.

Even from a distance Adrienne had been aware of the power and the masculine energy that Hugh exuded. He was a born leader; neither his proud stance nor his confident manner betrayed any of the inner torment she knew he was suffering. Only half realizing that she did so, she had placed her palm over the curve of her abdomen and felt an intense joy in the thought that her child had so handsome and courageous a father. Seeing her, Hugh had smiled and lifted his hand in greeting, and her heart had swelled to the point of bursting.

Adrienne had rinsed her face and was wiping the excess water out of her eyes with the towel when she heard the chamber door open, then close again. "I'm glad you're back, Lina. The water quickly grows cold."

She twisted her hair and held it on top her head with one hand so it would not get wet, but when she leaned forward so that Lina could empty the bucket of water into the tub, she saw the toe of a man's boot next to the tub, and she gasped.

Instinctively one hand flew to cover her breasts and the other gripped the side of the tub for support, but when she snapped her head around, her alarm shuddered into relief when she realized that it was Hugh. "My lord, you gave me a fright!" she said breathlessly. "I was expecting Lina."

Hugh set one of the two buckets he was carrying down on the floor and grinned boyishly. "I waylaid Lina on the stairs and promised her a holiday if she would permit me to take over her duties for this night," he said. "I wanted to find out for myself how my son and his mother are faring."

Adrienne was not proof against either that deep voice or the compelling smile, and she felt herself blushing beneath Hugh's possessive regard. She again lifted her hair and leaned forward. "You sound certain that the baby is going to be a boy."

Hugh poured the hot water into the tub, careful not to scald Adrienne's back. He set down the bucket and knelt beside the tub, then began rolling up his sleeves. His dark eyes twinkled. "Positive."

Hugh held out his hand, and Adrienne placed the soap and the washing cloth in it. "Your *son* is fine," she said. "But his mother has missed you terribly."

In spite of her attempt at humor, her voice caught.

Hugh's smile faded. Leaning forward, he slid his free hand into her hair and drew her toward him. His lips found hers, and he kissed her tenderly but with a heartfelt passion that came from deep within his soul. When he left Château Clairmont in the morning, he wanted to carry with him the memory of her lips soft upon his. Nothing else mattered—not Vernier, not Richard, not even his own brother.

Graeham was a grown man; he was going to have to stop jumping in and rescuing him every time he got into trouble. Granted, Graeham was not responsible for this latest trouble with Lachen; *he* was. But after this, Graeham was going to have to solve his own problems. His wife and his child came first.

His wife.

He wanted to marry Adrienne; he had reached that conclusion several days ago. That was why he was leaving in the morning. He was going to go to Paris to renew his oath of fealty to King Philip and to make his peace with the Crown. It was time to put aside his resentment and forget that two years ago Philip had turned a blind eye to Henry's invasion of Sainte-Croix. He needed Philip's help. This was no time to cling to false pride.

When Hugh finally pulled his lips away from Adrienne's, her eyes were huge and shining with unshed tears. The desperation he saw in her eyes caused his chest to tighten. "Why the tears?" he asked. "I used to be able to make you smile by kissing you. Have I become so inept these past weeks that my efforts make you want to cry?"

"My lord, that was a good-bye kiss."

Hugh drew back. "And you're an expert?" he teased, trying to coax a smile out of her.

"I had a good teacher. You."

When he saw that he was not going to be able to cheer her up by teasing her, he stopped trying. "You're right. Conraed and I are riding out in the morning to inspect our outer line of defenses." Hugh hated lying to her, but only Conraed knew of his real intent. Vernier, Toulouse, and Foix were not privy to his plans, and he felt that Adrienne would be safer knowing only what he had told them.

"I want to be certain I've left no weak spots where Richard's army might be able to break through," Hugh continued. "The longer we can keep Richard away from Château Clairmont, the better chance we have of holding out against a siege."

Adrienne's heart sank. So Hugh had decided to stay allied with Vernier after all, which meant that Hugh's betrothal to Alais de Vernier was still as valid as ever.

At Adrienne's crestfallen expression, Hugh chuckled. "I'm only going to be gone for a few days, *princesse*— a couple of weeks if I encounter any problems."

If I can't have you, you might as well be gone forever, Adrienne thought dismally. She forced a smile. "Please don't mind me, my lord. I'm merely feeling weepy tonight, which is vastly preferable to being sick."

Hugh grinned at her and began soaping up the washing cloth. "Do you think you could stop weeping long enough to enjoy having your back scrubbed?"

Hugh's grin was infectious, and Adrienne found herself responding to it in spite of her low spirits. "And just how long might that be, my lord?"

Hugh's expression softened. "As long as you want, *princesse*," he said quietly. "For tonight I am your humble servant."

I love you, Adrienne thought. "All night?" she asked.

"All night," Hugh said. "We will do whatever you want." He hesitated, then added, "Within reason, of course."

A dimple appeared at the corner of Adrienne's mouth. "Of course," she said. Then she gathered up her hair and bent forward.

Hugh ran the soapy cloth over her back, lightly at first, then gradually increasing the pressure as he changed the long sweeping strokes to tight circles that left her skin pink and glistening.

Adrienne shuddered with delight at the gentle roughness of his touch. "That feels wonderful," she murmured as his hand moved from her shoulders down to the small of her back. The tension slowly began to ebb from her muscles, and she thought she could sit there forever. Then his hand slid around to the front to cup her breast.

Adrienne sucked in her breath and lifted her head to meet his gaze. She had not realized that she was still covering her breasts until Hugh gently moved her hand away.

His gaze never leaving hers, he soaped her breasts, gently stroking and caressing them until her nipples were hard and erect beneath his palm. Then he began rolling one between his thumb and forefinger, and Adrienne's pupils suddenly expanded, making her eyes look almost black in the firelight. Her breathing quickened.

Hugh lowered his head, and suddenly his lips were upon hers again, hot and demanding and robbing her of whatever thought she might have entertained of resisting him. Her lips parted, and she kissed him deeply in return, taking every ounce of passion that he offered her, then giving it back to him tenfold. Whatever happened tomorrow, the night belonged to them alone, and she did not want to waste even a second of it.

He kissed her until her mouth burned, then tempered the fire with his tongue, running it over her lips and between them with a fierce tenderness that quickly broke down what remained of her defenses, leaving her quivering and breathless and aching for more. And then, when she thought she could stand it no longer, he possessed her lips again.

All the while he was kissing her, he never stopped caressing her breasts. He brushed his fingers back and forth across her hardened nipples with a touch that was almost maddening in its lightness. Adrienne rose up on her knees. Curling her arm around his neck, she leaned against the hand that was pleasuring her as she returned his kisses with a feverish passion, her body demanding all that he had to give.

Holding her steady with one hand placed securely in the small of her back, Hugh let his other hand glide down over her belly and into the tangle of curls between her legs. He parted the damp curls and began teasing and caressing the sensitive flesh, bringing her to a trembling arousal before sliding his fingers deep inside her.

Adrienne cried out against Hugh's mouth, and her body arched. Hugh caught her to keep her from falling and held her against him, while her muscles contracted rhythmically around the fingers still buried within her wet warmth.

He pressed his face against her hair, feeling her tremors as acutely as if they were his own. She was shaking, and her quick, shallow breaths were somewhere between being gasps and sobs.

Still holding her, he slowly withdrew his fingers, then gently eased her to her feet. He kissed her hair, then her cheek, and finally her soft mouth. When he lifted his gaze to hers, her eyes were wide and trusting in her flushed face. Steadying her with one hand, he bent and picked up the remaining bucket, and Adrienne held her hair aside and obediently responded to his instructions to turn while he slowly poured the warm water over her, rinsing off the last of the soap.

Water streamed down over her sleek, glistening form, made softer in recent weeks by its newly acquired roundness, and Hugh's body began to ache with the intensity of his desire for her and the effort of suppressing that desire.

Adrienne stepped out of the tub and stood by the fire while Hugh dried her off. He started with her shoulders and worked his way downward, briskly rubbing her lavender-scented skin with the towel until it tingled.

Kneeling before her, he lifted one slender foot and toweled it dry, then placed it against his thigh while he dried first one leg and then the other, beginning with her calf, then her thigh, and finally moving to the soft, sensitive skin of her inner thigh. Adrienne gasped and braced her hands on his shoulders as he eased his fingers into her and began pleasuring her again.

She did not know if it was her closeness to the hearth or Hugh's skillful touch or the passion that smoldered in his eyes as he watched her reactions to his caresses, or perhaps a mixture of all three, that made her body feel as if it were on fire. All she knew was that she wanted it to go on forever.

She clutched his powerful, muscular shoulders as he worked his pagan magic on her, seeking out her most sensitive spots and teasing them with his knowing fingers until she felt as if she would burst from an excess of pure pleasure. She could no longer stand without trembling violently, and had Hugh not been holding her she would have fallen. Suddenly a dam inside her broke, and every inch of her was flooded with a golden liquid warmth. She felt her limbs give way. Everything around her went dark, and she was falling, falling . . .

When the darkness began to lift, Adrienne realized dimly that Hugh was carrying her across the chamber. He lowered her to the bed, and the contact of her overheated skin with the icy sheets startled her back to reality. She shivered and opened her eyes just as Hugh released her and straightened up.

His smile flashed white in his tanned face. "Welcome back, *princesse*."

Still too dazed to make her mouth form coherent words, Adrienne responded with a drowsy smile. She was not certain exactly what had happened. All she knew was that she felt as if every ounce of strength had drained out of her. She felt groggy, as if she had been drugged. She felt as if she were floating.

Hugh began to remove his clothing, and Adrienne watched him without moving or speaking as the garments came off, revealing the sheer strength and power of the man who wore them, a man whose life was shaped by war and violence, yet who made love to her with such exquisite tenderness that she never feared coming to his bed. Firelight danced off Hugh's dark hair and sun-bronzed skin, making him look like a majestic pagan god.

And when he came to her, she felt pride and love and passion swell inside her.

He parted her legs with his knee, but did not immediately enter her. Instead, he began stroking the insides of her thighs with a touch so light Adrienne thought she would go mad. Her hips rose off the bed, straining toward the promise of fulfillment that he held just beyond her reach. "My lord, please . . . I don't think I can endure much more of this. I want . . . I want *you*."

In answer to her wish, Hugh shifted over her and eased his swollen shaft into her, and Adrienne gasped as the world melted around her.

The fire had long since died. Hugh tucked the covers around Adrienne to shut out the chill of the night. She stirred and snuggled closer to the warmth of his body. Her head lay against his shoulder, and beneath the covers, one warm, slender hand lay on his chest, close to his heart.

Hugh closed his eyes and rested his cheek against her hair. He had missed sleeping with her in his arms. Even more than making love to her, he enjoyed just being close to her like this, holding her.

As he lay there, waiting for sleep to come, he went over in his mind his plans for the morning. He was having second thoughts about taking Conraed with him; he wondered if it would not be wiser to have another knight accompany him and leave Conraed here at Château Clairmont to watch over Adrienne. Unfortunately Conraed usually accompanied him whenever he left the castle. If he changed his habits now, he might arouse Vernier's suspicions.

In the end he decided to stay with his original plan. Adrienne would be well protected; his men already knew they were to keep Vernier away from her.

He was just drifting off to sleep when the sound of a voice jolted him awake. His eyes flew open, and he lay rigid and alert, listening.

Nothing.

The only sound to break the silence was Adrienne's rhythmic breathing.

Hugh frowned. He could have sworn he had heard a voice, and that voice was close by.

He pulled back his head and looked down at Adrienne. She was sound asleep. At least she appeared to be. "Did you say something, *princesse*?" he whispered.

Adrienne sighed in her sleep and murmured groggily, "I said . . . I love . . . you."

Adrienne stood at the parapet atop the tower Hugh had shown her when they first arrived at Château Clairmont and fought the ache that filled her heart as she watched Hugh and Sir Conraed ride away. She tried to tell herself that Hugh was going to be gone for only a few days, but she knew she would not rest easy until he returned.

Had anyone told her a few months, or even a few weeks, ago how much she would come to love the man who had once been her enemy, she would not have believed him. But she did love Hugh, more than she had ever thought it was possible to love anyone. She remembered the lovers depicted in the tapestry in her bedchamber at Burg Moudon, and her own cynical conclusion that no woman would ever be foolish enough to love a man that much. If she had known then that falling in love would bring her as much pain as pleasure, she thought sadly, she would have taken greater precautions to protect her heart. No matter how much she loved Hugh, he was promised to another. She had surrendered her heart and her soul to a man who was not hers to love.

"Are you ready to go back, my lady?" Roland asked.

Adrienne had forgotten about the knight. Had he not spoken, she might have stayed on top of the tower forever. Now she realized just how cold it was up here. Drawing her mantle tighter around her, she nodded. "Thank you for bringing me up here," she said.

Roland bowed slightly. " 'Twas my pleasure, m'lady."

He held open the door, and Adrienne stepped inside the shadowy tower and began the long descent down the winding stairs. Neither of them spoke again until they reached the landing outside Adrienne's chamber door. Adrienne thanked the knight again and started to enter her bed-chamber, but Roland held back. "My lady, if I might be so bold . . ."

Adrienne stopped, her curiosity piqued by the urgency in Roland's voice. "What is it?"

"My lady, do you remember the day you were attacked by the renegade knights?"

"How could I forget? Every day I think of how you nearly lost your life to save mine. I am grateful to you, my lord; I hope you know that."

Roland was silent for a moment, as if weighing the wisdom of speaking his mind. "I've known Lord Hugh for years," he finally said. "When he sets his mind to something, he is tireless in his pursuit of his goal. Nothing can change him from his course, and he has little regard for the suffering of others if that suffering is essential to his purpose. He has been that way for as long as I've known him."

Roland hesitated, then continued in a low, concerned voice, "Something happened to him that day; something inside him changed. All his resolve was directed toward saving you, not because you were a necessary part of his plans but because he truly feared for your life. Lord Hugh takes risks only after a great deal of thought. That was the first time I ever saw him throw caution aside and unthinkingly risk his own life for another.

"What I am trying to say, my lady, is that, although his actions may sometimes indicate otherwise, he cares deeply for you."

Although Adrienne had not known Hugh long enough to know what he had been like in the past or when he had started changing, Roland's words were just what she needed to hear to keep her spirits from sinking any further. "Thank you," she said quietly.

For the next few days there was no change in the routine of the inhabitants of either the castle or the village.

Preparations for a siege continued. From the bank of windows in her bedchamber, Adrienne could see supplies being moved into the mountains where they would be stored in caves.

It puzzled her that more men seemed to make the trip up into the mountains than returned, and she wondered if perhaps they were entering and exiting the caves at different points. If there were as many caves in the region as Hugh had implied, then she supposed that some of those caves could be linked. She thought of the snakes that had been found in the caves, and shuddered. A warm, sunny day was often enough to bring the creatures out of hibernation.

There was a soft tap at the chamber door, and then it opened.

Adrienne turned.

Lina entered with a tray and a bright smile. "I brought your breakfast, m'lady," she said cheerfully.

"Thank you, but I'm not hungry."

"But, m'lady, since Lord Hugh left, you haven't eaten enough to keep a sparrow alive."

"Lina, please. I don't wish to argue with you, but I really don't want anything right now. If I get hungry later, I shall tell you." Adrienne turned back to the window.

Lina's face fell. Without another word, she left the bedchamber.

After she had gone, Adrienne sighed and rested her forehead against the cool stone wall. She had not meant to be short with Lina; she just wanted to be left alone.

Since Hugh left, the life seemed to have drained out of her. She spent her days either lying on her bed or staring out the window. She had no appetite. The longer Hugh stayed away, the more she worried about him. She could not shake the uncomfortable sensation that something terrible was going to befall him.

This time there was no knock at the door; it swung open and Marthe marched into the room, holding the tray Lina had been carrying earlier. Marthe put the tray on the table by the hearth and plunked her hands on her ample hips. "I don't want to hear any of this nonsense about not being hungry," she said. "You must eat for that child you're carrying, if not for yourself."

Adrienne shoved her hair away from her face in frustration. "Marthe, I told Lina I would eat later."

"You will eat *now*." As if to emphasize her point, Marthe pulled the chair away from the table and turned it toward Adrienne.

Adrienne's stomach contracted. Her face paled. "Marthe, please, I cannot."

Marthe's expression softened, but she remained firm. "M'lady, Lord Hugh has enough troubles on his shoulders without having to worry about you starving yourself to death. I want you to eat something and then put on your mantle and go out into the sunshine. Staying closed up in this chamber is not good for either you or your baby."

At Marthe's urging, Adrienne managed to get down some bread and some stewed pears, and she had to admit that she did feel a little better after having eaten something.

When she donned her mantle and followed Marthe down to the kitchen, Lina had just finished tying a pair of feathered pigeon wings and a piece of raw meat to a padded weight. Lina smiled hesitantly. "I made a lure for you, m'lady, in case you want to take Sperantia out for a while."

Adrienne took the lure and looked it over. She remembered the first lure Baldhere had made for her, and her throat tightened. "You do good work, Lina. Thank you."

A pleased grin split Lina's face.

Adrienne hugged the girl and kissed her cheek. "I don't deserve your kindness, but I don't know what I would do without it. Thank you for being so patient with me." She looked at Marthe. "Thank you both."

"Are you ready, my lady?" came a voice from behind her.

Adrienne turned to find Sir Roland standing in the doorway. She glanced from him to Lina to Marthe and breathed a sigh of exasperation. "I am beginning to suspect that there is a conspiracy afoot. Do you have a reason for wanting me out of this castle?"

"We want to see you smile again," Roland said.

Hugh and Conraed rode hard, pressing steadily north-ward. Once they left the mountains, the weather turned dis-mal. A damp chill hugged the ground like a cold, wet blanket, and the sun stayed well hidden behind the clouds.

Whenever they stopped for the night, they made camp well away from the main road, and they took turns keeping watch. Several times Hugh thought they were being fol-lowed, but when he mentioned his suspicions to Conraed, the knight looked at him oddly. He was becoming obsessed.

"I should have brought Adrienne with us," he said when they stopped to rest at noon on the fourth day.

Conraed tipped up his water flask and took a long drink. "We agreed it would be best to leave her behind," he reminded Hugh. "If Vernier even suspected you were about to betray him, he would turn his army on Sainte-Croix and destroy it. Lady Adrienne is our assurance that he won't."

Hugh shook his head. "I don't trust him, Conraed. I would not put it past him to try to harm her while I am away."

"Would you prefer that he harm your people instead? Is it worth protecting one life at the expense of thousands?"

Hugh thought of Adrienne lying in his arms and of her innocently whispered "I love you," and his chest con-stricted. His expression was unreadable as he regarded the knight. "*Two* lives," he said flatly. "And the answer to both questions is no."

Chapter Sixteen

THICK BLACK SMOKE billowed up from mountains left parched after a long hot summer and an uncharacteristically dry autumn.

The guards posted at the top of the tower turned to stare as Adrienne burst through the door with Sir Roland close on her heels and ran to the parapet. Her eyes were wide with horror. "My God!" she cried, trying to catch her breath. "The entire mountain is ablaze!"

Vernier spoke behind her. "Your intended husband is announcing his arrival," he said harshly.

Adrienne whirled around to face him. "Duke Wilhelm?"

The expression in Vernier's eyes was hard and unforgiving. "Were you expecting anyone else, *Lady* Adrienne?"

Adrienne winced at Vernier's deliberate insult, but she refused to be intimidated. She lifted her chin and eyed the count with the same lack of deference that she knew infuriated Hugh. "Surely you did not think Duke Wilhelm would peaceably accede to his bride's abduction?" she shot back.

Vernier's face darkened. "No more than I will accede to having my son-in-law's whore abide under the same roof with his wife."

"I might remind you, my lord, that you won't have a son-in-law if your daughter does not arrive here safely."

Surprise, then fury, flashed in Vernier's eyes. "Who told you Alais is coming here?"

Roland took Adrienne's arm. "My lady, you need not answer to him."

"*Who told you?*" Vernier demanded.

Adrienne resisted the pressure Roland was exerting on her arm. She met Vernier's furious gaze without flinching. She suspected Vernier was worried about his daughter, who should have arrived weeks ago, and she seized upon that worry. " 'Tis common knowledge," she said smoothly. "Sending for her when Sainte-Croix was preparing for a siege was hardly the act of a man in full possession of his senses, my lord. You had best pray that your daughter and her entourage do not meet up with Duke Wilhelm's men on the road."

Roland forcibly dragged Adrienne inside the stairwell and slammed the door shut. "My lady, what has possessed you that you seek to anger him?" he hissed in the darkness. "Vernier is a dangerous man!"

"I know that," Adrienne whispered. "But I don't think he will do anything foolish or try to provoke Duke Wilhelm into a fight if he thinks there is a chance that his daughter might be in danger."

"Lady Adrienne, the Count of Vernier cares naught whether his daughter lives or dies. 'Tis Sainte-Croix that he wants, and he will stop at *nothing* to get it."

Adrienne had begun to feel ill. "To include killing Hugh?"

Roland shook his head. "Not at the risk of provoking King Philip. Philip might have found it convenient to ignore Henry's seizure of Sainte-Croix, but he won't be so complacent where Vernier is concerned. He has enough to do to keep rebellion in Toulouse repressed. If Vernier were to gain control of Sainte-Croix, between Vernier and Toulouse, Philip risks losing the entire south of France."

"Then where is Hugh? Why hasn't he returned?"

Roland glanced at the closed door. "Come, my lady. 'Tis not wise to talk here where we might be overheard."

At Roland's suggestion, they went down to the mews.

The falconer's assistant had just finished feeding the birds. "Good morning, m'lady," he said when Adrienne and Roland entered the mews. "Had I known you were coming so early, I would have waited so that you could feed Sperantia yourself."

"I grew restless," Adrienne said. "May I take Sperantia out now?"

The youth nodded. "I'll get the gauntlet and the leash."

As soon as he left, Adrienne turned to Roland and said in a low voice, "Please, my lord, I cannot bear not knowing. Where is Lord Hugh?"

"I was hoping you could tell *me*," Roland said.

Adrienne's brows arched questioningly.

"My lady, 'tis no secret that Hugh spent his last night here with you. Before he left, did he tell you of his plans?"

Adrienne fought the embarrassment that consumed her face in a hot crimson tide. "He told me only that he and Sir Conraed were going to inspect Sainte-Croix's outer defenses and that he would return in a few days," she said defensively.

Roland persisted. "Did he tell you anything else? Anything at all that might give us some idea where he could have gone?"

Adrienne's embarrassment turned to alarm. "I don't understand. Has something happened to him?"

"We don't know. All we know is that he is not in Sainte-Croix."

Just then the falconer's assistant returned with a thin leather leash and a heavy leather gauntlet. Adrienne forced a smile and took the items. Her heart raced. *Dear God, let Hugh be safe*, she prayed frantically, trying to keep her fear from showing on her face.

The falconer's assistant picked up the pails in which he had carried kitchen scraps out to the mews to feed the falcons and harriers. "M'lady, I need to return these to the kitchen," he said. "I will be right back."

Adrienne nodded. "That's fine. If I need anything, I shall wait for you."

Adrienne waited until the youth had left the mews, then rounded on Roland. "My lord, is it possible that he went to Poitiers to negotiate a truce with Richard?"

Roland looked worried. "If he did, then we have more to fear from Vernier than from Lachen."

After talking for a few more minutes, Adrienne went to Sperantia and untied her from the perch, keeping a firm grip on the jesses as the falcon bated her wings and tried to fly away. Accompanied by Sir Roland, she carried the falcon outside.

Neither of them saw the man who was hiding in the shadows in the far corner of the mews, watching and listening.

Two days later the Count of Foix and his men abruptly departed, igniting a fine storm of speculation. Rumors proliferated. Some said Vernier and Foix had argued over an order Foix had issued to some of Vernier's men. Others said Foix and Toulouse and Vernier could not agree on whether to advance an offensive attack against Wilhelm of Lachen. One disturbing rumor that refused to die hinted that Vernier had proposed taking advantage of Hugh's absence to seize control of Sainte-Croix.

Wherever the truth lay, when Foix's men pulled out, the remaining knights and men-at-arms had to scramble to close the gap that left Sainte-Croix wide open to Lachen's advancing army.

Lachen's men scoured the countryside, ruthlessly destroying farmhouses and mills and laying farm fields and vineyards to the torch. Villages and keeps that had yet to recover from Hugh's march on the countship only a few months before were subjected again to attack.

Refugees from the outlying villages poured into Château Clairmont daily, fleeing hunger and cold and seeking asylum from the devastation that had driven them from their homes. Room was made for some of them within the castle walls; others were housed with families in the village. All day long, the gates were repeatedly opened to allow them to enter, and the ward was filled with men, women, and children with pinched faces and eyes dulled by despair.

Adrienne found her own refuge in keeping busy. She cut and rolled bandages. She helped Marthe in the kitchen, preparing food for the newcomers. She watched the refugees' children, giving the weary mothers a chance to rest. And when the falconer's assistant was put to work as a message runner, Adrienne took over his duties, feeding and watering the falcons and sweeping up the droppings and castings beneath the perches.

Lachen's encroachment into Sainte-Croix was no longer measured by smoke from distant fires or by tales told of his brutal, methodical devastation of the countryside; it could be *seen*. Great wooden siege towers and trebuchets were moved closer to Château Clairmont each day. In the valleys, skirmishes erupted between knights and foot-soldiers on both sides, and the opposing armies hurled missiles at each other with trebuchets and catapults.

There was a new flurry of activity inside the ward as men dismantled the heavy artillery machines and hoisted them to the tops of the towers where they were reassembled and readied for use against the besiegers.

With the increase in the number of soldiers quartered around Château Clairmont and with the steady influx of refugees, a new worry arose: how to protect the castle's dwindling water supply. The main wells were safely located inside the curtain walls, but the drain on them in recent weeks had been tremendous, and there were no guarantees that they would not run dry at a critical moment. Extra guards were posted at vulnerable points along an underground conduit that carried water down to the village from the mountains; if the wells failed, the conduit would be the castle's only source of water.

Throughout it all, Adrienne prayed constantly for Hugh's safety. The longer he was away, the more certain she became that he had gone for help, although in recent days a new doubt had crept into her thoughts and refused to be dislodged: suppose Hugh had abandoned them. Suppose he had decided to run rather than stay and fight for his people and his homeland. She told herself that it was not possible, that Hugh was too honorable a man.

But even an honorable man had his limits, Adrienne thought, and what better way was there for him to extricate himself from the mess in which he had entangled himself? What better way to escape his betrothal to Alais de Vernier, his obligations to Sainte-Croix, his responsibility for her and her unborn child?

Although Adrienne never voiced her fears to anyone, they began to take their toll. Dark shadows, a legacy of sleepless nights, ringed her eyes, and her skin grew pallid. Her hands became chapped and reddened from the work she did in the kitchens, and they might have been worse had Lina not rubbed a healing balm into them every night before Adrienne went to bed. Unable to escape Marthe's critical eye, she ate well for the baby's sake, but her appetite was gone and she derived no enjoyment from the food, no matter how tasty or well prepared.

Her pregnancy was beginning to show.

It was not yet daylight when Adrienne was awakened from a troubled sleep by a muted *thud* that came from somewhere outside her bedchamber walls. The sound had not been close enough to pose an immediate danger, but it disturbed Adrienne nonetheless because she did not know what had caused it or where it had come from.

She lifted her head and looked at Lina, who was sleeping soundly on her cot against the far wall. If there had been a noise, Lina was blissfully unaffected by it. Wondering if perhaps she had dreamed it, Adrienne lay back down.

She was just drifting off to sleep when she heard the sound again: *thud, thud . . . thud.*

Throwing back the covers, she bolted out of bed and ran to the window.

Lina stirred. "Is something amiss, m'lady?" she mumbled sleepily.

Adrienne threw open the window.

Fear wrapped itself around her heart and squeezed, robbing her of breath.

Lachen's forces had broken through the line of defense and moved their trebuchets into position just below the outer curtain wall. The noise she had heard was the pounding of the wall with massive boulders hurled by the trebuchets.

Adrienne closed the window and leaned against the wall. She was shaking. Something was not right; even without Foix's men, they should have been able to hold out against Duke Wilhelm indefinitely.

Lina clambered out of bed. "M'lady, what is it?"

Adrienne fought to get her churning emotions under control. "They're attacking the outer wall," she said shakily.

Lina crossed herself.

At that moment the entire castle seemed to come awake.

Footsteps pounded the stairs as men scrambled to take up positions atop the towers and the walls. Shouts filled the wards.

Shaking, in part from the cold and partially from nerves, Adrienne broke the thin layer of ice that had formed on the surface of her washbasin and quickly washed with the cold water before throwing on her clothes.

"Wh-what are you going to d-do, m'lady?" Lina stammered, her teeth chattering.

"I don't know," Adrienne said. Her hands trembled as she combed the tangles from her hair in the darkness. "But I cannot stay in this chamber and wait for the walls to crumble. I have to do *something.*"

Do what? her mind frantically pleaded. If twelve hundred men could not protect Sainte-Croix from pointless destruction, just what was she capable of doing to stop it?

You can surrender to Duke Wilhelm.

Impossible!

He wants you. Once he has you, he will stop the attack.

But what of Hugh?

Hugh is not here. There is nothing he can do. Only you have the power to stop Duke Wilhelm from destroying Château Clairmont.

I cannot!

You can.

Adrienne groaned and pressed her hands over her ears to shut out the conflicting voices. She felt as if she might lose her grip on her sanity.

"M'lady, you're trembling! Are you ill?"

Lina's voice brought her back to reality. Adrienne lowered her hands. "I'm fine, Lina. I just have a lot on my mind right now."

Whatever she decided to do, she knew she could not tell Lina. She could not tell anyone. Sir Roland would lock her in her chamber if he knew she was even considering turning herself over to Duke Wilhelm. Even Vernier, despite his animosity toward her, was astute enough to realize her value, both to Sainte-Croix and to the enemy. Whatever she did, she would have to act alone, without counsel, and pray that she had made the right choice.

The necessity for any sort of decision was mercifully delayed; when Adrienne went down to the kitchen, Marthe and Paschal promptly put her to work hauling water and firewood, stirring pots, carrying bedding to the great hall, and making up sleeping pallets on the floor. She worked quickly, without giving any thought to the passage of time, concentrating on the immediacy of her chores rather than on the dilemma that lurked in the back of her mind.

Lachen's assault on Château Clairmont continued without respite. At evenly spaced intervals, the same point in the outer curtain wall was subjected to repeated aerial bombardment from the trebuchets. Ballistae mounted on top of the castle walls rained a succession of giant arrows on the attackers below, and the archers maintained a steady defense with their smaller crossbows.

Some of Lachen's men managed to scale the wall at an inadequately guarded point, and a bloody bout of hand-to-hand fighting ensued before the intruders were beaten back or taken prisoner. Lachen's men fired torches of flaming pitch over the walls, and the defenders were kept busy drawing bucket after bucket of water from the well to put out the fires that were started in the ward.

It was midafternoon when Adrienne realized that she had forgotten to feed the falcons. Snatching up the slop pails in the kitchens, she filled them with scraps and offal, whatever she could find that was not destined for the stewpot, and hurried outside.

The buildings in the outer ward that were used to store grain and hay had been set ablaze, and the sky was thick with smoke that stung the back of Adrienne's nose and caused her eyes to water. The inner ward had disintegrated into chaos. Goats and chickens and pigs ran unchecked through the ward, getting in the way of those who were attempting to carry the wounded into the hall. Families who had taken refuge in the castle huddled close to the walls of the keep. Children clung to their mothers' skirts and cried, their pitiful wails mingling with the screams of the wounded. Adrienne dodged a supply wagon and ran across the ward.

Inside the mews, the falcons, frightened by the commotion outside, bated their wings and fought their restraints. Adrienne dropped one of the pails and threw her arm up over her face as a large peregrine that had managed to tear free of her perch flew straight at her. The falcon's wing struck her head with tremendous force, knocking her to her knees as it flew past her and out the door.

Shaking, and her heart pounding, Adrienne got to her feet and picked up the pail she had dropped. "Shhh, there is nothing to fear," she cooed to the terrified birds. " 'Tis only me. I've brought your dinner."

Without warning, strong arms seized her from behind and a hand clamped over her mouth, smothering her scream.

Chapter Seventeen

ADRIENNE DROPPED THE pails and clawed frantically at the hand that covered her mouth. Screams burned in her lungs, demanding release. She thrashed and twisted. Her foot struck one of the pails, sending it rolling across the mews.

A strong arm tightened around her middle, cutting off her air. "My lady, be still!" came a man's harsh whisper. " 'Tis I, Leland!"

Relief surged through her, and she stopped struggling.

Sir Leland released his hold on her.

Adrienne whirled around, joy and disbelief on her face when she saw the gray-bearded knight. He looked tired and gaunt, and the scar on his cheek seemed more pronounced than usual. To Adrienne he looked wonderful.

"My lord, how did you get in here? How did you *find* me?"

"I've been here for several days," Leland said quickly. "I tried to talk to you before, but every time you came to the mews someone was with you."

Leland handed her a friar's robe. "Put this on," he said. "We must hurry. The guards could close the postern gate at any time."

Adrienne hesitated, realizing that this meant she would be leaving Château Clairmont—leaving Hugh. Then she saw that this was the opportunity she had been praying for. This was her chance to end the fighting.

She took the robe and put it on over her mantle.

Dear Hugh, please forgive me. I am doing this because I love you.

"When we discovered you were missing from the barge, we found your trail and followed you as far as Burg Moudon," Leland said. "Once there, we learned of your whereabouts from Graeham de Clairmont. Pearroc and Guibert are waiting in the mountains with horses. We will meet them there."

Adrienne remembered Sir Pearroc lying on the deck outside her cabin door the last time she saw him. She was relieved to know that he was still alive, but her happiness was tainted by her worry for Graeham. "Marlys and Sir Eustace and the others were taken prisoner also," she told Leland. "But Hugh let them go before we left Burg Moudon." She paused. "Graeham de Clairmont . . . is he all right?"

Leland nodded, puzzled by Adrienne's concern for her captor's brother. "Lachen took him prisoner, but from what I saw, he is being reasonably well treated." It stuck in Leland's craw to say anything good about Wilhelm of Lachen, but he only spoke the truth.

Adrienne tucked her hair inside the robe and pulled the hood up over her head. "I'm ready," she said.

Leland went to the door of the mews and peered out. He motioned to Adrienne.

"I forgot the falcons," Adrienne said suddenly. "They need to be fed."

"There is no time, my lady. Hurry!"

Adrienne followed Leland. As soon as they were out in the open, Leland assumed a convincing limp, and Adrienne realized that he was not wearing his hauberk and surcoat, but was dressed like a peasant in a threadbare tunic and torn braies. He looked like a tired old man. As they crossed the ward, Adrienne tucked her hands inside the folds of her robe and bowed her head to hide her face.

When they reached the postern gate, the guards had just admitted an empty supply wagon and a deluge of refugees and were pushing the gate shut. "Wait!" Leland called out in a frantic, shaky voice. "My wife needs the last rites. I am taking the good father to her."

Adrienne's heart pounded mercilessly. What if they were found out? What if someone recognized her?

Just then there was a low, ominous rumble, and the air was filled with shouts and war cries. Adrienne twisted her head in the direction of the noise, as did the guards. Leland grabbed her arm, nearly wrenching it out of its socket, and hauled her through the open gate.

They ran.

Sliding and stumbling on the rocky ground, they made their way down the hill. Adrienne had assumed that Château Clairmont was completely surrounded by Duke Wilhelm's men, and she was surprised to see the stretch of unguarded hillside before them. Her hood fell back, exposing her hair, but she did not bother replacing it. A terrible stitch gripped her side, and she was already out of breath. She glanced back at the castle and saw that Lachen's men had succeeded in pounding an opening in the curtain wall and were pouring into the outer ward.

"My lord, please, stop!"

Leland skidded to a halt.

Adrienne clutched her abdomen and struggled to catch her breath. "We have to go . . . to Duke . . . Wilhelm," she gasped.

Leland stared at her in disbelief. "You don't have to marry him," he said. "I won't take you back to him. I will take you somewhere else, where you will be safe."

Adrienne shook her head. "You don't . . . understand. I *must* go to him."

Remembering her earlier unexplained concern for Lachen's hostage, Leland said, "Don't throw your life away to save Graeham de Clairmont. Lachen won't harm him; he doesn't want to incur King Philip's wrath."

"Duke Wilhelm wants *me*. Once he has me, he will stop the assault. I know he will."

"No, my lady. You're wrong."

"Sir Leland, please, you must listen to me! Duke Wilhelm sent word to Hugh that he wants to trade Graeham for me. I must go to him. These people are suffering terribly because of me. The fighting must stop!"

Whether it was because of the way Adrienne was holding her abdomen or the desperation in her eyes or the ache in her voice, Leland suddenly realized that it was not Graeham de Clairmont who was uppermost in Adrienne's mind: it was Hugh. Hugh de Clairmont, Comte de Sainte-Croix.

She was in love with him.

And she was carrying his child.

"Please?" Adrienne pleaded softly. "Please take me to him."

Leland's shoulders drooped in dismay. He nodded. "If you wish."

They resumed their descent down the hill, with Leland holding Adrienne's arm to steady her and to keep her from falling on the rough terrain. Before they had gone more than a few more yards, an arrow whirred out of nowhere and struck Sir Leland in the chest.

The knight stumbled and pitched forward.

Adrienne screamed. Clinging to Leland's arm, she fell when he fell. He landed face downward.

Adrienne scrambled to her knees. She gripped the knight's shoulder and shook him. "Sir Leland, are you all right? My lord, answer me!"

Even as she pleaded with him, she knew inwardly that he was not all right. He was not moving. With a strength born of panic, she managed to roll him onto his back. His eyes were closed, and his face was gray. Adrienne's stomach surged up into her throat when she saw the arrow protruding from his chest and the crimson stain spreading rapidly across the front of his tunic.

A sob tore from her chest. "My lord, please answer me!" Leland's eyes slowly opened, and he looked at her.

Adrienne bent over him, her long dark hair falling forward and brushing against his cheek. She began to weep, great sobs that wrenched her shoulders. "Thank God you're still alive," she said, sobbing. "I'll go get help for you. Just don't die. Please, don't die!"

Leland's voice was weak and raspy. " 'Tis too late," he whispered. His eyes drifted shut.

Adrienne shook her head in denial. "No," she murmured. "It's not too late. I'll get help. Please, don't die!"

Realizing numbly that she was not alone, she looked up. A dozen mounted knights and archers with black and saffron surcoats over their armor surrounded her, but her gaze focused on one man in particular. He too wore chain mail, but his surcoat was all black and unembellished. His face was sallow and deeply scarred, and there was a look of self-satisfaction in his heavy-lidded eyes. "I knew he would lead us to you," the man said smugly. "It was just a matter of time."

Adrienne slowly rose to her feet, hatred and disgust welling up inside her as she faced Duke Wilhelm's chancellor. Tears filled her eyes, and she was shaking so badly she could hardly stand. "You killed Sir Leland," she said in a strained voice. "He was taking me to Duke Wilhelm, and you killed him. *Why*?"

Lachen's men moved in closer, effectively blocking any chance she might have had of escaping. Theobald of Mainz turned his horse and extended one pale hand with long, tapered fingers toward her. "We had no more use for him," he said simply.

The guard prodded Adrienne awake. "Duke Wilhelm will see you now."

Adrienne pushed herself into a sitting position and shoved her hair out of her eyes with one hand. Her head hurt. Her body hurt. There was a dull, squeezing ache in her lower back. She had been given only a thin blanket to lie on, and the ground on which she had slept was rocky and uneven. Only total exhaustion had enabled her to sleep at all. And had she not had her mantle and the friar's robe to cover herself, she would have frozen.

Adrienne struggled to her feet and followed the guard out of the tent and into the open. Outside the tent, three other guards were waiting for her. She squinted at the bright sunlight. "My lord, please . . . might I have a few minutes of privacy first?"

The guard ignored her. With a sigh of resignation, Adrienne followed him. All four guards escorted her to the largest tent in the center of the camp. That tent was also heavily guarded. One of the guards held open the tent flap and indicated that she was to enter. She ducked through the opening.

For a moment she stood just inside the opening, letting her eyes adjust to the sudden dimness.

Soon shapes began to form. At the far end of the tent, opposite the opening, stood a large crucifix. A man clad in a long black tunic knelt before the crucifix, his head bowed in prayer. His hair was gray and hung over his bony shoulders in long, scraggly strands.

Then Adrienne saw Theobald of Mainz standing off to one side of the tent. His tapered, feminine hands were clasped serenely in front of him, and he was regarding her with those unblinking snakelike eyes. A cold smile touched his mouth, and he inclined his head toward her.

Adrienne thought of Sir Leland, and bile rose in her throat. Her mouth thinned, and hatred smoldered in her eyes. Never in her life had she despised anyone so much as she despised Theobald of Mainz.

The man before the crucifix crossed himself and rose to his feet. He turned to face her, and Adrienne's breath caught at her first sight of his severe, sunken-cheeked face. At first she thought he might be a monk, perhaps from an order that demanded extreme asceticism and self-discipline. Then she realized with a start that this was Duke Wilhelm. *This* was her betrothed husband.

Her stomach twisted into a hard, punishing knot.

Grappling with the horrible reality of the marriage her father had contracted for her, Adrienne somehow found the presence of mind to execute a bow of obeisance. "My lord," she murmured shakily.

Wilhelm did not speak. His critical gaze traversed the length of her, and Adrienne sensed that he was not in the least pleased with what he saw. His gaze lingered on her abdomen.

Adrienne nervously moistened her lips and fought the urge to shield her baby from Wilhelm's probing gaze. She clenched and unclenched her hands at her sides. "My lord," she began. Her voice was dry and strangled with fear. After witnessing with her own eyes what had happened to Sir Leland, she knew there was little chance that Wilhelm would listen to her pleas. But she had to try. She could not give up now. She began again. "My lord . . . I beseech you to release Graeham de Clairmont and to call an end to the assault on Sainte-Croix. I-I will go with you. I will do whatever you want. But please, please, don't hurt these people any more."

Wilhelm still did not speak, and Adrienne wondered frantically what it was they expected of her.

Wilhelm signaled to Theobald with a barely perceptible nod. The chancellor went to Adrienne. Before she realized what he intended, he grasped the neckline of her chemise and bliaud and jerked, ripping the fabric of both garments clear to her knees.

Adrienne gasped and her hands flew to cover herself, but Theobald knocked her hands away.

Choking back a sob, Adrienne squeezed her eyes shut against the shame that engulfed her as Theobald parted her torn gown, exposing her and the child she carried. Terror pressed down on her like an icy black cloud, freezing the blood in her veins and causing her to tremble as she endured the humiliation of Wilhem's condemning inspection.

When the duke finally spoke, Adrienne's body jerked as if he had struck her.

"Get her out of here," he spat.

The siege on Château Clairmont ended as abruptly as it had begun. The trebuchets stopped hurling missiles at the castle walls. The battering ram stopped its ceaseless pounding at the barbican. The siege towers were rolled away from the walls, and Wilhelm's men retreated.

Puzzled by the besiegers' sudden withdrawal, Vernier and Toulouse responded immediately to a guard's urgent summons and mounted the tower stairs.

When they reached the top of the tower, the guard pointed across the valley. "Look."

A large force of perhaps fifteen thousand men was steadily advancing toward Château Clairmont. Had the defenders not already been weakened by Lachen's assault, they might have been able to repel the newcomers. But everything that could have gone wrong in the siege did go wrong. Disputes had broken out within the ranks, and men who should have been united in their efforts to defend the castle wound up fighting each other. Warriors deserted their posts. And one of Lachen's soldiers, disguised as a peasant, had entered the ward and managed to poison two of the wells before he was caught.

Furthermore, neither Vernier nor Toulouse had any idea if the approaching army was friend or foe.

By nightfall that question was answered for all when a contingent of armed riders entered the castle gates under the banner of King Philip of France.

Each new shred of information to reach Hugh's ears served to increase his frustration rather than ease it.

Wilhelm of Lachen had halted the siege on Château Clairmont and ordered his forces to retreat.

Richard had agreed to parley.

Alais de Vernier and her escort, upon leaving the sanctuary of Collombey Abbey, had immediately been captured by the Count of Durgundy and were being detained under papal order until Vernier paid the fines and indemnities imposed upon him by the Church.

Adrienne was missing.

It was that last bit of information that drove Hugh to the verge of madness.

He wanted to go to Vernier and seize him by the neck and demand to know what he had done to her, but until a truce was negotiated and the kiss of peace exchanged, he was essentially Philip's prisoner. He had no rights. He was not permitted to leave his tent or even to ask questions. Only his skill at sniffing out guards who were susceptible to bribes had provided him with what little information he did have.

Upon reaching Paris, he had been placed under house arrest. But this time Philip had turned neither a deaf ear nor a blind eye to his plea; Sainte-Croix was too valuable to the Crown.

Philip had immediately mobilized his army.

At first Hugh had feared they were too late. By the time they reached the borders of Sainte-Croix, word had reached them that Wilhelm of Lachen had launched a full-scale siege against Château Clairmont and that his forces had broken through the outer curtain wall.

Philip had sent a messenger to Lachen, demanding an immediate cessation to the fighting and requesting a meeting with him to negotiate a truce.

He then sent messengers to the castle, summoning the defending counts to appear before him.

And finally Philip sent a legation to Richard, whose army was camped a two days' ride to the northwest, reminding Richard of the oath of allegiance he had sworn to Philip and requesting his assistance in putting an end to the fighting that was tearing France apart.

Miraculously, all parties agreed.

The parley was to take place three days hence on a rocky plain near Vallorbe.

Until then, all Hugh could do was wait and hope for an outcome that would pacify them all.

As for his request that he be allowed to marry Adrienne, Philip still had not given him an answer. And even if that answer was favorable, what good was it if something had happened to her?

As for Adrienne, he did not know what to think. Was it possible that she had managed to escape? Hugh thought of her previous efforts, and he realized that the odds of Adrienne attempting to flee were as great as the odds that Vernier might have harmed her.

Hugh raked his fingers through his hair in frustration and groaned. "Why now, *princesse*?" he pleaded silently. "Why now, when we are so close to getting what we both want?"

Adrienne had no idea where she was being taken.

She had been given clean clothes to wear, clothes that she recognized as having come from the chest she had left behind on the barge. Though worn and faded, the familiar feel of the fabric against her skin brought her a measure of comfort.

She was given her own horse to ride.

She could not tell how many knights formed the party; she guessed that there might have been upwards of three hundred, a fraction of Lachen's total army. Duke Wilhelm rode at the front of the column, as did Theobald of Mainz. She rode in the middle. Near the rear was Graeham de Clairmont. She had not known until this morning that Graeham was here, nor did she know why, but when she saw him across the encampment, she had nearly collapsed from relief.

They rode all day, camped for the night, then resumed traveling in the morning.

The weather turned hostile. A fierce wind howled down off the mountains, tearing at Adrienne's mantle and whipping her hair around her face. Her hands and feet were so cold that she no longer had any feeling in them. She kept her chin tucked in against her chest, hunched her shoulders against the wind as she rode, and tried to direct all her body heat toward the child growing within her. Hugh's child. The only thing she had left to live for.

At noon on the second day, they left the mountains and descended to a broad valley. Occasionally Adrienne caught a glimpse of the area below, and what she saw stunned her. There were soldiers in the valley. Thousands upon thousands of them.

Because Duke Wilhelm did not turn back but kept on a steady course, Adrienne could only assume that the valley was their destination.

Why? she wondered. Was Duke Wilhelm going to turn her over to those soldiers? Her and Graeham?

As they drew nearer to the valley, Adrienne spotted a standard whipping in the wind bearing the gold lions of Anjou, and then another emblazoned with the fleur-de-lis of the king of France. Her pulse raced with trepidation. *Dear God, will someone please tell me what is going to happen?* she prayed.

Finally they stopped and made camp. Adrienne was again given her own tent. She wished she could talk to Graeham, but it was obvious that they were intentionally being kept apart, and she dared not ask for any favors. She had seen neither Duke Wilhelm nor his chancellor, except from a distance, since that awful day in Duke Wilhelm's tent; and she did not want to say or do anything that might draw their attention to her or bring retribution down on her head.

After a meager supper of bread and wine, Adrienne wrapped her mantle around her and lay down on the blanket. But sleep was slow to come, and for a long time she lay awake, listening to the wind as it whistled across the valley, snapping the canvas walls of her tent.

*   *   *

In the morning, Duke Wilhelm and twenty of his men, his chancellor, Graeham de Clairmont, and Adrienne de Langeais rode out onto the rocky field and stopped. Adrienne glanced at Graeham and found little reassurance in his grim smile. When she again turned her head to the front, she caught Theobald of Mainz staring at her. Although she knew it was not wise to antagonize him, she lifted her chin and met his chilling gaze with a look of bold disdain. He turned away, and she felt a brief thrill of victory.

Others joined them on the field.

A sizable group bearing the arms of the king of England rode toward them. The wind carried the words of the knight nearest her, and Adrienne heard him tell another that the two men who led the group were King Richard and his brother, Prince John.

Although Adrienne had never before seen either of her half brothers, it was Richard who drew her attention because he was said to most resemble her father. He was tall and solidly built but graceful, and he sat a horse well. His complexion was ruddy, but whether it was naturally that way or had been reddened by the wind, Adrienne did not know. His hair was tawny, his gray eyes were piercing and their expression bold, and his bearing was magnificent. Rumors hinted that Richard's sexual preferences leaned more toward handsome young men than toward women, but Adrienne did not care. If Henry had looked anything at all like his son, then she knew now why her mother had fallen in love with him.

The counts of Vernier and Toulouse rode onto the field with their men.

Adrienne sucked in her breath when she saw them. Why were *they* here? Vernier said something to Raymond of Toulouse, and both men turned to stare at her in surprise and speculation. Adrienne glanced at Graeham and saw his jaw tighten.

Then King Philip rode up with an escort of more than a hundred men. With him was Hugh.

Adrienne's pulse leapt, and she nearly cried out. It was all she could do to keep from jumping down from her horse and running to him.

Surprise, then relief, then joy swept across Hugh's face in rapid succession when he saw her, and Adrienne felt a gentle warmth wrap itself around her as though he had reached across the distance that separated them and touched her. Her heart swelled in her chest.

I love you, she thought desperately.

Philip opened the parley. "I have asked you here," he began in a loud, clear voice, "to call upon you to put aside your differences and unite for the common good of France, of England, and of the Holy Roman Empire."

For the next twenty minutes Philip spoke. He reminded his French vassals of their responsibilities to the Crown. He reminded Richard of the oath of fealty that Richard had sworn to him little more than a year ago. He reminded Richard of the concessions he had won for him at his last meeting with Henry where he had gotten the king to cede Poitou, Normandy, Maine, Anjou, and Touraine to Richard. Judging from the disgruntled look on her half brother's face, Adrienne suspected that in recent weeks Richard had been reminded of both the oath and the concessions more often than he would have liked.

Philip reminded Count Raymond of the time he had intervened on his behalf when Richard invaded Toulouse.

Raymond stiffened and eyed Richard with open contempt. That the two men could barely tolerate being on the field together was obvious. It was also evident that Philip was calling in his favors.

Of all the leaders on the field that day, the only one who owed Philip neither allegiance nor debt was Duke Wilhelm. When Philip addressed Wilhelm, he appealed to the duke's love of God and his desire for all the nations of Christendom to unite in a joint effort to retake Jerusalem from the infidels.

Adrienne listened in amazement as Philip managed to appeal to Duke Wilhelm's sense of righteousness, his religiosity, and his vanity in a single swoop. In spite of the fact that Philip was younger than most of his vassals, he was remarkably astute.

Richard was the next to speak. His volatile temper barely under control, he let it be known that he was not about to surrender a countship that his father had worked so hard to acquire, and Adrienne felt herself growing angry at his hypocrisy. Richard, who had betrayed their father before his death, now expected to collect on an inheritance that was never intended for Richard in the first place.

Wilhelm's demands were simple and brutally to the point. To Adrienne's humiliation and utmost relief, the duke announced that he had no desire to marry a whore who was carrying another man's bastard and that he was nullifying their betrothal. In exchange for turning Graeham and Adrienne over to the French king, Lachen wanted compensation for the loss of his bride and her dowry.

The negotiations lasted more than two hours.

Finally Philip recited the list of concessions.

He declared Henry's seizure of Sainte-Croix illegal and called for its return to Hugh de Clairmont and his heirs.

He called for the release of all hostages.

He called for an end to hostilities and for the formation of a joint army for the purpose of retaking the kingdom of Jerusalem and returning it to Christian rule.

Sensitive to Hugh's beliefs, Philip excused Hugh from taking the cross. However, as a condition for the return of Sainte-Croix, Hugh would have to open his ports to those who would use them as a point of departure to the Holy Land, and he must guarantee safe passage to anyone who would traverse Sainte-Croix for that same purpose. He must also raise taxes and provide manpower to help support the venture.

Tears filled Adrienne's eyes as she listened to Hugh quietly agree to every one of Philip's demands. She knew how much this truce had cost him; the concessions went against everything Hugh believed in. And yet he had accepted them so that the people of Sainte-Croix might be spared further bloodshed. He had agreed to them for Graeham's sake, and for hers.

Philip's final announcement drew a gasp from everyone present. He declared void the betrothal contract between Hugh de Clairmont and Alais de Vernier. In compensation, Hugh would be required to pay Vernier's indemnities to the Church.

"There is one person present," Philip continued, looking straight at Adrienne, "who has everything to lose and nothing to gain in these negotiations. In the interests of restoring peace between England and France, and in deference to Henry Plantagenet's bestowal of Sainte-Croix, as her marriage portion, upon his daughter, Lady Adrienne de Langeais, I am ordering you, Hugh de Clairmont, to wed Lady Adrienne at once. May the fruit of your union, the true heirs to Sainte-Croix, bring peace and prosperity to the countship."

Adrienne stared at Philip in stunned disbelief. She glanced at Hugh. He was staring straight ahead, his face devoid of expression, and Adrienne felt her stomach clench. Dear God, King Philip had *ordered* him to marry her. Did Hugh find the thought of marrying her so distasteful? Would he grow to hate her because he had been forced to make her his wife?

Feeling faint and a little ill, Adrienne looked away from Hugh, unable to bear the thought that he was marrying her against his will.

She thought of her mother and of how she had condemned Isolde for being unwed. Adrienne, at least, was going to marry the father of her child, but at what cost?

She saw the Count of Vernier staring at her, his face twisted with rage, and a sob caught in her throat. *Dear God, at what cost?*

Hugh and Philip dismounted, and Hugh ungirted his sword and laid it aside. With an ache in her heart, Adrienne watched through a haze of tears as Hugh knelt before his monarch to publicly renew his oath of fealty to him.

Adrienne wiped her eyes with her fingertips, and when she did, she caught a movement from the corner of her eye. She blinked, not trusting herself, and then she saw it again: pale blond hair being blown about by the wind.

She stared at the young man as he inched his horse closer to the center of the gathering, not because his pale hair was unusual but because it was so familiar.

The squire moved into full view, and Adrienne suddenly recognized him.

Lysander!

The relief she felt at finally knowing that he had not drowned warred openly with the uneasy feeling that he had no business being here.

There was a look of single-minded determination on Lysander's face and a feverish light in his eyes that reminded Adrienne of Duke Wilhelm's fanaticism.

Lysander did not see her. He was staring at Hugh. Staring at him and moving steadily closer to him.

Then Adrienne saw the glint of a blade in Lysander's hand, and she cried out, *"Hugh, look out!"*

Hugh dived for his sword and rolled to his feet in one fluid motion.

Horses spooked at the sudden distraction, and riders fought to get them under control.

Philip's knights immediately closed ranks around their king, and Richard's knights did likewise.

The knight closest to Lysander saw the drawn dagger in his hand. Just as Lysander started to throw the dagger, the knight swung his lance, catching the youth across the chest and knocking him from his horse. Several knights leapt from their horses. They pinned Lysander to the ground and wrested the dagger from him.

In the midst of the commotion, when the attention was focused on Lysander, Vernier spurred his horse forward.

Adrienne saw him coming. The knights closest to her scrambled to get out of his way, but Adrienne sat, gripping the reins, terror frozen in her veins as he bore down on her.

At the last second Adrienne turned her horse and tried to dodge Vernier's advance, but the move came too late. Vernier seized her and dragged her off her horse and onto his.

Adrienne screamed.

Hugh spun around.

Realizing what had happened, several knights started forward, then stopped when they saw the dagger Vernier held to Adrienne's throat.

Vernier's arm tightened around Adrienne's rib cage, and she gasped in fear and pain. She squeezed her eyes shut and choked back a sob as the cold point of Vernier's blade pressed harder against her throat, breaking the skin.

His gaze darting madly about the crowd, Vernier slowly backed his horse away. "I'll not sit idly by while you abrogate my daughter's betrothal and seek to replace her with this Angevin whore!" he shouted at Philip. "Sainte-Croix is mine! I fought for it! I won't give it up!"

Hugh started forward, and Vernier turned on him, his eyes blazing. "I warned you," he growled. "I warned you what would happen should you try to break your betrothal to my daughter. You are a dead man, Hugh de Clairmont. I will wreak my revenge on every last one of your line."

Philip broke away from the protective circle his knights had formed around him. "Don't do this, Vernier," he commanded. "Don't destroy the peace we have sought here this day. Let us talk. I will listen to your demands and redress your grievances."

In response, Vernier spat on the ground. "I renounce my allegiance to you and to France!"

A murmur rippled through the crowd.

Holding Adrienne and the reins with one hand while he pressed the dagger to Adrienne's throat with the other, Vernier turned his horse, guiding the animal with his knees. "If anyone tries to follow me," he warned, "I will kill her."

Vernier gouged his spurs into his horse's sides, and the animal shot forward.

Hugh leapt onto his own horse. The crowd parted to let him pass. Conraed started after Hugh, but at a motion from their king's hand, Philip's men cut Conraed off. The message was clear. This fight was between Hugh and Vernier. It was to be fought between Hugh and Vernier, with no outside interference.

Vernier glanced over his shoulder and saw Hugh riding after him. Swearing savagely, he urged his horse to a break-neck pace.

As they neared the mountains, the land began to slope upward and became more broken. Vernier had to slow his horse to keep the animal from losing its footing on the uneven ground, and when he did, Hugh gained on him.

Vernier's horse slipped and went down.

Adrienne screamed as she felt the ground give way beneath them, and she was being hurtled over the horse's head. She hit the ground hard and rolled.

When she finally came to a stop, she lay there, dazed and bruised, but before the world could stop spinning, Vernier seized her arm and hauled her to her feet.

A searing pain shot through her abdomen and her lower back.

Vernier's arm went around her from behind, and he pulled her against him, using her as a shield as he inched his way backward up the hill. He had dropped his dagger in the fall, and now Adrienne was his only protection against Hugh's steady advance.

Hugh dismounted. In a gesture of goodwill, he put down his sword and lifted his hands to show that he was unarmed. "Let her go, Vernier," he said quietly. "She is nothing to you. I am the one you want."

Vernier's arm crushed Adrienne's rib cage, and she slumped against him, too exhausted and in too much pain to fight him. Still, she fought to ignore the pain and to clear her mind. She was the only one standing between Hugh and Vernier, and she knew Hugh would not attack if there was any chance that she could be hurt. There had to be something she could do. Something to distract Vernier . . .

"Don't come any closer, Clairmont! If you do, I will kill her. You're right; she is nothing to me. I would gladly see her dead."

"If you harm her," Hugh said in a low, deceptively calm voice, "there will be no place on this earth where you can hide. You will be a hunted man." He was close enough now to see the whites of Vernier's eyes. He did not look at Adrienne; he did not dare lose eye contact with Vernier.

The backs of Vernier's legs came into contact with a rocky outcropping. Muttering an oath, he skirted the protrusion, pulling Adrienne with him. "You betrayed me!" he spat at Hugh. "While my men were risking their lives to defend Sainte-Croix, you ran to Philip with your tail tucked between your legs like a whipped dog. You are a coward. A stinking, miserable coward!"

Adrienne turned her head and sank her teeth into Vernier's arm.

Vernier cried out in pain and surprise. He shoved Adrienne away from him.

Hugh lunged. He caught Vernier around the legs, bringing him down.

Vernier scrambled to his feet. He flung a handful of dirt and pebbles into Hugh's face.

Hugh turned his head aside, and the debris struck his cheek.

Vernier turned to run.

Hugh hurled his full weight against him. Both men crashed to the ground.

Several feet away, Adrienne managed to pull herself into a sitting position. Pain gripped her insides. Shoulders hunched, she watched in mute horror as Hugh and Vernier, locked in a death grip, rolled over and over in the dirt. Dislodged gravel skittered down the hill.

Adrienne shoved herself to her feet. Barely able to stand, she made her way down the hill to where Hugh's war horse waited patiently, as if nothing were amiss. Hugh's sword lay on the ground beside the animal. Hoping frantically that the horse would not try to attack her the way Sir Roland's had, Adrienne bent and grabbed the sword's jeweled hilt.

The sword felt as if it weighed a ton, and the muscles in Adrienne's arms burned as she dragged the heavy weapon back up the hill, all the while praying that Hugh would see her and claim the sword in time to save his own life.

Hugh broke the hold Vernier had on him. The two men rolled away from each other and clambered to their feet. Hugh swung. Vernier ducked. Hugh's unsteady footing caused him to skid and miss his mark. Vernier sprang out of the way.

Then Vernier saw Adrienne.

He staggered toward her, his expression savage.

Terror exploded inside Adrienne. With an inhuman strength she did not know she possessed, she lifted the sword.

Hugh snatched his dagger from his boot and hurled it at Vernier's back. The dagger lodged between Vernier's shoulder blades with a sickening thud.

Surprise widened Vernier's eyes, and his mouth opened in a silent *O*. Reaching frantically toward Adrienne for support, he pitched forward and fell on the point of the sword. His weight caused Adrienne to stumble to her knees as the blade sank deep into his belly.

Vernier clutched the front of her mantle, his mouth wide open in shock and his unseeing gaze fixed on her face.

Then he toppled over.

Adrienne released her grip on the sword and clamped her hands over her mouth to halt the silent screams that welled up inside her as the horror of what had just happened began to penetrate her consciousness. She had killed a man, she thought frantically. *Dear God, she killed a man!*

She was vaguely aware of being lifted to her feet and of Hugh's strong arms being folded around her. Then, mercifully, everything went dark.

An ominous silence hung over the camp. Hugh paced outside Philip's tent while the king's physicians tended Adrienne. Now that the worst was over and Vernier was dead, he could not stop shaking. He kept thinking of how close he had come to losing Adrienne, and how he might still lose her. He cursed himself for not having taken her with him when he went to plead his cause to Philip. He cursed God for letting this happen to her.

After listening to his blasphemous outbursts, Graeham calmly reminded him that he did not believe in God, and Hugh cursed Graeham too, for the sake of venting his anger.

Just then the tent flap opened, and the two physicians and Philip's astrologer exited the tent. The elder of the two physicians looked at Hugh. "She is asking for you," he said. "You may see her, but only for a few minutes. The next few days are critical. If she makes it through them without miscarrying, we might be able to save your son."

The astrologer frowned. " 'Twill be a daughter," he said flatly. "To be born under the influence of Mercury."

Annoyed with the astrologer's inane concerns, Hugh glowered at him before ducking through the tent opening.

Adrienne lay in the middle of King Philip's portable camp bed, tucked warmly beneath a mountain of furs. Her dark hair was spread out across the furs, and her long lashes cast shadows on her pale cheeks. She looked so frail and weak that Hugh wondered how she had ever survived the past several months, much less this morning.

He knelt beside the bed. "*Princesse*, are you awake?" he whispered.

Adrienne's eyes fluttered open.

Hugh reached beneath the furs for her hand. Finding it, he closed his fingers around it. "I was worried about you."

"We must talk," Adrienne said hoarsely. Her throat was dry, and every bone and muscle in her body ached.

"Shhh. We can talk later. Right now you must rest. Philip's physicians think there is a good chance the baby will live."

"Hugh, I can't marry you."

Hugh's grip tightened on Adrienne's hand as he stared into her pain-glazed eyes. He did not realize how tightly he was holding her hand until she winced. He relaxed his grip. "Why?"

"I love you," Adrienne whispered achingly. Tears filled her eyes. "I love you so much that I thought nothing would make me happier than to be your wife. But today . . . when Philip ordered us to wed . . . I could not bear the thought of spending the rest of my life knowing that you had married me because your liege lord *commanded* you to."

Hugh's defensiveness turned to bewilderment, then to disbelief. "*Princesse*, I am not marrying you because Philip commanded me to. I want to marry you. I went to Philip and asked—no, begged—to be permitted to marry you. The command he issued was intended not to force me into marriage but to keep Vernier from interfering. For all the good it did."

Adrienne shook her head in denial. "I saw the look in your eyes," she protested.

"*Princesse*, when Philip was issuing the edict, I was fighting with everything that was in me to keep from going to Vernier and throttling him. I saw the way he was looking at you, and I wanted to kill him."

Adrienne stared at him, her gray eyes clouded with confusion and longing. "My lord, if you're marrying me because of the baby—"

"I am marrying you because I love you."

Hugh saw the surprise on Adrienne's face, and a smile of regret touched his mouth. "I should have told you that before. I'm sorry I didn't. I love you. *I love you.*"

Tears pooled in Adrienne's eyes. She opened her mouth to speak, but nothing would come out.

Hugh's expression turned sober. Releasing her hand, he slid his hand down to her abdomen and rested his palm against the pronounced curve there. He could have sworn he felt something move beneath his fingers, but he could not be certain. "*Princesse*, I am not marrying you because you are carrying my child. Even if, God forbid, the baby does not live, I still want to marry you. There will be other children; and even if there are not, you are the one I love. I want you by my side. Always."

Adrienne took a shattered breath, trying to absorb what Hugh was saying. She placed a trembling hand over his, and together they felt the quickening in her womb. "I love you so much," she whispered.

One of the physicians stuck his head into the tent. "You must let her rest now," he said.

Hugh rose. He bent and pressed a gentle kiss to Adrienne's lips. "Take care of yourself," he said. "And take care of our son."

Hugh started to leave the tent.

"My lord?"

Hugh turned back. There was a smile behind the tears in Adrienne's eyes, and a dimple appeared at one corner of her mouth. "The astrologer says the baby is going to be a girl," she said.

In that instant Hugh knew that Adrienne was going to be all right. The baby was going to be all right. The entire world was going to be all right. Fighting the urge to jump up and down and shout for joy, he scowled in exaggerated affront. "That astrologer," he retorted, "is a fake."

Epilogue

June 30, 1190

INSIDE THE GREAT hall at Château Clairmont, the Comte de Sainte-Croix and the Baron of Foutreau were doing their best to drink each other under the table. Lord Baldhere had arrived at Château Clairmont only a few days before, to see for himself just what manner of man had caused him so much worry by abducting *his* daughter, carrying her halfway across France, then marrying her without *his* consent. Assuming, of course, that this young man was going to meet with his approval, Baldhere had brought with him chests of warm English woolens, clothes and household linens and other items that Lady Joanna had insisted were absolutely necessary, and one restless, travel-weary falcon that Baldhere said had not been the same since her mistress left.

"Oh, yes, and this," Baldhere had said, withdrawing a pouch from beneath his tunic.

Adrienne opened the pouch and gasped in delight when she saw its contents. Nestled in a bed of damp moss was a plant that Hugh had never seen before. Hugh frowned at the almost homely little plant with its pale leathery leaves. "What is it?"

"Mistletoe," Baldhere said.

"What?"

Baldhere grinned. "Ask your wife."

Over the past few days no one had spoken much about Lysander. He had been turned over to the custody of King Richard. No one knew what his fate was going to be, but it was rumored that he would continue with his squire's training, and if he managed to stay out of trouble, he would eventually be absolved of the charges that had been levied against him by King Philip. He was lucky. It was only his fervent loyalty to Richard that had saved him from being hanged for treason.

Eight of Henry's knights returned to France to fulfill their pledges to Adrienne, and this time Hugh accepted their oaths without question.

Marlys had stayed at Foutreau with Lady Joanna. She simply could not, she had insisted, make another sea crossing.

Hugh refilled his goblet and Baldhere's. Adrienne had gone into labor yestereve. She had been upstairs in their bedchamber ever since, and Marthe would not let him near her. The only way he could ease his worry was by drowning it.

Baldhere raised his goblet. "To my granddaughter."

Hugh took a hearty gulp of wine. "To my son," he corrected.

Baldhere eyeballed Hugh over the rim of his goblet. "The astrologer," he said, slurring his words, "said it will be a girl and will be born under the influence of Mars."

"Mercury."

"Are you sure?"

"Positive."

"I think 'tis too late for Mercury. It must be Mars."

Marthe appeared in the doorway. "The astrologer was wrong on at least one account," she announced, beaming at Hugh. "My lord, you have a son."

Hugh jumped up from the table, nearly knocking over the bench. "I have a son! Dear God, I have a son!"

Hugh downed his wine and slammed the goblet down on the table, then bolted from the hall. He took the stairs two at a time. When he burst into the bedchamber, Adrienne was propped up against the pillows with a tiny swaddling-wrapped bundle in her arms. She looked tired, but happy. "Come hold your son, my lord."

Hugh went to the bed and stood looking down at his wife and son. The infant screwed up his face and presented his father with a toothless yawn. Worry creased Hugh's brow. "He looks so small."

Adrienne chuckled. "Marthe says he is of a good size, and he is strong and healthy."

Hugh shook his head. "He gave me a scare a few months ago. You both did. I feared you would not live."

"This child has the blood of kings flowing in his veins," Adrienne gently reminded him. "Neither of us was about to surrender without a fight."

At his wife's urging, Hugh sat down on the edge of the bed. His hands shook as Adrienne passed the tiny bundle to him. Cradling his son in his arms, Hugh gazed down into the infant's reddened, wrinkled face and thought that this was the best gift anyone had ever given him. His throat tightened. "Thank you," he whispered.

Adrienne reached out and touched her hand to her husband's unshaven cheek. Hugh seldom revealed his deepest feelings, yet she had only to remember what he had sacrificed for her to know just how much he cared for her. She had everything she had ever wanted: a home, a loving husband, and a beautiful, healthy child who would never want for a father. She felt like the luckiest woman in the world. "It is I who should be thanking you, my lord," she said.

Hugh looked at her. "For what?"

"For abducting me."

"As I recall, *princesse*, you were not very happy about it at the time. You fought me like a tigress."

Adrienne traced her forefinger down the faint scar on Hugh's cheek, a permanent reminder of that fateful night when he had slipped into her cabin on the barge and forever altered her destiny. She lifted her gaze to his, and her eyes were bright with unshed tears. "And for capturing my heart," she said softly.